DEDICATION

This book is dedicated to those who long for love, bond and happiness. May you find the love you seek by shining your light inward.

Ryder's Route

A midlife search for happiness and love

"Life begins at the edge of our comfort zone."
Neale Donald Walsch

"Often we cannot get there on our own but need to
be pushed..."
Jeff and Nicki

Nicki Blumenau Bloch

Jeff Lomey

CONTENTS

ACKNOWLEDGMENTS

Jeff: This book is dedicated to my late mom Rhona, who taught me how the written word can inspire mental and visual images, as well as how to compose a decent photograph. Thank you Mom, my best friend ever, I love you. Thanks also to my daughter Maxime and my son Levi, whose love I feel in every living moment.

Lastly a word of thanks to Nicki, my co-author and friend, without whom this book would never have been written.

Nicki: Working on this book with Jeff has been an adventure I would not trade for anything. Together we created Ryder and Jack, then experienced their ups and downs all along the way. Jeff, what an amazing journey—thank you for traveling this path with me.

I would like to acknowledge the support of family and friends the world over, as this book grew from a vague notion to the content you see before you. And to my husband and daughters—thank you from the bottom of my heart, for always supporting me, and always seeing the good in all I do. I love you!

DISCLAIMER

This is a work of fiction. Names, characters, businesses, places, events and incidents are either the products of the authors' imaginations or used in a fictitious manner. Any resemblance to actual persons, living or dead, or actual events is purely coincidental.

ABOUT THE ARTWORK

Seascape looking out from
Brenton-on-Sea towards Buffels Bay

Original cover photograph by Jeff Lomey
Illustration and art by Trevor Donenburg, of LogoRhythm

1: Ryder and Sophia,
Plettenberg Bay, November

"I dunno, Ryder, if you're so smart then you figure it out."

This is what she says to me as we begin the drive along possibly the most beautiful road in the world. The ocean beside this part of the Garden Route is a brilliant turquoise, with the light fluffy clouds above reflected in the deep hue of the water below. The Beacon Island Hotel, instantly recognizable by its unique shape and location on a small peninsula jutting from the heart of Plettenberg Bay, is still visible in my rearview mirror.

Then she continues in her best angry tone. "I've lost count of the number of times we've had this conversation. I'm so sick of it, you have no idea."

How much of what I'm thinking do I dare say out loud?

"Sophia, do you think I'm not sick of it, too? It's not like we haven't tried to resolve things before, but I just don't know what you want. You never explain it properly, half the time avoiding touchy subjects at all costs. Then we take a long road trip, and you sulk and still avoid being direct. Why do you always blame me, make me the problem? Did you ever think maybe it's you?"

Thirty minutes ago, after settling up our hotel bill, I'd walked over to the expensive leather couches in the lobby near the exit door, where Sophia sat talking on the phone.

"Of course, that's what I want. Any TV presenter of my caliber would want that, so please get it done right now. And don't let it happen again."

She snapped her phone shut for emphasis, her lithe brown body bending forward as she stood up on her impossibly long, shapely legs. This time, she had not mentioned her extensive pedigree, her education in both politics and economics from the University of the Western Cape. Perhaps the person on the other end of the line was already familiar with that refrain; Lord knows I have heard it countless times before.

"You are definitely poised for success," I remarked as we walked out the door of the Beacon Isle together. "There is no doubt in my mind."

Then we stood outside waiting, giving me a chance to reflect on the incredible setting, a place used by whalers hundreds of years before. This iconic hotel is perfectly located, with giant rocks dividing the poolside gardens from the white beach below, and with soaring mountains in the background completing the picture. I reflected, too, on my country and my history, on how I've never been tempted to leave the land of my birth, despite the many chances I've had to emigrate over the years. Yes, the ANC is corrupt; Mugabe is taking all the farms from the white people to our north; the economy is on its last legs. So what else is new? Those who choose to focus on nothing else are yet another problem to be sick of. I'm a fourth-generation South

African and proud of it. So much has been achieved in the few short years since regime change here: schools and health care clinics built for the poorest of the poor; electrification and sanitation expanded to those who had none; tax collection efficiencies as never before. The list goes on.

Today as we packed up to leave, and as I stuffed my half-empty bottle of Jack Daniels into the backpack I slung over my shoulder, I had been congratulating myself for planning this trip so we arrived before the summer vacation and before the onslaught of the Johannesburg jet set.

Yes, as soon as the schools and universities let out, the crowd from Gauteng will descend on the beautiful towns along the coast, from Cape Town all the way to Port Elizabeth, ready to spend their plentiful rands and throw around their considerable weight. Already I could picture them, the old money and the nouveau riche, with their designer-label clothes and high-end electronic gadgets, talking loudly on their cell phones and behaving rudely, with their whiny, equally ill-behaved children wreaking havoc in the beautiful hotel lobbies. But today, we were well ahead of the crowd, and the lot outside was mostly empty of people and vehicles—which did not explain why we had been waiting over forty-five minutes for the valet to retrieve my car and bring it up the hill to the hotel entrance! Well no matter, I decided when he finally screeched to a halt in front of us, then climbed out and stretched out his hand for the obligatory tip. I wondered what he thought when he looked at me, a tall guy with a fancy car sporting personalized number plates. "Previously advantaged," I guess he would call me, a white male who grew up in the days of apartheid. And I guess that would make him a part of the "previously disadvantaged." As I fished for a few five rand coins and handed them over, my thoughts were interrupted by her, reminding me that I was already being annoying, already missing the point. Taking too long, talking too much, not listening enough. Yes, all the same old ongoing problems between us, arguments recycling the same dynamic, invoking an endless array of different topics.

Now I think about what she has said as I silently navigate the twists and curves, tree-lined on one side of the road, and sea-filled on the other, in my new Lexus 250 SE with SatNav and voice-controlled climate and audio systems. God I love this car! Sophia and I are returning from a romantic, sex-filled, four-day vacation, something I eagerly planned a couple months ago. And this get-away was significantly enhanced by two things: the absence of her interfering parents, and the free upgrade to the honeymoon suite. The first came courtesy of her brother, who invited those parents to his home for the long weekend, and the second came courtesy of the Beacon Isle after my successful flirtation with the concierge upon our arrival. Great good fortune on both counts, that's what I say!

I try to pull my mind away as unbidden images appear. Her pale father, working at our kitchen table, the New Testament and his notepad spread before him. Writing and rewriting the sermons he delivers every Sunday to his obedient congregants. Her mother, sitting with regal posture, carefully marking her students' exams, her curly black hair and ebony skin always perfect no matter the occasion. The oppressive silence interrupted intermittently by his throat clearing, and the taint of her disapproval permeating the entire house.

Instead, I force myself to focus on our next stop before we return to Cape Town, the small town of Knysna. Sophia sits next to me in the passenger seat, eyes closed behind her oversized Gucci sunglasses, which means the subject she brought up should be considered closed, too. She's wearing her usual traveling attire: tight black leggings, casual Nike cross-trainers. At her feet is an accumulation of gum wrappers and tissues, this despite the trash bag I pointedly handed to her before we departed. She has thrown a pink Roxy hoodie cardigan over her shoulders, complaining that the air conditioning in the car is too cold.

Perhaps it's because the top you're wearing is too skimpy, I think bitterly. *Or maybe it would be less chilly in here if you quit giving me the cold shoulder.*

What is it about travelling together in the car that brings on arguments between us? Nowhere to go, except an awkward climb into the back seat for a nap? Last month we drove from Cape Town in the other direction, a trip to Saldanha Bay. We had just driven past the Koeberg Nature Reserve, a stop I suggested but she rejected for reasons unknown. We passed Grotto Bay off to the west, then continued up the coast past the rocky beaches of Yzerfontein. One beautiful vista after another unfolding all the way from home in Camps Bay to our destination. And I wondered then how it was possible that she seemed more interested in arguing with me than with looking out the window, at the breathtaking views of the Atlantic Ocean, the mountain ridges, and the indigenous flowers growing all alongside Marine Drive, the R27.

"Sophie—what's wrong?" I asked on that day, as the silence in the car became more oppressive.

"Nothing, Ryder. Nothing's wrong."

"Oh, okay then. I'll just turn up the radio, and—"

"Why do you do that? Again, avoiding confrontation."

"But you said nothing's wrong. I asked, and you—"

"So you just drop it, is that it? Typical. Fine, then, it's as if you don't even care."

"First you say nothing's wrong, then you get mad because something is wrong. You can't have it both ways, Sophie. I don't even know what to say to you anymore."

"Precisely. You never do."

Unable to flounce off in the moving car, she had done the next best thing, turned her back to me and curled up in the passenger seat, and remained that way for the rest of the drive. Come to think of it, she never did tell me what was bugging her that day. At least not that I remember.

2: Koos, Knysna, November

The policeman shifts uncomfortably in his chair, his slightly ruddy complexion reflected in the glass-paned front door. Anyone who enters here will see him at his desk, he knows, and he tries to maintain a stern demeanor.

With the newspaper resting on his protruding stomach, he reads it squintingly while simultaneously keeping an eye out for visitors. He has already finished the back sports page, and has surreptitiously read page two where the bikini-clad luscious ladies are a daily feature. Now he sees a picture of a rhino, prominently located on the top right side of page three, and he grunts as he reads the latest poaching article.

"The government said yesterday that poachers slaughtered a record 668 rhinos in South Africa in 2012 as demand for their horns continued to surge on the black market in Asia. Over sixty percent of the slaughtered pachyderms were from the vast Kruger National Park, the largest wildlife reserve and the country's top safari destination. Poaching-related arrests climbed from 165 two years ago to 267.

South Africa is home to just over three-quarters of Africa's 20,000 white rhinos and 4,800 critically endangered black rhinos. Authorities have launched inter-related campaigns to slow the killings. Unless reversed, at this rate these rhinos will be extinct in less than thirty years."

He imagines himself roaring across the Highveld in a powerful *bakkie* (pickup), chasing poachers and making arrests. Then he clucks his tongue, shakes his head sadly as he thinks of his job as a cop in this small town of Knysna, with no excitement and little opportunity for advancement.

"If I were hunting those rhino poachers, instead of being stuck here, I would be travelling all over, making some real money. I would be catching those guys, getting my picture in this paper, and no more arse end of the world. Then I could finally say *tot siens* (goodbye) to Knysna. *Tot siens* forever."

He sighs and turns the newspaper page, then winces as he sees the accompanying photos of the mutilated animals, their horns brutally hacked off and their carcasses strewn about on a deserted road.

"Bloody animals themselves," he declares as he looks more closely at the pictures of the captured poachers. "Just the tip of the iceberg, and now I bet they get off because some stupid *ou* (guy) didn't do his job properly. *Fokken* rich criminal animals—makes me sick!"

He folds the paper up and drops it impatiently in the wastebasket at the side of the desk, then leans back heavily. He tries to prop his feet up on the desk but gives up when the chair refuses to recline.

"Furniture in this dump is falling apart," he mumbles, then he reaches around, scratches his ample behind. "Only another hour. That Klaas better not be late again tonight."

He leans forward and turns on the computer at his desk, ignoring the prominent "No personal business at work" note affixed to the side, and types in a web address. By the time Klaas arrives, Koos is no longer staring at the door.

"Hey Klaas, come look at this. You won't believe all the stuff I'm finding out about rhinos, poaching and—"

"Koos, not again. Did you fill out the forms on the shoplifters? What about the report about the stolen library books? *Jissus* (Jesus), man, catching poachers and whatnot is not our job. Don't leave here tonight until you finish that paperwork—I'm not gonna do it for you."

3: Ryder and Sophia, Plettenberg Bay to Knysna, November

Well, today's discussion with Sophia seems once again to be headed in a disagreeable direction. A different topic from the last time, maybe, but still no good can come of my current sarcastic and unhappy thoughts, so I do my best to brush them away from my mind. I'm feeling perfectly comfortable with the climate in the car, in my loud checked shorts and bright yellow Bafana Bafana soccer shirt, but I adjust the air conditioning to suit her just the same. I've kicked off my sandals and placed them on the back seat so I can drive barefoot. I figure the trip will take about an hour, and I have a carefully selected George Benson CD playing softly in the background.

"Do we have to listen to this again? And would you please quit humming along. Seriously, Ryder."

She folds her arms across her chest and sighs deeply. It is clear things are deteriorating rapidly here, and that I'm in over my head. I have to try to clarify—clear the air.

"Please, let's talk about this," I say, while attempting to keep a whining, wheedling tone out of my voice. "You're still angry, I can tell. I really don't want you to feel like this.

I do want a shared future with you, Sophia, I thought you knew that. Why would you think otherwise?"

"Well, I don't know," she replies sarcastically. "Let's see. We have been together for what, almost three years now, right? But sometimes I think I will wake up one morning and you will have just buggered off. What have we built together, jointly? We're not married, we no longer talk about getting married. The best you can do is get an upgrade to the Honeymoon Suite."

"Yeah I thought that was pretty cool. And funny in a way—" I say, trying to lighten the mood, steer the conversation differently.

"Well, you don't hear me laughing," she replies coldly.

"Sophie, I moved in with you, into the property you share with your parents. Doesn't that count for something? You know that was a big step for me, giving up my own place. We have talked about all of this—"

"Yeah, yeah, whatever, Ryder. I'm just saying, we live together, fine. You have your business, I have my career in television. But what do we have together as a joint dream, a joint aspiration? Not your work, not mine. Basically nothing." She shifts in her seat, then impatiently re-crosses her legs. "So we just live together, that's it. So what do we really have?"

I glance over at her, notice her lips pursed in disapproval. Are we going to go back over this territory again? Marriage, negotiating around her nagging parents? I realize I'm willing to do almost anything to keep her happy, and I also realize reluctantly that there is some truth in her observation about our parallel, somewhat disjointed, lives.

"What is it you want Sophia? Do you want to be married? Do you think that would be best for us?"

I glance out of the side window, notice the ocean way in the distance, and silently wish we could spend this drive time just enjoying the journey, instead of rehashing old business. "Remember, we have both tried this before, this marriage thing. Didn't work so well for either one of us, as I recall, and let's face it, your parents aren't that fond of me. When I moved in, that seemed traumatic enough."

Now I hold my breath, scared of what she might reply.

"No, Ryder, that is not what I want," she responds, and silently I resume breathing. "I just want, I don't know, something to look forward to. A dream we can share, a certainty of a future together. Something we can work towards, together. Instead of just living side by side, each doing our own thing."

It's at this point that we round the corner and spot the town of Knysna in the distance, sitting as if perched delicately on top of the lagoon, the sun reflecting all around. I drive down the long steep hill, passing Hornlee on the left, and turn off at George Rex Drive, choosing the road that winds out along the east side of the lagoon.

"Ryder, why are we going this way? We have to get there soon. I told my mom we would call when we arrived, so now she'll be waiting. You're going to make us late."

"Okay, okay," I say, "just an extra ten minutes, please. I have to show you something."

I'm taking a chance here, postponing the looming return to real life. We pass Mo's on Rex, a popular pub and grill, and I take the turn-off towards Leisure Island, the playground of the rich and famous. We reach the Coney Glen turn, and my car glides soundlessly up the steep and twisty road, bringing us to the perfect viewing point. I pull over.

"Ryder, what the—why are you stopping here?"

She peers around, over her sunglasses, then looks behind the car at the steep incline to see if she can figure out why I've stopped. I act quickly, knowing I'm on thin ice. I grab my sandals and slip them on, then jump out of the car, walk around to her side and open the door.

"Sophie, please, come here. Climb out, I want to show you this."

I pull on her arm, coaxing her from the car, and she reluctantly unfolds her legs and steps out. I hustle her along the tree-lined path that winds between the huge multi-million-rand homes, and we emerge at the conveniently named View Point, where we're both immediately drawn in by the breathtaking view of the lagoon hundreds of feet below. The Knysna heads are clearly visible, that treacherous opening from the Indian Ocean into the lagoon where so many lives have been lost over the years. From here, we can also see the upper-class suburb of Thesen Island in the distance, and we stand staring, both momentarily silent.

I can't help myself around this woman, never could. Even after almost three years, I look at her and my heart lurches, every time. Now I glance over, remembering the appreciative stares she drew as we walked through the hotel lobby this morning. Everywhere we go, there are always other men desiring her, yet she only has eyes for me.

And I think about being back in that hotel in Plett, back in the privacy of our room, just yesterday evening. I recall her standing looking over the railing of our balcony, our room situated so perfectly on the top floor of the hotel. Outside was a sweeping vista: white beach sand, turquoise ocean, the dip in the Robberg Peninsula clearly visible across the bay. Her profile from the waist up, with her perfect pale-brown breasts visible through her thin cotton blouse, was silhouetted by the setting sun. Her hair glinted and she was smiling, relaxed, as we reveled in being alone with each other, away from the world. No arguing, no distrust, just harmonious silence. I remember the breathless feeling, the excitement I felt as I moved to stand behind her, still shirtless from my shower, and encircled her with my arms. And how she had leaned back into me gently, pressing her round hard cheeks against my thighs, rubbing gently and then more insistently. I knew what she wanted then, just as I wanted it too. Always totally irresistible to each other, no matter the angry words between us, for as far back as I can remember.

Again now I feel it—the overwhelming attraction, the intense desire to meld, merge, become one with her. Last night she had turned around, put her arms around my neck and looked deeply into my eyes. And I was totally hers, lost in her. I could see fifty dolphins gliding through the waves, below us and just meters from the shore, a perfect backdrop to what was fast becoming another climactic evening. What more could a man want, I thought then. We have it all, love, happiness, a bond made in heaven. I remember feeling her hips moving slowly, gyrating, and how quickly my body responded, getting hard. I had lifted her up easily and she wrapped her legs around me, holding me tightly. We kissed for an eternity, long and hard, soft and gentle. Slowly she had reached down and unbuckled my belt. Then I put her down and spun her around so she could see the dolphins. I hurriedly pulled her shirt off over her head, her jeans down over her slender hips, and followed this quickly with her thong underwear. I threw them all in a heap on the floor, and then removed my jeans hastily. I smiled to myself as I thought of the old ad "Jockey or nothing"—nothing it was! And I knew then as I know now—she's mine—and I love her. I took her from behind knowing exactly how to please her. Moving my hands over her, until we were both moaning, groaning with anticipation. We know each other so well. Know this as a favorite position for both of us. I can still picture her, her profile visible to me, as she arched her back, still pressing against me from below—

"Okay, enough standing around. What're we doing here Ryder? Do you want to show me some indigenous plant life or some other nonsense—you know that does not interest me," she informs me sharply.

"Wait, just take a minute. Look over there," I say, as I point out across the cliffs, to the far-off bay, framed by the mountains and the clouds. "Tell me what you see."

"I see the ocean. I see mountains. I see a lagoon. I see the sun in the distance, and I see my mother's angry face when we're late checking in with her and Daddy. Okay?"

"Do you see the couple way off over there, sitting on the bench?"

"The old *tannie* and her even-older partner? Is that who you're talking about? Ryder, c'mon, get to the point."

"Yes, them. Sophia. What if that were us? What if we decided to move here in a decade, retire here?"

"Retire? Ryder, you are fifty, I'm forty-five. We are not exactly—"

"I said in a decade, Sophia. But in the meantime, look, we love being out here, you said it yourself."

"Yes, true—"

"And you know I'm not looking forward to going home. Admit it, neither are you!"

"Ryder, we have jobs, bills, responsibilities. We can't just—"

"But what if we did decide to build something together, something right here, in Knysna?"

"With whose money would that be, Ryder? Certainly I don't have—"

"Just hear me out, please. I know I could find the capital for a small business. I've been setting money aside for a while now. A business would allow us to return here, live here part-time in a few years, and then stay here when we're like that old couple over there."

"Are you being serious?"

"Of course I am Sophie. I would hope you know that by now."

She opens her mouth to interrupt, but then closes it, remaining uncharacteristically silent.

"What about if we open something small here in Knysna?" I continue. "Together. It'll be our retirement investment."

"But I still don't see how something small will help, Ryder. We would need something that can support both of us."

"Sophia, we can grow this together. I'll do all the work to get it off the ground, and then eventually we can move here. And I'll provide the upfront capital."

"So where do I fit in, exactly?"

"You can join me when the business takes off. And we will build it together."

I lean my back against a tree, encircle her waist and pull her so she's leaning against me, facing away and looking towards the ocean. I rest my chin on top of her head, her lean frame fitting perfectly against me. I point into the distance, to a small building with a for lease sign barely visible in front of it.

"Look, over there. A perfect location for what could be our new business. A finishing school to groom local talent for television, just like you've always talked about. I'll bet a place like that is not even that expensive to rent. We could do this, you know! Tell me you like the idea."

As we head back to the car, I take her hand, feeling her responding, opening up to me again, her anger and frustration dissipating. I love this woman, all I want is her happiness—my happiness depends on it.

Now once again my thoughts are rudely interrupted, this time by a face only a mother could love, attached to a skinny, non-too-clean body, fast approaching and speaking to me.

"Hey Boss, *ek kyk na die kar* (I'm looking at the car), nice car Boss, *lanie* (fancy)! Vee Pee number Boss, you from

Cape Town?"

I reluctantly acknowledge the presence of the nagging colored car guard, looking like a *bergie* (down and out), glassy eyed and dressed in torn jeans, but with new Nikes on his feet. He's anxious to make sure I see him, anxious to ensure a tip. Does he really think I need him to stand guard? To prevent someone from stealing my car while I'm standing looking at the stunning view, just meters away?

"Jesus man, it can cost a guy twenty rand a day just for stopping and parking five times in this country," I say, as I reach into my pocket, fish out a few coins and hand them to him. I turn to Sophia and shrug. "Oh well, at least he's trying to do something to earn a buck."

Sophia frowns at me and shakes her head slightly. "*Ag* please, he can't be doing too badly out of this, with those new smart trainers," she says. "You're a sucker Ryder—you know that? I would just tell him to *voetsek* (get lost). C'mon, we need to get a move-on if we want to get to Knysna already, and if we want to get away from these guys hassling us on the road—"

Again she's becoming impatient with me, turning back towards the car, ready to press on. I release her hand, step over and open her door. We climb back in, but now the atmosphere has changed. She sits with her body angled slightly towards me, no longer disengaged. I can tell from her intense stare that she's mulling my idea over. Yes! I've said the right thing, made the right suggestion.

"Okay, when we're in Knysna over the next few days, let's do some legwork." She speaks breathlessly. "You're not just doing this because of what I said, are you? Just to shut me up maybe?"

"No Sophia, you're right. We need to build something together. We've decided we're not going to do the traditional thing, the tying-the-knot thing, so honestly, I have to agree with you. When I think about my future, the only one I see is with you. The only one I want is with you. So let's build it together."

We get back on the road again, turn left from George Rex onto the N2 and drive straight into the quaint little town. The sun is slowly sinking over the lagoon, creating yet another stunning image, capping off a glorious day. Now we're both filled with extreme hope and unbridled optimism. We can do this! We have money, time, ideas, and the will to build this wonderfully vivid dream together. This is it, I think, the start of an exciting new chapter. Sophia and Ryder. We've been a couple for years now, but this shared dream, built together, will ensure that we'll be a couple for years to come. Ensure that we spend our old age together. This feels so good, so right. She wants a shared dream, well so do I. Don't I?

4: Jacqueline, Wilderness, December

She sat with the sketch pad in her lap, trying desperately to relish the moment and turn her thoughts away from the past few months.

"Focus. That's enough anguish for one day," she admonished herself, not for the first time. "Frank would not want you to be so miserable for the rest of your life. Get on with it, Jacqui."

She leaned against the semi-rigid backrest of her beach chair with a sigh. Her pastels were scattered on the blanket at her feet, many of them worn down completely now. Most other artists preferred to sketch from photographs, but she had always liked to do her work surrounded by the real thing, giving the drawings a more dynamic feel. Now, she quickly added two seagulls floating above the drawn clouds, and then turned her gaze back out over the ocean. Behind her, she could sense the *fynbos* (sparse bush), covering the low scrubby dunes, with the Outeniqua Mountains looming across the N2 highway in the background. Stretching out on either side and into the surf were rocky outcroppings, the sea-sand coarse with ground shells and coral, but where she sat it was fine and white. The waves of low tide splashed out in the distance, the sea relatively calm today. She closed her eyes and adjusted her wide-brimmed straw hat, trying to envision the scene from three hours ago, when she had first arrived. Wilderness Beach was known as one of the premiere spots for shell picking, yet there had been only one other person wandering along it then, an elderly woman. Jacqui thumbed through her sketches, pulled out the one of that woman with her collection of clam and conch shells, and then made a small adjustment. Satisfied, she closed her eyes, again forcefully ignoring the uneasiness at the edges of her consciousness, the darkness that pulled her down and threatened her concentration. The beach was now totally deserted, the sun almost level with the horizon, the sound of the water faint in the background. She allowed herself to drift off.

"What in the world—?" she muttered as an object went whizzing by, waking her from a dreamless sleep and landing a few meters from her blanket. She looked over, noticed a bright yellow ball with a smiley face painted on it, half buried where it had landed. She glanced behind her just as a brown-and-white blur ran past, and then stopped abruptly in front of the ball.

"Oh is this your ball?" she asked as the dog picked it up with his mouth, then walked over to her and dropped it at her feet. She looked around, noticed someone cresting the dune and looking over in her direction, before she glanced back at the dog.

"Ah yes, I see you've noticed. I am truly adorable, aren't I? Please, allow me to introduce myself. I'm Jack. Believe me, the

pleasure's all mine. What's that? Oh yes, him, bringing up the rear over there, headed towards us. Why, that would be Exhibit A. One fifty-two year old man by the name of Ryder. Stylishly dressed, slender, neat and well-groomed. Fond of whimsical footwear, including the Haviana Pac-man flip-flops currently on his size ten feet. Bald, over six feet tall. Capable of charm and wit, although some may find his jokes corny. Kind and reliable, with a ready smile and strong white teeth. Enjoys swimming, sailing, and most other outdoor pursuits. 'Is he handsome?' I see you already wondering. Well, what do I know in this regard, best you judge for yourself. Certainly the women find him attractive—there never seems to be a shortage, that much I can assure you. Good company, generous; in possession of one rather overpriced vehicle of which he seems inordinately fond. My best friend."

"I'm so sorry—sorry we disturbed you," Ryder yelled out, his words barely audible over the rhythmic sound of the surf. "C'mon Jack—that lady is not going to play fetch with you. Over here, come play with me instead."

He whistled for the dog, who remained where he was, the ball covered in sand and slobber still resting at Jacqueline's feet.

"Here I've got it—I need to stretch my legs anyway," she said, as she stood shakily and picked up the ball, then threw it. Once again Jack retrieved it, and once again he delivered it to her feet.

"Well, it seems you have a fan. I'm Ryder by the way—looks like Jack and I interrupted your drawing," he said, walking across the white sand towards her.

"No, not at all—I was really done for the day. I'm Jacqueline. Guess I'm just going to have to throw this again, aren't I, Jack?"

"Well, that would be the general idea—I assume you've played fetch before?"

As she threw the ball repeatedly, Jack kept retrieving it and bringing it to her, ignoring Ryder. She looked him over surreptitiously, noticed that he was indeed a tall, dark and handsome stranger. About fifty years old, she guessed, flip-flops, brightly-colored Hurley swimming trunks, no shirt and a tanned, hairless chest. Kind eyes. The silence stretched awkwardly between them as Jack ran back and forth.

"So, um, are you from around here?" she asked. "I'm sure I would've recognized Jack if I'd seen him before."

"No, no, just passing through. Couldn't resist a walk on the beach though, and how 'bout you?"

Just as she was about to reply, a third voice was heard, coming from the far side of the dunes.

"Ryder? Jack? Where the heck are you guys?"

"Ah, here we go. Time to introduce Sophia, and yes, I'm afraid she does go with Ryder, more's the pity. Quite the mismatched pair really. She is of a totally humorless breed, guaranteed to be displeased to make your acquaintance. A killjoy, you might even say. And so now, undoubtedly, we have reached the end of playtime."

Jacqueline watched as a tall woman, fashionably dressed in a black-and-gold bikini with a matching cover-up climbed up the hill. She had her gold strappy sandals clasped in her hand, with her oversize designer sunglasses completing the outfit. Suddenly Jacqueline became uncomfortably aware of her own crayon-smudged clothing, the baggy t-shirt and cargo shorts chosen for utility only. Her hat flapped in the slight breeze and she raised her hand to hold it in place.

"We're over here Sophia. Just retrieving Jack's ball. We're coming," Ryder said and waved. As they hurried away and towards Sophia, Ryder turned back to Jacqueline. "Hey, thanks for playing with Jack. Nice to meet you, Julie."

"It's Jacqueline," she called out, but they were already gone. Ah well, it was time to pack it in anyway. The day at the beach had been productive, the small pile of drawings easily exceeding her goal for the day.

She thought of Jack and Ryder as she gathered her belongings, how glad she had been for their company, and wondered briefly about Ryder and Sophia, the nature of their relationship. Did he seem nervous when she called for him, or was Jacqui imagining it?

"Ah pointless," she decided, "trying to figure out the private lives of perfect strangers. Will probably never lay eyes on them again."

Over the past few months, she had deliberately simplified her life, and she resolved, again, to let go of any second thoughts. Yes, there had never really been any choice. She was simply here, now, for better or for worse.

"Enjoy the given moment," she reminded herself. "Nothing to be gained from gazing backwards, wistfully, or forwards, expectantly."

She trudged across the sand, beach-chair slung over her shoulder and art supplies jumbled together in her arms. She drove carefully from the easternmost side of the beach parking lot, along the road heading to her temporary home. First, a right turn into Station Road along the railway line, then over the National Road, into and through the village of Wilderness. This late on a Friday afternoon, the hawkers were already collecting in front of the small strip of shops under the milkwood trees on the left. The visitors buzzed about, buying exotic foods and local goods, and the smells of the schwarma, felafels and sweet pancakes filled the air.

"Has this place still not left the sixties?" she asked herself, as she slowed down to take it all in: the live music; the assorted stalls and booths selling leather adornments, beadwork and clothes; and the usual collection of shoeless hippy locals smoking something sweet-smelling under the trees.

Driving deliberately now, she cruised past the handful of restaurants serving the town: Pomodoro, with the wafting smells of fresh pizza, pasta and garlic; the Blue Olive with the famous large jam jars of outlandish mixed drinks with multiple straws visible even from the road; and of course Cocomos, a venue for live music and an eclectic assortment of foods. Very briefly, she wondered if tonight, finally, she would venture out, instead of eating at home alone.

The rest of the town, the general store, pharmacy and doctor's office, had already passed quickly by. Each day as she completed this drive, going to and from the beach, she was struck anew by how fortunate she was, with this unique opportunity to be here in the heart of Eden, on the Garden Route. The sight of her little yellow rented house as it appeared on the left, with its thatched roof and welcoming porch, lifted her spirits, and she drove up the winding driveway, lined on both sides with colorful hydrangeas and blue and white agapanthus flowers. Yet despite her efforts to focus on the pleasant book waiting open on the arm of the sofa inside, still she thought about the vacant passenger seat next to her. She parked the car, climbed the steps and stared back at the Touw River, clearly visible from this vantage up on the hill. Then she opened the front door and let herself in to silence.

5: Ryder, Cape Town to Riebeek Kasteel, March, two years later

He flings the spare bunch of keys onto the cold, beige-tiled floor, muttering angrily, then storms out into the cool air. He glances briefly at the overcast sky, before turning and forcefully slamming the door shut. Now cursing more audibly, he locks it with a lone key still held in his hand. Then he bends down, about to slide it through the gap above the threshold. Already he knows that the bunch lying inside the door in the foyer will serve as a clear communication to whoever sees it, nothing more required. Yes, he wants this to be his message to Sophia, and no, he's not looking for subtlety. That has never been his style.

Reminding himself of one last thing, he straightens up and re-inserts the key, opens the door. Then he glances back outside and over at the patio, catching sight of his dog. Jack's ears perk up immediately and he raises his head, watching intently, a slightly bemused expression on his face.

"Oh no, please Ryder, go ahead. Take your time, just standing there lost in thought. Perhaps you think I have all day with nothing better to do, and well, I suppose you're right. So I'll just lie here, as I've been trained to do, waiting for word that you're ready. Because I do so want to accompany you on this long-overdue voyage. After all, as I ponder this more deeply, I really am here only for the sake of service

to you, the underlying reason for my existence. And so I will wait, patiently, and when you're ready we can start out together."

Moving deliberately now, Ryder takes off his drab wool sweater and tosses it so it lands in the middle of the slate floor of the entry way, right next to the house keys. *Won't be needing this anymore,* he thinks grimly. Then, he replaces his cap on his cleanly-shaven head, reaches down and firmly tightens the laces on his sneakers. He stands up, shuts and locks the door more resolutely, then slides the key easily underneath. No turning back now—not possible, with literally no way back in.

He looks again at the stone exterior of this house. The grey, shaded facade has always seemed so clean and tidy, but so inhospitable. No hint, inside or out, of the natural warmth and beauty inherent in the setting overlooking the beaches of Cape Town. Instead, the house ensured blocked views, sharp angles, and a cold, stark feel. Small wonder he reached for that sweater each time he walked in the door, regardless of the season. And small wonder so much time was spent in this house planning for the future, rather than acknowledging the unwelcoming present.

Determined to get going now, he crosses the garden, reaches his car and opens the door, then whistles for Jack. Twenty pounds of brown and white energy bolts out and jumps right in, immediately making himself comfortable on the back seat.

"Ah so now you're all set—well, then, I guess we shall begin. Off we go."

There are no neighbors around, no one to call a simple greeting to, making the mid-morning departure a convenient choice. Ryder slides behind the wheel, inhales deeply of the leather smell, his trusty steed waiting here, warm despite the gathering clouds. He thinks of how the car, the clothes on his back, and the thoughtfully chosen items folded neatly on the back seat and in the trunk are all he can depend on now. Then his thoughts turn to Jack, half-asleep in the corner, but with one ear always cocked, waiting.

"Really, Ryder, don't look at me that way. Do you think I care about our destination? How many hours have I spent in this car with you, always the dependable travelling companion? Always holding my own counsel, yet providing for comforting company. This warm seat, this soft blanket, you my best friend steering the way. How could I ask anything further?

And as long as I know one thing for certain, that we're headed away from here, away from Sophia, I'm content. You can rest assured that it pains me deeply to even think about her effect on you right now. She has cast you from her bed, and now finally she's forcing you from your home, setting you on this quest. Look at yourself—discarded, dejected, banished from love. Why, I think you're dangling dangerously on the edge of the sanity precipice. What a precarious beginning to our journey!

It's a good thing you have me, you know—pulling you back, guiding you onto the road to reason. Ah Ryder, Ryder, it is going to take a lot of work to get you to see how much better off you are going to be. Are you even aware—all you ever do with that Sophia is compromise? Give in here, give in there, and now, see for yourself— you have nothing left to give. And typical Sophia, she chooses now to ask you to leave."

The clouds start to amass, even as the drive begins.

Ryder reaches over, turns up the volume on the radio. He resolves to focus on the road, on his breathing, on remaining calm. The car descends slowly down the hill, exiting the neighborhood. On the way driving through town to reach Kloof Nek Road, he pulls into the parking lot of the corner store. His usual routine includes a stop off here, just before getting onto the N2 and then N7, to buy snacks for the trip: two cans of Red Bull, some chips, and a small beef stick for Jack. Today, as an afterthought, he grabs a box of tissues as well, then waits in line to pay, while compulsively checking his phone. But there is no call. No message.

"Hey, you forgot your change." The pierced and tattooed cashier comes out from behind the counter as Ryder exits, and hands him some money. "You all right man? Somebody die or something?"

"Sure as shit feels like it, I tell you. Sure feels like it," he replies as he walks out the door. Yes, that describes it exactly, he decides on the way back to the car. Something has died, he's in mourning, yet he's going to have to keep on going. After all those months spent in denial, he feels the depression closing in, and knows his fall from grace is complete.

How the heck will I land gently and get up and go again? he wonders, as he climbs in, buckles up, and sets forth on the long drive. *Won't be needing these fancy sunglasses with how this weather looks. Useless as all the other stuff she has given me over the years.*

He takes off his Levi sunglasses, places them carefully in the glove box. And now it starts to pour in earnest, and the emotions he has struggled so mightily to keep in check, overwhelm him. As the windshield wipers flap frantically to keep up with the showers, so he wipes impatiently at his eyes to keep up with the flow of sad and angry tears. Somewhere up ahead, the road is clear but he's not yet able to see it. Swirling fog blows in from all directions, clouding his vision and leaving no discernible path to any destination. Just a drive, onward and through the mist, with the vague hope that he will find his way, the waning trust that eventually the storm will subside and the sun will emerge.

He pulls over to the side of the road, deciding to wait out the worst of the weather. Jack jumps over the seat, nestles in his lap and they sit in contemplative silence. Ryder strokes the white-and-brown fur absent-mindedly, feels Jack's heartbeat so closely in synch with his own.

"There, there Ryder. All will be well. Everything happens for the best, you'll see."

Ryder stares into the rearview mirror at the passing storm, catching intermittent glimpses of Cape Town. He sees the clouds covering the mountains behind him, a sure indication of foul weather.

"This is it, Jack," he mutters. "I'm finally going to have to accept it. I'm leaving, for good. Good bye Cape Town— Lord knows when I'll be back."

Ryder thinks back to his simple dream as a young man: to find happiness living at the seaside, enjoying the sun, surf and sailing offered by this enviable location. Why was that so hard to achieve, what was so difficult about that plan? Or perhaps he did achieve his dream, he thinks mournfully, and now he has used up his allotted measure of happiness, and will be condemned to spend the rest of his days in abject misery. No, he reminds himself, he will not think that way. He focuses instead on more deep breathing, and less contemplating. The storm abates, he dries his eyes, and adjusts his cap more firmly on his head. He needs to get back on the road, resume this journey in earnest. Yes, he thinks, he has wasted enough time already.

"Go lie down in the back, Jack. On your bed, good boy."

He hands the beef stick to Jack, who wags his tail briefly, then settles down and munches on it, content as ever. He merges back into the traffic, driving north out of the city. After all of this time, all these trips, he knows the details of the road ahead, the straight shot on the N7 as it makes its way to Malmesbury. From there, he will detour onto Ceres road, cresting the top of the pass before descending into Riebeek Valley, at the foot of Kasteelberg Mountains. Without any effort he anticipates his first glimpse of the valley, the colorful patches of green and yellow, interspersed with the inevitable brown, now that it is late in the summer. The road stretches forward as the mountains keep watch in the distance, the clouds looming above.

Figures, he thinks bitterly. *Of course it would be raining today, even though it never rains at this time of year. Not exactly helping my mood.*

As he drives, fond memories of Table Mountain, flanked by Devils Peak to the east, and Lion's Head to the west, seem to pull him back to Cape Town, despite the increasing distance. He thinks of the many afternoons spent outside, lost in thought, as the tablecloth clouds delicately descended over the magnificent Table Mountain. Beauty, strength and danger, all juxtaposed here on the Cape of Good Hope and the Cape of Storms.

He recalls one of his favorite pastimes, driving visitors, family and guests around the peninsula, all the while pointing out the sights and sounds, and telling stories of this most incredibly beautiful part of Africa. Talking about the settlement below the mountains, founded in the 1600's by Jan van Riebeek, for the Dutch East India Company. Prattling on about how ships sailing around the Dark Continent would stop here to collect fresh meat and vegetables to avoid the dreaded scurvy. Yes, he would watch with pride of ownership as his visitors gazed out over the beautiful vistas at every turn, as they took in how the ocean stretched around the city, and how the three kilometer flat surface of Table Mountain formed the perfect backdrop.

He tries to avoid the obvious question, the one screaming out for an answer: will he ever come back to this place, his home for almost three decades? He drums his fingers on the steering wheel angrily, turns up the volume on the radio, trying to force a focus on the sheer beauty of the scenery, trying not to dwell on the sad reality that it might be a long time before he sees it all again. He looks back at Jack, his little dog with the huge personality, snoring on the back seat, and he feels momentarily comforted.

But hard as he tries, he's unable to gather his presence into the present, the time and space he's occupying; the thoughts and feelings from the past emerge again, and he's pulled backwards in time. Back into his memories of the many days spent hiking to the top of the mountain, climbing to reach the amphitheater overlooking the city. At over a thousand meters in the air, at one of the most popular tourist attractions in the world, he would sit, communing with the local landscape, the flora and fauna.

He remembers walking along the paths carved into the craggy, grey, erosion-resistant sandstone, his long, loping stride matched by Jack's short fast trot. Sometimes they would ascend the mountain by foot; even the most straightforward path through Platteklip Gorge would take him and Jack at least two hours and leave them both panting and breathless when they finally reached the top. There they would look out over Cape Town, Table Bay and Robben Island to the north, or the Atlantic seaboard to the west and south.

Or sometimes they would climb one of the other popular paths, traversing only the lower slopes of the mountain, beginning from Constantia Nek, Cecilia Park, Kirstenbosch, Newlands Forest or Rhodes Memorial, pausing intermittently to watch the rock climbers map out and then ascend their varying routes. Now he thinks about his indigenous origins, much like the 2,000 unique species of plant life, many of them endangered, which are found in this small corner of the world. And he pictures the more-exposed slopes with their covering of *fynbos*, the fine-bush that burns off every year through the natural wildfire cycle, and then rejuvenates at the start of the growing season. He tries desperately to recapture the thrill of unexpectedly discovering a phoenix protea, a plant that regrows every year after having been burned and left for dead. He thinks about this national flower superimposed upon the image of the phoenix, a symbol of his country that has emerged from the fire of racial hatred to become a rainbow nation. Can he, too, emerge from this barren place he now finds himself in, to return in triumph? Or will he never come back to Cape Town, a place where he found true love for the first time? This city, with its famous mountain, a modern member of the Seven Wonders of the World, how can he leave it when it holds such a huge part of his heart? How can he accept that he might return as a visitor, an outsider, but perhaps never again as a resident?

He tries to imagine himself a lion, the ruler of his domain. And once again tears of self-pity and regret for his circumstances well up in the corners of his eyes. The king of the jungle indeed, now forced into retreat. Feelings of disconnection and isolation threaten to overwhelm him, and it is only through grim determination that he steers through the last of the raindrops, the bleak road ahead gathering him in with every passing minute. Driving away from home, family, and love, and driving toward uncertainty, homelessness, and rootlessness. Suddenly, he sees he's suspended between two worlds, the past and the future, and he feels shattered when he realizes he has no present. No focus, no awareness, no hope in his circumstances.

He swallows hard, takes a few chips out of the bag, and begins eating them slowly and methodically. He tries to engage his senses, concentrating on the salty flavor, the slightly oily crunch. With effort, he pulls himself back into the present, again forces his concentration on the road ahead. And as the miles disappear behind the wheels of his car, and the distance between him and the city of his dreams grows, he focuses on a new beginning. Yes, he will start over. Without anything except his car, his dog, and his meager worldly possessions packed into the trunk. And without her, the once magnificent love of his life.

6: Ryder, Cape Town to Riebeek Kasteel, March

Raining? Really?! Could this day get any worse? The first part of this difficult journey and now I have to drive it in the rain, on my own again, naturally. Let's face it, crying doesn't make seeing the road any easier. Pull yourself together, man. Probably nothing but static on the radio. Nah here's a good song, "*Forget You.*" Yeah sure, that's going to be easy. Five years and now nothing left! Nothing! I should turn around and go back to Cape Town. Tell her what she's done to me. Bargain with her. Talk her into rethinking and starting over. But I already know, she won't listen. Her words, repeated to me over and over:

"Just because you want it, Ryder, doesn't mean I want it too."

How many times, in so many different ways, did I get this response from her? Directly, indirectly. Passively, aggressively. Yet, all it did was make me more frantic. More desperate to hold things together, to fix what was broken.

Well, today I finally did it, moved out, and left while she wasn't home. I deliberately planned this so she wouldn't know I was choosing today—of all days—to be gone. Do I hope she'll come back, sadly realize that I've finally left, and then suddenly see the light? Maybe it could still happen. What if she called me right now? My cell phone—no missed calls. I wonder if the damn thing is switched on, if it's working correctly? Yes it is—full signal. And she's definitely home by now. She'll already have seen the obvious signs of my being gone, and there have been no phone calls. No big surprise there.

Screw it, why should I spend this ride waiting for her to call me? I've already squandered too much time wishing and hoping. Yes, I'm tossing this phone onto the back seat, out of my reach. Whoops, sorry Jack. Hope that didn't wake you up. Sleeping through my anguish, a best friend indeed. Imperturbable as always. No suggestions for me, Jack? Useless, talking to my dog now, expecting words of wisdom. I'm so sad, it's truly pitiful.

I need to think of other things, to focus. What was it she said, exactly?

"It would be best if you moved out, I think you know that."

Stunning words! I wonder how long she waited to say them, or all the words that followed, as I stood there, despondent and crying.

"Ryder, I want to be on my own for a while. You can take your time, but you WILL need to leave."

Did my inadequate response only make things worse?

"Jesus, Sophia—I thought you wanted to build a future together. What about that? It was all your idea, you know it! Since when do you prefer to be by yourself? I thought you wanted to be with me, I thought—"

And yet I couldn't bring myself to ask her that one big

question, did she really want to be by herself, or had she found someone else?

I'm such a fool. Small and large incidents are coming back to me now, like the time I expected us to go away together for the weekend, just a few months ago. And so I sat, waiting, bags packed, full of eager anticipation. That anticipation faded as I endured the next three hours, wondering what was happening, why she was so late. Finally the phone call came.

"Oh Ryder—I'm sorry, I thought you knew…"

"Knew what? I've been waiting for you for hours now," I responded, more than a little drunk by then. Yes, alcohol, I admit it—my ready solution looking for a problem.

"Oh, a simple misunderstanding," she said with a small laugh. "Well, nothing to be done now—I'm already at the resort with the others. I thought we arranged it all a few days ago."

"What? Who're you with? Sophia, we were supposed to go together," I answered, confusion from both her response and the alcohol swirling together.

"Whatever, what's done is done. See you in a few days," she had responded before she abruptly hung up.

And now, where am I supposed to go? We built a home together, dammit. I gave up everything for her. Everything! And here we have the root of the problem— right here! I merged my dream with hers. Moved in to her home; involved myself in this new business at the expense of my own, then tried to coexist with her family, while keeping my own on the periphery. On top of that, I over-reached and began our new business guided by her hopes and her dreams. Did I really think those were my hopes, my dreams, too? With each effort and compromise I made, I saw it as a deposit into our future together. But in actuality, each represented a withdrawal against my personal store of pride and self-worth. I plundered my chances for a viable future, and willingly! Now all of my accounts of self-reckoning are empty, overdrawn. I sit holding on to investments in nothing, at such a high cost. Worthless. That's me—desperate and worthless.

Okay there it is, the sun, finally, already beginning its slow descent in my rearview mirror. Now I can catch occasional glimpses of the farmlands, vineyards and mountains. I can see the neat rows of grape vines lining the valley, with what is left of the unharvested fruit, adding a purple hue to their deep green. I can spot small lakes and ponds, as well as the occasional animal in the distance. I can even see a farmer or two out there, trimming the smaller grapes from the bunches with tiny nail scissors to increase the size and sweetness of the table grapes. The peaceful rural life in beautiful wine country—these are all good things.

I have to remember—there are lots of good things left. Just because my life is in shreds, and I have no future; just because I'm middle-aged and single; just because I've invested time and considerable money into a failed love venture, and an at-risk business one. Just because all of my friends have now become her friends, and are therefore lost to me; these are not things to cry over. I can move forward. Let her keep her fucking friends, and her horrible parents, and every other thing we built and planned together. See if it makes her happy. Lord knows I tried to do so; let some other sucker give it a whirl. It's time for me to build my own future. No more shared vision. No more fusion of dreams, emotions, desires. I know I need to do this but dammit, does it have to be so hard?

7: Jack, Cape Town to Riebeek Kasteel, March

One thing you may not know about me—I used to live in the inner city. Yes, to look at me you might think I'm more of a creature of the suburbs, but really, I was a big Man-About-Town back in the day. All right, technically, Dog-About-Town, but the finer points of semantics are lost on so many. Don't you agree?

And my best friend Ryder? Well, I feel he could be very happy becoming a small-town beast despite having lived all of his life in the 'burbs of the big city. And I will do my best to help him discover this, but I can already tell, it's not going to be easy. So much ground to cover, so much self-awareness to be achieved.

Look, the man is somewhat unoriginal: naming a Jack Russell terrier Jack. Need I say more? Moderately bright, but lacking in imagination, would probably describe him best. For the most part, I've tried not to interfere with his behavior, which we all know has been somewhat erratic thus far, and in return, he allows me a certain latitude to live my life as I see fit. All-in-all, our coexistence forms a nice symbiotic relationship, which is why I refer to him as my partner rather than my master. It has a certain ring to it, don't you think? Come to think of it, best friend is probably how he would describe me, and I suppose that pretty much covers it. Let's settle for best friend and throw in worst critic. How about that.

Anyhoo, being stuck with a Best Friend who is not that cerebral can have its plusses and minuses. As a matter of practicality, I get my way more often than he realizes. Definitely in the plus column. And for intellectual stimulation, I can always look to outside resources. So all in all, we manage nicely, thank you very much. Also, if I'm to be perfectly honest, I've grown kind of fond of my name. Evocative of "Jock of the Bushveld," one of my all-time role models, although I doubt my best friend was thinking that way when he bestowed it upon me. More likely thinking about his favorite libation, Jack Daniels, if you must know. However, I prefer not to dwell on that. And I'm certainly thankful to be a step above "Patches" or "Spot," or some of the other unoriginal monikers with which my peers are saddled. Yes, I think despite the obviousness of it all, my name is pretty much reflective of my character. Happy coincidence perhaps, but there you have it.

Now you may be wondering why I mentioned my inauspicious origins. I believe they give me a unique perspective on small town existence, what with my having arrived in Ryder's life as an outsider. Some of the details of the old days are hazy, but I recall very clearly a wrinkled, brown hand alternately feeding me and feeding himself. What was his name—Gatiep? Gammaat? Let's simply call him Old Brown Sherry. The names most of these humans are endowed with don't bear repeating, and in any case many sound all the same to me. So Old Brown Sherry it is—OuBies for short.

Oh yes, during my time as OuBies's companion in the Big City, there was always a variety and an occasional bounty: a discarded hamburger, not too elderly, with plenty of meat still remaining; a lamb shank bone, nice and gristly. Lest you think I spent all of my time concerned with such pedestrian pursuits as filling my belly, let me assure you that it was during this time that I began to hone my talents as a keen observer of human nature. Life on the streets certainly provides a unique perspective here. And it was also during this time that I learned something very special about myself: people think I'm adorable. Not just fetching, like your average miniature poodle, or even cute like your average cocker spaniel. No, I'm talking adorable. As in irresistible. And it didn't take Old Brown Sherry long to realize this either—increased handouts when holding me in his arms was probably his first clue. As I said, the details are hazy, but I'm guessing OuBies took full advantage of this. Let's face it, although OuBies didn't have any leg up on my current best friend in the brains department, he was no fool either.

Okay, so between what I gleaned on the streets, and what I observed at the hands and feet of Old Brown Sherry, I would say, without invoking any false modestly, that I was primed to become the perfect companion. Problem was, OuBies was more in need of spare change than a cool, composed, capable companion of the canine variety. Perhaps you can see where this is going.

On the day that I became known as Jack, I do recall that it was raining. I believe OuBies was huddled next to the fire-pit cum trashcan, as was his wont, with the remains of a cigarette, a so-called stompie, clamped between his ragged, chapped lips. Funny how some details remain etched in one's mind: the pungent odor from the brown paper bag never far from his side; the smell of tobacco or something stronger and sweeter from the collection of butts hidden in each of his pockets. I know that, simply by virtue of the fact that I was a key player. I must have been witness to what followed. Yet I remember very little of it, only that one moment I stood between OuBies's legs sheltered from the incessant rain, and that the next, I was being whisked away in a purring vehicle. I recall a fluffy white towel surprisingly absent of any smell, and some rather annoying music. The rest is a veritable blur. I have to presume some money changed hands.

Does it make me excessively vain to assume that it was a large amount?

After that fateful ride, my life changed considerably. I could dwell on the obvious: two squares, no more wide variety of questionable provenance: regular baths, walks, classes and socialization sessions. I had always been somewhat particular about my personal hygiene and elimination habits, so to have them recognized, praised, and even rewarded, seemed a little condescending. I was already an adult, after all. It has been my experience that low expectations lead to poor results. Luckily, I take a certain amount of pride independent of external influences, because the bar was set pretty low, let me tell you. However, playing right along—my relationship with my new best friend proceeded very smoothly. He believed he was "training" me, while I came to see that I could easily transfer my affection for OuBies to this new guy while simultaneously molding his behavior to suit my needs. And naturally, he became very devoted to me as he fell further and further under the spell of my irresistible adorable-ness. Basically your classic boy-meets-dog story, albeit with a slightly older boy and a slightly altered initial chapter.

Now it seems my Best Friend has been contemplating the subject of happiness for quite some time. A central part of this Quixotic quest he's on, in fact. How do I know this? Do you really have to ask? Is it not in my job description to intuit this type of information? Let me just say this: the pursuit of happiness is a lot like chasing your own tail. And again, here is a subject I know a thing or two about, as both a keen observer of human behavior and also, well let's simply say I've been there, done that, a time or two over the years, believe me.

Let's go back a few months. It's hard to be exact about the timeframe, of course, but it is helpful to have some history in order to understand why Ryder has set out on his own in the first place. I had been spending a lot of time hanging out under the bed, a place not at all conducive to my usual sociable nature. Why? Well, the atmosphere around me had become somewhat poisoned. I had been doing my darndest to help Ryder, but was getting nowhere. Delusional does not even begin to describe how he had been acting. Frankly, it had become painful to watch him keep trying so hard and keep failing so badly. Look, I can be as smitten as the next hound by a wily bitch. All it takes is a coquettish look from one of those stuck-up thoroughbreds to get my heart racing. I know you know the type. But forgive me if I fail to understand how human males can be so clueless when it comes to the opposite sex. Here he was, being rebuffed consistently, so what does he do? Well don't make the obvious guess because of course that is not what he chose to do! No, rather than walk away, he simply tried harder and harder. Denial! Delusion! Willful blindness! And I'm supposed to be the dumb animal!

Yes, just like chasing his tail. I'm glad you're keeping up. There cannot be anyone more foolish than a human in love with another human who does not return the feeling in equal measure. I believe that this imbalance of affection and the resultant behavior is responsible for a great deal of the disharmony in the world. But I digress...

Well, it seems pointless to go into the details of all the miscommunications and misunderstandings. I might have been under the bed but I'm not deaf; therefore I was privy to most of the discussions. And really they all boiled down to the same things: she was disappointed and dissatisfied; he tried harder; she got further disenchanted. Between the accusations and the sadness, there were reconciliations and promises to be better, intervals of noisy discussions followed by noisy lovemaking. Forgive the cynicism if I state, once again, that I knew where this was headed. Two people on two divergent paths, each trying to mold the other to their own desired form.

Sometimes I get so weary of human problems, so tired of people's inability to see their own actions more clearly.

The details of the eventual breakup are superfluous, with so many occasions leading to this unfortunate ending. An example: poor delusional Ryder, sitting waiting, bag packed expecting a romantic weekend for two. A silent telephone, no word of warning, just a no-show, and a grim weekend spent in solitude and misery. Yes what we had was a true cycle of loneliness, powerlessness and heartbreak. And this eventual departure on his own in his trusty vehicle came far too late, in my opinion.

I will certainly acknowledge that today has been a long and tough day. Oh, the work of man's best friend is never done! I truly believe without my comforting presence, Ryder might not have survived this past month. Today, with bags hastily packed, we took off with only one end-point destination in mind. Knysna. And all the preceding crying, wailing, moaning, gnashing of teeth—all of this for naught— which, believe me, I would gladly have explained had I the capacity to do so!

I would like to think I've always understood that together we would embark on some exciting adventures, Ryder and I. But certainly I could not have anticipated that we would begin our latest journey heavy with loss, heartache, sorrow and pain. Oh, for a renewed sense of courage and purpose, or even a vague hope that we might someday emerge in optimism and inspiration, as we continue on our noble quest, the never-ending search for happiness. And from my perspective, which perhaps one day Ryder will become enlightened enough to share, this quest is nothing more than searching for something that already exists within. Yes, that is right. Slow down, breathe and let your tail come to you. Be your own tail. Namaste.

8: Ryder, Riebeek Kasteel, March

The Obiekwa Mountains form the backdrop to this tiny town eighty kilometers from CapeTown, with its population of less than five thousand, around seventy percent so-called "colored folk."

"Yeah, my mood matches perfectly with these mountains named for Murderers," Ryder thinks bitterly, then remembers a new joke about the cemetery he has just passed. "Dead bodies. Always good for a laugh. Morbid. Guess I'll tell that later, after we're all suitably inebriated."

Approaching the town of Riebeek's Kasteel, there are vineyards as far as the eye can see, with the Elandsberg mountains visible out on the horizon. Ryder has pulled up into the dusty central square, the area usually populated with wine makers and artists, along with tourists busily shopping and sightseeing. At this time of year, there are few visitors and Ryder finds a parking spot easily. He unbuckles, takes off his long-sleeved shirt and replaces it with something more suitable for the warmer weather, the light t-shirt carefully selected and placed on the passenger seat just last night. Jack leaps over into the front, and Ryder clasps his leash to his collar. Then they clamber out together.

"Are you hungry? Who's a good boy?" Ryder murmurs to him as they begin walking down the street, looking for a cafe for a quick lunch. He finds a place with a large cool *stoep* (porch). The tables and chairs scattered about are a mish mash of furniture collected randomly, with all pieces a little rickety. Ryder selects a taller table so his legs can fit underneath, recalling previous visits when he sat with his knees uncomfortably pressed against the table edge, eating with his food more than an arm's length away.

He stares at the menu, unfocused, as thoughts overwhelm. Love, happiness, bond. LHB, BHL. Life with all three is like a sandwich, he thinks. A BLT? No, a BLH. Is that bacon, lettuce and ham? Well, what about the sandwich without the B—no bond, no bacon? Is it even worth eating the sandwich? Certain to be tasteless— experiencing love and happiness without a bond with someone special. An LH, hold the B.

"No sandwich for me today, that's for damn sure," he mutters.

"*Meneer* (Sir)?" The waitron has walked up to his table and looks at him questioningly. "*Ek het gevra* (I asked)—*ietsie om te drink?* A drink sir?"

She sets down a small bowl of water for Jack.

"*Ah thank you, you're a dear. Please, don't mind him. He's just a little distracted—a rough day. I'm sure you know how that goes.*"

Ryder hesitates. It's past lunch time and he considers ordering a double Jack and Red Bull, lots of ice and lemon, his drink of choice.

"Just water please," he says reluctantly, as he thinks how one drink inevitably leads to two or more. "And I'll have one of those wonderful thin rectangular shaped pizzas you have, why not."

Ryder watches as a few people drift in, seeking a late lunch, yet he avoids making eye contact or talking to anyone. Consumed with grief, anger and despair, he barely notices when the food arrives at his table, but instead keeps thinking about his life with Sophia, back there, back then. What should he have done differently, all the time they were together? Or even in those last few weeks of deciding and leaving, of setting in motion this new lonely path? As the questions flow across his brain, he feels himself becoming more inured, less able to think cogently of any answers to the questions constantly swirling through his mind. When is a shared dream real and worthwhile? When is compromise worth the end result? How did I let myself go so far into this, that now I'm lost? How will I manage the pain and despair? How will I even get through the day, or every day from now on? How can I manage being alone, all by myself, all the time, every day and every night?

"Will there be anything else, *Meneer*?"

He looks down in front of him at the empty wooden board, and realizes with a start that the pizza is gone, yet he has no recollection of having eaten any of it. He silently chastises himself—a wasted opportunity—dwelling on the past, while sitting surrounded by beauty, eating yet not tasting a delicious meal. Without any awareness of the present, he might just as well not have been here. Disgusted, he pays the bill, and he and Jack return to the car.

Now he steers his way past the local schoolyard, past the church, and past the local inn and bar. Education, salvation, damnation, all conveniently co-located. The guest house appears around the next corner, just past a field of unusual wildflowers, purple balls of fluff growing on long stems, and he navigates up the unpaved driveway.

"Ryder—finally! We were getting worried about you."

Vinnie and Maia come out to greet him. Ryder's old friends, married for over twenty years, are the owners of this small inn. Vinnie is dressed in his usual attire, khaki shorts with a cotton shirt that fits loosely over his barrel-chested frame. His now-balding head is slightly sunburned, as are his sturdy forearms and large ears. Over his shoulder is his trusty Nikon, and on his feet are the obligatory hiking boots and thick socks. His arm is around Maia, who stands shoulder-to-shoulder with him, dressed in jean capris and a matching t-shirt. A no-nonsense straw hat to protect against the sun completes her casual outfit. Jack jumps out through the open car window, lands with ease on the bare earth near the front entrance. Then he bounds over to Maia, leaps into her arms and stares into her eyes imploringly.

"This dog—Ryder, I swear, he's part human. Okay, all right, I have a biscuit in my pocket. Here you go. Poor bugger—doesn't Ryder ever feed you?"

"Don't mind if I do, thanks, although truthfully, Ryder sees to my nutritional needs quite well. Today we're in need of help of a different sort—well, it's probably easier if I allow him to explain it for himself."

Vinnie walks over to Ryder, clasps his hand in a firm

shake.

"It has been raining so hard, and you sounded so down when we spoke, we were starting to worry about you, driving these roads—"

"Nah, I'm fine." Relief floods him as he sees his friends, their smiling faces so welcome after the last few days of anguish.

"What do you have there—looks like all of your possessions?" Vinnie cups his hand and peers through the window into the car.

"Yes, well, pretty much so. I told you—she kicked me out. What was I going to do—leave my stuff for her to put out on garbage day?"

Ryder grabs a small bag from the back, and then walks with Vinnie up the stairs to give Maia a quick hug. "God, it's good to see you guys. It's been way too long."

"Ryder, you know you're always welcome here. And now that tourist season is almost over—you can have your choice of rooms at our little place. Come see, we finished the work on our pool a few months ago. Why not put on your *cossie* (swim suit) and we'll have a swim before dinner? It's certainly hot enough."

Within fifteen minutes, Jack is settled in the shade with a second bowl of water, and Ryder, Maia and Vinnie are in the pool, with the guest cottage on one side of them and the vineyards on the other. A selection of *fynbos* surrounds the pool, the landscaping designed to thrive in the heat and sparse water conditions. After the rain, the pool water is cool but the sun still warm, even as it continues its slow descent.

"Guys, I don't know how to thank you for letting me hole up here for a few days. Bury myself so to speak," Ryder begins. After all the time of solitude, and the lonely and pitiful lunch, he finds himself feeling gregarious. "You know on the way here I passed a cemetery, decided to go for a walk. There were four guys carrying a coffin around. I thought, now that is odd."

"Wait, why would you go for a walk in the cemetery, Ryder? It is so hot here in the middle of the day, are you *mal* (crazy)?" inquires Maia.

"I'm getting to that! Okay, cutting a long story short, I thought maybe a walk in the cemetery would help me decide if I might be better off dead. After an hour of that, as I was leaving, I see that these guys are still there carrying the coffin around. I thought to myself, wow these guys sure have lost the plot!"

This has Vinnie laughing out loud and Maia pulling faces.

"Ryder—dammit—you get me every time!" Vinnie says, paddling to the side of the pool to get his drink. "Always with the jokes—"

He glances up just as Jack moves across the patio, then lies down again, making certain his entire body is in the growing shadows.

"Flung into a deep pit of despair, is that it Ryder? Is that the reason for this visit: you, me and your fancy car, all the way out here in this sweltering climate? And what now? Is it time for you to swear, again, that you're retreating into permanent exile, that you're forever giving up tilting at windmills? Well, let's get it over with then."

"I'm telling you guys, I'm done. I've lost the plot too. I

will never find a partner to bring shared love and happiness. That's all there is to it, and after the cemetery visit, I think perhaps I will die trying."

"And—there it is. Back to this refrain again—"

Maia and Vinnie glance at each other. This dejected version of Ryder is new for them, a huge contrast to the person they have come to know over their fifteen-year friendship. And perhaps now is not the time for them to tell Ryder how they always felt about Sophia, how they never liked the way she treated Ryder. How she never seemed to trust him, but preferred to argue with him at every available opportunity. But Vinnie feels he must say something helpful to his pal, who is in such obvious pain.

"I must tell you, you remind me of an old friend who was addicted to brake fluid. Just like you're addicted to beautiful women. Only one difference, he could stop whenever he wanted to."

At this Maia shrieks with laughter.

"Ryder, did you ever think that you might be looking for the wrong quality in all the women you land up with?"

"How so? Vinnie, I really thought this time was different. I really thought Sophia and I would be together forever. Joke's on me, I guess."

"Well, I can tell you one thing I've noticed, something about all the women you've dated since I've known you—" Vinnie says tentatively.

"There've been a few, Ryder, and usually you tell us that this time, this is the one—" Maia interrupts. Ryder simply shrugs guiltily.

"Yes I agree, quite a few," continues Vinnie. "And

guess what? All these women have been real lookers. Think about it. So what does that tell you—maybe you're choosing these women based on the wrong criteria? I mean seriously, how many of the women you have been with have put Ryder first, before themselves, ever? I think you put too much emphasis on their appearance, too little on what motivates them."

"Now wait a minute Vinnie—" Maia interrupts. "Just what're you saying? That he should choose an ugly girl? Is that what you did? Well is it? I'm waiting—"

"Ah Maia, I was lucky enough to find someone beautiful, kind and caring. My soul mate, my ideal partner!" Vinnie backtracks quickly, leans over and pecks Maia affectionately on the cheek. "But just think about it, Ryder," he says over his shoulder.

"I don't know," Ryder turns serious again. "I just don't think there are too many women out there who think like me, who want someone like me, and who wants to give as well as take in a relationship. It's too damn difficult to keep trying so hard."

"Ryder, you will find someone, but first, you have to get past this. Use this as an opportunity—"

"Opportunity? Five years, Maia—"

"Technically, four and a half—"

"Whatever! That's a long time to spend with someone, and then to find out they don't want you anymore. Did she ever want me? Did she ever love me? Lost chance is more like it. Why was I so—"

"Ryder, stop." Maia climbs out of the pool now, grabs a towel and then hands another to Ryder. "You have no control over her and her emotions. Why doesn't she want you anymore? Does it matter anyway? She doesn't deserve you, never did. Time to move on."

"But how? I feel like I've got nothing to build on, nothing left anymore." Outside of the pool now, Ryder wraps the towel around his waist, aggressively tucking the corner under to hold it in place. "No love, no happiness, no bonding for me. Hopeless."

Again, Maia and Vinnie share a secret glance, then Maia speaks up. "Ryder, you have your own family, your dog, your work, your friends, and your pleasure in so many things. And your stupid bloody sense of humor!" Here, she rolls her eyes. "Why would you say you have no love, no happiness? From where we sit, you have that in spades. You'll get over her, you know. And all the other good stuff in your life will still be here for you, as ever."

"I don't feel it, Maia. I feel like it's gone, all of it. What I want to know is how people like you make a relationship work, because I think I can't be truly happy without being bonded to someone. Perhaps that is just how it is for someone like me. You guys have been together for two decades already; see, that seems so bloody impossible for me now. No, I think that I'll never be in a relationship that lasts. I should just accept that. Misery for the rest of my life."

Vinnie hauls himself out of the pool. He stands drying off in the cooling air, the pool water running in small rivulets down his hairy chest, and collecting at his feet. "Ryder, here's your big mistake. You're trying too hard to anticipate what these women want and then give it to them.

They don't really know what they want!"

"Yes we do!" pipes up Maia. "We want someone who'll stand by us, love us, support us, and keep us warm at night! Even in the middle of winter."

"Well then—it's gonna be a long cold lonely winter for me," Ryder says. His eyes are red and Maia wonders if it is the chlorine, the high pollen count, or perhaps the hidden tears. "Hey, I bought a bottle of red in town earlier. Let's toast to the end of the world. How about that?"

"Well, I need to go get things ready for the braai," Maia says. "During dinner how 'bout let's talk about something else, anything else. Okay?"

"Yes Maia, I have a few other things to talk about. How about how my business in Knysna is barely treading water? Or let's talk about how I really don't have anywhere to live now that Sophia says I'm no longer welcome in "our" home in Cape Town." Ryder is on a roll, his face becoming flushed with emotion. "Sorry, I don't mean to take it out on you. I'm just so upset. Tell me Vinnie, I'm serious, what's your secret?"

Vinnie looks into his glass reflectively. He pauses, either for effect, or perhaps to wait until Maia is out of earshot.

"Well," he says, "judicious use of the following two words, YES DEAR." With that he smiles and laughs, leaving Ryder confused as to whether he's serious or not.

"Man—you can't solve all your problems tonight," Vinnie continues. "Let's just sit here, have a drink and enjoy the sunset, enjoy the evening." He walks over to the small table outside, picks up the bottle of wine and a corkscrew.

"We can just relax okay? No more depressing talk! How about our national rugby team, Ryder, what do think their chances are this year?"

Maia brings out the glasses, then returns indoors to change and begin cooking. Ryder and Vinnie sit in silence, sipping a notable red from Darling Cellars, one of the local wineries that has achieved worldwide renown.

"Ja, this is good stuff Ryder. Thanks for picking up a bottle."

"L'chaim Vinnie! You guys are good friends. Lord knows I need some of those."

"Ryder, everything will be okay. You'll see. Next time you visit, you'll be happier. I promise."

9: Jacqueline, Riebeek Kasteel, March

After a small breakfast of fruit, yogurt and coffee, she packed up her car with her remaining seaside and vineyard drawings, shoving them haphazardly on top of her small suitcase. She glanced at the practical, large-faced watch on her wrist, then rushed back inside the inn to gather the last of her things. As she dashed outside again, she dropped her recycled canvas bag, spilling the contents in the empty parking lot.

Exasperated, she scooped up her wallet, lipstick and phone, and pushed them back inside, securely zipping everything shut, then she steadied herself as she waited for the slight dizziness to abate. She climbed into her car and raced to the town center, parking crookedly in front of the yoga studio.

"Hard to summon the energy to even climb those few stairs," she thought as she paused behind the wheel. But she forced herself from her car, made her way up the small flight and to the studio door.

'Open up my heart, embrace the love.' she reminded herself. *I have to keep trying—even if those good days seem so far away now, so hard to remember. God Frank, I miss you every day—how could*

you leave me like that? Forever is going to be so long without you.

She entered via the side door, cautiously wiping her eyes on her sleeve, and avoiding contact with the four other students already stretched out on their mats. As she lay down on her back and waited for the start of class, she wondered if they could see it, the black cloud of grief that hung over her wherever she went, making her so tired of trying so hard. Trying to come to terms with her life, trying to come to terms with his death.

She focused on a small spot on the ceiling, willed her mind to empty of all thoughts. She struggled to remain present through the hour of bending and stretching, fought valiantly against distracting negative thoughts. She knew she needed this yoga and meditation class to fortify herself before commencing the drive back home to Wilderness.

"Hey, Jacqueline, long time no see," the instructor said as she approached her after savasana. "Are you in a hurry? How 'bout we go across the street to Beans About Coffee? They make a fabulous breakfast to go with their java, and we can catch up."

Rebuild connections, Jacqui reminded herself silently, *stop spending so much time alone.*

Yet she shook her head, unable to contemplate sitting across the table and accepting the proffered sympathy from her well-intentioned friend.

"Actually, I think I had better head out of town right away," she said as she rolled up her mat. "Perhaps we can catch up the next time. Sorry, I have to get back—looks like there might be another storm coming."

They hugged briefly and she exited the studio, and

then made her way to her car, the feeling of disturbed equilibrium returning despite her best efforts. As she started the engine and then backed quickly out of her spot, she glanced worriedly at the huge black clouds rolling in over the mountain.

Take heart, Jacqui, she consoled herself. *All storms pass. Internal, external, eventually all of this will abate. Time is all you need.*

She drove slowly through the center of town, passing the old cemetery on the left and the obligatory Cape Dutch church on the right. Then she turned and headed out towards the highway, heading east, resigned to another lonely day back at Wilderness Beach.

10: Izzie, Knysna, March

Webster scratched his unkempt beard, and then pulled at his snug shorts that had crept up uncomfortably over his stocky thighs. He stomped his foot impatiently, his hi-tech hiking boot ringing hollowly against the wooden floor. Staring across the sparsely furnished room, he deliberately ignored the nervous flutter of the hands, and the tremulous quiver of the chin, of the skinny woman seated on the sofa. She pressed her knees together, her nondescript uniform of sensible black shoes, black pants and Chinese-collared white shirt giving nothing away. Her eyes revealed a lack of sleep, and she sat up straight, trying to hide the ever-present undercurrent of fear. He smoothed his moustache carefully with his index finger, then handed her a dense package wrapped in butcher paper and sealed with heavy-duty packing tape. The heft took her by surprise, a good thirty kilograms at least.

"Look, Izzie, all I'm telling you to do is to stash this somewhere where no one will find it," he said testily. "It's just for a week or two, a month, tops, until I can figure out how to get these pounds out of the country."

"How many horns did you trade to get all of this?" she asked. "There has got to be a fortune in here." She attempted to hand the package back to him "No wait; I can't have this in my home. You know I'm already on probation. What if the police decide to search my place? All this cash in foreign bills. You will have to think of another plan. This isn't—"

"Stupid—I don't want you to keep this at your home." Again, he stamped his foot. "Use your brain woman! No, you need to hide it at work. That workshop you teach at— the owners aren't even there most of the time. It's the perfect place."

"It's an academy, for those wishing to enter into the world of television production and presenting. And I don't know, Webster. I think that's a mistake. Ryder, my boss, I heard he's coming this weekend. Who knows how long he'll stay this time."

She stood up, turned and walked to the other side of the room, but Webster followed her. He put his arms around her, then nuzzled her neck as he pushed the package back into her hands.

"Yeah but you're always telling me what a nice guy he is, Izzie. What a pushover. He's not going to suspect anything."

"Well, what about his partner Sophia?" she asked "She's a real bitch, and suspicious and jealous of everything! If she comes here, she'll definitely find out, I know it. All I need is to get into a fight with her. She scares me—"

"C'mon Izzie, you said she never comes here, makes

him do all the work."

At this, he placed the package firmly in her arms, then moved away from her. She stood examining it.

"They will never find it as long as you don't do anything stupid. The horns are long gone, and now this cash is wrapped up all nice and tidy." Webster went back to the front door, picked up an empty bag lying near the entrance. "Take this, it's one of my gym bags. Fill it with old clothes, old shirts and stuff. We'll hide the package in the middle of all of that."

"But Webster—how much is in this? You know this poaching business makes me nervous."

"Izzie, you're nervous because you keep reading all of those articles. So stop reading them! Look never you mind about how much is here. If we get to keep only half of it, that is still going to be a couple hundred thousand. Pounds not rands!"

He took her hand, steered her towards the bedroom to begin the task of selecting the clothes for the bag.

"And I don't want to hear another thing about the poaching—what you don't know, won't hurt you. Just you forget about all of that." Now he moved toward her, took her chin in his hand. He moved her hair from her forehead, spoke more gently. "All you have to do is hide this package, and when I find a way to do the exchange, give it back to me. You'll see, Baby, we will be so rich in a few months, we can get out of this town, go anywhere we want. Mr. and Mrs. Sloane—as soon as this is over, we'll get married. I promise."

"I like the sound of that," she said, but still looked at

Webster worriedly. "Tell me, do you ever think about the baby rhinos? Don't you wonder if they miss the mommy rhinos? It doesn't seem right—"

Webster gave up trying to disguise his impatience. He responded sharply, determined not to give her any more details about the package he was entrusting her with.

"What the hell—are you changing your mind now? It's too late. The rhinos are already dead, and we're in this together. Take this package, hide it and I will tell you when I want it back. Or else we will both be in huge trouble. Do you understand?"

"Okay, okay. I'll bring the bag to work." She backtracked nervously, obviously uncomfortable with his brewing anger. "But, Webster, maybe... uh, maybe you can find a way to deal with all of this quickly? I really don't like—" she continued, then stopped when she saw the look on his face. She opened the bottom drawer, gathered up an armful of shorts and t-shirts. "Here, this should do." She carefully folded each item and placed it in the duffel, then inserted the package in the middle and filled up the sides.

"Perfect," he said as she laid the last of the shirts over the top of the package. "Now take it to work tomorrow, just put it in one of the cabinets, and then forget it's there. Can you do that, Izzie? For us?"

He lifted the bag and set it on the table, and she nodded slightly. Now he took her in his arms again, kissing her passionately. She responded immediately.

"Webster—for you I'd do anything. You know that. And this—it's for our future. I'll take it in tomorrow, I promise."

"Good—now let's not talk about it anymore. We have other things to discuss," he said as he steered her toward the bed. Then he dimmed the light, and began unbuttoning his pants. "Come here, Izzie. Let's talk about what I have right here for you, instead of all that other nonsense. There's a good girl—"

11: Ryder, Riebeek Kasteel to Knysna, March

Why Knysna? Ryder's car driving there as though pulled by a magnet, or by force of habit. Ever since opening their small business together in this town, some 450 kilometers from Cape Town, he has driven there dozens of times, with and without Sophia. Trying to get the academy up and running, trying to make it into a viable concern. The motivation for this investment is now turning over and over in his regretful mind. Their retirement proposition, their way to plan for a future together. Oh yes, it was to be Ryder and Sophia with their version of happily ever after, a way to merge their separate lives and establish a joint retirement plan. A pipe dream? For a time there, it had felt so real, so doable. And now, focusing on this last vestige of life as he knew it had become more urgent, more crucial. Because it was all he had left of their lives together, after being forced to leave the home where he was no longer welcome.

Navigating his way to route 62, driving through Malmesbury, Ceres, over the Hottentots Holland Mountain, then on through Worcester, Robertson, Ashton, Montague and Barrydale. Turning left to Swellendam, then right to the N2. Deliberately bypassing the turnoffs for Albertinia,

Mossel Bay, George, Wilderness, and Sedgefield, and concentrating only on getting to Knysna. Driving, yet refusing to acknowledge, the journey as a retreat, a pause for licking his wounds. Allowing town after tiny town to fly by, ignoring the pull of the markets along the way, with their endless variety of cured cheeses, dried meats and mouth-watering confections on offer. Focusing on misery and sorrow, not noticing the historic wine farms and fruit stands lining the road, nor sparing a glance for the local vendors headed to market with their homemade biltong, koeksisters, melkterts and bobotie. Dwelling on the silence of the phone on the back seat, waiting for the call begging him to come back. And holding on to the vain hope that this Knysna business would serve as a link in their tenuous chain, something binding them together. Hadn't this happened before, this parting of ways? A stubborn refusal to acknowledge that all along, throughout the course of their relationship, there had been an abundance of these oft-soldered, poorly repaired and weakened ties, with each break lessening the chances that they would remain permanently bonded together.

Now he's finally arriving, after all those hours on the road from Riebeek Kasteel. He heads to his small rental cottage, tries hard to discern the surrounding lagoon in the dusky twilight. For now, this will be home; a comforting thought as he remembers the light and airy interior, the views of the water from the bedroom window. He clambers out of the car, stretches, then rolls his shoulders, trying to relieve the tension built up from clutching at the wheel. Jack scampers up the steps.

"Come along—you do remember the way I assume. And if you pick up the pace just a little, we can still squeeze in a walk along the beach or even a trot near the lagoon."

He runs back down to the car, circles Ryder, then charges up the stairs again. Ryder rummages around in his pocket, produces the key, attached to a ring from a local real estate company. He recalls getting a duplicate cut at the local hardware store on one of his first visits to Knysna. And he thinks of the conversation he had with a smiling woman who had been inside the store, chatting with the owner.

"Well hello. You must be new in town," she said, turning her head towards him. The purple streaks in her jet-black hair shimmered in the sunshine. "I don't believe I've seen you around here before. I'm Demi."

She extended her slim arm to shake his hand. She was attractive and eccentric-looking, and she seemed to immediately notice the absence of a wedding band on his hand. He in turn immediately noticed her interest. Yet, his instinct that day was to look over his shoulder, make sure they were not being watched. He had lived with Sophia's jealousy and mistrust for so long that adaptive behavior had become second nature. Even while travelling on his own, in those days, he was cautious. Either don't engage in conversation, or else be forced to lie about it.

Today he thinks ruefully of that day and realizes that there is no longer anyone to be jealous, for better or for worse. He enters the dark cottage, carries in his small suitcase. He sets it down in the entry, turns on the light, and then crosses over to the tiny kitchen. He sighs audibly as he opens the compact, apartment-style fridge. Empty, of course, it has been several weeks since he was last here. And he's always careful to clean up before departure, so why even bother looking? As he closes the fridge, he sees it: Demi's business card, held to the door with a magnet. A phone number in big, bold type superimposed upon an abstract, whimsical picture of a flower pot, with her name and the address of a store centered across the bottom. He recalls the rest of the conversation with her in that little key shop.

"Well hi there. I'm Ryder, yes I am new here in town. I'm opening a business, an academy for those youngsters wishing to get into the world of television."

"Television? Tell me more." She perched on the edge of the counter and tucked her black-and-purple hair behind her ears. Swung her muscular legs, covered in tight leggings and cowboy boots easily back and forth while they spoke. Her long wooly top had ridden up slightly as they talked and she had not paused to pull it back down. "What, exactly, will your academy be teaching these youngsters?"

"Well, the main idea is to provide some opportunities for the locals, teach them skills to become more employable," he had explained. "At any rate, I'll be spending a lot of time driving up here from Cape Town. Just getting some spare keys made. You never know when I might need them."

And Demi had slipped her business card into Ryder's breast pocket—her touch lingering there a little longer than required—with a promise to show him around when he was ready. He was flattered but had no intention of calling, no wish to complicate his life further. But he had patted his pocket atop the card, and made sure to save it, even while committing the address of her store to memory.

Now Ryder remembers, too, the multiple times he has come to Knysna since that day, the many times he had almost bumped into Demi. He thinks back on his walks around town during these regular visits, with Jack at his heels, how he deliberately chose the path that wound its way past Demi's little store. How he peered in through the window, trying to catch a glimpse of her, yet not be noticed. And how he had reluctantly avoided striking up a friendship, not wishing to rock the boat at home any further. No, he wasn't totally oblivious to the stormy seas he was sailing even back then.

What else did they talk about on that first day? Without too much effort, he recalls the rest of their first conversation:

"Well, it's nice to meet you, Ryder. I live right around the corner. You know everyone lives nearby in this town! Unlike the big city."

"Oh, so you know all about the big city, do you?"

"Oh yes, got *gatvol* (fed up) with my job working as personal assistant for the CEO of a big company, so I moved here. Now I own a small shop. Peat's Pot Spot."

"Oh I see. A pot shop. You sell pot then, clearly. And who is Pete?"

Was he feeling slightly apprehensive when he asked this, trying to determine if she was single or attached to the store's male proprietor?

"Yes, pots but no, not pot, not cannabis, and there is

no Pete either. Just me, myself and I, but I have a friend who does sell pot, if you're interested. Her store is called Get Off. Never mind, just kidding about that part. Or maybe not."

"So let's see. If I need pot, then I'll call your friend, but if I need something to put my plants into, then—"

"Yes, you've got it! Oh, you're going to fit in well in this town Ryder! Where all is not as it seems, obviously—"

Tonight, momentarily, his heart feels a little lighter as he picks up the card, examines it. Yes, he will settle in. Take that damn dog for his damn walk before he barks his damn head off. Go to the nearby grocery store, stock up on some provisions, and then maybe, just maybe, he will give this Demi a call. What could it hurt?

But even as he thinks this, he's already dispirited, disgusted. Why bother? She will just be like all the others. Why get involved again, simply to repeat all the same mistakes? Witty conversations, enticing dates, eager anticipation, then disappointment and regret. Fighting and arguing, distrust and jealousy, then denial and retreat. His pattern, repeated time and again over the years, with the same woman, or with a series of different women. Either all the women are the same, or he's useless at understanding how to get along with them. All of this in the pursuit of love and happiness, and of the perfect bond to cement them both.

Now he pauses, recalling the times in his life when in that bond, when he felt the daily confirmation of the care, respect, and lust of and for another. And when he and she were that special complement to each other; how he had felt a supreme validation of his unique greatness and usefulness, in the relationship and therefore in the universe. This view, knowing that another person loved him, in turn produced a craving in him. Was this always temporary, lasting only for a few months, or even for a few years? Or was it possible for this to evolve into a deep caring companionship, a love of doing and being together in the moment, an ability to let go of past hurts and lost dreams? And into pleasure at simply being together, and a wistfulness for each other when apart? Now all he feels is the hurt and pain of trying to get over it all again.

With a bitter laugh he recalls the words of one of his friends shared a few months ago "the best way to get over a woman is to get under another one."

"Ah what difference does any of this make?" he asks aloud, sighing heavily and shrugging. He puts the card back on the fridge, promises himself he will call, but no, not today, too much chaos. Looking around the apartment, he spies an open bottle of Jack Daniels, left over from a previous visit. Yes, that's how he will end this difficult day. Grabbing an almost-clean glass he finds on the counter, he pours himself a stiff drink. No ice, no lemon available; he knocks it back in one large gulp.

"Bottoms up, Jack. *L'chaim.*"

"Ah another night of this then. I suppose I can just forget about my walk, forget about any chance of fetch this evening. Most frustrating."

"Screw this forcibly concentrating on the present, Jack. Trying so hard to think positively when all I am is angry— damn angry! As of today, there'll be no more denial."

Ryder slams his glass down on the table, then picks it up again and stares at it, his eyes welling up. He raises the empty glass in Jack's direction.

"It's really over now. A toast to that—to the wasted years." He looks into the glass ruefully. "Yes, I can be in the moment, the here and now, as long as I drink enough. Here's to me, Jack, and to my state of limbo, is that somewhere between here and nowhere? You know all I really want is to feel okay, reach some sort of acceptance, find a way to move on, enjoy life again."

He refills his glass from the ready bottle, splashing the contents carelessly over the side.

"One thing's for sure, Jack, my boy. I'm never going back." His words are beginning to slur, the volume rising and falling unpredictably. "No, Sophia, this is the last time, and for any future relationships I'll be sure I have new rules, codes, and guides. This is never going to happen to me again. Never! If I can just figure this all out, I know I'll be able to find true love and happiness. One day. In a real bond with a companion lover. The here and now without any concerns."

He lifts his glass in another toast, throws back the contents. Sighing, he takes off his cap and places it on the table, then angrily brushes it on to the floor. He throws himself into the empty chair, kicks out his long legs and stares sadly down at his feet, noticing how the red and black trail shoes are scuffed and spotted with grime, the laces worn and frayed. Damn *takkies* need replacing, he thinks absently as he reaches over to the bottle, losing count now of how many refills he has had.

Another two shots of Jack in the glass, a few more sips, and now, his head is spinning. With no energy left to make the bed, he moves into the bedroom and simply lies down on top of the covers, closes his eyes and prays that sleep comes quickly. And that it lasts through the dark hours of the night.

"How can tomorrow be any worse?" he wonders aloud. "Surely it can only get better."

12: Ryder, Knysna, April

Usually so careful to screen his calls, this time he grabs the ringing phone in the dark, then answers before rolling over and switching on the lamp.

"Hello?"

"Ryder. Hey, it's me."

Stunned, he holds the phone away to look at it, then brings it back to his ear.

"Sophia—why're you calling me? What time is it?"

"Oh, did I wake you? Sorry. I was just lying in bed thinking about you, Ryder. Thinking about how much I miss you. We haven't spoken in over a month now—"

"Yeah—pretty much since you asked me to move out, and then I did. Don't suppose you remember that?" he responds with sarcasm.

"Please Ryder—I just wanted to say hello. How're you doing, really? How's everything going?"

"Look I sent you all the information about the business through email. You shouldn't have any questions. And if you want to know why the academy is doing so badly, you only have to look to—"

"Ryder, I didn't call to talk about the business. I know

all I need to know about that. I wanted to talk to you, hear your voice. Don't you miss me, even a little bit?"

"Why are we talking like this? You knew how I felt all along, yet you asked me to go. You kicked me out, Sophia. What are you doing? Do you enjoy picking at scabs? Opening them up, and making them bleed?"

"Please, don't make me feel even worse. We both knew it wasn't working at that time. I didn't call to fight with you. Can't we be friends? Surely, we don't have to be on such bad terms. We were always so good together Ryder. Please say you remember! If only we could've kept up the physical part of our relationship. God I miss that so much. Do you remember when we went to Plett that time? We virtually never left that hotel room—"

"Do you think I could forget that, Sophie? Do you think I don't replay that over in my mind, even if I don't want to?"

"Ryder, why don't we get together, talk things over? Wait—please don't say what I know you're going to—"

"What—that it's a bad idea? That we can't just simply go back to the old days?"

"It doesn't have to be the way it was. We can be different. I really want to talk, I do."

The silence stretches endlessly between them as Ryder contemplates his answer. He sighs deeply, thinking carefully before he speaks.

"Do we still have things to talk about, really? Because if we do, then perhaps we should try get together, but it has to be on neutral ground, not at our house. Or I mean— YOUR house."

Suddenly, Jack bounds over to the bed, then sits, growling at Ryder's feet. Ryder reaches down to pat him, but he bobs and weaves, then cocks his head to the side, and begins to howl.

"Look, I've got to go. Jack needs to go out and—"

"Oh how is Jack? Does he miss me too?"

"Too? Did I say anything? Say that I miss you? Sophia, I'm hanging up now. I need time to think. You know you have me all worked up again."

"You used to like it when I got you all worked up, Ryder. Remember? You know we could have it all again. Please don't make me beg you. What I wouldn't give to have you in bed with me right now. To have you hold me in your arms all night. Yes, just like before. Will you call me back, really?"

"No promises. Bye Sophia." He gently presses the red call-end button, and then sits staring at his phone. Should I call her back, he wonders? Why did she call? Is this message of reconciliation a ruse? "Lying in bed," she said. So her bed is as cold and empty as mine, is it? I guess that means she hasn't taken up with someone else after all, and maybe she's really missing me. After all, if she doesn't genuinely want me back, then why call at all? Yes, I should call back right now; strike while the iron is hot. Is this a chance to reclaim the bond, to regain our love and happiness?

He enters the number, then hits send, but hangs up just as he hears the first ring. No, he has come too far to fall for this. He has to think it through all the way. Angrily, he flings the phone onto his bed, then pulls on his shorts and t-shirt, slips on his sandals.

"Get a grip," he tells himself. "She might be lonely right now, but has anything really changed?"

He moves towards the front door. "I'm going for a walk Jack. Are you coming or not?" he growls, then steps out into the foggy night air.

Now his fragile peace, so hard-won over the past month, is gone, and replaced with a sick feeling in the pit of his stomach. Only this time, he feels it magnified as he reflects on how deluded he was, thinking he had gotten over Sophia, resolved his feelings.

"Jack—she's done it again! Will I never get past this? Is this all it takes—one call from her, and I'm a mess, again?"

After a short walk, he's breathless and ready to return. He marches inside, sits down on the bed, and pulls out his phone, staring at it.

"Misses me in her bed? Dammit—I miss her in mine. I'm so lonely right now. Why is this so damn difficult?"

He stuffs a pillow behind his head as he lies down, his mind swirling. Okay, now is the time to put in to practice the lessons I've learned, he finally decides. To understand that I will never control her actions, only my reactions. Finally he begins to see the power he has. The power to control this situation, totally, by what he chooses to do or not do. Now, decisively, he sets the phone aside, and resolves never to answer it again without checking the caller ID first.

Is this progress? he wonders. Resisting temptation even while getting emotionally sucked in? With a wry smile, he acknowledges that he has behaved maturely, giving only a small indication to her of his emotional state. Well, he thinks, at least there's that victory, however minor. And if I ever talk to her again, it'll be on my terms, and because I decided to do so.

With that, he turns out the light, rolls over and tries to deal with what promises to be a long and sleepless night.

13: Ryder, Knynsa, May

"Well, that's that then. I wish you the best of luck. Ciao."

I hang up the phone gently, wishing I could throw it against the wall instead. Dammit, another student calling to say their funds are not approved. It's no use. Nobody has any cash, and so they are unable to get an education, despite the obvious dividends it will pay off in the future.

"What do you mean you won't help them organize a loan?" I had tried desperately to explain a few days ago to yet another faceless bureaucrat. "Don't you understand— once they have this training, they will be able to earn a living, and pay it back with interest—"

"*Ja Meneer*," they explained to me, speaking slowly and loudly. "Two years ago when you opened your academy, we had this funding. Now we don't. *Miskien* (maybe) don't call us back anymore because we can't help you."

Well it is clear that the needed class size, small as that is, is becoming impossible to obtain. Across the ocean, America sneezed and we in South Africa caught the rinderpest, the economic ripple effect drying up any possible government funding pipeline.

"How is any of this my fault?" I demanded of Sophia

last week when my patience with her accusing tone finally ran out. "You know as well as I do, the crippling poverty here is precisely what this television training academy was supposed to help alleviate."

"So you have to be the one to rescue them, 'give them a chance', is that how you see it? Well, someone has to pay for the training, Ryder. We can't afford to keep the doors open like this. We are not running a charity here—"

"Do you think I don't know that? I have been dealing with the nightmare of red tape and the inefficiency of the National Youth Development and other government agencies for months now. I've spent countless days approaching local and national authorities, municipalities, private funders, school headmasters, charity organizations—"

"Well, all I know is, you claimed we would have a limitless supply of students, yet now—"

"Sophia, listen to me." Did the fact that I was now shouting make it any more likely that she would actually hear what I was saying? "The pile of applicants on my desk is over one hundred. Supply of students is not the issue—why can't you understand this?"

Even now, I am struck by the irony: the number of potential students, the possibility of economic freedom for the graduates, but the inability of any of the authorities to connect the dots and write the school a goddamn check!

I didn't even bother telling Sophia about my struggles to keep a decent instructor—really, why would I? Sometimes I think it's just my pattern to be screwed over by women, personally and professionally. I have had one

instructor leaving town to chase her errant boyfriend—
following hard on the heels of the previous one who quit
when she got pregnant. At least right now, I have a decent
one, this Izzie seems pretty smart and knowledgeable. But
that is assuming she does not disappear like the other two
did. And also assuming that the useless boyfriend, that
Webster character, she has been hanging around with
doesn't distract her from her duties here. Well, if my
students keep withdrawing, what will it matter anyway?
Yeah, I think I'll have another drink while I sort that
question out.

Was I wrong to think Sophia might have spared five
minutes to ask about my personal frame of mind, instead of
dwelling only on the business woes? And why does it still
matter whether she knows that I am fretting about my path,
about the life and love I left in Cape Town? Or that I feel
so unsettled, living as a semi-nomad in a town that seems
populated with some of the craziest people I have ever met.

"We are so lucky to live here," I was told just this
morning by some random stranger at the grocery store.
"Isn't Knysna the most beautiful place?"

"Well, sure," I was tempted to reply, "as long as you
like living amongst some of the weirdest people in all of
Africa. Or perhaps you haven't noticed—maybe you are
one of them?"

Most days, I stumble around feeling hurt, stunned, and
in disbelief of my circumstances. I observe the townsfolk
and sometimes I wonder: is it by chance, or is it some sort
of affinity that has drawn me here? Is it possible that I, too,
am on the brink of insanity? I've left my home and my

family, and I have no clear idea of what the heck I'm doing here. I spend most of my days in my so-called office that does triple duty as the reception area, the interview room and the supply chain head office. Come to think of it, this is the crying room too, what with the constant drama between the instructors, the students, and the various crazies that come and go from these premises. Is the good view from the window opposite my desk the reason I can't summon the energy to pack up and go home, despite the late hour? Does this pretty scenery really make up for the helpless chaos that swirls around me at all times?

God, this is making my head hurt. Where the heck is the Tylenol? I know I left it here in my desk. Top right hand drawer—dammit—who the hell put back the empty bottle? Something as simple as throwing away empties, replacing what you use. How hard is that? Everything is my responsibility; no one else does anything around here. Shit—now I have to deal with this pounding in my head on top of everything else. Maybe if I close my eyes for a few minutes—

14: Ryder, Knynsa,
May

Suddenly the door clangs open and the blinds on the window rattle, waking me from a deep sleep. I must have forgotten to lock the front door, and now the wind has blown it open. What time is it anyway? It was already almost six when I dozed off. Then I look up, startled, as the regular delivery guy appears in the doorway. The irregular, unreliable delivery guy, that is.

"Meneer! Dis nat buite, bliksem se reen, Hier is jou goed, waar moet ek dit sit?"

(Mister. It is wet outside, raining like a mother. Here is your stuff—where should I put it?)

It is Bernie November, or is it October, September or even April or January? This last-name-month-thing was explained to me by the last colored delivery guy. Seems if you have a white father who doesn't want to lay claim to a mixed-race child, then the kid can't use his father's last name. So why not use the month of birth instead? A certain logic there I suppose. Yet another explanation is that the surname was used to determine the month in which the person would be eligible to be sold as a slave. The fleeting thought crosses my mind that my problems are so first-world by comparison to Bernie's: can't find a parking spot, my cell battery has died, no Tylenol in the drawer. I stare at him, my mind whirling. Annoyance, embarrassment, guilt.

Bernie has on blue jeans, Guess no less, and a Mr. Price t-shirt with a brightly colored skateboarder design on it. On the left breast pocket of his grimy jacket is the whoosh of the latest courier logo, and on his feet a pair of fancy Nike shoes, undoubtedly the latest air jump pump or whatever. The odor of stale cigarettes wafts off him, magnified in the fresh clean confines of my office. He must have smoked non-stop in the truck all the way from George where the depot is, the nearest "big" town. What a life he has, I think, driving up and down this coastline. Probably has girlfriends all along the way. No doubt stopping here and there for "*a dop and a stop*"—and probably a *shtoep* too, why not? (Drink, marijuana, intercourse).

"*Hai—luister! Waar? Dis heavy Meneer.*"

(Listen. Where? It's heavy Mister.)

"Bernie. Where the Hell have you been, *ou*?" I bark at him, switching into his linguistic style. I'm in no mood for his bullshit banter and lame stories. "*Jis man, is jy gerook?* (Are you stoned?) I've been waiting for this stuff for three days. You promised it to me last week."

"*Yislaaik Meneer—what makeer jy Boss?*" (What is bothering you) comes the rude reply as he carelessly slams the supplies for my students onto the floor. Nothing too fragile in those boxes, I hope.

"*Ons kannie so ver ry net vir een doos!*" (We can't ride so far just for one box). He strolls over to where I'm still sitting at my desk. "*Kan ek saam drink? My bek is droog—wat het jy daar?*" (Can I drink with you? My mouth is dry—what do you have there?)

I hand him a warm can of Coke I have sitting on my desk, although I know he's greedily eyeing the Jack Daniels. And I refuse to relent as he stands there, one hand in his pocket, waiting expectantly. Finally he turns to leave.

"Here, next time try get this here when I ask for it, *verstaan* (understand)?" I say as I peel off a couple of pink fifty-rand lion-embossed notes and hand them to him. "And *miskien* (maybe) then *kan ons saam drink* (we can drink together)."

Everyone has a palm stretched out to me, everyone! And this business is slowly draining me dry. As the insolent wretch disappears through the door, I pour a few more fingers into my glass, add another splash of Red bull. Screw it, the day is wasted anyway. Might as well have a few, then go home to Jack, the only one who asks nothing of me. Yes, at least he's always happy to see me. A smile tugs at the corners of my mouth as I think of him, waiting patiently at home. Is he truly the only soul I can converse with these days without getting angry or upset?

The rain is intensifying, booming thunder and lightning streaking across the sky. I need to get home; this foul weather will make poor Jack nervous. I walk through the rooms checking that everything is locked up, all the items powered down, all the various goods restored to their designated places. Why I even bother with all this neat labeling, when the damn instructor cannot trouble herself to train the students to put the stuff away, is beyond me. All so frustrating, with no one willing to do the small things I expect of them. I have to clean up everyone's mess, all the time. I look around, see how a closet of training manuals, recorded tapes and camera equipment has been filled haphazardly, despite the clean, lined shelves. And dammit, who left this trash can in the middle here for me to trip over? More mess, this time all over the floor. Now searching around for a broom, I find a surprisingly heavy duffel bag, filled with old clothes stuffed in the back of one of the storage closets. Sophia's initials, SM, embroidered on the top.

"Dammit Sophia," I mumble. "More of your crap. This cabinet is for towels—it says so on the door." Sighing heavily, I drag it to my office, put it with my keys so I will remember to take it home. I don't know who is worse: Sophia, the staff, or the students, ignoring my instructions. Useless, the whole bloody lot of them. I feel the waves of anger rush over me as I sweep up the spilled garbage, attempt to restore order to each of the small training rooms. Now I will never get out of here tonight. And then when I do, in ten or twelve hours, I have to turn around and come back to all of this crap again.

"This is the shared dream, is it? What the fuck was that all about, Sophia? A shared nothing! Did you even want this, any of this?" Muttering to myself, I look around and honestly, there is nothing, absolutely nothing, here that any sane person could want. And certainly not me, this pathetic man with a broom in his hand, and an angry red flush on his face, crazy talk spewing from his mouth.

What a way to begin my new life in Knysna. Backward reflection is pointless and fruitless, and forward projection is impossible without any concept of where to go. How did I get here, so low down, in such a deep pit?

So many critical and interconnected events that all seemed to come crashing in at the same juncture: the downward spiral of the economy with the accompanying loss of income; the increased arguing and disconnectedness at home; and yes, the loss of self-respect as I sought to repair the relationship no matter the cost to myself. And then finally, the inertia that came along with knowing it was time to move on, but somehow the inability to do so.

I have to ask myself: how can I have allowed one person's actions to lead me so far astray, so far away from myself and from the love, happiness and bond I so crave? I thought I was moving towards this, and yet instead all of my actions have taken me so far from it.

I can look in the mirror and see how I've changed, from happy-go-lucky to sad and despondent. And just because I'm changed does not mean I'm a better man for it. No, not hardly! I want to say this is all her fault, but I know that's not the whole truth. I've been rejected and exiled, and it was Sophia that did this to me. That much has been covered. But perhaps I'm not quite ready to take responsibility for my past actions or for my life going forward. Today, as I contemplate whether or not I'm becoming quite mad-in-the-head, I'm still going to cling to the belief that all the blame for my undoing can be laid at her feet.

Yes, growing up in Africa might have prepared me well for many things, but what I'm not so well prepared for is the need to meet my new life head-on without feeling broken or further defeated. The need for something—a lifeline, anything—is overwhelming. Drowning.

15: Demi, Knynsa,
May

"So tell me what you know about him, this new guy." Demi sidles up to Farrell at the bar at Mo's and links her arm through his, then adjusts her mini skirt so it covers fractionally more of her slim thighs. She sips her club soda, then turns her head towards Farrell and focuses on him with her green eyes.

"I used to see him around town with that tall, stuck-up brown-skinned brunette, but lately I only see him by himself, and only from a distance, and always with his dog, of course. What is he—a vampire? Only going out at night, in the full moon?"

Farrell is slouched over at the bar, dressed in traditional khaki pants, a blue-and-white striped long-sleeved shirt with wrinkled collar and slightly frayed cuffs, and shiny office shoes. Just your typical Fort Hare business graduate turned local businessman, transplanted from the Transkei. His brown skin and distinctive features give away his Xhosa heritage, despite his name change from the tribal *Fikile* (Arrived) to the anglicized Farrell. He looks up from his glass and into the mirror above the counter, taking in his thinning layer of coarse grey hair, his rheumy dark eyes, and his already-aging neck weighed down with a heavy gold chain. He checks the expensive Rolex on his wrist as he nurses his fifth or sixth drink of the evening. The night is young, but after a hard day of peering at computer screens, helping his near-broke clients try to market their useless products, he's exhausted. Alcohol is always the perfect remedy. Besides, being out at Mo's on Rex, the main watering hole of this sleepy town, is preferable to being home alone, his only other choice. Demi is good company, always seeming to be smiling and positive. Yet, she personifies that unique blend of *plaas* (farm) culture and European sophistication, an opportunist who searches for the angle in any situation.

"Why do you think I know anything about the guy? What's his name again?"

"I told you, Farrell, pay attention. His name is Ryder. He used to come to town every few weeks for a day or so at a time, but now I think he's moved here full-time. You know everything that goes on in Knysna, or so you keep telling me. I've been seeing his car, his Lexus with the personalized "Ryder's-WP" plates, parked around town these last few weeks."

"Why so interested, Demi? He's just another honky city boy, another tourist, if you ask me. With a fancy shmancy car—is that what caught your eye, maybe?"

"Well, firstly, he's not a tourist. I already told you that. He has come here to start a business."

"Oh yeah, trying to make a small fortune in Knysna. Well you know what they say is the best way to do that—"

"Yeah, yeah. Start with a large fortune. Old joke,

Farrell, but completely apart from the nice car, I think he's cute! He has a nice smile. Well, I think I remember his smile. I only talked to him that one time. But he was really funny and charming. You know, I think we—"

"What, don't you think I'm cute, funny and charming?" Farrell smiles up at her, tries in vain to wink. "By the way, did I mention you look really hot tonight? Have you lost weight? Cut your hair?"

"Shut up. Stop flirting with me! C'mon Farrell, I'm trying to pump you for information here."

"You can pump me any time you like." Farrell leers at her, reaches over to grab her knee, and then almost falls off the barstool. "Hey, I'm only a few years older than you. All I need to do is give up drinking and smoking, and drop about twelve kilos. Then I would be your ideal man, no? If you would be my girlfriend, I would do all the website work for your shop for free."

"Well, Farrell, if you want that to happen, I suggest you raise your prices. Considerably." Demi smiles at him affectionately. "And in any case, *Koekie* (cupcake), maybe I shouldn't remind you, but you do my web-work for free anyway."

Farrell laughs. "True that! And you know I know, you need someone with money—preferably lots of it. I'm certainly not wealthy enough. I see you staring at my bling—you know it's all from ill-gotten gains, many years ago. No more of that for me."

"Yeah that's right, I do need someone with money," says Demi, disregarding his offhand reference. "So let's focus on the subject at hand. Are you telling me you know nothing about this mysterious Ryder guy with his fancy car?"

"*Aish*, nope, zero Babe. So can we stop talking about him and resume our previous conversation?" Farrell signals to the bartender who brings him another drink.

"Why is it so ridiculously hot in here when it is so cold out there?" he asks no one in particular, as he spins clumsily around on his stool at the bar.

"*Siestog* (shame), Farrell. You know you're always complaining about something or other! Take off your shirt and give us all a show if you're so hot, why not?" Demi is becoming frustrated, despite her usual tolerance for Farrell and his quirks. "Fine, if you have nothing to add, then let's change the subject. But I don't even remember what we were talking about. Was it love, lack of love, relationships, our usual crap?"

"Well, as I recall I was trying to enlighten you about what men really look for in women."

"Farrell, I'm forty seven years old, and you know I am nothing but a realist. So do you really think I need you to explain this to me?" Demi picks up her drink, swirls it around in the glass. The ice has long since melted and the soda is flat. Perhaps she should have left an hour ago, she thinks. "It becomes clearer every year that men are more interested in youth, good looks and good bodies than anything else. I suppose you're going to tell me they see inherent worth in more mature women? Hah! You know they will reject an older woman if some young thing waltzes through the door."

"I told you—I would take you anytime over any of

these girls—" Farrell looks around as he attempts to gesture to other women in the bar, but alas, they are the only customers left. Unless you count the two off-duty policemen sitting at a table in the corner, each staring glumly into his half-empty beer glass. "Ah well, never mind then—"

"What about you Farrell? Have you changed, ever, what you're looking for in a mate?"

"Seeing as I've never actually found a true soul mate that lasts longer than six months to a year, I can't really say—"

"Yes well—that is your problem isn't it? You've always been afraid of getting too involved with someone—"

"Are we being serious now?" Farrell is trying to focus through the fuzziness, knows something important is being discussed. "I don't like needy bitches, okay? You get involved with them and then suddenly it's all about where are we headed, what's this all about, I need you for this, help me with that, take me here, buy me the other thing. Oh and marry me too, while you're about it—"

"Bad attitude, man. At least we women reassess what we're looking for as we get older, and wiser. Men never grow up. They just want pretty toys."

"Demi, perhaps it's time for you to take up drinking again. This conversation is no fun anymore."

Demi smiles ruefully and drains the last of her club soda. She slides off the stool and pulls on her sweater, followed by her warm coat, then gives Farrell a small kiss on his cheek and a quick hug. As she walks towards the door, her high heels clatter on the wooden floor.

"Wait. Come back tomorrow. I'll be here." Farrell calls out as she leaves.

"No doubt," she says as she rolls her eyes and waves. "*Tot siens* (bye bye), Farrell, and if you should happen to see Ryder, find out what his story is. Tell him to call me. Why not? Maybe I can be the pretty toy he's looking for, you never know."

Demi walks out of the bar, glances anxiously around and then hurries across the parking lot. Her old VW sits where she deliberately parked it in full view under a bright light. She looks at the broken side-view mirror hanging listlessly despite the duct tape repair, the dented bumper and passenger wheel cover, and then she sighs as she unlocks the door. She looks around one more time, then quickly jumps in and relocks the car. Was that simply a shadow she saw, or is there really someone hiding in the bushes? Going out at night on her own means she has to remain vigilant. A single woman is an easy target for robbery, rape or worse in this crime-torn town in this crime-torn country.

"This constant worry is no way to live," she thinks, "but can't very well lock myself in every night, never go out just because I'm not with a man, now can I? And how am I supposed to catch Mr. Right if I never leave the safety of my home, anyway?"

She drives slowly and cautiously, arriving at her small apartment in less than fifteen minutes. As she pulls up, she pauses to look around. The lagoon, visible around virtually every corner, looms black in the distance, sparkling with reflected light. Again, she makes sure to park beneath a bright lamppost, then sprints across the lot, hurriedly unlocks and opens her front door. She slips inside and locks and bolts the door behind her. Relaxing now that she's safely home, she leans against the wall and kicks off her heels, then walks down the hall directly into her bedroom. No need for her to turn on the lights, with the whole place bright from the full moon. Before she draws the drapes shut, she wonders if Ryder is looking at this same moon tonight, at this same time. "What is it about this Ryder guy?" she wonders. "Maybe he's destined to be the one who will take care of me for the rest of my life. Am I the type of woman he's looking for? Or could I possibly become that for him?"

This evening has left her feeling unsettled, nostalgic for something she never had. Throughout her childhood, as she watched her proud and beautiful Dutch mother slowly fade into the background of their humble Afrikaans home, she resolved never to waste her life in the same way. No living on some remote farm in the African bush with a dour Afrikaner for me. Yet now she finds herself living a small existence in some forgotten town, with no love and no direction. She wonders if her current thoughts about Ryder, a man she has not really met, are futile, and if someone like Farrell is bound to be her destiny after all. All her life she has lusted for more, for better, but now, the choices are dwindling, and she has a nagging feeling that time is running out. That she might be compelled to settle for a life here with this crumpled alcoholic, or with some other middle-aged man with no ambition and nothing much to offer.

"Ah best not to dwell on things that are certain to look brighter in the morning," she decides as she shrugs out of her sweater, steps out of her skirt. Then she slips into her unmade bed, pulls the covers over her head and closes her eyes. She wonders some more about Ryder; if he's merely an older guy looking for some young female diversion, or if he's after a deeper connection. If he's looking to start a family, or if he has one already. If the sexy brown-skinned woman he used to hang out with is permanently out of the picture, or if she will show up soon to lay claim to him. She resolves to find out more about him, with or without Farrell's help, and then rolls over onto her stomach, her arms folded beneath her, and wills herself to sleep.

16: Izzie, Knynsa, June

Izzie is on the sofa again, this time sitting on her hands to hide their tremble. The tiny room is dark and gloomy, and the cup of coffee beside her on the wooden table has long since grown cold.

"I'm not going to be helpless," she tells herself repeatedly. "This time he's not going to bamboozle me. I'm strong. I can do this—I mustn't allow him to control me. And I know more than he thinks, I need to remember that."

Now she hears Webster at the door, opening it abruptly, then slamming it shut loudly. She sits up a little straighter.

"Izzie, are you home?" he bellows, and then wanders into the living room, glancing around before his eyes settle on her. "There you are—what're you doing? Why're you sitting here in the dark? Does this mean you haven't made dinner yet?"

"Webster, we need to talk," she says resolutely. "We have something important to discuss, and you can't keep putting me off about this—

"What? I've had a long day, and I've told you before.

Don't crap all over me the minute I walk in the door."

"Webster, there is always a reason why it's not a good time to talk. Now I'm asking. Do you realize that it's already June?"

"And so—?"

"Webster, you gave me that bag to hide at work, just for a couple of weeks, you said. That was three months ago! When are you going to be able to get rid of it, cash those pounds in so we can use our share? You promised me we would get married, we would pay off our debts, and we would leave here—"

"Is there a problem?" Webster asks as he walks towards her, clenching his fists at his sides. "Did your boss, that Ryder asshole, bother you about something? I know guys like that, all they want is one thing. I will go over there, learn him a thing or two—"

"No, Webster, no, please. It's nothing like that, he's nothing like that! And I stuck the bag way in the back of a closet the day after you gave it to me; haven't opened it since. Nobody has. But still—I'm scared, Webster. Please, when are you going to be able to take care of this? You promised—"

"Izzie—for crying out loud. What has come over you—you used to be adventurous! Don't start bringing up the setbacks now, I'm—"

"Setbacks? What are you talking about? Webster, don't tell me the police are going to find out. And what if Ryder does find the bag, what if—"

"I told you—this is not your problem. You don't have to worry about the police, I assure you that is taken care of.

I will find a way to exchange the money, after which we will get married. I already told you. But it seems you have a problem being patient."

"But Webster, you know I've been patient. I can't help it—I'm finding it hard to keep waiting—"

"Well, if you think I'm not worth it, then maybe it's time to reconsider our arrangement, Izzie," he says, turning his back and retreating towards the door.

"Honey, no," she replies, her strength dissolving as she walks towards him, grabs for his arm. "Baby, I'm just getting tired of all of this, but it's only because I want to marry you. I want us to be together forever, I love you so much. I'll just pretend the bag's not there until you ask me to retrieve it. I'm sorry—I won't bring it up again, okay?"

"If we don't ever have this conversation again, then it's okay. I will let you know when to bring the bag home. Until then, the topic is off-limits. Got it?"

Now she knows instinctively to remain quiet, and instead leads him to the bedroom. He petulantly resists at first, then allows her to steer him towards the bed. Then, he allows her to start making amends for bringing up this difficult subject in the first place.

"Oh yeah, just like that," he tells her. "Oh Izzie—you know just what I like—"

17: Koos, Knysna, June

"How much longer are we going to sit here?" Koos asks, as he rests his arm in his lap. They have been sitting inside their car, the cruiser concealed by a large bush, pointing the radar gun at the road for over an hour, but all they have seen are three cars, none of which have remotely approached the posted speed limit. Now he shakes out his right arm, trying to restore the blood flow.

"Feels like the captain sent us here to get us out of the way. What else could it be? There is no point to this, watching nothing. I'm telling you Klaas, I don't like how he speaks to us."

"What—because of what he said, that I'm new and you're stupid?"

"Yes, Klaas, that's exactly—"

"Ja man, that's definitely insulting to me 'cause I'm not new anymore." responds Klaas, then laughs out loud. "*Luister* (listen), how should I know what his point is— when the boss tells me what to do, I don't ask questions. Go out there, set up a speed trap, he says. Guess what I do? Ag man, you got somewhere else to be *miskien* (maybe)?"

"It's bloody cold out here, and ja I have somewhere

else to be," comes the impatient reply. "I could be at Mo's, for example."

"Oh ja, picking up a woman, no doubt. Serious like, they're all there just waiting for you," says Klaas as he stares pointedly at Koos's protruding belly. "I see you had to add a new notch in that old belt of yours, maybe you should skip the *koeksisters* for a week or two, neh? That might help."

"*Luister* Klaas, you haven't seen your toes since you were tickie high to a mailbox, can't even fit another notch onto the end of your belt—fuck you talking to me about *koeksisters*."

"I can still make time with the ladies. Always. Next time we go out I'll show you—"

"Ag nonsense. And take this blerry thing—it's your turn to hold the radar gun. I'm not staying out one minute past midnight, no matter what the captain says."

At this, Klaas grumbles his assent.

"*Jy weet* (you know), there's a lot of things we could be doing instead of wasting our time out here," Koos says now, a serious tone creeping into his voice. "You think I'm happy like this—no woman in my life, no excitement in my work, no reason to get up in the morning? And also the boss thinks I'm *doff* (stupid)."

Klaas shakes his head sympathetically, and Koos continues, encouraged. "But I've been reading about the rhinos *boet* (brother). It's some serious *kak* (shit) going on there. It's a pity we're in Knysna, no rhinos here, dead or alive. Imagine if we could bust a poaching ring and save some of them. We'd be heroes, man. When I was a *lightie* (youngster) my parents took me to the zoo. Man, I'll never forget seeing those ancient animals. Huge man, could belong in Jurassic park—you remember that *fliek* (film)?"

"That's what I like about you Koos—*vol kak* (full of shit) about how you're going to capture some big criminal. Save the world, become famous. Jurassic Park—*jyslaak* (Jesus). Why do you care, dead rhinos on the other side of the country are not our problem."

"Look, I'm trying to tell you. These bad guys, the poachers, they're all over. Do you know everyone says the problem is from the Vietnamese, that they are the ones who use the horns? But the problem is here in South Africa, man. I met this *oke* (guy) Jan once, in a bar in Malelane, outside Kruger—"

"I've never been there, Koos. I told you, it's the other side of the country—"

"Man, this Jan guy, he works for the Kruger Park as a ranger, and he told me all about the army, the helicopters, and the planes with cameras that are used in the park to look for poachers. There's always a shortage of pilots and fuel, and, of course, the rands needed for all of this."

"In the old apartheid days, I think some of the army officers were involved in these activities—"

"Ja Klaas, they turned a blind eye to all of it. It's true. Some army guys would work together with local farmers near the borders to hunt and kill rhinos, get the horns. It's only in the last few years that the Vietnamese have come along. In any case, still today, if there were no locals on the ground, the poaching couldn't even take place. Those are the bad guys that need to be caught, I would—"

"All right—when someone calls you, invites you to come to Kruger to help fly a chopper with a space age camera, let me know. In the meantime—"

"Yeah I know. Shut up and watch the traffic. Got it," says Koos glumly.

They continue sitting in the car on the cold, deserted road, no view of the lagoon or the ocean. The night stretches on endlessly without a sign of any goings on, illicit or otherwise. Eventually, at midnight, they engage the car, drive slowly back to town and return to the station to sign out of yet another pointless, eventless shift.

18: Jack, Noetzie Beach, June

Another day, another road trip. Where to this time? Oh does it really matter? I wander out of the house, jump in the car and fall asleep immediately anyway. No sense wishin' and hopin', we will go where Ryder wants to go, and get there when Ryder is good and ready. Really, so what else is new?

Do I sound resentful, annoyed that I'm not the one selecting the destination or the timetable? Well, maybe a little, you say. Yes, perhaps a little, but as I said, not really of much consequence to me. I go, I sleep, I provide moral support, and then I return home. Food in the morning, food in the evening. Makes no never-mind, as the less eloquent might say. So why the attitude? Why the edge of irritation? My usual equanimity has been disrupted by something. What is it that is sticking in my craw this morning?

What is it about Ryder that I find so endearing, when half the time I am at my wit's end with him? Yes, he "rescued" me from the harsh streets of Cape Town, and yes, he provides for all of my physical needs. But just to be clear, and I believe we have covered this ground before, with this face and this personality, it is not as if I was in danger of starving or being neglected in any way. This much I'm sure you can see for yourself. If not, then I suggest you take another look at the profile pictures attached! So no, in fact he "rescued" me only from an excess of attention, if you must know the truth.

Now watch Ryder, ever the kind fellow, as he waves to the little kids playing in the sand at the side of the road. Look—he is even pulling over and handing the scruffiest of the bunch a small bag containing a few sandwiches, our precious biltong and a roll of wine gums. What are we to do about lunch? I wonder as he pulls back onto the road. Perhaps he cannot hear the rumblings in my stomach as we continue on, now approaching, and then driving alongside of, an enormous chain-link fence.

Wait, I recognize this place. We are headed to secluded little Noetzie Beach, another stunning location. I hang my head out of the back window, my tongue drooping as I take in the expansive Pezula Estates. I can't help but admire these multi-billion-rand homes soaring out of the steep cliffs overlooking the Indian Ocean. Each resembles a small modern hotel, with perfectly landscaped gardens and bright blue swimming pools dotting the mountains. I think I catch a glimpse of the world-famous golf course and clubhouse just before we make our way to the small beach parking lot. As Ryder parks the car, I retract my head and then jump over into the front.

"C'mon Jack," *he says as he opens the door and climbs out.* "Time for some exercise."

What, no leash today? Usually I welcome the freedom, but right now it's kinda hard to keep up, what with those long legs and that vigorous stride. He's usually a kind fellow, but today he shows me no consideration as I trot behind, three steps to his one.

"Please," I implore silently, "let's pause for a minute, catch our breath and take this all in. Let's stop and admire this path, crafted from stone and sloping so steeply down towards the beach. What about the castle here, appearing on our left, can we not stop and stare at it for a few short moments? Look, it's been converted into a hotel complete with swimming pool. Perhaps we can obtain some refreshments here?"

But no, we continue on, the fast pace almost making me forget why I am so enervated. With my tongue hanging out, panting hard, I'm hard pressed to analyze any issues, let alone how I feel when it comes to Ryder and his unfortunate behavior. Keeping us in the here and now, with no time or energy to think about how—over the past few months—I've been unable to help him, to hold a mirror up to him. I've sat with him, walked with him, eaten with him, and even shared the sofa-bed with him when he was exiled there in disgrace. I know he has the power to help himself, if only he could see how much in need of help he is.

After we cross the beach we finally pause and look back at the castles, his feet and my paws in the ocean. I feel a renewed surge of affection for my best friend here at my side. But still, I am consumed with worry. He is becoming a mere shadow of his former self. Even his corny jokes have been in short supply of late. Will he continue to change, to move away from whatever it is that makes him so special? He gave up his work to attend to hers, never a good idea. Now slowly but surely he seems to be giving up his sparkle and charm too. And to think, it all began in the name of happiness, compromising until there was nothing left to compromise. Today, still and again, there is every danger he is going to backslide irretrievably. Notice as he selects a spot in the shade, close to the mouth of the river that empties into the ocean right here on this beach. Watch as he parks himself on his towel, then pulls his phone from his pocket and stares at it. Here we go again.

"Well she did call me. That should count for something," *he says as he begins the rationalization process.* "I think I've cooled down; it has been a few weeks you know. I don't have to be so inflexible—I can compromise a little here."

"Haven't we already gone over this?" I yell soundlessly. "A

pointless, endless discussion about calling Sophia. A terrible idea, Ryder."

Oh thank heavens, he is putting the phone away. He leans back on his elbows, staring out at the distant breakers before turning to me.

"Jack, I swore I wouldn't do this. What am I thinking? Why would anything be different with her now?"

Okay, well, seems we're making progress. Perhaps he's actually figuring out the difference between flexibility and complete compromise. No one can spare the brain cells he's sacrificing beating his head against the Sophia wall, that's for sure. Just yesterday, we had another close call.

"Wait a minute," *he had said, looking up from the TV guide with a vaguely hopeful look on his face.* "Sophia is probably wondering where all of her stuff is. What's in that duffel of hers I brought home, anyway?"

He fetched the duffel, then sat down again and hoisted it into his lap. He opened the zipper and peered inside.

"Oh, this must be some of her summer things. I really should call her. I'm sure she'll be looking for these clothes."

"What—what?" I yelled in my silent fashion. "Let her go naked for all we care. Do you honestly think she will thank you for all of this, any of this? Has she ever thanked you for anything in the past?"

I walked over to where he sat on the sofa, duffel between his legs, telephone in hand. He was stuck, paralyzed. I had to do something, anything. He swore to me that he would not do this; actually he swore this to himself. Not that I was surprised by this backtracking, mind you—I've become accustomed to this from him lately. But then, he surprised me.

"Oh for crying out loud," *he had said suddenly, zipping up the bag without disturbing any of the contents and shoving the phone back deep into his pocket.* 'I'll wait and see if she calls me again. Maybe she will—what do you think Jack? I'll keep the phone handy, just in case."

Now do you see my problem? I'm disheartened by the Herculean tasks ahead of me. Not only do I have to teach Ryder that there are some things that should never be compromised, shared goals be damned, but I also have to race back up that steep path to get to the waiting car. Oh go ahead, say it already, I know I have stubby little legs. And that I lack the patience needed to explain esoteric ideas to out-of-touch humans. Always willing to admit my own shortcomings, that's me, despite what you might have heard to the contrary.

Ah finally back in the car, with all four windows slightly open and the air flowing gently over my tired body. The motion lulls me to sleep as we set off again, continuing our journey without knowledge of where it will end. And I suppose there is always the chance that tomorrow will point us in a more favorable direction. Please send positive energy because, Lord knows, Ryder needs it now more than ever.

19: Ryder, Knysna, June

Where am I going to find any answers? I've been living in limbo, brought here by denial. De Nile—a river in Africa. Sometimes the jokes in my head are as irritating to me as they obviously were to Sophia! Why must my thoughts keep returning to her? She who set me on this path in the first place? Dammit—enough!

I have to admit it, over the years I've spent a lot of time denying what my mind was saying, allowing my heart to refuse to hear. Dumb, stupid—I've seen this over and over again, in countless conversations with others suffering the same pain. My pattern is their pattern, and it is clear— all of us are foolish in love and happiness. We go for instant gratification. Indulging because our hearts want it, all the while knowing that we're choosing something that is not good for us. And we justify the bad choices by concentrating on the immediate return. We ignore and deny the facts. We refuse to face reality. Living in hope of what may be, and the farther we go down this path, the harder the extraction and ultimate acknowledgement of our own stupidity becomes. After this denial, if we begin to admit that we erred in our judgment, then we're doomed to a downward spiral, into the depths of sorrow and sadness. That must be where I am now—mourning the loss of love, happiness, bond; disappearing deeper into limbo.

If I ever want to emerge from this, I know I have some work to do on myself. Rummaging around in my virtual toolbox, that bag of tricks where I keep all the things I need for mental repairs. Strange coincidence? Or perfect synchronicity, that these are the very tools I've used over the years to help others with their self-repair projects? Oh yes, I was quite the expert at this before getting involved in our "shared dream;" my life's work had always been about coaching others who found themselves at a crossroads, stuck and discouraged. Now I have to use these same tools to assist me.

Step one: Recognition of how my last few months in Cape Town mirrored the stages of others I've worked with. Who had, in one way or another, experienced loss. I considered myself the expert, and yet there I was, well past stage one before even recognizing this. Again, stuck in denial, the most intransigent stage of all, and apparently no one is immune. Not only did I deny my circumstances while actively living in them, and simultaneously reinforcing them, but also denied my feelings about these circumstances.

How did my whole process of loss begin? Just as every journey begins with a single step, so I must have started out with a seemingly innocuous movement in the wrong direction. Was it that first or second compromise, maybe? And I never thought compromise a bad thing, that basic principle we're taught to embrace from a young age. "Here, I will give you this toy if you give that sharp object back to me." The bending to the will of another, giving way to make for a more peaceful path.

But I never understood the danger, the peril of giving way until I was no longer on my own path, but had been forced onto the path of another. The giving and compromising eroded quintessential parts of me until what was left was barely recognizable.

I ultimately lost myself. Lying to myself that I was merely discarding that which was not important, only working with her to arrive at a shared purpose. But it was all her purpose, not mine, and not shared at all. I thought I was doing what she wanted—letting her take charge of all the decisions, make all the plans. But now I have to confront the sad truth: towards the end, I no longer knew how to stand up for myself. What a conundrum—she wanted me to be in charge, be my own man, yet take care of her, and do everything her way, all at the same time.

But no, no bitterness, no blame. We both failed to see that we were on the wrong path, until the only way back was to reverse directions, and go our separate ways. Yes, shared guilt and shared blame.

Should I decide I don't believe in compromise anymore? Compromise leads to loss leads to denial? The solution can't be that clear cut. From now on in a relationship, I resolve to look for mutual purpose. With at least one condition, from the outset, that each person gets to preserve their own essence. Allow the head to rule when asked to make a concession, and not accept anything that goes against my nature. I will always be willing to discard meaningless obstacles that stand in the way of achieving and building something together. That is a given. But if integral parts of me are distasteful, if my head knows parts of her are unacceptable, then the relationship is doomed. Willingly discarding things that are important to me, or willfully overlooking things that should not be ignored, is not a way to build a shared future, based on mutual goals. It is a recipe for loss, emptiness, ultimate imbalance and limbo.

20: Ryder, Knysna, July

Tonight outside it's freezing cold, the wind howling off the water. It's a poor choice for a first evening out, especially when Ryder has been cooped up for so long. But he decided earlier, he will go to the party. God helps those who help themselves, or so he has always been told. Tonight is the night, it is time for him to help himself. Introspection and examination is getting old, and he has finally reached the point where he's even annoying himself. So he made a spur-of-the-moment decision, prompted by an invitation from a potential student.

"Hey Ryder, a few of us are getting together tonight to celebrate my birthday. Are you free? Please come, it will be fun."

Ryder realizes with a start that this is one of the first connections he has made in months. This isolation has been tough, made all the more difficult by the constant emotional upheaval. If he's going to make any progress, finally begin on a road to recovery, here is the opportunity for some real human interactions as a first step.

He pauses in front of the mirror hanging next to the front door, and begins the preparation against the damp wind. Wraps on his scarf, pulls on the woolen hat. Coat, gloves. What else? Heavy boots. Again, he glances in the mirror. Is that the almost unrecognizable ghost of a smile he sees crossing his face?

Now he's ready. Jack glances at him from his bed next to the sofa, then rolls over and sighs.

"Sorry Ryder. You're on your own tonight, Mate—there's no way I'm braving that weather for another night of your crying in your beer. What's that? Planning on socializing with others, not sitting by yourself at the local, knocking them back? Well seeing is believing. Another time, I'm afraid. And please, try not to slam the door on the way out. There's a good lad."

Ryder goes out quickly, hoping the brisk one kilometer walk in the frigid air will bolster his confidence. And as he arrives and rings the doorbell, he feels excited. It is time and he's ready. This party is being hosted by Leeza and her partner Julie, a couple Ryder was introduced to earlier in the day. They open the door together, then usher him in.

"Ryder, come in. It's freezing. Quick, shut the door behind you! We're so glad you're here." Leeza is the first to speak. She's dressed in a loose colorful gown, belted at the waist, with her high heels adding a few extra inches to her chunky frame. Her bluntly-cut hair falls in strange angles all around her face and she peers at him through her owl-eye glasses. Definitely an eccentric, he thinks, as he hugs her quickly.

"You can hang up your coat over here, and then come join us. We're all in the kitchen," Julie says as she smiles warmly, and Ryder finds himself grinning in return. Julie is tall and spindly, with her wrists and hands adorned with so many colorful tattoos, bracelets and rings that it is hard to distinguish where the skin ends and the jewels begin. She, too, has an odd haircut, and Ryder has a fleeting image of the two women inexpertly cutting each other's hair. Simultaneously and haphazardly. He blinks this odd image away, then steps over to the small coat closet. He's reminded of the camaraderie he has missed, while spending night after night brooding, fretting, and drinking alone. Now, as he turns to remove his coat, another guest walks through the door. They stare at each other.

"Wait a minute. I know you," she says.

"No you don't. I just moved here. You have never seen me before," he replies, as he tries to determine if she's simply mistaken, or if it is at all possible that she's flirting with him.

He glances at her as they continue the process of removing scarves, hats, coats, boots, when suddenly, black-and-purple hair comes tumbling down.

"Now I get it. You're the pot store girl, Demi! You do know me after all! I'm—"

"Ryder, right? You see I was correct! I never forget a face, most especially yours. How the heck are you?"

They wander to the kitchen together, where they encounter the guest of honor, the birthday boy, Duane.

"Ryder, you're so late," he says as they shake hands. "Where have you been?"

"Well I just came from a pleasure trip, took my mother-in-law to the airport," Ryder replies, as if on cue.

He laughs at this, but Demi looks on, a worried frown fleeting across her face.

"So you're married?" she asks bluntly.

"No, no, I'm not. These guys are already learning about my weird sense of humor."

"Oh I see—" Demi stalls, trying to think of a smart response.

"But he does have an ex he can tell you about," Duane eggs him on. "Go on Ryder—"

"Well, she was at the beauty shop for two hours today," Ryder begins. "But that was only for the estimate. Last week she got a mudpack and looked great for two days. Then the mud fell off."

Now with an audience, he's off and running, showing off, trying to impress Demi with his wit. They wander deeper into the kitchen together laughing, falling into a natural conversation. He realizes with a start how happy he is to see her again.

"So, how did that spare key work out for you Ryder? Did you ever find someone to give it to?" she asks at some point.

"No, still looking—do you know someone who might be interested perhaps?" he answers with a grin.

And so it begins. The welcoming hosts, the celebrated birthday, the pleasant guests. This gathering of unusual souls starts to feel most normal to Ryder and he embraces all of it, from the shared pot of mielie pap, to the hotly contested game of Taboo. He feels as though he's waking from his self-inflicted hibernation, and he realizes that his instincts to force himself into a social situation tonight were correct. Any time there is a lull in the conversation, he's ready with a comment or a quip.

"In the big city, the new drunk driving laws are getting very serious," he says as he refills his glass. A generous splash of Jack Daniels, some Red Bull. Lots of ice. "Roadblocks and the like. Pull over and breathe into the gizmo. Did you know that our drink-and-drive limit is much stricter than in the US or the UK, where they allow a half gram per hundred ml of blood, compared to 0.08g? I'm telling you, these *okes* are very serious about the death toll on the roads now."

"Well, being here in Knysna it's really great. You can drink as much as you like, and go from party to party, just walking. Nothing is too far away," interjects Leeza.

"Yeah, true," continues Ryder, unwilling to relinquish the spotlight. "You know, this party reminds me of my good friend who was brought in front of a judge just this past Monday morning for drunk driving. The judge said, 'You've been brought here for drinking.' So my friend said 'Okay, let's get started.'"

The room is now filled with both laughter and groans; the serious drinking is well underway already. Demi walks to the narrow bar counter, where she eyes the bottle of wine, then shakes her head almost imperceptibly. Instead, she pours the last of the club soda into her glass, then walks over to sit down.

"Hey, mind if I squeeze in over here?" she asks as she lowers herself between Ryder and another guest. He immediately notices her thigh pressed against his on the crowded sofa, and wonders if she, too, is feeling this budding attraction. He sneaks a sidelong glance, and notices again how striking she is. Don't get carried away, he cautions himself, even as he wonders what it would be like to take her in his arms, kiss and embrace her. It dawns on him that he was right to avoid contacting her until tonight, even though he has been alone for a few months now, and deeply lonely long before that. Because now he's finally free of all other relationships, free to call whomever he likes, converse with whomever he wants, and free to pursue Demi with no guilt or fear.

With the alcohol flowing freely, the conversation skirts the awkward topics of religion and politics, and instead turns directly to sex. A perfect opportunity for Ryder to test out some of his factoids, gathered over the years from random encounters.

"So, have any of you been to a sex therapist?" he asks, apropos of nothing.

Demi is quick off the mark, asking "Wait, are we going to be talking about your ex again?" to laughter around the table.

"Ah, too fast Demi. She's probably there right now! But you know, recently I met this woman in a bar—"

"Wait, what? You met a woman in a bar?" interrupts Leeza. "Say it ain't so—"

"Shut up," Julie says to her partner. "I want to hear this."

"Yes, Leeza, quiet. Back to my story. This woman I met was a sex therapist and we had a very interesting discussion. Did you know that the number of affairs with a married woman cheating on her husband is now almost equal in number to the other way around? This is a big change from previous generations, apparently. But tell me, is this news to anyone?"

Julie pipes up, "About time someone was keeping count. But honestly, this surprises me. I always thought men screwed around, period, hence my gay preferences."

"Really?" inquires Leeza. "And I thought it was because, as a woman, I could understand your body better than any man. Because I know how to stimulate those special places—"

"Hey can I come to you for lessons? Needing help over here, desperate!" Ryder says laughing. "Well, perhaps a verbal description will suffice—"

Demi looks on, intrigued by the openness of this man with her friends.

"Men all think they know exactly what their partner wants or needs because, duh, it worked for the previous one," she begins, then zeroes in on a sensed weakness. "Here's a question for you Ryder. If you were so clued in? Then why are you now single?"

At this Ryder shrugs helplessly, the answer beyond his understanding.

"Men are so dumb!" Julie exclaims. "But then again, males are known worldwide for thinking they know everything about what the whole world wants, in and out of bed! In fact, all women have different turn on buttons, both emotionally and physically."

"Absolutely," Ryder agrees. "Believe me I know—as if it is not enough that all of those secret places are different for each woman. Then we have to understand that it is all complicated by the head space, which has to be aligned to the guy and his approach. Not to mention the planets, where the kids are or are not, the dog's latest illness, the peak time of traffic, the boss's schedule, her work team—"

"Yeah, we get the picture Ryder. Sounds like maybe you have struck out a time or two. You can blame it on the traffic, if that helps you feel any better. But take heart— even women find this complicated and don't understand their own bodies, and often don't know how to get into the right headspace."

"Nothing a little alcohol can't sort out," responds Demi, and they all laugh knowingly.

"Well, most men are not so different from each other sexuality wise, a lot of it is mechanical," says Leeza, as she winks at Ryder. "A good pair of heels and they are good to go, am I right?"

"Certainly helps," he says, blushing just slightly. "But seriously, the big difference is men can get it on without much of the "headspace" requirement. I believe this is linked to men as hunters trying to spread the most seeds, with women as nurturers. You know, trying pick the most-likely-to-have-success genes. That's why women have to be convinced that he's worthy. Damn, it is so hard to be worthy!"

At this, most of the women present nod their heads, raise their glasses in a complicit toast. Encouraged, Ryder now hopes to appear both knowledgeable and curious.

"Well, I read that women's sexuality evolves over time, unlike us men who stay pretty much the same. So basically everything I've learned, and keep learning, becomes useless with every passing year. Starting from scratch, over and over," he continues.

"Oh, I think you might know a thing or two—" says Demi, now blushing slightly in turn.

"C'mon Demi—you're the budding cougar in the crowd," says Julie. "Don't be bashful."

"Is that so?" asks Ryder, turning his full attention her way. "In that case, tell me what you think about this. I hear that the older guys enjoy sex only if their partner is really into it, whereas the younger guys don't care one way or the other. Look, we older guys have less testosterone, so I'm guessing we're just more discerning in how we use it. What do you think?"

Demi is now on edge, knowing what he's after, and wondering if he's all talk, or if he can walk it too. She feels his thigh pressed up against hers, warm and toned, feels the beginnings of both desire and arousal. Then she sneaks a glance at his lap, trying to see if there are any telltale signs that this conversation is having the same effect on him. He shifts slightly.

Leeza decides to expand on the sex therapist theme. "I have an anecdote about two lesbians in sex therapy. One of them—like me—had been married before, but then came out. While her partner was out of the room, the therapist asked her who she preferred having sex with, her ex-husband or her female partner. She replied that sex with her ex-husband was much better! Why? Because he was easier to please, and less complicated. I found that funny—"

"Then why am I not laughing?" asks Julie, before Leeza continues

"—but totally unrealistic, Jules, baby. Not to worry!"

To the sound of chuckles around the room, Julie says

"I hear that as women age, gay or straight, they need three things. Reading glasses, hearing aids and a vibrator."

"What's that?" Leeza responds quickly. "Speak up, Honey. I can't hear you over the buzzing—"

Now they all laugh, and Julie gets up to serve coffee before the guests stumble home. After this long evening of drinking and socializing with new friends, the walk home feels infinitely shorter. Is it because he's no longer going against the frigid wind? Or is it perhaps because he's preoccupied with thoughts of this new woman? And with thoughts of how, now that he once again has opened himself to new possibilities, the universe is providing these very possibilities for him, seemingly in abundance!

When he reaches his building, he takes the steps two at a time, barges in to the small place.

"Jack, get up! Time for your evening walk! Let's go. Up and at 'em. Good Boy! Let me tell you about my night."

"Ah back home finally, are you? I sincerely hope you appreciate me, your best friend and sounding board, waking me up and dragging me outside in frightful weather. Ready to talk, I suppose."

But tonight Ryder's story is different, more hopeful and less depressing. They walk to the corner, then turn around and race back. Ryder is eager for bed, eager for the next day. A new leaf, a new chapter. Is it finally time to get on with it? To move on? Months ago, he put himself in a new place geographically; now his emotional self might finally have made it there to join him. *Yes, about time I got over myself,* he thinks, as he falls asleep with a slight grin on his face.

21: Jack, Knysna, July

Ah Ryder—finally I'm able to recognize the fellow I see before me. This morning, a quick breakfast and then a walk alongside the lagoon. Playing fetch with you again—one of the simple pleasures in my life. And then we sat and watched the sailboats on the water for a while, after which we went to the town square for a snack and some people watching. Joking with the wait staff, interacting with the other customers as they paused to admire me. Oh yes, a comfort and a joy that you and I enjoy the same things! Finally I feel like I'm getting my best friend back, and no, I never really gave up hope. Perish the thought. Certainly my patience has been severely tried over the past few months, but surely that is forgivable.

I wonder if this change of attitude and change of heart is due to Ryder's new "person of interest?" What is this name Demi? Is it short for Dementia perhaps? And if so who will warn Ryder of this? No, no, I won't think like that. He's an adult, and as such, is capable of drawing his own conclusions about the women he chooses to date. If he learned very little from Sophia, surely he has at least learned how to approach this cautiously, take a new relationship one step at a time. And to let his head govern his heart, just a little. Yes, I feel sure he will think things through very clearly if he chooses to get involved here.

So now we walk from the town square in a different direction, towards Demi's little shop. It is still chilly out, but Ryder has on a warm jacket and I, of course, have my usual fur coat. Does he hesitate before approaching the entrance? Perhaps he does, because as we linger on the corner, I see someone exiting the shop. A woman with long blonde hair, carrying an artist's leather portfolio.

Ryder stands there as I debate taking off after her, and I take a few steps in her direction. But then he sets to whistling and calling for me, and I obey. This much I know, being the disciplined and obedient fellow that I am, when my best friend calls, I must come running. Demi emerges to see what going on, and Ryder attempts to explain my behavior.

"What, wanting to chase after my customers, are you?" *Demi asks as she pets me on the head. She turns to Ryder.* "That woman drives all the way up here from her home along the coast, visits town every few months. An artist. But tell me, Ryder, what brings you by today?"

So here it is, the moment of truth. Oh Ryder, do you still have it? Your magical way with the fairer sex?

"Demi, I really need to get ahold of some pot."

"Hmm—so you appear to have forgotten that I sell planters, not pot—"

"Actually, I remember every word of our conversation. And I would very much like to continue it. Over dinner maybe?"

"I close up tonight at seven—and I happen to be free after that—"

Well, that was easy enough, and the look of relief on Ryder's face is so endearing. I wonder if Demi notices this as well. We walk back home quickly, Ryder excited in a way I haven't seen in a long time.

"You see, Jack, I'm going to be okay. I feel so much better than I did a few months ago. Or even a few days ago."

As if I need him to tell me this obvious piece of information, but I cock my head to indicate I'm paying attention. After all, I am his dog, his partner. Listening to him is my job, my work, and I'm good at it. He goes into the kitchen, busies himself making a cup of tea.

"And you know what else? I'm never going to call Sophia back. Never! Yes, the best way for me to deal with that situation is to blot her out of my mind completely. As for that bag of clothes of hers, if she wants them she's going to have to come to Knysna to get them."

Bound and determined, I would say. Finally, finally we have heard the last of this woman, this Sophia. Is Demi going to be the solution to all of Ryder's problems? I doubt it. Perhaps you're familiar with his extensive list of issues? But my hope is that she can help pull him out of the doldrums permanently. Love, happiness, bond—the three things he goes on and on about. Perhaps Demi will help him recognize the love and happiness he still has, despite the breaking of past bonds. Whether she will be the one to help him intensify these, to ensure deeper levels of happiness and love, well that remains to be seen. Because a bond with a new woman must be carefully considered, and not entered into lightly. I believe Ryder knows this now. At least I hope so!

22: Ryder and Demi, Knysna, August

The pearly white Lexus winds silently up and around the narrow, tree-lined road to the very top of the Knynsa heads, leaving the town and its residents way down below. Ryder, in the driver's seat, can focus on the beautiful scenery instead of the map and directions. Oh the joys of this car with its Japanese Satnav technology.

On the dash is the elaborate invitation to tonight's party. Ryder is looking forward to this evening, pleased to be included by Mack and May as a part of their crowd of friends. He has visited their inn on the heads before, and is eagerly anticipating an evening of international guests, great South African food, and perhaps most importantly, vast quantities of the famous regional Cape Wines. Ryder is an innocent, a relative newcomer, and has no idea what the party has in store for him.

He parks the car and exits, looking around. He walks to the deck at the entrance to the inn, and marvels anew at the magnificent view from the marble tiles leading up to the guesthouse—eye boggling! The blue hue of the under-lit swimming pool and Jacuzzi is enhanced by the tiny lights of the town below. There are lagoon views in all directions.

The seductive vistas, the seductive niche boutique wines, and the seductive local girls, all complement and reinforce each other. He basks in all of it, his attention pulled in multiple directions.

Then he returns to the car to escort his new girlfriend into the party. Yes Demi, that slim, smiling, purple-and-black haired woman has been a large part of his re-entry into communal life. After their first real date, they instantly became an item, naturally falling into a pattern of spending time together whenever possible. And Ryder is grateful for the easy company, the seemingly uncomplicated relationship. She seems so willing to have him take over and make all plans, organize all joint activities, a stark contrast to the demands of Sophia, those dark days with her now seem so long in the past. Wearing cowboy boots, leather jacket, and hip hugging black jeans with a tiny sliver of flat belly skin showing, Demi is welcomed by the hostess who emits friendly wild shrieks. Ryder is fast becoming familiar with this form of greeting, performed seemingly in unison by these Knysna women even though Ryder had introduced them only one week before. The hostess is well-groomed with striking features, a dark-haired woman of generous proportions, wearing a colorful pink-hued flowing gown. Ryder attributes her youthful appearance to her gentle personality and calm lifestyle living in this mansion on the lagoon hilltop. Yet her unruffled exterior belies the fact that she and her man, the Mack and May of this establishment, have physically built and decorated the magnificent place themselves. Through their collective sweat-equity, they have created a first-class resort.

Ryder has already become accustomed to some of the Knysna traditions—drinks are poured for the two of them before introductions to the other guests are made. Priorities! Demi walks onto the deck, greeting the guests as she is introduced, with Ryder following closely along, turning on the charm. Glasses are raised by way of greeting, and they're welcomed as the newest additions to the crowd of regulars. *Salut! L'chaim!*

They walk across the deck to the top of the staircase, where a huge table stands. On it, the five selected bottles of white wine from local farms cool in a huge, ice-filled, silver bowl. The same number of reds are displayed, open and breathing, alongside. Already there are empties, and already the two wine merchants in attendance are overly happy, despite the early hour.

"That's Wendell," Demi whispers to him, as they approach the duo. "He's a fixture at all parties around this town. And despite the upper-crust British name, he's a stoner from way back."

"Yeah, I think that's already apparent. But, ah, who's the other one?" Ryder asks, perhaps a little too eagerly, indicating the sexy, provocatively dressed woman next to Wendell. She turns and flashes herself to them in an ultra-short, sleeveless gold dress with stiletto heels. She's almost anorexic in build, well-stacked, a real head turner.

"Their relationship is somewhat unclear," Demi whispers out of the side of her mouth, as they walk up to them for the obligatory greeting.

Ah, Ryder thinks after being introduced, *that's what all small towns need, a local wine merchant to spice things up. And the quirkier the better, to be sure.*

It is readily apparent that Wendell will have no problem spicing things up, and his red nose and continual sniffing indicate that his fondness for vices goes beyond mere alcoholism. He explains to Ryder that he and his assistant work the local small town route, doing wine promo parties all along the coast. Actually, the assistant is the real wine expert, a knowledgeable source and marketer of local wines, while Wendell is the party guy, always charming, friendly, and fun. And obviously a ladies' man, beloved by all. He schmoozes and she sells, a perfect arrangement. Ryder wonders if that's all the partnership consists of, because it is immediately clear she has eyes for her business partner, another sort of business in mind for him! Ryder is beginning to realize, albeit slowly, that in Knysna all will become clear sooner or later. Alcohol appears to have certain illuminating effects—

While the girls giggle and the wine flows, Ryder leaves the deck and goes to find his host in the kitchen. More smiles, laughter, warm hugs. Ryder feels at home immediately, welcome as part of this newfound family.

"Hey Mack, you did not have to get all dressed up for me you know," Ryder remarks facetiously.

"No worries man. I'm a Knysna beach boy, all the way. Like my new slops? Fancy! Same as the old slops, I'd say! New Hawaiian shirt though. Cool, no? Matches my shorts. Well, sort of matches. Hey, where's your drink? C'mon, you have some catching up to do."

Ryder knows he will learn a new recipe tonight, to modify, enjoy, and make his own for years to come. He's well in time to help with food preparation.

"Now get busy, man." Mack hands him a knife, which he can tell from the heft is of hand-forged steel. Extra-sharp, of course. "Here you go—chop up these chilies—and when that's done there are onions and garlic to prepare. Just put them next to the cucumbers when you're finished."

A little male bonding over drinking, a little chatting over chopping and dicing.

"So Mack, I hear you ran a huge corporate empire for all those years, worked really hard, and then you and May cashed it in, came down here, and built this stunningly beautiful place."

"Yep, Ryder, all true. And we don't regret it, not even for a minute."

"Man, I'm in awe of you. And you've been married for so long, too."

"Yep, twenty-eight years next February."

"So tell me something. What is it that you would advise a woman to look for in a man, something that would point towards the likelihood of a successful relationship?"

"Check this out," Mack replies, taking two paper plates from the top of a large stack on the counter. Then he opens up a kitchen drawer and pulls out a permanent marker. On the first plate he writes "Things that matter" in big, bold letters, and on the second "Things you can control." He carefully places the plates so the overlapping edges form a small intersection. He points to this small oval of overlap and says "See, Ryder, this segment here is the key, the part to focus on. What matters AND what you can control."

"Are you talking about here at the inn, or in general?"

"Actually, this little trick can be applied to almost any challenge we face in life. Simple and obvious, sure, but it's not often in our awareness. Hey, we both know emotions get in the way of logic, all the time. So let's see—if we're talking about the inn—the part that matters is that our guests get both May and me as full time hosts, all day, every day."

"Yeah—I see that very clearly. I know you cook for them—"

"Yes, and take them to town, book dinners for them, have parties for them. This is what we feel matters to them, and that's the client base we attract. We become friends, do business, have fun with them, and they come back year after year, each time bringing more friends."

"Really? Even with this recession, they keep coming back?"

"Well, Ryder, that is moving into things we can't control. You know we can't control the global recession, the economy, and especially the rand-dollar exchange rate."

"Yeah, I know that to be all too true—"

"But you see, we can control the daily interactions of our friend-guests when they are here. That's what we do, make the most of our time when we're with them, put our focus on that. It separates us from all the other inns, and truly it is a simple and clear way to run our business."

"Hey that's awesome!" Ryder exclaims. "I really see evidence of it too, because any event at your place is always special. Now I understand—it's exactly as you describe the focus. But tell me—how does a woman apply this lesson to her dealings with a man?"

"Well, it's basically the same idea, Ryder. She has to decide: what matters in finding love? What can and cannot be controlled?"

"You mean, finding out what drives a man will let you know what matters to him? Then she has to figure out if those things matter to her as well, right?"

"Yes, if the same things matter to both people, you have match. May and I both love to entertain, and have made this passion our livelihood together. We have different roles to play here, but with the same view of what matters. Our independent actions lead to a combined value-add to our clients."

"And to your relationship, I'm guessing."

"Yes, of course. This totally enhances and complements our personal relationship. Hey, May knows a woman can't control a man when he's way from her. Only when I'm with her can she be fully present in my life. Then she can control her own behavior and see how I respond. She knows she cannot control other things like my sport, hobbies, work, so she doesn't try."

"Yeah, that never ends well—when someone tries to control every aspect of your life," Ryder says, shaking his head slightly.

"Yeah, Ryder, so maybe she can control my diet, or how we spend our vacation time. Just basically because I have given up control of the things she cares more deeply about than I do. And between you and me, hopefully she can control my credit card as well!"

"Ha!" says Ryder, "reminds me of something that happened a few years ago. Someone stole all my credit cards, but you know I did not report them to the cops. I figured the thief would spend less than my ex-wife did."

"Funny guy you are Ryder! As always. Do you record and practice these jokes?"

"Actually, when we used to go shopping, we always held hands. If I ever let go she would start to spend! But to be serious for just a minute—"

"Yeah, for just a minute—"

"Mack, a lot of this is becoming clearer for me. And I guess what you said is also true for a man looking for love and happiness with a woman, looking to form a bond. Things that matter to me, things I can control. The intersection. Got it! Now back to work—"

The prepared olives and feta sit soaking in the oil; the pile of empties grows. Ryder helps with the finishing touches of the preparations for the evening's feast, noting that all of this celebrating, this wining and dining, takes a lot of hard work. But at the inn, there is always the kitchen help, assisting with the prep work. And as Ryder looks around, he imagines that his two bedrooms, two bathrooms, lounge and open plan kitchen, deck included, would fit comfortably into the middle of all of this. They all work side by side at a huge granite-topped island work-station, the double sink and gas hob to his left, the double ovens and free-standing rotisserie to his right. The lagoon is visible from the kitchen, as are the guests outside around the blue hued pool. An awesome, remarkably unforgettable space.

23: Ryder and Demi, Knysna, August

With the salads, sauces and trimmings completed, Ryder and Mack move out to the poolside deck where the two fires are roaring, and the flowing Merlot, Shiraz and cabernet reds keep the arriving guests warm on this clear evening despite the slight chill creeping in with the setting sun. The iPod is plugged into the outdoor speaker system and songs from the sixties, seventies and eighties play in the open air. "Call Me," "It's Still Rock and Roll to Me," "Sailing," and, ah, here's a good one: "(It's Just Like) Starting Over."

When the cooking is done, they lay out the black fancy plates with red edges, fill them with huge steaks, piles of cocktail sausages, marinated chicken kebabs and chopped salads and trimmings. Ryder takes careful note of the recipes, thinking vaguely of loading them onto a website, and compiling them into a book someday. Tonight's menu includes the inn's special Rump Steak. South African men are very particular and passionate about the fire making and the meat cooking. Indeed a gas barbeque is never an option. Wood is definitely the first choice, preferable to charcoal briquettes. Ryder reflects on the fact that the ritualized process of fire making and tending is almost as enjoyable as the eating. And there are always two fires, one for ambiance and warmth, and the second functioning in the more important role of producing, on demand, the fresh hot coals to be used for the cooking fire.

Recently-arrived guests stand beside the wall of fire or seat themselves at the large wooden table, surrounded by twelve chairs. The whole town lies below them, lit up by streetlights and traffic lights carving paths through the houses and down the main road. Yes, this is to be a dinner party of note, with locals who arrive one by one, or in some cases two-by-two, in their four-by-fours. Included in the guest list tonight are some out-of-town guests, long-time friends and business partners of the hosts. Rumor has it even the mayor and his estranged wife will be here eventually, as they work on their umpteenth reconciliation.

But how did it come about that Wendell's girlfriend suddenly showed up? No, not the anorexic female wine merchant in the revealing dress, another woman in this endless cast of quirky characters. Yes here, added to the mix, another beautiful, sexy woman, also seductively attired. Another mini dress again paired with stiletto heels, elaborate jewelry snaking its way around her lean upper arms. Prominent zipper pulled halfway up the front, or is that halfway down? And all of her attention focused on her man, who she's here to claim. With two femmes fatales in attendance now, both with the hots for Wendell, it seems clear that male wine merchants are a rare and popular commodity. And this merchant, this apparently irresistible guy, keeps disappearing into the bathroom, then reappearing looking more glazed and loaded. Ryder observes the arrival of the half-clad nymph and the possibilities for ensuing chaos from his position on the deck. He is learning, observing, watching the interactions and taking mental notes. Farrell, also a guest at the party, sidles up to him, looking for all the world as though he has just bitten into something distasteful. His long-standing friendship with Demi seems to make him want to confide in Ryder. He leans over and speaks, his boozy breath hitting Ryder full in the face:

"These people—all of them drunk!" he exclaims.

"But, but you—"Ryder begins, but Farrell interrupts.

"Listen, don't make excuses for them. I can handle my alcohol. Unlike some of these people."

"Is that right? I think maybe you have had a few too many yourself," Ryder says to the increasingly inebriated, and increasingly agitated, Farrell.

"I'm going to go climb up on that there table, tell them a thing or two, Ryder. Right after I finish this drink. Wait, don't take the bottle. Top it off. There you go." He grabs the bottle back from a passing guest, makes sure to pour the last drop into his glass before casually dropping it into the bushes surrounding the deck.

"I give up, Farrell. There is no talking to you. You're too drunk to listen." Ryder looks around, realizing that for most of the guests, arriving slightly drunk has meant becoming progressively drunker as the evening has worn on. Bottoms up.

"Is there anyone left here who is sober?" he turns and asks Demi who has moved over to stand beside him.

"Did someone call my name?" This from Wendell as he stumbles across the deck. Who is he walking away from, who towards? "You know my name is Wendell, right? Stiff upper lip, a solid Brit all the way. At all times, Mate, all times. Ryder, we're going to become good friends, I can feel it. Have you met my girlfriend, or my business partner?"

"I don't know Wendell—which one is which?" Those within earshot snicker, waiting for the clarification. Ryder playing dumb, innocently waiting for a response.

"You a funny guy, aren't you? You see the blonde over there with the big tits? No, the other blonde with the big ones? That's my girlfriend. The other one is my business partner."

"Oh, the one with the plunging neckline is your girlfriend, not your "business" partner. I got it. Wendell, why does it look like they are arguing? Surely they're not fighting over you?"

"Nah, it's all good. We all love each other, *bro*. It's all business and also all love." Then he leans over, lips against Demi's ear, and whispers those words any woman is dying to hear: "Hey, Gorgeous, wanna join me in the bathroom for a few minutes? Know what I mean?"

Ryder shakes his head, laughs, as Demi squirms away, moves to stand somewhere else. Wendell stumbles off, meeting and greeting as he goes.

Drunken shenanigans ensue. At some point, the anorexic assistant, now well into her second or perhaps third bottle of wine, leans over and reaches for a glass. Her ultra-short skirt rides up even further, all secrets revealed! And Ryder cannot help himself, he sneaks a peek at the half-naked woman, easily assessing that yes, she is wearing underwear. Black lace, of course, but that no, it does not cover much.

Ah Wendell, he thinks somewhat wistfully, *you're going to have your hands full when you leave here tonight!*

Then Demi pulls him away, unnoticed by the crowd. She leads him up the circular staircase, and across the lobby towards the honeymoon suite, knowing it is unoccupied tonight, having confirmed this with May, her newest friend and confidant.

"Don't you be concerning yourself with her lace," she says to Ryder. "Oh yeah, I saw all that, with you pretending not to stare. Did it turn you on, looking at her like that?"

"Well ummm—" he mumbles guiltily. "It did make me wonder what you have on, I'll say that. But where are you taking me, Demi?"

By now they have reached the bedroom, and Demi opens the door, pulls him in by his arm.

"Look at this bed. It's huge, a waterbed no less," she says. "My ex-husband and I had one like this."

"Is that right?" asks Ryder, "and what was it called, the Dead Sea? Is that why you drifted apart? Ha ha."

"Funny guy, you won't be laughing soon," Demi responds, as she walks over to the bathrobe hanging on the back of the door, then removes the terrycloth belt which she wraps around her arm. "Now stop fooling around and pay attention."

She places his hands firmly on her hips, and then pulls his head towards hers for a long intense kiss.

"I know what you men like," she says now, her voice

becoming raspy. "And tonight I'm going to show you. You want to be hunted and taken, don't you Ryder? Just like you do with your women. Tonight it's time for role reversal."

"Ah Demi, you know I'm your slave," he replies casually, still chuckling to himself. "Whatever you want, darling."

"I want you to take off your shoes," she commands. While he sits down on the edge of the bed and complies, she pulls off her jeans and boots. He looks up startled, and she pushes him back suddenly, forcing him to hard onto the bed. Then she sits astride him, leaning in to kiss him again.

"Wow no lace, no nothing—Demi, that's great," he says. "You sure know how to excite a man. If you had told me about that, downstairs or even in the car coming here, it would have been me pulling you into this room."

"I don't see any jockeys holding you back either," she says as she rubs her nakedness up against the growing bulge in his jeans. Ah the old Jockey or nothing story, he thinks and giggles, a flashback to another time, another honeymoon suite. Easily he lets the thought go as he focuses on Demi, her plans for him still unfolding.

"Shouldn't we close the door?" he asks.

"No. It's more arousing this way," she answers. "Now shush, no noises or someone will hear us."

The risk of discovery, the open door with the guests clearly visible below, heightens the excitement.

"Ryder, you dare not move or make a sound. Do you understand my instruction, my slave?"

He reaches up to touch her face tenderly, but she takes his hand and pushes it down onto the bed.

"I said don't move," she reprimands him, then takes the belt from her arm and loops it around his wrist. "Give me your other hand too," she instructs, then loops the belt around both wrists and ties them together and to the headboard. She unbuttons her shirt slowly, pausing and wriggling, then shrugs it off her shoulders. Next she unclasps her lacy bra, removes it, and drags it across his chest, while he lies helpless, watching her lustfully. He licks his upper lip, bites the bottom one, determined not to disobey.

Now the bed rocks and sways beneath them both as she reaches down and unbuttons his fly. A well-practiced move. She has done this before with these jeans, knows her way around. Ryder breathes heavily as she leans her whole body forward, grazing his mouth with her breasts, first the right and then the left. He lifts his head and strains to kiss them, but she moves just out of his reach. He pulls against the belt, but cannot free his hands. His breath is getting heavier and heavier as she moves her body backwards, then takes him in her mouth. She moves rhythmically, building tension. He starts to moan and she raises her head.

"I said silence. Or we will stop," she says sternly. He immediately complies, desperate for her to continue. She places one hand on his cock and caresses his balls at the same time with the other, as he grows harder and harder. Tonight, she knows she has him where she wants him, totally at her mercy. All of him to herself, to do with as she must. Now she sits on his hardness and plunges him deep inside her, again and again. First slowly and with control, then faster as she moves towards reckless abandon. She's so hot and wet, his heavy breathing and stifled moaning bringing her along on a wave of intoxication.

She wants to scream as she rocks back and forth with him inside her, grinding her hips and forcing him to lie still so she can take what she wants.

"Yes, it's all about me tonight—you pleasuring me," she says as she rubs her clitoris against his hard cock, slowly, quickly, moving at her own pace and rhythm. "Perfect. Keep still and be quiet."

The silence, the beautiful people visible below, the moon shining in the window, the knowledge of what she has beneath her on this moving, swaying bed, all contribute to the building climax.

"Demi, I love you. You are my mistress, I will be your slave forever!" he says as he comes inside of her, just as she feels herself explode and then dissolve into him.

She unties his hands and they dress quickly. As they walk back down the stairs, she holds onto his arm, then whispers in his ear.

"Next time I will be your slave, I'll do anything you want me to! You know I'm just crazy about you, Ryder. You have changed my life in this little town."

To this he replies "Peter's Pots, well I never!"

"But now you have—"

"Yes, now I have—ah Demi, you're such a great lover. I would be lost without you too."

24: Ryder and Demi, Knysna, August

They arrive back downstairs just in time to witness a car pull away, tires squealing.

"The mayor," they overhear the whispered comments.

"I guess those two are at it again."

"Surprised they even arrived here together. No surprise to see them leave separately."

Ryder looks around, sees Farrell fumbling for his keys.

"Uh no, I don't think so," he cautions him. "Let me drive you home, Farrell, you're in no condition. We can return for your car in the morning."

"The hell you say. I'm not drunk. I can drink you under the table. All of you all! Don't tell me I'm—whoops. Just my shoelaces. Fuck off. I'm driving."

Ryder grabs Farrell's keys and hides them, then goes looking for Demi. He finds her at the bar, huddled in deep conversation with another woman.

"Ryder, this is Irene," she says and Ryder nods. "Well, it seems her husband has already left the party."

"Stormed off is more like it," interrupts Irene. "I'm sure you've heard—everyone is talking about it. His Honor the Lord Mayor—bloody hell. "

Ah, thinks Ryder, *that infamous situation.*

"So I think she needs a ride home," Demi continues, to which Irene nods sadly.

Soon it is settled. Demi will drive Irene home in Farrell's car, while Ryder follows behind in his own, with Farrell buckled firmly into the passenger seat. They set off, the hour growing late, and the passengers in each of the two vehicles far from sober. Farrell is singing softly to himself. Ryder leans over to hear what he's mumbling, but is driven back by the exhaled fumes. Then Ryder receives a call from Demi, warning of a roadblock with a sobriety check up ahead. South African police with their over-eager policing, collecting and jailing drunken drivers along the roads. But all drivers in this case are sober, right? So what is the problem now? Ryder shakes his head as he remembers. Demi does not have her license because her purse was stolen a few days ago. Now she and Irene are detained at the roadblock as Ryder and Farrell pull up. Typical hijinks on the back roads of the Western Cape!

They sit at the roadblock and wait. Farrell surreptitiously reaches into his pocket, pulls out a bottle he secreted there earlier in the evening. He's thirsty, perfect time for a quick *dop (*drink)—the police will never notice. Really? Here, in the middle of everything? Ryder snatches the bottle away, corks it and throws it into the back of the car. The policeman catches his eye, shrugs his shoulders. He glances at Ryder's proffered documents and waves them all through. A stroke of luck! Through the window Ryder hears him mutter to himself:

"*Eish.*" Ah, the standard expression of exasperation,

disbelief and resignation, that surely says it all.

Wow. 1:30 am and they finally arrive at Irene's house, the empty drive and garage signaling that her husband, the mayor, is definitely not home. Ryder takes Farrell for a walk outside near the lagoon, hoping the fresh air and bracing breeze will do him some good. Farrell rants and raves about the party, about Demi and shady business dealings, and about unpaid bills, cash flow problems and rental arrears. Ryder pays no attention; he just wants Farrell sober.

"Farrell—wait. Don't go so close to the water. It's muddy and slippery over there."

"What? Can't hear a fucking thing Ryder, come here and talk to me. Look, isn't that a—oh shit! Help! Damn this water is cold. And bloody wet."

Now Farrell is stuck with one leg in the lagoon, one on shore, with no concept of how to disentangle himself and get back to dry land. He's slowly doing the splits on his drunken, wobbly legs as he sinks deeper and deeper into the mud. Ryder is forced to half-carry his drunken friend, pulling him as they both stumble out of the water. After the rescue, they are filthy, soaked through and shivering, and they go into Irene's house to dry off. Then suddenly it is decided. Farrell will spend the night on the sofa here, then drive his car home in the morning when he has sobered up.

"It's fine. No, I will be okay. Spend the night here. What a good idea. Yes, too drunk to drive my car. Quite agree. Bye-bye now. *Totsiens,* as they say. On your bicycles, off you go." He has become strangely compliant.

Finally, both Ryder and Demi depart. One car now, and at last homeward bound, back to Ryder's little place where Jack waits patiently. A long night that can be analyzed and dissected by the light of day. Or not. And had they merely glanced rearwards in their respective mirrors, they might have noticed Farrell, slightly more sober, sidling up to Irene. Or if they had kept on looking they would have noticed Farrell climbing the stairs, arm in arm with Irene. Wait, the sofa is downstairs. Opposite direction. Are you that drunk that you cannot find it, or … ah, got it. Now we know how this particular evening ends for the Knysna mayor's wife and her unlikely suitor.

And in this way, Ryder discovers some more secrets about the Knysna community, the subtle and not so subtle nuances around sex, drugs, money and power, and begins to realize the implications.

25: Ryder and Demi, Knysna, September

On the now-frequent occasions that I'm invited to a party at the inn on the Knysna Heads, I arrive in plenty of time to help with food preparation. This is the part of the meal I enjoy the most; taking simple ingredients, working together with others in the kitchen, and turning these ingredients into a feast. Keeping my hands busy constructively, instead of the naughtiness that I am usually inclined to!

"Ryder, where the hell have you been?" roars Mack, his large voice reverberating in the equally sizable kitchen. "Get in here, and get busy!"

Being a guest at the inn, which is also home to him and his wife, is always a treat and an adventure. There is always an interesting array of visitors from around the world clustered around the table for mealtimes. Conversations range across multiple diverse topics, often in many languages. Food is served in generous proportions, with locally sourced meat, fruit and vegetables, a step ahead of the world in the locavore movement. And as always I'm struck by the merging of cultures and foods: the Afrikaans *potjiekos*, the Cape Malay *bobotie* and *konfyt*, and the Jewish challah gracing the table all at the same time, serving people from all over the world and introducing them to our little cuisine melting pot in this corner of the earth. Knysna has developed into a popular tourist spot with people from Germany, France, and many African countries. And with the beautiful accommodations and setting, wonderful food and gracious hosts, the inn has a well-earned reputation as the place to stay.

Tonight's festivities begin in the usual way. We all sit on the deck, admiring the breathtaking view of the distant Knysna Heads and Thesen Island, the old railway line running across the lagoon, and the small boats sailing up and down. We chat about nothing as we listen to some golden oldies. Bruce Springsteen, the Beatles, all the familiar sounds from our youth. Someone puts on some old Rodriguez tunes.

"Searching for sugar, Sugarman…"

And regardless of how often I visit, each time I'm struck anew by the vistas from this balcony, sweeping down from the house to the town and lagoon. As the sun sets, the lights go on in town and they reflect off the still water of the lagoon. From up here on the hill, it is hard to tell where the stars end and the city lights begin. Tonight, I'm once again in the company of Demi, once again sitting back and relaxing, reveling in the present moment, enjoying the view from the deck at the inn. Soon dinner will be served out here in the cooling night air. With the music playing and the alcohol flowing freely, we reign like kings, looking out over the town with a full view of any who might seek to drive up unannounced.

Did I perhaps forget to mention that Demi has now

moved in to my little cottage? Well, all right perhaps we did rush into it just a little, but surely no harm in that. She was desperate for a home free from crime after a series of break-ins in the neighborhood, and I was trying to step up, to be the chivalrous boyfriend. Just tonight, on our way over, we talked about our new arrangement.

"I'm so comfortable living with you in our little place now, after all that trauma and emotion," she said.

"You know, Demi, it's fine for now," I replied cautiously, "but obviously the place is too small for any type of permanent arrangement."

"Yes, I know Ryder, too soon for this, we've been over it before," she said. "Going from the frying pan into the fire. See, I already know how you think. Look, we'll see what happens. We agreed that it's probably only temporary, until I can find something more suitable."

But we both know the thought is there—temporary unless we decide to make it more permanent. I mean, that could happen, right? Circumstances have forced us to take steps in the relationship in a different order, but it can all still work out.

Tonight, the unannounced guest that shows up to the gathering is Jill, a lawyer of some renown in Knysna. I've met Jill a few times before, even flirted casually with her in the local bar. And I know her line of work, how she manages legal issues for a local real estate mogul. I recognize her car immediately as she drives up, her bright-red convertible with the lame personalized plates eliciting a small groan from one of the other guests. She climbs out and stretches, her ample breasts encased in a tight t-shirt briefly visible above the car door. She steps over towards the stairs and I see she's wearing a short skirt that shows her chubby legs and slightly dimpled knees. Not the most flattering look for her body type, I think fleetingly. She has on high heels of course—there are some woman in Knysna who would never dare leave home without them. She flips her auburn hair over her shoulders in the fading sunlight, pausing for a few minutes. Mack and May go out to the stairs to greet her, and the three of them stand there engrossed in conversation.

"Heads up Demi, looks like Jill is here."

Farrell is providing a warning to Demi, but for what reason? I had no idea she and Jill were even acquainted, although this should not surprise me in this small town. After all, seems everyone here has some connection to everyone else.

"Wait, what's this? What's the problem?" I ask Demi, in response to Farrell's warning. Somehow I sense that now is not the time to confess that Jill and I are already friends.

"Ryder, please. Let's not talk about this. It's not important. I have a headache. Can we go home now?"

"But Demi, dinner has not even been served," I say as I trot after her. She's dragging me by my arm now, trying to get me to leave via the staircase that exits through the kitchen. This confuses me. Demi is a fun-loving party girl, never the first to leave and never one to use the old headache excuse, or to enter or exit via the back door.

"What's this about a headache? Is this because Jill is here? Is there something going on between the two of you?" I'm becoming breathless, chasing after her as she quickens her pace.

Farrell follows behind us, whispers to me so Demi cannot hear.

"Jill is helping with the legal work to settle some serious debts, man. And Demi is in the middle of all of this. My advice? Keep out of it, *boet*. You don't know how deeply involved she is, man—over her head."

This confuses me further. Usually Farrell is the fool, the clown who is sure to get totally wasted before the evening is out. Tonight he's giving me advice, on a subject I should know all about. Demi is my girlfriend; we have been together for a couple of months now. Yet she has confided none of this to me. If she's in trouble, in debt, surely she would have told me about it? I follow behind her and we leave through the kitchen, making sure we avoid running into Jill. As we drive off, she turns to me.

"Listen, Ryder, it's no big deal. I don't like her, that's all. She's a bitch and we've had some run-ins. Can you just drop it?"

And because I'm new, and unschooled in these small-town affairs, and also because I don't want Demi to know that I'm already acquainted with Jill, I do drop it. I let it go, as she requests, and we drive back to our place in silence. Not everyone can like everyone else, right? But it nags at me, that despite our relationship, she's not comfortable confiding in me. And it bothers me further that Farrell knows more about this, is warning me off. What is it, exactly, that he knows and that I don't? But once again I lie to myself, force myself to ignore that little voice of warning in my head. The sirens go off, yet I keep pressing mute. It's nothing. Her business.

Ah, but now it's two weeks later, and the result of this willful blindness comes back to bite me.

"Ryder—thank God you answered."

It is Demi on the phone, I'm busy at work, but I answer when I see her number on the caller ID.

"Demi—what's up? Make it quick, I—"

"Oh please help me. They are here, at my store. I can't stop them. Everything is outside. I don't know—Ryder, you have to help me."

Now I'm worried. She's crying, acting incoherently. Her part of town has been hit by several robberies and I fear something bad is happening.

"Call the police. Now. And I'm on my way," I yell into the phone.

"You don't understand. It IS the police. I can't—"

What is she saying? Rather than try to decipher, I hang up, run out to my car and speed over to her store, once again ready to rescue my girlfriend in her hour of need. Ryder, the knight in shining armor. I arrive at that pot shop that sells no pot, expecting the worst. And there she sits, outside the store on the pavement, broken planters and potting soil scattered all around her, crying, seemingly at a loss.

"This is what happens when you don't pay the rent." The uniformed captain speaks to her with obvious distaste as he emerges from the store with another armful of supplies which he dumps unceremoniously at her feet. "And clean this fucking mess up—creating a public nuisance here on the city street."

I need someone, anyone, to explain to me what is going on. I turn to the two rotund policemen standing nearby.

"Wait. Hold up a second. Can you tell me what this is all about?"

But I get no response. They stand silently, somewhat sheepishly, awaiting orders from the captain.

"Six months she didn't pay. What did she expect?" the captain finally spits out in my direction. "Here: the official filing, if you want to see."

He throws a piece of paper in my direction, and I snatch it out of the air, then look it over. The notice of eviction, drawn up and signed by none other than Jill, on behalf of the landlord. So this is the nature of Demi's ongoing clash with Jill, and I'm left standing there, amazed that I've lived with Demi for months now, yet she mentioned none of this to me. She failed to tell me that she's delinquent in her rent and who knows what other debts. As her gallant rescuer, am I expected to go to battle for her, to argue on her behalf with the captain and his flunkies as they continue to clear her stuff out of the store, throw it outside? Again and again, I'm struck by how clueless I am. Ignoring warning signs and alarm bells going off in my head. If she has been capable of hiding something this large from me, what other secrets and surprises does she have in store for me? A relationship of reduced expectations—hah, now I'm involved in something unsavory that feels somehow sinister. I've always honored my debts, yet now I'm being forced onto the dishonorable side of the balance sheet. How can this be? Good intentions gone awry.

Another lesson for me, hard earned as usual. No good deed goes unpunished. Is that it? Or rather, I'm experiencing the direct results of ignoring my inner voice of truth. The one that told me not to rush into things, not to ignore Farrell's advice, and not to ignore the friction between Demi and Jill. The inner voice that I have to learn to listen to more attentively, because when I don't, this is the result. Now I'm going to have to make a choice, and also face the fact that my relationship with Demi is built on a crumbling foundation of half-truths and lack-of-trust. For someone who is trying to rebuild and move on from hurt and devastation, this feels a lot like a setback. Especially because by this stage of my life, I should know better!

26: Jack, Knysna, October

Oh dear Lord—must I do everything myself? Here we are, well into our journey, far from what was once home and supposedly making progress towards a newer, healthier destination for both body and soul. And here is Ryder, sitting on the sofa, second drink in hand already, pouring from the bottle as he pours over online pages of spreadsheets and numbers. Reading and writing emails frantically, muttering to himself angrily. We had made so much progress; I really felt I was getting through to the man. Lead by example, that's the way I approached it. Projecting a calm, peaceful existence, focusing on the moment at hand. Yes, I really thought he was getting it! All right, I need to look at all of this from a different perspective. Perhaps this behavior is simply the nature of the human, to attain a level of enlightenment for a period, but to constantly backslide and need propping up and encouragement just to maintain the status quo, never mind the forward motion! But I have such high hopes for him. We need to regain our momentum.

As I might have mentioned previously, sometimes it is most effective for my Best Friend to believe he's getting his own way. Using this to my advantage, and therefore indirectly to the advantage of Ryder, has been how I conduct most of our interactions. I start with the following premise: for some reason, ideas are always more palatable when thought of personally rather than suggested by others. Come to think of it, this sentiment is probably true for Man and Beast alike. Naturally, this makes my work of assisting Ryder in overcoming inertia that much more difficult. Not only must I prod him into action, but I need to do it in such a way as to convince him that all action was his idea in the first place! Challenges and opportunities in abundance. Perhaps this won't be the first time I mention to you how fraught the path of Man's Best Friend can be. And it won't be the last, of that I'm certain.

I should now explain how I'm trying to leverage a sudden abundance of chances from an unexpected source, namely Ryder's rudimentary understanding of my needs. For some inexplicable reason, there has always been the assumption that we dogs need to play with other hounds, whether in the park, or in some other public place deemed suitable. Where this idea came from remains a mystery. For my money, I prefer to keep the company of humans. This is where I believe my life's work must be done. However, Ryder appears to have bought into this one hook, line and what-have-you, so we regularly set out for the park in order that "Jack can make some friends." Things that seem so obvious to me that they bear no repeating or explanation seem to be lost so much of the time. Emphasis on my social life serves as a perfect example of one of these things. Sigh; this is the burden of the enlightened I suppose—to see so clearly that which is invisible to others.

So although it is not easy for me to mask my growing impatience and feign enthusiasm, I grab my leash from its convenient location near the back door. With the leash firmly grasped in my mouth, I walk back and forth in front of the sofa. Pacing. No effect whatsoever. This is going to be more of a challenge than usual! I stroll casually to the basket of toys. Slapping the leash against the side of the basket by whipping my head back and forth does not seem to be working either. Well, as I said, today is a bad day for Ryder, that much is obvious. I lean my head into the basket and start shaking back and forth. Pretty soon a ball goes flying—let him try ignore that! And yet he does. Well it appears I'm going to have to empty the entire basket and then push it across the floor before Ryder will look up. Yes, he certainly seems slightly dazed as he appears to notice me for the first time since he parked himself in that seat. About bloody time you paid attention, I might add (but don't, obviously).

And we're off to the park because Jack needs the exercise. Oh yes, indeed, "Jack" needs the exercise. As I said, sometimes it helps that we're not always dealing with a "deep thinker" here. Let's examine the facts: only one of us has been sitting around, sighing ever more deeply and sinking farther into a funk. Only one of us has totally ignored the other for the entire day, something I'm going to try very hard not to dwell on. Yes, I can now focus on the task at hand. Dragging Ryder out to socialize, to make some friends at the park, while I pretend to frolic with a random assortment of mutts performing the same service for their respective owners. Ah what a great idea to be out in the fresh air and sunshine. Wish I had thought of that.

27: Ryder and Demi, Knysna, November

"Demi, all I mean is that things would work much more smoothly if you simply told me the truth," I say as the discussion begins to escalate. Out of the corner of my eye, I see Jack slink off into the bedroom and crawl under the bed. Funny, I remember how he hung out in that same spot in our last few months in Cape Town too, but since moving to Knysna, he has usually preferred to stay at my side. Tonight, however, he seems eager to leave the open-plan kitchen- sitting- and dining-room, as Demi and I continue our heated exchange.

"Well Ryder, I think this evening will go much more smoothly if you could find it in yourself to top up my glass. The bottle is over there on the bar."

She points her demanding finger, not moving from the cottage-style sofa. I walk over to the fake marble counter and pause to look out at the view of the lagoon in the fading light. I reluctantly collect the bottle and fill her glass.

From never drinking to this: I return from work and she's already well into the first bottle, with the second one on ice, ready when needed. I've lost count of how many days I've come home to her in this drunken, disheveled state, and I'm exasperated. I notice once again her frizzled hair, her bare feet and her crumpled dress.

"Look Demi, I know your shop is closed," I begin. "And I know you don't know what to do next. But you have never yet told me what exactly happened. How things spiraled downhill so quickly. And drinking like this is not going to help. You need to sober up and—"

"So you think I need a man in my life to tell me what to do? Is that what you think?" she asks, clearly not expecting a reply.

And I can't tell if she's crying or simply slurring her words, the two seem to happen simultaneously virtually every night now. I observe the two of us, locked in this battle, and am shocked anew by my circumstances. What am I doing here? Why am I once again involved in a relationship that asks for such huge compromises, that strays so far from what I need for happiness and connectedness? I've been lying to myself, again, thinking I was growing, evolving, maturing. I see how little I've learned about selecting a partner to be my helpmate, a source of mutual support. Love, happiness, bond—all three are conspicuous in their absence from this room tonight, and every night lately. But I can't help myself. I'm not done with this conversation, despite a dawning realization that I'm done with waiting for change, and done with enabling destructive behaviors.

"Demi, you lied to me about your shop and your finances. You lied about so many other things. How can I trust you ever again?"

"How dare you say that to me?" She stands up

abruptly and I can see she has become completely enraged. "I haven't looked at another man since we have been together! Just because I like a glass of wine now and again, is that a reason not to trust me? You're a fine one to talk, with your love of Jack Daniels, and your—"

I've stopped listening. Why is acknowledging the truth here so difficult? The fact is, I've been drinking a lot more since Demi moved in with me. The words "double Jack, Red Bull, lots of ice, large glass" rolling so easily off my tongue. Yet another negative consequence of our incompatible arrangement, an increasing need to escape.

"Demi, this is not working out. You're going to have to move out," I say, the same words I heard just a few months ago from Sophia.

"No, Ryder, we can fix this," she answers, her anger replaced with something much more pitiful. "Please— you're just upset with me right now—"

Is this the same plaintive note I struck back then, is this how pathetic I sounded? I remain firm.

"No Demi, you can take your time but you're going to have to leave. I need to be on my own."

There. I've done it. Acknowledging that I have no control over her, her drinking or her poor lifestyle choices, but I do control my own life, my own future. And my future path is not with her. Difficult, but not insurmountable. I will be fine, I tell myself. I've lived through this disentanglement before. And this time will be easier, quicker and simpler, it has to be. No shared dream, no shared business, and our shared time together was of a much shorter duration.

Yet still, I feel the old clouds gathering, swirling on the periphery. A change of mood from calm bond to foul feelings—from contentment to deep sadness. Once again a failed relationship, a repeat failed performance. The familiar trio of anger, blame and guilt; the inevitable confusion over how to assign responsibility.

This time, I gather all the negative thoughts and emotions, visualize pouring them all into a glass. A bloody big glass! I see the vessel, standing in my line of sight on the coffee table in front of the TV and within easy reach, a trick to help me separate my past feelings from the present moment. I watch the level in the glass from my comfortable seat on the sofa, and see the emotional contents bubble and boil, yet I'm able to remain calm and dispassionate. And finally I see them simmer, then settle, then ultimately cool. And I know the storm has passed, and now I'm free to choose what I say and do without being ruled by my emotions.

Jack emerges from the bedroom, takes his place beside me. Then he lies across my feet, his weight both warming and comforting me. Yes, Demi will move out and I will move on. This relationship will not disrupt me nor throw me from my path. My mistakes will simply inform my future choices; I am learning, growing and evolving. There will be no going back as I reclaim the Now. I take a deep breath in, then slowly let it out. And then repeat.

28: Jacqueline, Riebeek to Wilderness, November

She merges into the traffic on the national road, distracted with thoughts about her last appointment. These visits to art galleries are what keep Jacqueline going these days, the chance to interact with a few store owners up and down the coast. That, and the idea, slowly germinating, that she will one day hold her own exhibition, perhaps even open her own studio.

"Drawing is all well and good," she mutters, "but sometimes you just need conversation. With someone, a real person. Oh Frank, I think what I miss the most about you are the conversations we used to have."

She looks at the passenger seat beside her, imagines she can hear his sympathetic reply. Then, not for the first time, she wonders if she's finally losing touch with reality, if the extended periods of solitude have finally taken their toll. She finds herself once again worrying about the descent into madness, if it is something that happens all at once, or if it is slow and gradual, barely discernible until too late. Never having been particularly tightly wound, these days she feels as though the fabric of her being is unraveling, becoming less expertly woven; loose and see-through. Gaps opening up between the warp and the weft, suddenly allowing for light, air and a measure of craziness to seep through. How long has this been going on, she wonders, since the death of Frank, or did it begin before then? Before or after the onset of these debilitating headaches? Maybe all of this time alone caused some sort of tipping point to be reached. She wonders if her psyche is like the last batch of clothes donated from her closet, bright, beautiful, and attractive when first acquired, in perfect condition. And each wearing seemed to leave them unaffected, but cumulatively, one day she looked at them and thought "How can I still be wearing these old things? They are rags, *schmattas!* Goodwill. Garbage. Anything! Just get them out of this closet!" She wonders fleetingly if this is what has happened with her sanity, a gradual wearing away until it, too, lies in rags and tatters. And again she asks herself if she's living this life of exile because she can no longer envision herself walking around with the normal people.

Sighing, she resolves to pay more attention to the drive, to the road ahead. Onward and upward. This time after visiting and selling paintings in Riebeek Kasteel, she's taking a detour before driving back to Wilderness. She has gotten an early start, before the sun was too high in the sky, and headed towards Paarl. From there she's taking the N1 East, driving inland instead of back out to the coast. She goes through the Huguenot tunnel, past Worcester and De Doorns, then drives on through the Hex River Valley. Finally she turns at Ceres, heads to the Aquila Private Game Reserve.

She thinks about the reason for her visit here, the

opportunity to get involved in a grass-roots effort to save the white rhino from extinction. Although she has always felt drawn to these slow lumbering beasts, with their calm exterior belying their internal ferociousness, she barely remembers how or why she decided to sign up for this conference. Was it one article in particular from all those she had read, then carefully clipped and saved, the articles all still stacked in the trunk of her car reminding her daily of the urgency associated with the dwindling numbers? It seems the rhino are no longer a match for the ever-more aggressive poachers, who hunt them down and brutally cut off their horns, leaving them to bleed in agonizing death. Perhaps it was the item describing the hopeless corruption and woeful inadequacy of the government protection programs that finally spurred her to action, that finally persuaded her to sign up to help conservation groups eliminate poaching in private reserves. But first she knows she must educate herself, must discover firsthand how to rally support in her little part of the country.

She pulls up to the reserve, wedged between the Langeberg and Outeniqua mountains. The gate is on a dirt road, fronted by a small thatched-roof canopy with a rocky, sparsely-planted flower bed beneath. As she passes through the gate, she marvels at the carpets of Karoo wildflowers spread out behind her, with the stone exteriors and thatched coverings of the chalets juxtaposed upon the hillside before her. She pulls up in front of one of the small round structures, enters and then immediately steps out onto the balcony, taking in the expansive view. In the distance, she can see the pool, the blue sparkle tempting, with the temperature steadily climbing in this desert spot. But no, not right now—she heads to the main lodge to meet with the rest of the group of activists.

The oversized log cabin is constructed from large yellow-wood poles, the expansive roof mirroring the one covering the entrance. The large windows, simply cut-outs in the side walls, allow those indoors to look out over the dry grassland plains scattered with acacia trees. Small herds of gemsbok and kudu graze far off in the distance, their apparent laziness belying their constant vigilance. And today, a herd of zebra appear close by, the young ones frolicking about, yet never straying too far from their watchful mothers.

The meeting begins as a tall bearded man greets the assembled group. His khaki shorts, matching shirt with epaulettes, brown leather ammunition belt and dusty boots easily identify him as a local game ranger. He introduces himself, describing his background as a tracker and conservationist, then talks about his current role, the one of driving foreign tourists on game drives, educating them about South Africa, and about preservation of the local flora and fauna. He leans forward earnestly, casually resting his left hand on his binocular case, while in his right he holds a sheaf of papers filled with statistics. His soft, firm voice is welcoming, the guttural rolling of his r's instantly recognized as the familiar "West Coast Brei" accent.

"*My naam is Piet. Ek werk al 20 jaar in die bos* (My name is Piet, I have worked for 20 years in the bush)," he begins, introducing himself and explaining his years of expertise and service.

Jacqui listens intently to his sing-song voice while looking around the room at the casually-dressed group, their bush gear conforming to the expected "Cape Union Mart" style. Piet continues, reading now from his list of numbers, the harsh statistics demonstrating that time is running out to save the rhinos from extinction.

"Seven hundred easily killed in a year, with more many years—" he explains, then continues. "The numbers are only climbing higher."

The tone of the meeting is pessimistic, and they all listen with dismay to story after story. Piet tells of his close friend who was killed in a helicopter filled with anti-poaching law enforcement agents, the purposeful downing never proven, but all agents dead nonetheless. Then he tells of the Taiwanese poacher, captured but ultimately set free because no translator could be found to ensure a fair trial. The list of stories, an absurd collection of missed opportunities, stands only to highlight the facts: a fast-diminishing population and a growing profit margins for poachers. By the end of his speech, the attendees sadly acknowledge that without a rapid turnaround, all will be lost. The idea that within a few years, there will no longer be a rhino population to save seems to discourage everyone, and they all head out the door towards to their respective chalets, wrung out and depleted.

"Um Jacqui, would you like to join me for a drink at the bar?" Piet asks, glancing appreciatively at her curvaceous hips and ample chest.

"Piet, right?" she replies politely. "Well, thanks for asking, I don't really drink much. Truthfully, I was hoping to go on a sunset game drive, maybe even see a rhino close up in the wild—"

"Say no more! I have my game vehicle right here, and I know where the rhinos go at sunset. I'll take you, right now. What do you say?"

"Wow—thanks!" Jacqui responds, suddenly excited. "I'll just go to my room, grab my camera and a warm sweater. See you back here in a few minutes."

Piet helps her climb into his bush-green, customized Nissan *bakkie* (pickup truck) then gets in, starts it up and deftly steers it along the dirt track. The car bumps and rolls, the open roof and folded-down windscreen allowing for unobstructed game viewing all around. Jacqui wraps her sweater around her shoulders as a cool breeze blows through the open vehicle.

"See, I can take three rows of tourists in this car," Piet explains proudly, pointing out the rows of seats that climb upwards. "And everyone has a good view, 360 degrees!"

Then he fiddles with the CB radio, checks his cell phone, two important tools for the modern tracker.

"Check this new app hey!" he says, showing Jacqui his phone. "All the *ous* put in their game sightings, and that way we can all know where the lions and leopards are, instantly." He turns wistful, sighing. "Maybe one day they won't need trackers anymore. What do you think Jacqui? Do you think an *ou* like me is going to be useless in the new world?"

"Piet, my guess is someone still has to find the game, then enter the information into the app. So I wouldn't be too worried," she replies reassuringly. Despite herself, she notices the ropey muscles of his tanned forearms, then sneaks a glance at his chest through the open top buttons of his shirt. *Not too bright*, she muses as he concentrates on the road, *but really quite hunky. And those are some seriously gorgeous blue eyes.*

Piet has taken an unused lane, with grass growing tall on both sides. Now he steers the vehicle down an incline, stopping just short of a small, almost-dry river bed running about a meter beneath the road.

"I know the rhinos usually come this way at the end of the day, their path back from the watering hole," he explains as he turns off the engine. "They follow the river bed from the dam down there, on their way to where they crash."

"Crash, as in sleep?" Jacqui asks innocently, referring to his use of slang.

"Ja, ja—but it's also a joke. Get it? Because do you know what a lot of rhinos are called? A crash! And you don't wanna get in the way of that crash—"

As Piet chuckles, Jacqui feels herself drawn by his engaging personality. *Yes, definitely kinda cute*, she thinks. *Maybe a bit slow, but definitely funny.* Then she watches, amazed, as Piet magically produces a cooler, complete with two glasses, a bag of ice and a bottle of champagne. She realizes that she has not eaten since lunch, her stomach growling loudly when he produces a packet of biltong along with some cheese and crackers.

Wow, is this really special treatment, or has it simply just been too long since I've been out with a guy? she wonders as she accepts the offered glass, then clinks it against Piet's in an unspoken toast. They sit quietly, the peaceful silence broken only by intermittent squawking, wild birds warning each other of possible predators in the bush. An hour passes as they sip slowly, with Piet refilling her glass whenever the level gets low. A giraffe struts by, eyeing them elegantly from atop its long neck, its long tongue deftly removing juicy green leaves from between the Acacia thorns. Then a small elephant family follows, the baby walking so close to its mother, it seems in danger of being trampled beneath her heavy hooves.

"Perhaps we should go back to the lodge," Jacqui says finally, realizing that she has had more to drink than she planned. *Not sure I trust myself alone with this man, feeling slightly tipsy,* she thinks, her earlier elation fading as she pictures the lonely sadness waiting for her, along with the inevitable tearfulness resulting from excess alcohol. And then, soundlessly, except for the whiffle of grass being pulled from the earth, a huge shape emerges. A male rhino stops less than twenty feet from her window, staring right at her, not pausing in his grazing. Jacqui feels paralyzed, overcome, as she stares at the unimaginably large, prehistoric, armour-plated beast. His huge head and even larger shoulders, his small and big horns, are all just an arms-length away. Her eyes move along his full length, taking in every scar, every patch of hair and skin. She notices the flies on his back along with the small, yellow-beaked pecker bird looking for mites and ticks. Finally, her eyes come to rest on the deep red grooves around his neck, raw and still healing. Tears well up in her eyes, as she stops herself from reaching out, desperate to touch the majestic magnificent hide.

They sit together, staring as the animal slowly pulls grass, feeds, and then moves away and out of sight into the thicker bush.

"Ah Piet, what an incredible sighting. I don't know how to thank you," she says, turning towards him.

"Well, maybe you can thank me back at the lodge—" Piet begins, but then pauses as he notices the tears welling up in Jacqui's eyes.

"Piet, this was truly a life-altering experience," she begins, "but I'm feeling really emotional right now, somehow really sad. I think I need to go back, get some sleep."

"Anything you say," he replies, a slightly disappointed tone in his voice. He starts up the truck obligingly, swinging the wheel expertly and heading back to the camp. The setting sun seems larger than ever, a round orange ball sitting low on the horizon, casting the acacia trees in silhouette, and turning their edges vibrant shades of pink and purple.

Jacqui goes straight to her room, lies down on the soft mattress and closes her eyes. The drive, the information, her situation, everything feels overwhelming. Tears flow slowly through her lashes and down her cheeks as she thinks about the uselessness of her efforts, the incessant trying through personal growth to achieve serenity, to restore herself to her former happiness. First, there was that relentless journaling, then the frequent yoga and meditation, now the possibly futile attempts at advocacy. And today, a failed romantic evening with a totally unsuitable candidate. A small sob of self-pity escapes her, and she settles lower down on the bed, then pulls the covers up to her chin.

"Ah Frank—thank God I had my time with you," she begins the one-sided conversation anew. "Unconditional love—how will I ever find that again?"

She pictures Frank's face as she falls into a deep sleep, hoping to renew her strength for the drive back home the next day. And for the uphill battle of conservation and education that she has resolved to undertake, armed only with her will and the meager resources provided at the conference.

29: Ryder, Knysna, November

It is the middle of the day, still bright, yet Ryder decides on a whim to wander down to Mo's on Rex. He's once again feeling sorry for himself, and lacking the energy to focus on the lessons he's attempting to assimilate. It's too difficult to remain in the Now, too difficult to avoid this self-pity. Demi has moved out, reluctantly. Their relationship progressed too quickly, became something it was never meant to be. Once again he had lived in denial, seeing—but not acknowledging—that he would have to make unacceptable compromises for her needs. Two different people with totally different values, both desperately trying to live in the Now, but with Demi unwilling to take responsibility for events of her own making.

How did he fall into this trap again? Not realizing that a relationship was detracting him from pursuing his own path? Hadn't he only recently vowed to himself that he would never again be dissuaded from travelling according to his own light?

Yes, he's doubly aggravated, disappointed that his relationship with Sophia did not at least teach him this lesson. Well, he rationalizes, perhaps a quick drink will lift his spirits. Nothing better to do this afternoon, no work, no playmate. Now he becomes maudlin as he thinks of his failing business venture and his latest failed relationship. He pulls Jack along inside and sits at a corner table. Cool and dark in here after the bright sunshine reflected off the water outside. He orders his usual, a double Jack prepared in the usual way, then turns around, trying to adjust his vision to the dim interior. Immediately he's spotted by Farrell, who is sitting up at the bar, holding forth about something with the bartender.

"Hey Ryder, I thought that was you! Come sit over here. What are you drinking? Innocent my man—did you know this bartender's name is Innocent?—this is my good friend Ryder. Innocent, one more for me and another of whatever Ryder is drinking."

"Farrell, jeez, how many are you up to already? It is only three in the afternoon!"

"Never mind about that. What is going on with you? You look like crap, man. Where have you been and what's with the gloom-and-doom attitude?"

"I've had a rough month, Farrell. My business is not doing well, touch and go I think, and things with me and Demi—well, I suppose you heard she moved out. That we're both moving on."

"Yeah I heard. You know how word gets around in Knysna! I'm gonna tell you something you should already know. How old are you anyway? Thirty-nine? Forty?"

"Add another decade there, *Oupa*! Shit, I'm over fifty. I think I'm going to end up a single, lonely old man. I'm already almost there."

"Whatever. What the fuck do I care how old you are? I'm always gonna be older than you and I'm still in the prime of my life. Deal with it! My point is—what are we talking about again?"

"You were about to give me some great advice, I think. Thanks, Innocent—put it right here. I thought your name was Temperance. Maybe that is your brother?"

"Isn't he a funny guy? A bartender named Temperance. No return in that! Well, here you are, words of wisdom from yours truly. Have you seen the cover of this month's Femina magazine? Sure, sure, I know you don't read it. Glamor, maybe? No? No, Ryder, I don't read them either, why would I? Okay fine then, what about Playboy? Seen the cover of that? Or the centerfold, eh! Now we're getting somewhere. Who is featured this month? Doesn't matter. Here is my point—"

"Yes, okay, what is the point Farrell?"

"Doesn't matter how good looking the chick is, or how many guys are out there lusting after her. I can guarantee you one thing. Wait, do you have a light? I have to go outside to smoke—can you believe that! Can't even enjoy a cigarette with my drink anymore."

"Farrell—will you spit it out already, the great advice you have for me."

"Oh yeah. No matter who the girl is, no matter how hot, there is some guy out there who is sick of looking at her face over the breakfast table every day. Guaranteed! You allow a woman to get inside your head and it's overs. You think I'm just a drunken sot, don't you?"

"Well, you do lift your elbow quite a bit—"

"Yeah, yeah, okay. But let me tell you—I've been watching you. You arrived here what—three, four months ago? You were like a beaten dog. That's what I thought when I first saw you. No offense, Jack. Nobody is going to beat any dogs around here. That's a promise! God that dog of yours—I swear he understands this conversation."

"Ah yes, well thus far not much of interest has been said. But do continue, my dear chap."

"As you were saying, Farrell. I arrived here four months ago and—"

"Yeah. That woman you were with before. She screwed you up big time. So what? You're a smart guy, good looking. Heck you have the girls eating out of your hand wherever you go. When you're not sulking, acting all woe is me and shit—"

"Again, what is the point here?"

"So you get in a relationship with a girl and it goes bad, but you still have your health, your work, your charm, your whatever. But you—you let these women throw you so far off track! After you got over that other girl, what was her name, Sophie? Seemed like after a while you figured it all out, picked yourself up, and started again, this time with Demi. And now—what the fuck man? So what if it isn't going to work out with her? Are you gonna go through the whole cycle again?"

After this long speech, Farrell picks up his glass, then drains it in one large gulp. He signals to Innocent, who is poised at the beer tap, already reaching for a fresh glass.

"That's it. Keep 'em coming, and while you're about it, how about a fresh water bowl for my little pal down here?

Can't beat the service in this place, Ryder."

Innocent moves out from behind the bar, places a bowl of water at Ryder's feet, and then absent-mindedly scratches Jack on the head.

Thanks, mate. Just put it on Ryder's tab. Seems I'm going to be here for a while, what with Ryder ruminating on his old underlying questions: how to find love with a suitable companion, how to form an ever-deepening meaningful bond. Between you and me, I don't believe he ever thought the answer to his quest was going to be found in the arms of that Dementia Detour. But once again, despite past lessons, he ignored his inner voice of truth.

What's that? Oh, don't bother to deny it, Ryder. You ignored that still, small voice that cautioned you, that said you were moving too far, too fast. You willfully blotted it out with loud music, drink and reckless abandon. And so now it's true, all of your questions about love, happiness and bond remain unanswered. Best you ask yourself this one—how likely is it that you and Farrell will find the solutions at the bottom of those glasses in your hands right now? Hmm, thought as much.

"Farrell, I'll be honest, man. I don't know what it is. Seems like I should know better, and you're so right, my whole world did not come crashing down, just the male-female relationship part of it. So why did it feel like it? Was that part so huge it overshadowed all the other stuff?" Ryder pauses, stares into his glass. "I must have told you all this before, the last time. How I allowed another's behavior to lead me to such a bog hole of despair. Must be my own mental and emotional weakness, allowing this to happen again."

"But c'mon, you're a strong willed, intelligent, and self-aware person," Farrell says, nudging Ryder roughly with his elbow. Jack lifts his head slightly.

"Debatable, but let's not split hairs. As you were saying—"

"You see, this is the responsibility I have to take, and not just blame the other person, or persons," says Ryder, his face becoming flushed. "Seems like there has been a whole string of persons, all females! Farrell I know this stuff. I can't control how others act, only how I deal with their actions. Why can't I practice what I preach? Why must I learn this lesson over and over? Or not learn it, it seems."

"Cause you're an idiot. Same as me. If it helps any, just remember this at all times: they're all the same as that Playboy centerfold. So there you have it, my lesson for today. Important, don't you think?"

"Seriously. We're never gonna understand them, and whatever we do is never gonna be quite enough to satisfy them. So this male-female thing can never be allowed to overtake everything else in our lives."

"Ryder, I think you finally get it. And remember, if you feel lonely, you always have me to drink with. But seriously—you know you have close friends who will be there for you always."

Don't forget about yours truly at your feet over here—the one who has stuck by your side through thick and thin. Just sayin'—

"Look, I may be an old soak," Farrell continues, "but I say it's time to get over yourself and stop dwelling on the loss of something you never really had. Sophia, Demi, the failing fucking business—whatever. We're going to drink to you, Ryder, your family, true friends, and the successful parts of your life. Bottoms up! Innocent my man, another round if you please."

30: Ryder and Izzie, Knysna, October

Woke up way too early this morning with a new word on my mind: compassion. A trying few months with a lot of progress and a lot of lessons learned. But why this word? Why now? I really cannot afford to have sleepless nights chasing random words around my mind. I need to be clear, refreshed. I look over at Jack, snoring softly on his bed, and wonder how I can achieve that peace. I'm the one who is dog tired, but also the one who is sleepless. Sigh—time to get up and face the music. As I swing one leg out of bed, Jack is instantly alert. How does he do that? My right-hand man (dog). How would I have made it through these last few months without him at my side?

Outside, it is another beautiful day. The harbor and the lagoon both beckon, with the air still crisp after an early spring rain. Instead, I force myself to drive the short distance to the television academy, to sit down at my desk, to power up my computer. Time to take a hard look at these numbers, I remind myself as I stare at the hourglass on the screen, which eventually gives way to the company logo and, finally, the abysmal balance sheets.

A door closing on the other side of the building has

me startled. No deliveries today and no students. What now? I grab the cricket bat I keep under my desk, and then walk on tiptoes down the hall, glancing into each of the training rooms as I walk by. The door to the last one is closed, and I approach it cautiously. I lean in and listen, remaining poised and ready in case someone emerges suddenly. Instead of the expected noises of someone rifling through drawers and cabinets, I hear sniffles and sobs. What on earth?

"Who's there?" I ask as I turn the handle, slowly opening the door, then lean the bat in the corner of the room as I see her. "Izzie, what's going on here?"

She's sitting hunched over in the corner, a box of tissues in her lap. Her usually perfect attire is replaced by dishevelment, her red-rimmed eyes and tangled blonde hair adding to the unusual sight. She jumps slightly as she sees me.

"Ryder—I didn't think you would be here. It's just—I needed somewhere private. Sorry, I'll get out of your way," she says as she stands up, blotting her eyes and grabbing for her purse lying on the floor.

"Please. You don't have to leave. I'll go. But maybe I can help?" I ask as I cautiously approach her, pulling up the extra chair behind me. "Would you tell me what's got you so upset, Izzie?"

And even as I ask, I know the answer. The boyfriend, that Webster character, I just know he must be the cause of this morning's drama. So of course I can be empathetic here, love, relationships, loneliness, angst. It's not as if I'm unfamiliar with these same struggles!

She indicates that I should sit, then immediately starts sobbing harder.

"I'm always in the total dark with him," she exclaims without further prodding. "And he never ever does what he says he will! He's an absolute jerk. I hate him. I wish he was dead, I wish we were both—"

Her body is shaking with emotion, her head hung so low I swear it is in danger of hitting the floor.

"Webster, right?" I say and she nods. "I know. Let's kill him now, what do you say?"

She laughs reluctantly, then breathes deeply, beginning to calm down a little.

"What can I do? I'm powerless when it comes to him," she says, shaking her head emphatically. "God, sometimes he even makes me hate myself when I get like this!"

"Izzie, you need to be gentle with yourself. You must have faith in yourself as a strong, beautiful, capable woman. How can you think you're powerless? All of this, your feelings, your actions, they are simply choices you're making."

"But Ryder, I love him. Honestly I do! What am I supposed to do? What if he left me? I would be lost without him."

"Here is a useful way to think about it," I say, my old-time coaching and training effortlessly kicking in. I think of Mack and his paper plates, and glance across the room looking for a useful prop.

"Can you think of the two of you as if you're these two circles here?" I ask, picking up a marker and drawing

181

hastily on the whiteboard hanging on the wall.

"Okay…"

"Now look. I'm going to reposition them so they are intersecting," I say, erasing one circle with my fist, then redrawing it so it is partially on top of the other.

"That's good, right? That they are coming together?" she asks.

"Well, if the circles overlap too much, then they are in danger of becoming fused, indistinct from each other. That represents a loss of independence, often a lot of over-compromise," I say as she stares at the board intently. "That is the point where you both feel like you would be lost without each other."

"Over-compromise?" she asks. "Like you mean if I did something for him that I didn't want to? That I thought was wrong?"

She continues, talking almost as if she's unaware I'm still in the room. "But of course I did it anyway, because otherwise he might leave me. And now, I'm becoming lost, losing myself."

A tone of despair has crept into her voice.

"Yes, Izzie, each time you do a little of what you don't want, it becomes easier to get used to that. To let his circle take over yours. We have to be careful, slowly that behavior can become the new you, and then one day you will wake up and have forgotten who you really are."

As I continue, I see the pain of realization in her eyes.

"For what it's worth, I'm only telling you this from my own difficult experience. And it is so tough to get back to the person you used to be. It takes so long, involves so much pain! You know my history with women, the bitches made me their bitch!"

At this we both laugh, although neither of us is truly amused.

"Today I can say, I allowed them that opportunity by over-compromising. Believe me, Izzie, I won't make that mistake again."

Now she nods her head in silent acknowledgement, staring at her hands.

"Well of course, totally separate is no good either, I know you don't want that," I continue, now erasing the drawing completely, then replacing it with two disconnected circles. "Let's assume he doesn't want that either."

"What do you mean, separate?" asks Izzie, looking up at me. "Living apart? But then it's like we're not even a couple anymore!"

"Have you heard of a LAT relationship?" I ask her. "Living Apart Together. Your house, his house, the best of both worlds. Privacy and togetherness, romance and special meals, but without the complicated logistics of shared living space."

"Ryder, that's no solution for me. That's not what I want."

"Huh, to me this sounds perfect. But of course, it's only great until one partner wants more, and then guess what happens? You move in together and suddenly reality sets in," I say, thinking back to Demi and our ill-fated cohabitation. "But no, Izzie, that's not what I was talking about, not what I meant about being too separate. See here, when the circles don't overlap or overlap only a tiny bit, it means the couple has nothing much in common anymore. Maybe he works late, brings in the money. In his spare time he plays golf or whatever."

"'Whatever' is right—"

"And then she has her book clubs, her mall rat pals, and her own career to run. Maybe she becomes a fanatic at the gym. The kids are out partying with their friends, or maybe they don't have kids together. He likes reading and movies, she likes gardening and outdoors. Not much of an intersection between the two of them."

"But isn't it possible to do all that without compromising our feelings? Can't we do different things but still feel our love?" asks Izzie, a puzzled frown on her face. "Webster and I have very different work, we—"

"Yes, of course," I reply. "That's not the issue. But if a couple has nothing to do together, then they spend no time together, and they become separate eventually. Even couples who have kids together, as the children grow, the couple needs to find common ground in new ways. Maybe learn how to compromise with each other on the things that are not in their control or not that important. One thing I know—living totally separate lives cannot strengthen their relationship."

"But Ryder," she says, "so you're saying there is no hope. Too much compromise or too little ... no hope!" and she starts to sob again.

"No, no, what I'm saying is that you need some sort of balance," I say, handing her a tissue and trying to reassure her, patting her gently on the back. "The key is, it has to be the same for both of you. Do you understand, Izzie? You have to both want the same shared space, the same amount of dependence and independence, but without compromise of things you value."

As I explain this to her, I realize I'm describing the fundamental question I have to answer for myself, one I've struggled with repeatedly. How can I be fully engaged in a relationship, both emotionally and mentally, deeply in love, bonded to another, but still independent enough to pursue my own ambitions, enjoy fulfillment in my own joys of life? Is it ever possible to be able to do what I want, to say no when I want, and to still be accepted?

"Izzie, is this how your life is? Total compromise or total disconnection? You can be honest, it's only me here."

"How can I know the answer to any of this?" she answers, a note of franticness returning. "He never levels with me. So then I feel like we're both just dishonest with each other. It's his fault! He keeps promising me, saying we will get married, leave here and—" Now she blushes guiltily, realizing she has told me too much. "Wait, I shouldn't have said that. I—"

"Izzie, let's be frank. I've wondered how long you would stay here working for me," I reply, hardly surprised by what she has told me. Then I continue, "But actually, that does bring up a difficult subject, something I've wanted to discuss with you."

"Oh?" she asks, her interest piqued.

"Yes, but just one more thing," I say, delaying the inevitable for a few more minutes. "You want him to level with you more, but ask yourself: have you ever really leveled with him?"

"But Ryder, how can I possibly do that?" she asks, a panicked look on her face. "Give him an ultimatum, tell him—"

"No, not that," I quickly reassure her. "Izzie, you don't have to tell me the details of what you really think. I'm only talking about being honest about your thoughts and feelings with Webster. Face it; you can control what you tell him but not what he tells you." I hold up my hand to stop her protested response. "You know I know what I'm speaking about. I should have leveled with Sophia and with Demi long before I did, but I was too scared. And then—"

"Then it was too late to save anything, right?"

"Yes, Izzie. Sophia had checked out. Demi had deceived me. All was gone. But really, neither cared enough for my needs, I know that now. And so I have to accept, it wasn't real love in either case."

"Okay," she says, "I will think about it. About telling Webster what's on my mind, how I really feel. I know you're right, that it's the only thing to do. I am really scared, but I'm going to try, Ryder, really."

With Izzie finally calmed down, I switch subjects. And as I begin speaking, I realize I'm relaying decisions made long before today. I begin uncomfortably, staring at the ceiling, then at the floor, then anywhere other than Izzie's tear-stained face. But I find myself more at ease as the words pour out.

"It's about the business, this business, Izzie. There is no other way to look at the numbers, much as I've tried not looking at them at all," I say, as I pull my chair closer, rub my bald head with my open palm. "If you must know, Izzie, for months now I've been trying to ignore what has been staring me in the face. No need for a trip to Oudshoorn, with the ostrich right here in the building with us."

She chuckles slightly, and I continue.

"But now—there is only so much looking the other way I can do. All these facts, figures, and numbers—I have to make decisions, take action. You know where this is going—with these dismal financial returns, I'm going to have to close the academy."

Izzie stands abruptly, reaches for the eraser and cleans off the white board. Then she picks up a pile of desk supplies and starts putting them into an empty box. I grab her hands, take the pens from her and place them gently on the table.

"No Izzie, we will do all of that later. We need to talk about how to approach it. I'm going to need your help, as my indispensable, capable assistant. I can't face this alone. It's too daunting. You have the closest relationship with the students, and you know how things work around here," I say.

"Yes," she answers slowly. "We're going to need to make sure they all finish their training somehow. We can help them with that, Ryder. Let's come up with a plan."

Now it is her turn to demonstrate understanding and empathy for my situation and responsibilities, and we spend the next hour discussing some detailed logistics. She surprises me by leaning over and giving me a quick hug along with a kiss on the cheek, thanking me for leveling with her.

"Ryder, look at the two of us," she says as we get up, and make our way towards the exit. "What a pair we are. Life constantly trying to beat us down."

"Yes, Izzie, it's true. My battles with Sophia and Demi, yours with Webster, and the economy fighting us at every turn. This shutdown is going to be a huge setback for me—"

"No Ryder, let me be the one encouraging you for once. Just think—this business is the last thing tying you to Sophia. Why not think of it instead as shedding something?"

"Yeah, the snake skin of Sophia. Shed and left behind while she slithers off. I like it," I reply, smiling slightly as I recognize the wisdom of Izzie's words.

I so need to think of it that way. As I move away from the past and all the associated sadness, disappointments and failures, best that I separate completely. Is this the final segment of the rope binding me and Sophia together, the last frayed and unraveled strand that somehow connects us still? Today, without denial and without anger, I see the path becoming clear. Acceptance, no more bargaining. Forward motion with inertia overcome, I can do this.

"Izzie, can I tell you something? This morning I woke up thinking about compassion," I confide in her. "You know, even before coming here to Knysna, there have always been sad circumstances for me to reflect upon, empathize with. The dire situations of the homeless on the streets of Cape Town, the fractured families torn apart by emigration that I was enmeshed in. I could go on—"

"And now you have to deal with me and my pathetic story too," Izzie says apologetically.

"But don't you see. Not having compassion for ourselves first, that is what makes us powerless!"

And even as I say it, I understand. THIS must be why I woke up with this on my mind. All of my problems, all of my sorrows, always I've harbored the idea that it is somehow of my own making. But where has been the compassion for myself? The empathy I've strived to show to others? Suddenly I feel it! And all it took was fifty-something years of trying to project what needed to be turned inward first. Fifty-two years, one dream, and this entirely unexpected conversation.

31: Jack, Knysna, November

By George I think he's got it! Or getting it! Eureka and hallelujah!

I've just spent the most incredible day with Ryder. Happy, carefree. No wringing of hands, tearful pity parties, no excessive checking of voicemails, and no aimless drives to dreary (or should I say beery?) destinations. No, instead, we set off for Sedgefield and the Wild Oats Outdoor Community Market.

We parked in the nearby lot, then paused in the sunshine at the entrance. Ryder absent-mindedly examined the unique southern Cape blooms at the flower stand, taking in the scene before him. Beyond the entrance a large expanse has been set up for this permanent market. Tree stumps form both the chairs and table bases for the picnic area, with green umbrellas, folded and placed strategically, surrounding it. Chalkboards are arranged in front of the various farmers' stands, indicating daily specials and pricing. The crowd of shoppers, both tourists and locals, was already beginning to build when we arrived.

We stood together, inhaling deeply, enjoying the present, and embracing the here-and-now. Naturally, I began analyzing the complex blend of aromas from the various stands: roasted meats, fresh fruits, vegetables, baked goods, coffee. And thank goodness, no sign or smell of those silly little hand-crafted artsy gimmicks. If you want those, best you head next door to the Scarab market, specializing in second-hand goods and books and locally made clothes and wood products. Here at the Wild Oats, only good, natural foodstuffs, organic and locally-sourced.

I know you're already suitably enticed, ready to make a small trip of your own immediately, forthwith. And why not? Select any Saturday year-round, get on your bicycle, and off you go. Head out on the national road from Knysna towards Cape Town and you can't miss it. But don't say I didn't warn you: with the food as delicious as this, you had better get there before 11am or risk everything being sold out.

Now where was I? Right, right, continuing on. I distinguished the unmistakable odor of homemade dog treats emanating from the back, and eagerly anticipated a walk to that heavenly booth for a sample or two. The anticipated cat-shaped rawhide variety seemed particularly enticing this morning. Or perhaps Ryder will steer me towards the smoked biltong—we are, after all, such creatures of habit, he and I.

So, I hear you asking, what was different on this particular day? Well for starters, Ryder was so chatty on the ride over, it automatically triggered my feeling of gratitude for his trust in me, and his eagerness to discuss things of great import with yours truly. Especially since, as you know, I keep my own counsel pretty much all the time. Perhaps that is why we make such a great team. He uses me as a sounding board and I remain inscrutable. Then he takes this neutrality of mine as encouragement and delves ever deeper, discovering and revealing more of himself. Oh the give and take of it all, the yin and yang. So perfect!

Now as we entered, he glanced around, then noticed Mack and May at one of the picnic tables. Ryder quickly purchased a snack, then slid over onto the seat next to May and put his arm around her. Small talk, chit chat—you don't really need me to revisit all of that. But *pretty soon they tackled more complex topics.*

"Guys, you're looking at the new and improved me," *Ryder said.* "I've realized that a lot of my unfortunate situation was of my own making, and I'm now taking steps to improve things!"

"Really? Are you using the lesson we discussed in the kitchen?" *asked Mack.* "Things that matter, things you can control?"

"So helpful, Mack. Yes! But it is so much more than that. I'm beginning, from this moment on, to live here, now, in the present! Let's take a day like today—"

"What a gorgeous day," *May interjected, as she closed her eyes briefly and leaned back, bathing her face in the sun.* "Perhaps you have spring fever, Ryder?"

"No, May, it's more like life fever! I'm finding out, constantly, that every moment has just what I need in it to be happy. The here and now! I'm not going to dwell on my past mistakes and misadventures anymore."

Here I saw May cup her hand, whispering 'Sophia, Demi, that crazy lot," *to Mack.*

"And I'm certainly not going to obsess about the future," *Ryder continued, not noticing the aside from May.* "Regret and guilt alone are enough to kill us! Look, here and now is all we really have. Am I right?"

"Absolutely Ryder. This is how May and I live our lives, don't we Honey?"

"Yeah, why do you think we have to go to the grocery store every day? Because we never plan in advance," *May said, rolling her eyes as they both blushed guiltily.*

"You guys know what I mean. This is not about lack

of foresight or forethought. It's about reveling in the moment, worrying less about what's around the corner."

"Yes totally," *agreed Mack.* "Why worry about something that might never happen, and that we can't control anyway? Ryder, I don't care what they say about you. You're not such a slow learner after all!"

With that they all chuckled, and Ryder got up, made his goodbyes. Hooray, I thought, off to dog treat stand. I strained at my leash and we moved forward. But as we approached the next group of tables, who should we stumble upon, but Farrell. Do I need to mention that we found him with a Mitchells draft in hand? What better expert to sample the wares from the local micro-breweries? Oh please don't look so shocked. None of this should surprise you. Let's simply continue with the tale of our unique morning of discovery and resolution.

"Ryder, I bet you didn't know that Knysna is the original home for Mitchells, now popular throughout South Africa," *he greeted us as he raised his glass.* "Begun in 1983 by Lex Mitchell, he started off brewing Forester's and Bosuns, for Knysna only, but the beer became so popular that they had to move to bigger premises in Cape Town to keep up with demand. Oh and I just finished a pint of Darling Slow brew, from Sneeberg Mountain at Nieu Bethesda—another good one to try."

'Farrell, the aficionado. And I see you're not wasting any valuable drinking time,*" Ryder said, then once again took a seat, this time next to Farrell. I resignedly lay down under the table, understanding that my snack time would be further delayed. And the subsequent appearance of Irene, obviously there with Farrell, made it certain that we were in for another lengthy chat.*

"So tell me—what are you doing out here so early in the morning?" *Farrell asked, finally registering surprise to see him. I guess it wasn't just I who had noticed Ryder withdrawing, becoming isolated again over the past few weeks.*

"Yeah, I know—unusual, right? Was it that obvious, that I was becoming a hermit?"

"Ryder, do you mind if I'm completely honest with you?" *asked Irene, who then barreled on, not waiting for an answer.* "I don't know what it is about you, really I don't, but I've become truly fond of you in the short time I've known you. I think we all have." *She turned to Farrell, who nodded in agreement.*

"But lately, I've been getting this vibe from you, like you feel you lack any sort of meaningful future. Like you're always thinking about the hurt from the past, or else worrying about some imagined hurt to come in the future. Can you forgive me for telling you all of this? Sometimes I can get carried away? But maybe it makes it clear how deeply I care for you. How we all just want you to be happy, and how we've been concerned about you."

"Irene, Farrell, it's like you have read my mind! But hey, that was weeks ago! You're right of course, but I've decided, no more—I'm done with that. I was just talking to Mack and May about this—"

"Oh ya, we saw them over there," *said Irene, indicating the entrance with an incline of her head.*

"Let me tell you, I've been doing a lot of thinking, and a lot of reading since Demi moved out," *Ryder continued.* "A lot of philosophy and psychology stuff. I suppose you guys know all about my business difficulties as well as my romantic ones."

"Yes, Ryder, Knysna is a small town that way," *replied Farrell with a shrug.*

"True, true. But anyway, all of a sudden, I feel empowered to control my own destiny. I'm telling you, reading all of this stuff has changed my life, maybe because I was finally ready to apply the message."

"Tell us, what is this message? Some of us would like to be enlightened," *asked Irene, leaning forward eagerly.*

"It's simple, really. Basically there are three parts to it, and if you think about it, this message has been repeated throughout the ages, by both biblical and philosophical sources."

I noticed Ryder's face beginning to change, his breathing becoming heavy with excitement. He continued intently.

"The first part is that to be in control of your own happiness means to concentrate on being present in every moment."

"What, like sitting here, enjoying the sunshine, not worrying about the rain predicted for later this afternoon?"

"Precisely," *Ryder said as he nodded towards Irene.* "That's what I mean—be completely present, drink it all in."

"Hey, you know I can handle the drinking part—" *said Farrell at which point Irene poked him in the ribs.* "What? I'm just sayin'—"

"Farrell, I'm being serious here. To live more fully you must live in this very minute, without excessive emotional energy devoted to the past or the future. That was my mistake—dwelling on the past, the loss of Demi, and Sophia, and my business, and—well, that's enough of that."

Now Farrell and Irene both listened intently. Ryder's face was glowing, and I felt myself so moved I could no longer control it. I let out a small yip, and Ryder leaned over and patted me as he laughed.

"Well not sure if you guys are on board but I know someone who is," *he said, and I felt as if my heart would burst with pride.*

"I'm certainly in favor of being at one with universe, a way to permanent happiness. Something for me to work on in the future I suppose," *Irene said thoughtfully, but Ryder stopped her with a small shake of his head.*

"No Irene, I'm not talking about all of that hippie nonsense, or some future happiness goals—and no one can be happy all the time, always. We have to be realistic."

"But what then?"

"All I'm talking about is this, the third part of my new outlook: the Now is the sacred time, the only time of certainty. All other moments are either gone or have no guarantee of ever even arriving."

"Yes I think I get it. Irene, if we can hold on to what we have right now, experience the most out of this moment—" *began Farrell.*

"Then, you have grasped your connection with time and space. That is what makes you feel fully alive and powerful. That's it precisely, Farrell. You create your own future right in the present moment. You don't need any of this 'one with the universe, one with all things spiritual' nonsense—for most people it has to be more concrete."

"So it's kinda like the people here, like life in this small town, Sedgefield," *said Irene, an awareness slowly beginning to build.* "I can see how a person could live in the moment here. Away from the despised big city, just exist in peace. Walk your dog, have everything stay the same day after day, then I suppose ultimately die in peace too."

"Yes, definitely. Everything happens slowly here, no rushing, and everyone seems happier," Ryder said as they all turned to look at an old man sitting nearby, painstakingly carving a figurine from a piece of wood.

"The idyllic country life would make me feel antsy, Ryder, like I need a drink or something," *piped up Farrell.*

"And is there any situation that does not make you think you need a drink?" *Ryder asked, naturally not expecting a reply.*

'To me, peace within, and therefore peace without sounds like something I need to strive for—I've lived so long without either one," *declared Irene.* "But Ryder, how does one go about letting go of all the hurts we have inside of us? That's a challenge for me, for sure."

"Well, none of us will ever make any progress until we acknowledge our own power in our own circumstances," *said Ryder as he stood up, then reached for my leash.* "But you're aware of all of this already, Irene—I know you are."

"It's what I keep telling you, Babe," *said Farrell as he turned to Irene."* As we go through life, we can't help collecting negative emotions and carrying them around with us. And then they become an intrinsic part of us. We all do this, consciously or subconsciously."

"Yes, Farrell, there is no point in denying that," *Ryder said before he sat back down, making it clear that he wasn't quite done with this little chat.* "See, we all know, this negative collection in our psyche, let's call it a semi-dormant beast, gets activated in so many ways. It just keeps sticking around, inflicting hurt as long as we let it. It colors our perceptions, affects our viewpoints—believe me, I know. And all of this happens when we're least aware."

"So what are you doing about it? What do we do?" *Irene asked.* "How do we keep the beast at bay, so to speak?"

"Well, think of it like those dusty mongrels that you sometimes see, scrapping for food in the city. You know those dogs, darting in to grab any food they see, sometimes dashing in front of moving cars."

"Man, Ryder, I know just what you're talking about because I think I hit one of them last week," *Farrell said.* "I felt so guilty, but I was afraid to pull over, afraid he would bite me. And besides, it would have made me late for my standing appointment with Innocent—"

"No, can't have that Farrell," *replied both Irene and Ryder sarcastically, and they all chuckled.*

"Well, I think most of us have a natural instinct towards sympathy for any poor creatures," *continued Ryder.* "But in this case, when the creature represents the embodiment of all things injurious, we have to abandon him at the side of the road. Do not give him a meal; deprive him of the opportunity to feast at your expense! And resist the temptation to relent and go back and get him, no matter what!"

We walked away then, with Irene scratching her head and Farrell resuming his drinking. Why was this esoteric information so hard for them to digest, I wondered. Instead of longing for the past or gazing wistfully into the future, they had to learn to grab life by the horns and get the most out of every day.

"C'mon Jack," *said Ryder now, pulling on my leash, acting as though I was the one who had been delaying our progress.* "Let's get some shopping done, perhaps buy some lunch before everything is sold out."

We continued deeper into the market, bypassing the dog treats, but instead investigating the various varieties of biltong. On the way back, Ryder held forth again, revisiting the conversations, and of course expressing his appreciation for me.

"Jack, you were such a good boy today—so patient," *he said, as I settled into the back seat and he handed me a rubber bone he found where I had strategically placed it earlier.* "I do wonder if the others get it—this idea of living in the here and now. I know for sure Sophia never understood. She forced us into a miserable situation, didn't she? Planning for a future that never came, destroying the present. And that Demi, no planning, but really a totally untrustworthy present."

On and on he went as I settled in for the ride back to Knysna. But the last thing I heard, before I fell asleep on the back seat, touched me deeply.

"Maybe there is something to the idea of a Silent Watcher, Jack. I think it could be helpful to picture a benevolent presence existing only within our own mind, observing all of our deeds, overseeing our own unique path, always in a non-judgmental way."

So do I flatter myself to think Ryder sees me as his own Silent Watcher? If so, I have my work cut out for me, trying to be the benevolent presence Ryder seeks in his life, leaving all judgments behind. We can grow in this together; I will begin this work immediately. First by becoming my own Silent Watcher, judging nothing but merely observing.

Ryder has come so far, picked himself up by his bootstraps, armed with nothing except his virtual toolbox of which he seems so proud. Suddenly, I feel so hopeful for his future. So much progress in so little time, travelling from despair to joy, and bringing me along with him on this path! My life's work and his life's work—harmoniously complementing each other for mutual gain. Oh happy day!

32: Ryder, Knynsa, December

It is late evening. Ryder has spent the day at the beach, body-surfing and swimming with Jack. He's pleasantly tired, but by no means ready to turn in for the night. A little music and a drink at the local pub, just the ticket, just what he craves. No female company tonight, but no regrets. Not today, no more of that. His relationship with Demi reached its logical conclusion; he's done with recriminations and remorse. Instead, he feels only contentment, something he has been experiencing intermittently now. A slow realization that time does, indeed, heal all wounds. Grasping the difference between being on his own and being lonesome. And no longer wasting time wondering whether today was more or less lonely than yesterday, or tomorrow for that matter. The past and the future—irrelevant! Today is what matters. Here and now—acceptance of what is.

He dresses carefully, hesitates as he tries to decide between two pairs of boots. Attention to detail is always important to him. His reasoning: if a woman's feet and shoes are the first thing he notices, she might possibly return the favor. Yes, classy shoes to attract classy women, and so he decides on the black cowboy boots. Definitely.

The pub is a mere fifteen-minute walk from his apartment, and he pulls on a light jacket, attaches Jack's leash and off they trot. Old pals, time for a quick nip, or a protracted stay. This neighborhood bar now always welcomes them both, always gives Jack a bowl of water under the table, and always greets Ryder with his regular Jack and Red Bull, made just the way he likes it, to his exact specifications. The regular barman begins preparations as soon as Ryder enters and nods in his direction. Eccentric or not, this has become Ryder's signature drink.

"Fancy seeing you here Farrell!"

Naturally, the first person he encounters. Ryder has a sneaking suspicion that any bar he wanders into, at any time of the day or night, would feature Farrell sitting there, chatting to the bartender. What was the name of this chap, Abstinence? No—that would not be right! Innocent. Yes, that's it. There is an empty stool next to Farrell at the bar and Ryder crosses the bar in three easy strides, then claims it for himself.

"Yeah, well maybe I'm a mayor too, just like Irene's asshole husband," Farrell replies. "Mayor of this square meter of the bar, at any rate! So what can I do for you this evening Ryder? You're still looking pleased with yourself, so I guess you really are done with the crying in your beer."

"For sure. You know what they say: it's not easy having a good time all the time, but somebody has to do it!"

"Yeah I guess you're just the man for that job. Nice work if you can get it, hey! So it seems you really have discovered the secret of how to be happy despite the circumstances."

"Yes and you know, when we met up the other day, there was one more thing I forgot to mention—"

"That's okay, Ryder. I think you covered all the highlights quite well."

"Well, here is one more important tip I left out. It all comes down to managing your expectations, setting them at a level where they can be met!"

"Here and now, all that other stuff. Now managing expectations too. Ryder, not sure I can follow along with all of this," says Farrell, motioning as if to take a pen and paper out of his shirt pocket. Then he waves his hands dismissively, frowns slightly and shakes his head.

Ryder looks at him askance, then feels suddenly inspired, hoping to impart yet another deep lesson to Farrell. He asks Innocent for an empty beer mug along with a pitcher of beer. He fills the glass halfway, and then hands it to Farrell.

"Look, the level of the beer represents your expectations in life. Now drink it down."

"I can do that," says Farrell as he eagerly obliges.

"Ok, now let's say you meet a woman, and you ask her—"

"Wait, Ryder, you mean a woman who would actually give me the time of day?"

"Yes, Farrell. Just use your imagination, you can do it. So you ask her, Woman, where is my beer?"

"I KNOW I can do that," says Farrell with a slight smirk.

"Now what if she brings you a glass that looks like this?" Ryder asks as he refills the glass, this time with only half as much as before. "How does this make you feel?"

"Yeah, Ryder, I think I get it. The bitches normally do exactly that, take away half my beer. Come to think of it, that's exactly what disappointed me the last time. Gloria, Samantha—screw it, Irene will probably act just the same way." Farrell is exasperated, scowling slightly as he reaches for the glass. "Screw it, I'll drink it anyway."

"All right—you understand that part. Now, say you meet a woman and—"

"What, another woman? How many women am I going to be carrying on with here, Ryder?"

"Hold on, pay attention. This time, once again, you say 'Woman, where is my beer?' and she brings you a glass that is almost full. Now how do you feel?" Ryder says as he refills the glass, this time almost to the brim.

"That's what I'm talking about," Farrell says as he reaches out eagerly, then lovingly caresses the glass.

"Taking it one step farther—can you handle that Farrell? What if all you thought you were going to get was water, yet somehow the woman gave you a glass of beer?"

"Damn, I think I would marry that woman. Even for a half-full glass of warm flat beer!"

"Yes, Farrell, otherwise known as being grateful and happy with whatever you get. Remember: you control the level you set. What you can't control is the level you get. Beer, life, it's all the same thing. So if we live in the here and now, and we appreciate what we get regardless, that is how we get to be satisfied."

"So as long as she keeps bringing the beer, who cares how much is in the glass? But what if I'm still thirsty?"

Farrell protested.

"Mate, that is the point where you need to go get your own beer, and top it up how you please. Don't rely on the woman to keep your glass filled, instead find a pal to drink with. Be responsible for your own level in your own glass!"

"Okay, fine. Tell me how all of this relates to my life. 'Cause all I've been doing tonight is sitting here, thinking about Irene."

"Woman troubles—here we go," says Ryder, now turning to face Farrell. "What's going on?"

"Well as you know, me and Irene have been together since that night out at the inn—I mean, that was after you rescued me from almost drowning."

"Oh yeah, I remember that night well. Don't forget—I rescued you from almost killing yourself driving drunk as well."

"Ok, ok, I told you before—and I'll tell you any time you ask—I'm an idiot. But that's not my point. Here's what I don't get. Why is Irene still married to that asshole? Can it really be just because she wants to be the wife of an important person? How long has she been in this situation? Thirty years? I think she's been unhappy for thirty-one."

"Farrell, I can't answer—"

"Stay with me here, Ryder. I want to understand this. Why does she stay married to a guy who treats her so badly? I'm a nice guy. Don't you think I am? Well, I am. I'm not married. There have been times when I've wanted to be married. And then I look at these women, they go for the assholes, marry them, and then they're unhappy. So what do these women do?"

"I have a feeling you're going to tell me. Go ahead, Farrell. What do they do?"

"I think there are two types out there. The first type, they run screaming for the hills. These are usually the ones you want to keep away from. They throw those husbands out like yesterday's trash, even if some of them are perfectly good trash. Hello—case in point." Here he pauses, gesturing towards Ryder with an open palm.

"Thanks Farrell. Always nice to be recognized as perfectly good trash. 'Preciate it," Ryder says as he fakes a small seated bow.

"No offense I hope," Farrell continues. "Anyway, it's like they decide, no need for him anymore. They have taken their pound of flesh—you know a donation of sperm for a baby or two—and they are off. Send your monthly check to this address please, child support and alimony both. Thanks and bugger off. Ryder, you following me? Ready for me to move on to type two?"

"What is type number two, Farrell?"

"Glad you asked. I'm afraid Irene is type number two. Guilt—that's it! They get married, have a kid or two and then they can't leave. They're worried their kids will hate them, scared their husbands will hate them even though they can't stand being with them anymore. Does this make sense? They stick around, feeling sad and unappreciated, often abused. Seems like the worse the husband is, the more likely the wife will be type two. Do you agree with me?"

"You're talking about the Pleasers now, aren't you?"

"Yeah Ryder. Where is the woman who is going to try

to please me for a change? Huh? I'm so tired of this business with Irene. She won't leave her asshole husband, says without him she would be lost. Maybe if she left him decades ago things would have been different but no, she had to stick around out of guilt. Maybe she didn't want to rock the boat. A big fucking boat in this small lagoon, if you know what I mean."

"You mean Irene's husband, with all his connections and—"

"Yeah, this particular pool of incest and nepotism. She moved here with no family and no friends when they first got married and never reconnected with anyone from her past life. You know what the two of us need, Ryder? Women who are a combination of the two types. Who stick around if they find a good guy, but say get lost if he's really an asshole. Who don't wait too long to do it, and who tell their families to mind their own business. Let's not forget that."

"Farrell, if you're serious about Irene, why not try talk her into making a big change, permanently?"

"Do you think I haven't tried? But here's what I've figured out. She's not going to leave him unless I plan on stepping in and stepping up, taking over as the caretaker. Which means I'll become the asshole. *Verstaan* (understand)?"

"Yeah, I'm afraid I do. You don't want to marry her, have her depend on you. Maybe that is why you have never—"

"Okay enough. Let me cry in my beer without making this my fault. I suppose next you're going to say I expect too much—"

"All right. Let me see if I understand what you're saying about women. We have type one: bitches, and type two: dependents. Now what about that number over there at the end of the bar? What type do you think she is? Think I can convince her to come over here and have a drink with us?"

"Not a chance Mate. She looks classy but high maintenance."

"What do you mean not a chance? I saw her looking at my cowboy boots and she half-smiled. These girls, you know, they always check out the shoes. The ones with class. If you want to get a chick that is fussy and full of shit, wear nice shoes. And we need a woman's perspective on all this nonsense. Innocent, send that lady at the end of the bar another round on me."

33: Ryder, Knysna, December

Candy looks up when Innocent delivers the drink, smiles and raises her glass in a toast. The guys beckon her over, and she stands up, sashays over to Ryder and Farrell.

"Thanks for the drink. So you're looking for a female's perspective, eh? Well, I'll give you my opinion, but you better be sure you want it."

At this, both Farrell and Ryder nod eagerly.

"Well, I'll tell you about some other types of women if you like. Seems both of you could use a little educating."

They are both a little taken aback. They did not think she could hear their conversation over the music. Ryder assesses her, a not-very-subtle glance, moving his eyes from her head to her toes. Early forties, good shape. No wedding ring. But a faint tan line where the ring ought to be, so it must have been very recently removed. A short, tight skirt. Low cut blouse, not too revealing. Toned ass. The cleavage, definitely fake, he decides, without a doubt. At forty, they would not be so high, so firm. But still, one can never be too sure, and he's paying attention now. Not a local or he would have noticed her before today. So a tourist, recently separated, hanging out in the local bar, on her own.

Looking to get lucky perhaps?

"Yes, please, come sit with us over here, educate us! We're just dumb guys, as if there is any other sort. Tell us about these other types of women!"

Farrell and Ryder, falling all over themselves to invite her to sit with them. A study in contrasts, vilifying women until one of them shows them any attention. Now they will compete head-to-head for her interest. But it is clear, she has her eye on Ryder. She pulls up a stool, which she positions between them, so her bare knees are touching Ryder's jean-clad ones. She carefully crosses her legs, exposing more of her thigh. Tosses her long dark hair back over her shoulders. Ryder glimpses diamond earrings sparkling in her delicate earlobes. A matching diamond pendant hangs around her neck, positioned perfectly just below her throat, directly between her beautifully shaped collar bones. His heartbeat quickens slightly.

"So here's the scoop. Listen carefully! Not all women are like either of those types. It's a lot more complicated than that. You should know that by now! Some women kick the guy out, you're right. And some of them stick around out of loyalty, feeling all trapped and stuff. Right again! But the next type, well, they stay married, but we find other ways to keep ourselves, er… they find other ways to keep themselves, happy."

She leans forward just slightly, so Ryder can see the shadow between her breasts. Slow down, he cautions himself, but already he knows it's useless. He recognizes this delicious, helpless feeling beginning to well up inside of him. Before the night is out, he will be at her mercy. Gladly.

"You know, when the cat's away? Are you starting to understand about type number three?"

"That depends." Ryder responds as if on cue. (Flirting—he's a natural!) "What type of feline do you have?"

"Oh, hmmm, an old brown tubby tabby, a house cat that didn't get out much. But I had to put that cat down, put him out of his misery."

At this, Candy chuckles, then flips her hair back off of her shoulders. "Anyway, I don't think you're ready to hear about any more types of women. That will have to wait for a possible future lesson. My name's Candy by the way. Ryder is it?"

"Yes, I'm Ryder, and this is Farrell. A real pleasure, Candy—as in Eye Candy—I assume?"

"That's what I've been told. I take it you like Candy, Ryder? Most boys do—" She's dangling one of her high-heeled sandals on the end of her foot, showing off her bright orange toenail polish and high-arched feet. How does she do that so effortlessly, Ryder wonders as he stares, entranced.

Farrell is starting to think he's superfluous to this little conversation. Certainly, he cannot keep up with the double entendres flying about, so he resorts to the next best thing.

"Innocent, another round. Candy, what are you drinking? Tequila shooter eh? The good stuff. You don't mess around, do you?"

"No, never mess around, unless I get good and drunk, then all bets are off. Just in case you want to know—I'm now on my way to being good and drunk. And, um, Ryder, you were telling me how much you like Candy, whether you ever indulge…"

Jack looks up from his spot beneath Ryder's chair, but Ryder studiously ignores his disapproving stare.

What is this, yet another woman? Didn't we just stop in here for a drink? So now I suppose you are too intrigued to pay any attention to me, too fascinated by Candy and her evident charms.

"I have to confess that I have a very sweet tooth. A real weakness for Candy you might even call it."

And even as he says it, he realizes how true it is, how truer it is becoming with each passing moment. Back and forth it goes. The small three-piece band in the corner begins its second set. The sultry, sexy singer is belting out some old songs and the sound of the saxophone is unmistakable. As the bar becomes increasingly crowded, the volume intensifies.

They all sing along in unison, the familiar words ringing out throughout the bar. Ryder grabs Candy's hand and pulls her on to the dance floor, while waving at the regulars he recognizes. *Wow, this woman can really move*, he thinks as they twirl around. Suddenly the band switches to a slow song and Ryder pulls Candy into his arms. He hums softly along, the words of love and devotion adding to the suddenly romantic atmosphere.

Candy whispers something in his ear, or did she simply just blow in there, with the band playing he cannot tell. The crowd, the noise, the alcohol, he's becoming intoxicated. He feels himself tingling all over, holds her tighter and presses himself into her. She responds with equal pressure, moving in his arms in time to the music. Her fingers brush the back of his neck, then move upward to slowly caress the back of his head. He closes his eyes.

Too quickly the song is over and the band announces a short break. Hand-in-hand, they return to Farrell who has now moved from the bar to a table, with Jack repositioned underneath it, his head resting on his front paws.

Farrell shrugs guiltily, mouths "Can't live with them, can't live without 'em," as he puts his arm protectively around Irene, who now occupies the seat beside him. Ryder hugs Irene in greeting, and then introduces her to Candy. They sit down at the table and resume the earlier discussion, eager to get Irene's added perspective.

"Irene was just about to explain to us all why she has not left her husband," Farrell resumes, seemingly hell-bent on getting an answer to this issue tonight.

"Estranged husband!" Irene corrects him, swatting him affectionately atop his head.

"After all these years. Go ahead, tell us why it is 'cause I sure as heck don't understand any of this stuff."

"Farrell, Ryder, and Candy is it? Look, I got married so young, I wasn't even nineteen. My parents were dead set against this marriage. A Jewish girl and a colored guy, they told me flat out it would never work, that they would not come to the wedding. That was it. They kicked me out, I never heard from them again. Then before I even knew it, along came the kids. No chance to think if this was what I truly wanted. My ex—well, he's not my ex—I guess we covered that. Let's just call him His Lordship. Whatever. He started being really controlling right from the start. God, if I hadn't been so naïve I might have figured it out even before we got married."

"So why didn't you tell him to *voetsek* (get lost) when you did realize? Surely you have had choices along the way. Isn't your happiness important?" asks Ryder.

"Ryder, I have no relationship with my family. They live so far away, and they barely speak to me, even after all these years. After our kids were born, I knew my choices had truly dried up. The only work I've ever done has been on his campaigns, getting him elected, and working in his office. This is a small town with limited opportunity. You know that. And his family has been around here for generations. In any case, I've asked myself this before, how much happiness are we actually entitled to in this life? Don't we give up our options as we make our choices ? Make our beds that we will have to lie in? Forever, you know, until we drop dead."

Even through the sarcasm, the seriousness of Irene's answer and her perceived plight is evident.

"Jeez Irene, you're making me want to cry. Innocent, please, another round, quickly man!"

Although he's the one who is asking the question, Farrell seems uncomfortable with the answers. Yet Irene continues.

"Look, I'll admit it. I don't want my kids to hate me. They have enough problems, more than their share. Sorry Candy, I won't bore you with the details of their run-ins, or how they get off just because their daddy calls the shots around here. But part of me still thinks I owe it to them to stay with him. I never want them to say I just gave up, didn't try to work it out. Farrell, I know you tell me my husband's abusive, but I don't really agree. You know I would certainly have left him if he actually raised a hand to me! I'm not that pathetic!"

"Sorry Irene, none of us think you're—"

"It's okay Ryder; I know how people see me around here. But think about it, what am I supposed to do? I work for the town, so I am his employee. I don't own my own car. The only place I can live is in our house because I have no money of my own, no family ties, nothing set aside. You guys are the only friends I have that are not his friends first. Does this sound like loyalty or captivity? I think both, if you must know. So now, like I said, no options anymore."

"Well, the women I've been with have had no compunction about kicking me out! Kids or no kids. Why has it been so easy for them?" Ryder blurts out, then immediately wonders if he has made a mistake bringing up past relationships. He looks quickly at Candy. Will she walk away now? Damn! Let the band start up again before he says something else really stupid. At least on the dance floor he can lead successfully.

"Perhaps because you're one of the good guys. Could that be it, Ryder? Are you one of the good guys?"

A relief, Candy is not walking away after all. She wants to know some answers too!

"That's right, just like I told you. The good guys get the shaft!" Farrell is starting to slur now. When did he cross that line? "You and me Ryder, we're gonna suffer the same fate. Get tossed aside because we're too good, too great."

"Riiight. Believe that if you like." Irene pats Farrell's hand affectionately. "I suppose another reason I never left was because I don't want to be alone. You know, the older a woman gets, the harder it is to find someone. The available pool keeps shrinking. Let's be honest, you guys keep looking at younger and younger women, the older you get."

"But Irene, Honey, you have me now." With this, Farrell leans in, kisses Irene drunkenly.

"Yeah, Irene, there's the solution to all of your problems, right there!" Ryder chimes in and they all laugh, although Farrell somewhat wryly.

Ryder glances over, sees the band about to begin their last set. Finally! They start out with a big crowd pleaser and the regulars surge onto the floor; now all four of them join in. Ryder longs for another slow song, another chance to take Candy into his arms. She smells so delicious, he can't wait to bury his face in her hair again. And as the set winds down, and the crowd finally thins out, his wish is granted. "Unchained Melody" a personal favorite. This surely must be a good omen.

As he listens to the words of love and hunger, Ryder seizes the opportunity, kissing Candy gently and she responds, tentatively. Again, she seems to whisper in his ear, seductive suggestive words. The song ends, closing time and the crowd all move towards the exits. He takes her by the hand, escorts her to her car. As they walk alongside the lagoon, he sees the full moon glimmering on the water, another good omen. She indicates her vehicle, naturally the most expensive one in the lot. Ryder notices that there are no people around, and that her car is shielded from view by a huge four-by-four off road. He opens the door for her and she gets in, reaches forward to turn the ignition. He bends his lanky frame over inside and kisses her again, this time long and hard. No more tentativeness in her response! He grins sheepishly and steps away slightly. She laughs and smiles.

"Wow," she says breathlessly. "Who taught you to kiss like that? A girl could be persuaded to do anything for a guy who kisses like that. Seriously."

In a wordless reply, he pulls her out of the car and pushes her up against the big black shiny four-by-four. He can see the moon and water over her shoulder, can feel her under his hips. As he starts kissing her again, thrusting slightly, she moans and starts moving with him. She clutches at him, pulling him closer. He lifts her hair, kisses her neck and she groans more loudly.

"Ryder, oh God, it has been so long. You have no idea how good this feels. How good you feel. My husband—he has not touched me in eighteen months."

"Wait, what? You're married?" Ryder steps back, holding her at arm's length. "So that type three discussion was all about you? Dammit Candy, all that talk in there. I thought you were single or at least separated. I don't go with married women, a rule of mine. Shit." Ryder rubs his hand over his bald head, frustrated and conflicted. Candy has him all worked up, horny. When did he make up this rule anyway? Would it kill anyone if he broke it, just this once, he wonders fleetingly.

"Ryder, it's okay. I think he has a mistress, and anyway, he'll never know. I promise. At least kiss me some more. C'mon, please? Do you live nearby? Can we go back to your place? I would invite you to my hotel but unfortunately there's something wrong with my room."

"Well, I can definitely help you out if you have a problem with your hotel, Candy. The least I can do."

"Oh I seriously doubt it. Seems the bed over there has my husband sleeping in it!"

Ryder is at a loss. Here is a beautiful woman, offering herself to him, seemingly without complications. And yet, her husband slumbers less than a mile away. Ryder is lonely and horny. It didn't take long to go from contentment to this, to be sure. And Candy is so hot, just raring to go. The horns of a dilemma indeed; once again he is faced with a choice. He can spend the next few hours in the arms of a married woman who he will probably never see again, or he can go home on his own. And contemplate how stupid he was to bypass the opportunity for a night with an exciting, enticing new female. But over the past few months he has come to understand that there are consequences to every action, and actions that betray your essential self have the most grievous consequences of all. And so he resolves to stay true to his guiding principles.

"Candy, it was wonderful meeting you. Truly a pleasure. Goodnight. Drive safely."

With that he turns around and heads for home, Jack trotting at his heels.

"Is it really possible, Ryder, that you avoided the obvious perils here? Oh I'm so proud of you, shunning the actions your head screamed at you to avoid. You're showing so much promise, old chap. Finally making choices that are in keeping with your instincts. Jolly good show. Now your actions can reflect who you truly are. Great progress, well done."

34: Ryder, Knynsa, December

Does becoming cynical mean I'm becoming wiser? Last night was an occasion for me to either choose the high road, which some might say I did, or succumb to my baser desires in the hope of finding love, a bond, and happiness.

So what? So I resisted temptation, realizing just in time that no hope of happiness is possible if there is another player in the picture. That does not make me feel any better about what this is all really about, the messed up relationships between men and women. And how little I still understand of this topic. Farrell and I, fumbling about for answers. I don't even know how many relationships he has had, but I do know one thing—I no longer have any faith in marriage as a viable institution. Well, maybe for the purposes of child rearing, but that phase of life is over for me now, at least I can acknowledge that much.

But why do I keep coming back to these same old questions? Round and round until I'm totally exhausted. Every time I meet up with my friends—Irene, Farrell, Julie, Leeza, Jill—are we destined to have the same discussions over and over? Just two weeks ago, at the local bar on a quiet night, it happened again. On that night, there was no live music, only some tunes playing softly in the background. Innocent worked the bar alone. Patience should be his middle name, with all the nonsense he has to listen to, day in and day out. We took our designated seats around the table, Farrell with his back facing the wall as always. Then he rocked backwards on his chair, hooked his feet around the front legs, and leaned up against the brick surface. Loafer-clad feet up in the air, drink in hand. Now he was ready to listen. And, of course, I started the conversation—my quest to find answers, the questions constantly burning and churning.

"I have a theory," I said, ignoring the eye-rolling from the others when they heard these familiar words from me. "Basically, these days we live way too long for us to have just one life."

"*Ag* please Ryder—don't get all heavy on us now," Jill replied. "Are you going to hold forth on reincarnation? No politics and no religion. You know the rules."

"This is not about religion," I answered, leaning forward, trying to engage their attention. "Let me explain. I think we each have about three or four lifetimes within one life. Life One: age zero to leaving home, before or during the college years. Life Two: after leaving home until marriage. This could be any amount of time, from no time at all to ten years or more."

"You see Farrell, that is your problem, too much of life two!" Irene chimed in.

"Yeah well, at least I've avoided my first divorce," came the smart reply from Farrell.

"Okay," I said, slightly annoyed at the interruption.

"Let's keep going, moving on to Life Three: marriage until divorce. I suppose, on average, this would be ten years. In the USA, they say now the average marriage lasts less than nine years! Can you believe it?"

"And amen to that!" shouted Irene, as she raised her glass in a toast. "Get out of there, get on with it."

"Calm down, Irene. Wow, someone is ready for Life Three to come to an end," I said, to which she nodded her head vigorously. "Okay, to continue. So now we're forty or fifty years old, depending on whether we waited for the kids to grow up or not, during this Life Three. But we still have more life to live and so we have Life Four: this is post-divorce or post kids leaving home, and it includes getting old, with about twenty years of retirement. For people who get married young, Life Three and Four can be sixty years or more as people live longer. Do you think, in this day and age, that it is possible to go forty or fifty years, our lives three and four, with the same partner, remaining faithful and loving, keeping a meaningful bond and staying truly happy?"

"Ryder, if you stick with the same partner, then you don't really have a Life Four, now do you?" asked Farrell, evasively poking holes in my logic.

"Just because you will forever be stuck on Life Two, you want to deny everyone Life Four. Is that it?" Irene asked, deliberately baiting him. "See, Ryder, you're asking the same thing I've been asking myself for a decade now. How the hell can any two people stay married undergoing all the changes and challenges that occur from when they get married until they die? Are financial or family value reasons good enough to make someone just hang in there?"

"But what about religion?" chimed in Jill. She who had asked me to keep religion and politics out of this discussion, "You're saying the institution of marriage is cracking up? Cases in point!" she said as she looked at each one of us at the table. "But you know religions are all pretty fixed on this married-for-life part. No such thing as a ten year renewable contract."

"Correct, and—as you well know—the law is on the same page. No financial free obligations for the man," I answered. "This probably explains why ninety percent of women will not look at an unemployed man for a relationship. S'true fact—look it up! Even if these women are capable of earning, the old fashioned role of the man being the bread-winner still applies. So why do we keep doing this? Keep admitting marriage is obsolete, yet keep wanting to get married, keep actually getting married, and then, oh yeah big surprise—keep getting divorced?"

Well, that conversation ended without any meaningful conclusions. And then again last night, how can I parse the idiotic musings between me and Farrell into any semblance of meaning? Talking of marriage and classifying women into two types, both of us weighing in with so much perceived knowledge and expertise, when really we're as clueless as the next fellow. Sigh. All the while I think we overlooked the obvious: marriage was invented so long ago, back in the day when men and women were lucky to live to see the far side of thirty, and when birth control wasn't quite so reliable. So yes, in those days all of that "til death do us part" mumbo-jumbo made a lot of sense. Get married, stay that way. No point in separating once the kids are raised, because your last child would reach the age of majority about twelve hours before you kicked the bucket. Sad but true. The historical proof is out there everywhere.

I recall asking Demi a long time ago about her failed marriage, why she decided to call it quits after being married for a decade or so. I was surprised by her reply, well-thought-out and carefully considered, yet way more cynical than expected.

"I can see why you would ask this question Ryder. Everything is so much easier for a man."

"How so?" I stupidly, naively asked, providing her with the perfect lead-in.

"I will try to simplify—pay attention! For a man, at any stage of life, when the hunt is on, the rules are pretty much the same. He identifies his prey, hunts her, stalks her, and pursues her, and then if he's so inclined, marries her. In this way, he wins. A game, a race to the finish. A competition with the rest of the males. Usually for the most attractive of the opposite sex. Youth, beauty, all are prized no matter the age of the man."

"Okay—I got that. Men like to pursue beautiful women, and men like to compete over them. Nothing new to me there. To the victor go the spoils, something like that. Is there something wrong with that?"

"No, not at all. And I'm glad you agree so far, but you see, for a woman, even the process of identifying the prey is more complicated. Who a woman desires depends on her age and her station in life. When she's young, this is all governed by the process of finding that ideal father for her offspring. Consciously, subconsciously—some women have no clue as to what motivates them, but basically she's engaging in the process of finding a suitable sperm donor. Appearance, intelligence, blood lines, financial security, all must be considered."

"C'mon Demi, don't you think that sounds a little harsh? What about love, what about—"

"Oh please, Ryder, listen to what I'm telling you—don't act all surprised. It's true and you know it! Now after the child bearing stage is over, that's when a whole different set of criteria emerge. Maybe this is why so many women wake up at this stage of their lives, take stock and find that their chosen one is no longer who they choose to be with."

"Is this what happened with you Demi? Is this why your hubby was kicked to the curb? Is that all he was to you? A suitable candidate for a genetic donation?"

"Okay, Ryder, you're going to have to learn to distinguish between generalities and specifics. I'm telling you about how women think, what the main issue is here. I'm not necessarily talking about me and my situation. Are you following me or not?"

"Well, I guess so but I—"

"Women will always tell you they marry for love, but women are also very good at lying to themselves, and their reasons for zeroing in on a man vary depending on their age and their circumstances. Believe me; love looks very different when you're eighteen versus when you're thirty-eight. Or forty-eight."

"What are you saying? Don't most women desire a partner who will care for them, nurture them?"

"Of course they do. But in this later iteration, they seek passion."

"Passion? What the heck—"

"Yes, passion, Ryder. An ingredient that wasn't as crucial when they were seeking to procreate. Most men don't understand that for some women, this urge is strong enough that they will alter their life's course, and set out on a quest for a new partner when they realize it's missing. That is why so many marriages fail at this stage, after the kids have been raised. Of course, there are many women who suppress this urge and simply make do with what they have, and maybe there are some who find they have enough passion in their marriage after all. I don't know. That wasn't my experience, or quite frankly, the experience of any of my friends."

"Stupid me," I responded. The conversation was winding down—Demi's words had made me feel totally discouraged. "Here I always thought true love was enough to conquer all. Meet a girl, fall in love; the rest will take care of itself."

"And how has that worked out for you so far, Ryder? Tell me that. Rule of thumb—don't bring only a fist to a gunfight; don't take a simplistic approach to matters involving women."

In the back of my mind, yet remaining unsaid was the model marriage of Vinnie and Maia, a builder and a decorator respectively. A bond now strengthened by common complementary interests in Life Four, with matching careers in teaching leaders and children in Life Three. Their similar expectations had formed the foundation of life Number Two, all those years ago. With their relationship grounded in a mutual love of food and wine, cooking and entertaining, and respect for all people, these two selfless souls embody my concept of Ubuntu. And somehow, they have no need to compromise themselves on important issues, proving that a marriage can work, even though this is a rarity. Sadly, I think it's time for me to acknowledge, this happy progression from one life to the next is not my reality.

My conversations with Farrell and Irene, the subsequent situation with Candy, all of this leads me to one conclusion: attempting to understand the inherent pitfalls of the sacred institution of marriage by grouping the fairer sex into two types is like removing a splinter with a sledgehammer. Or sewing on a button with a screwdriver. With the wrong tool for the wrong job, it's not gonna happen.

So now what do I do? Decide that I will be on my own for the rest of my life, or accept that if I ever get into a serious relationship again, my beliefs about marriage will have to be altered? I have such a poor track record with building serious relationships, one decade of marriage ending in divorce, a subsequent long-term relationship ending in exile and total loss. Continuing with my relationship with Demi that ended when it was clear that her ethics and mine were not the same, and so we could never establish a foundation of trust between us. Have I ever really figured out what exactly my goals are here? Have my mistaken beliefs around women and their motivations become barriers to setting or achieving realistic goals? It is painfully clear that there have been large gaps in my understanding, and that my habitual behaviors have not served me well in the long term. And the pain of moving on, of being rejected and landing in limbo, seems to totally overshadow all the love and joy leading up to it.

Surely I should be able to use all of this to learn and reflect, instead of spinning uselessly? What about active learning, experiencing something in the moment, and then using this experience to inform future belief systems—isn't this what I've taught my students? I have to remember, connecting deeply with another person is only the first step. Having realistic expectations, understanding the desires and expectations of the other person, these are possibly steps two and three. "Catching my prey," Demi's projected metaphor, has been so easy for me. Is it the subsequent tending where I keep falling short, or is it simply a mismatch at the outset? Or both?

Yes, I think some clarity around goal-setting and belief systems will help considerably here. So, note to self. Don't allow what I believe to get in the way of the truth. And don't allow false expectations to ruin what might otherwise be a good relationship. Be realistic and always keep the motivation of others in mind when forming or growing relationships. I guess this does not solve the thorny marriage-as-passé issue, but, for now, my goal is an ever-deepening relationship with a worthwhile woman, one who shares my belief system. I can strive for that, can't I?

35: Jack, Knynsa, December

Asking my opinion, indeed. That Farrell, did he think that I would so casually dispense my advice, my pearls before the proverbial swine? Not bloody likely, as they say. No, not bloody likely. And yet there they sat, for what seemed like hours, holding forth at the bar. The two of them, fools, I tell ya, fools!

Now I'm sure even the slowest of readers can deduce that those two were not going to make any progress in figuring out the psyche of the female. Clueless would best describe them—perhaps I've already covered that. And now, today, Ryder rails on about marriage, how it was invented decades or perhaps centuries ago. Well, what of it? He might think it has outlived its useful purpose, yet it still exists today, so men and women must still be finding ways to navigate in and out, and often times around, it. Surely those two knaves can see that much. Let them classify and clarify away—they might as well be a two-headed Sisyphus—pushing that great boulder up that steep hill, for all the results they will achieve. Men have been trying to understand women for centuries, yet failing repeatedly. No wonder Ryder finds this all so hopeless. Does anyone really believe that, before another century has passed, we males might achieve some clarity around this convoluted topic? Ah me, all so depressing. And just pause and imagine how I feel. For you, a century is a mere one hundred years. For me, it is seven hundred.

Now I'm going to depend on you to keep me on track from here on out as we try break this down. There is no point in railing against what is—boys will be boys, and men, men. That is the way it has always been. Women, on the other hand, are way more complex. Please don't argue—again, acceptance of what is. Deal with it. And perhaps this is what Ryder and Farrell touched upon last night, somewhat ineptly of course. The notion that some women no longer find happiness with their spouse after they have made their suitable genetic donation, and subsequently kick them to the curb. No, not like a dog—please don't use that analogy. Believe it or not, it truly offends.

Here is the question I believe Ryder should be pondering—and it differs substantially from the misguided foolishness under discussion last night—Who is happier, the woman who sticks with the status quo? Or the woman who takes the leap? And to bring the men back into the equation, who is happier? The dupe who is ejected and forced to re-examine himself and his motivations? Or the equally foolish sucker who is allowed to stay, and remains oblivious to the unhappiness of his partner? Perhaps now it is becoming clearer why a simple discussion of the types of women will not provide any real clarity on this complex subject.

Can we talk about Irene? She decided to stay, to endure. To walk the responsible path. Is she happy? Would she be happier had she left? The answer to the first question is easy—a resounding no. To the second—very uncertain. For now, she's forced to live without any hope for a happier future. Again, here is someone who grasped perhaps one aspect of the road to happiness, reduced expectations, yet failed to blend it with the others.

Or let's have a discussion around Candy. Another who decided to stay, yet she chooses to grab at what she can to make endurance more acceptable. Living for the Now, certainly. Reduced expectations—absolutely. Sticking to principles and not compromising self, well, unfortunately not. And were we to observe her today, I've no doubt she would be either actively seeking her next clandestine tryst, or weeping into her cereal with regret.

Then we can discuss Sophia. After all, she was the impetus for all of this, providing the initial momentum for Ryder's journey of discovery. She found that Ryder no longer fulfilled her needs, made a choice, and refused to compromise. But who can tell—is she really happier now?—or does she long for the good old days, when Ryder was around? Is she able to live in the Now and not feel lonely when she reflects on the past? Were her expectations of life without Ryder realistic? Well, as Ryder's best friend, I must admit that I care not a whit about her happiness, but I do find it interesting to ponder all of this nonetheless.

Okay now we need to talk about Ryder. Over the last few months he has made progress, I will grant him that. And he has discovered the valuable concept of living in the Now, without dwelling on the past or the future. Certainly at least one key ingredient to a happier life, and to this I say, good show old chap. Further, he has at least paid lip service to the idea of never compromising to the point of loss of self. Again, jolly good. Finally, he now has a rudimentary grasp of the concept of setting realistic expectations. Three out of three so far. But, here is where he falls short—he's unable to blend these concepts together. So even while resisting Candy and her advances, he second-guesses himself. He's unable to recognize that by remaining true to his convictions, he's actually travelling along his own path towards enlightenment. Instead, he wakes up this morning bemoaning the missed opportunity, cursing himself for not having seized the moment last night. Is this merely a small blip, or is he backsliding? I was so proud of him for not breaking his own rules, for not acting like a helpless pawn in the Candyland game. But alas, that was then, and we're by no means out of danger.

Last night, he and Candy ill-advisedly exchanged telephone numbers, and now observe: Ryder sits at his desk, frequently checking his phone, looking for a message, deliberating whether to send one of his own. And I know what he's thinking, as I always do, that surely she's longing to see him just as he's longing to see her again. I can see him vacillating, on the verge of creating his own imbroglio. Honestly, if I didn't know better, I would think he makes these messes on purpose.

So what is to be done? How do we move from here to there? From Misery to Happiness? Being in the Now does not mean acting impulsively; reducing expectations does not mean passively allowing life to pass one by. And persisting with moral fortitude—well, that requires an innate confidence to stick with one's principles regardless of temptation (or temptresses). Is this what Ryder's quest is all about? Dare we hope that as Ryder grows and assimilates all of his experiences, he's able to consider all aspects of a situation before choosing a path of action? And then to act, modify expectations, and never go against instincts. The jury is still out, but there is always hope. Are we agreed?

36: Ryder, Knysna, Christmas Day, December

He rounds the corner on foot, his Docksider-clad feet dragging slightly while Jack pulls eagerly ahead. The Knysna yacht club is now directly in front of him, the sun glinting off the modest white building and the surrounding picket fence. The steep imposing cliffs of the Knysna Heads can clearly be seen from the club deck, marking one of the most treacherous entry points into any estuary or river in the whole of Southern Africa. A dangerous outlet to the ocean, the cause of many deaths, with only the most experienced skippers able to take boats out to sea this way. As always, walking alongside the water brings a fragile peace and pleasure to Ryder, despite his generally foul mood.

He leads Jack through the gate and into the small fenced-in area, studiously ignoring the no-dogs-allowed sign. Tied up along the quay are a few small boats, along with the tenders used to access the large yachts anchored farther out. He walks to the water's edge, stares out into the distance, enjoying a vista of Hobie Cats, small canoes and large boats—all with different names, shapes and colors—mostly deserted on this day. Once again, the scattered clouds reflect his unsettled thoughts, refuse to dissipate and mar an otherwise perfect day.

"Ok, fine, I don't have a partner," he mutters. "Or a girlfriend—yes, dammit, I'm all alone again. But even if I did—then what? If marriage is not forever, not until death do we part, then is it even worth entering into a relationship? Why even bother if it will simply end in heartache?"

He looks over at Jack, continues with his muttering.

"Do you know it has been a decade since I got divorced? Yeah, before your time, I know that."

"*And your point?*" Jack stares at him attentively.

"What do I have to show since then, tell me that? Ten years of sequential monogamous affairs, some short, some long. Shit, Jack, some have been great and loving, I know that. But in the end, right now, what do I have left?"

"*Oh please, I hope you're going to spare me the details of the intensity of the sex, the allure of the romance. Is it not enough that I've had to bear witness to some of this in the flesh? No pun intended.*" Jack looks on imploringly.

"It's starting to seem like I'm to entice or be enticed by an endless number of women for the remainder of my life," Ryder continues, now deep in thought. "So is my challenge just to learn how to transition from one woman to the next, with minimal heartache, while keeping my integrity? Go to the doctor for a checkup between times, clean bill of health to present when requested. Is that it? Is that even possible? Or does there always have to be pain and suffering?"

His thin t-shirt flaps loosely as a sudden breeze blows in over the water, clearing the sky almost instantly, and he resolves to put all of this angst from his mind. Looking to his left, he notices how small his shadow is, and then feels how the top of his head is starting to burn.

"Dammit—shoulda brought a hat," he mutters, then begins to look around for something to use as a makeshift water bowl. "Jack, you must be getting thirsty. Come, this way."

"*Yeah, was wondering if you would notice,*" observes Jack, his equanimitous expression betraying nothing of his exasperation as he trots after Ryder to a nearby trough. "*But since you asked, there is always the option of staying single for a while you know. No judgment, naturally, but isn't all this promiscuousness becoming somewhat tiresome?*"

They pause while Jack drinks and Ryder gazes out over the lagoon. At first, he thinks he's imagining it—a fleeting echo coming across the shallow water—but then Jack's ears perk up too, and they both hear the voice calling out.

"Yoo-hoo. Over here. It's me, Candy."

Ryder looks behind him and sees her, just as she stands up in the small dinghy. Her denim shorts and colorful bikini top glimmer in the reflected sunlight as she reaches her arm in the air, vigorously waving him over.

"Well if it isn't Daisy Dukes, bikini on top!" calls out Ryder, as he runs over to the dock, Jack dragging reluctantly behind him.

"*No Ryder, please. What of your resolve? This looks like trouble to me. Let's head home, let's go somewhere else. Oh please don't make me beg.*"

"I knew it was you, Ryder, and I bet you thought you would never see me again!"

"Well, there's thinking I wouldn't, but there was

always hoping I would," Ryder replies enthusiastically. "Wow, Candy, what are you doing here? And what are you doing in that little boat?"

They begin the shouted discussion with so many questions forming in his mind. Isn't she with her family today? Where is that husband? The one she forgot to mention until quite late in the game, the last time they met?

"This little boat? Making my way out to the real thing, of course. Hey, I have an idea. I don't suppose you know how to sail?"

"Are you telling me you have a sailboat?" to which she nods vigorously. "Really? I've been sailing since I was a kid, quite the expert in fact."

Now he bounds across the dock and then he and Jack climb aboard the dinghy. Candy starts up the small motor and they head out into the lagoon. Ryder is thrilled—a chance to go sailing with Candy and possibly revisit a missed opportunity. He willfully puts all resolutions, all thoughts about marriage, fidelity and adultery, aside, as Candy points out her boat in the distance.

"There she is—you can't miss her—a forty-six footer," Candy says as they chug along, closing the distance.

Ryder takes in the black hull, the folded blue mainsail, the generous prow of a large and very expensive boat. And when he spies the name painted across the side, "The Honeymoon Suite", he can barely suppress a giggle. The tender bumps gently up against the sail boat and they drop anchor, then board quickly. Candy opens the main hatch leading down to the large cabin. Fitted with teak and oak, it has a small lounge area next to the captain's chart table and instruments. It can sleep ten easily with two private double-bed-en-suite cabins, one fore and one aft. Ryder whistles, impressed.

"Pass up the winch handles, Ryder, and switch on the battery. Let's get the radio and instruments going. We're going out through the heads. No time to mess around. I checked the weather and the tide table, and the conditions are perfect. We have eight hours to get out and back in again."

"Are you sure? If we don't make it back in on the tide we have to stay out at sea all night," Ryder cautions. "Going out through the heads is no joke, Candy. You have to have an extra engine on board. My friend the harbor master is usually on call for the small fishing boats that go out, and let me tell you, he gets called out a lot. When these boats capsize, the crew can easily drown. A guy died last year exactly that way, and the rescue boat could not get out in time, it all—"

"Afraid?" she asks, at which he stops speaking, then vigorously shakes his head. "Well okay, let's do this," she concludes, indicating that they need to speed things up. They work quickly together, raising and unfurling the genoa, then lifting the anchor. The boat accelerates as the wind catches the sails and the silent powerful gliding machine, fine-tuned for top speed, surges forward. Candy expertly adjusts the sail settings then glances over at Ryder. They smile at each other, mutually aware of their love for the wind and water.

With the boat now stabilized on a starboard tack, they pour drinks and sit in two built-in deck chairs, enjoying the motions and sounds of the water running along the line, from bow to stern. Jack has made his way below and lies curled up on the bunk, enjoying the 800 thread count linen. A dog who knows his place amongst the finer things in life.

Surrounded by the mountains on all sides of this beautiful estuary, Ryder decides to speak aloud the thoughts that have been weighing him down.

"Candy, if we live as serial monogamists," he begins, and then backtracks slightly. "Well, some of us do, I think we covered that already. Really my question is simple: how do we know when to stay, and when to go? When is the right time to transition into a new relationship? Or when to let one die a natural death? Have you ever thought about that?"

"Thought about that—are you kidding?" she says as she looks at him wide-eyed. "That's possibly the only thing I'm able to think about some days, trying to sort out my situation. Serial monogamist huh? Interesting terminology. Look, Ryder, cards on the table, okay?"

"Most definitely," he responds eagerly.

"It's obvious you and I have a sexual attraction. We also have a lot in common, drinking and dancing the other night, sailing today. We're both here in the same town at the same time for various reasons. For all I know they might be similar reasons. Does all this mean we will be able to be together until we die, that you're right for me or me for you? Frankly, I don't really want a full time relationship. Great sex, good company when I want it, that's about all I can handle. I like my own company, would rather be alone than deal with some random guy who claims he fancies me, then runs away. What good would that do me? A few years together, maybe? Leaving me with what, exactly?"

Ryder remains silent, wondering if someone in Candy's past has hurt her deeply, her sentiments mirroring his own so closely. Somehow he knows not to interrupt, and she continues.

"I've learned over many years of marriage with the same person, that there are some things I have control over, and some things which are important to me. That's where I choose to focus my energy. I can't change my husband's attitude and behavior."

She looks over at Ryder now and notices the quizzical look on his face. "No, I can't go into details about any of that now. My husband is a sick man, that's all I can say. Bottom line—he loves me but I don't love him. And, quite honestly, his type of love is incomprehensible to me, acting like he owns me and so many other things I won't talk about. But Ryder I assure you, he knows now it's finally all over. I've empowered myself, and I'm now making my own choices." She looks up at the sails and lets a long breath escape, then focuses on Ryder again.

"Let me explain it another way. I saw how you looked at me last night, how you have been staring at me today—"

"Candy, I can't possibly help it. You know how attracted I am to you," Ryder responds, blushing slightly, but returning her gaze.

"Well, none of what I have comes without hard work, you know. Whether I'm on vacation or not, I have my routine, including hectic workouts at the gym. All of this," she says, sweeping her arm in an indication of the boat, her clothing, her large diamonds in her delicate earlobes, "you have to understand, I work very hard to have it all, to enjoy my life. I love to travel, which costs plenty. And of course I love to shop—let's not discuss the expense there. You know, I resolved very recently—I want what I want, when I want it, and now I intend to have it. All of it. Does that sound selfish to you Ryder?"

"No Candy—I think basically the world is an unhappy place and life is short. Perhaps it's best, as you say, to get on with it."

"Well precisely. The world I cannot control. My husband I cannot control. But my life I can, and I will."

Ryder is stunned into silence. How can he argue with this amazing woman, with her eloquent reasoning and her irresistible body? He knows he need not worry about breaking her heart, feels almost sure he will not allow her to do the same with his. So can he find a way forward with her, at least in this moment? The boat tilts sideways suddenly and rockets off the power of the wind towards the dangerous heads of Knysna. Candy grabs the wheel, he's once again on the main, and together they harness the speed, working in harmony, understanding the precious moments as only true sailors are able.

And suddenly he comprehends it all! He has his answer to Candy, the here and now, with no compromise required. The Ubuntu of the sailing community, controlling the boat but not the wind. And moving as if guided, he integrates all these into the moment, into acceptance that while love, bond, and happiness are not possible with this woman, he does not care. Married or not, she makes her own choices, she has been honest with him, and he will simply seize the moment, and all the rest of the moments they have together.

The sun is setting on the horizon as they return to harbor, with the boat now cruising down to the club, sails folded on the boom. Candy adjusts the radio, selects a mellow jazz tune. The sax wafts along the flat water, lit by the reflection of the dying rays that turn the sky pink and finally a flaming orange. They drop anchor near the club, then make a toast to the here and now.

"Ryder will you run again, now you know my truth?" she asks, approaching him tentatively.

"No, of course not Candy," he says, as he takes a step forward, moves a little closer. She reaches behind her back with her free hand, grasps the strap of her top. And with one quick tug, she loosens it, then removes it over her head and tosses it aside. She stands facing him.

"Or maybe you left so quickly the other night," she says coyly, "because you're just not that attracted to me. Is that it Ryder?"

Ryder groans, the hunger in his eyes apparent to the semi-naked woman before him.

"Candy, you're gorgeous, perfect. Beyond beautiful. How can you even ask if I'm attracted to you? Come here."

He reaches his arms around her, pulls her closer, and then stares into her eyes.

"Tell me, Candy, what are you looking for, what are we doing here? Why are you so interested in me, what...?"

"Ryder, please, I already told you. I'm not looking for anything, only looking for us to enjoy each other. Today, tonight, without thinking beyond that. No more talking, okay?"

She takes his hand and they walk to the pulpit at the bow. The sky darkens and they stand watching the stars brighten in contrast. She's in front of him looking out to the heads, shielded from the town by the mast and sails. He wraps his arms around her waist, then moves his head to the side, kissing the edge of her mouth and then up to her ear. She leans backwards into him and sighs. The warm sea air starts to cool and he looks down over her shoulder, noticing her nipples harden in the slight breeze.

Ryder wonders what her thoughts are, if she wants him as desperately as he wants her, or if she really meant what she said, that she doesn't need a man. Could they actually grow to love each other, or would the fear of lying, cheating, controlling, never allow them to find out? He holds her tighter, feels her skin getting warmer to the touch, and feels dizzy with desire.

Now they allow the alcohol, the incredible view, and the urges of their bodies to take over. No more thinking, no more talking, just feelings, lust in the moment, the culmination of a day filled with meaningful looks, honest conversation, powerful wind and beautiful water. Candy turns around to face him, hastily removing his shirt, and then pulls him over to the mast. She bends down, takes off his shorts and Docksiders, letting her hair brush against his penis, deliberately teasing him. He stands before her, stripped naked, barely able to contain himself. Then she lets him expertly remove her shorts and lift her to the boom, seating her on the canvas sails. They kiss for hours, both wet now from the day and the night.

"All I want is you Candy," he says. "But just for as long as you like, then I will let you go. To be the free powerful woman you are."

He lets his hands travel slowly down her belly, then begins exploring her deeply with his fingers. She feels him on her inner wall, how he easily finds and then begins probing and pressing against that spot, driving her to the edge of orgasm then retreating, over and over. Finally she cries out as she explodes, her juices soaking his hand and the sail. Then she grasps desperately for his hard head, pulling his throbbing cock deep inside of her. They stay embraced and locked together, thrusting, breathing, groping and kissing until they come together. Then they stand together, supported by the sail, naked and exhausted, warming and shielding each other from the wind.

Ryder glances around, relieved in more ways than one that Jack is nowhere to be seen. And yet, for those who are attuned, his cynical opinion is very much in evidence.

"Oh good grief. Can you believe it, Ryder out there, now seeking true love with Candy? Oh sure, he's going to steam up a few windows, wrinkle a few sheets, no need to alert the news media. But we're talking momentary gratification, when he claims to be seeking a true bond. And surely he knows all of this—even a meeting of the minds, along with the merging of flesh, does not substitute for real love. C'mon Ryder—time to get with the program."

37: Ryder, Knysna, Boxing Day a.m. December

Jack looks up from his bowl, a perturbed expression on his face.

"What is it, Boy?" Ryder asks, a minute before he hears the banging outside.

"Police. *Maak oop* (Open up)."

He rushes to the door, barefoot and dressed only in his boxers, and peeks through the peephole. Outside stand two policemen, both stocky, both sporting buzz cuts. One white, one black, both with stern expressions on their faces. Koos and Klaas, sent to investigate another dead-end case.

"One minute," he says as he fumbles with the lock, convinced they have simply come to the wrong address. He pulls the door open.

"Yes, officers? What seems to be the problem?"

The two officers push in, one on either side of Ryder. He turns around, follows them as they look around. Then he walks behind them as they make their way towards the window on the far side of the room.

"Perhaps you would like to take a seat?" he asks, but they shake their heads, seemingly in unison.

"*Ons soek* (we are looking for)... *askies* (sorry)... we're looking for Demi Rodgers. This is her address, right?" asks Koos.

"Well, she doesn't live here anymore. We—"

"Describe the whereabouts of your wife, *Meneer* (Sir)," demands Klaas as he takes a notepad out of his pocket. He fishes out the stub of a pencil, then licks the tip.

"Wait, so you're here about Demi? Why are you asking?"

"*Meneer*," says Koos sternly. "We ask you the questions, *verstaan* (understand)? Where is this Demi? We understand she's your wife, says so on this warrant."

"Uh no, she is, or was, my girlfriend, not my wife. But she moved out, she doesn't live here."

"Well, then, whose gym bag is this *Meneer*? This looks like it belongs to a woman." Klaas picks up the duffel bag that has been lying neatly in the corner ever since Ryder brought it home from the television training academy. With difficulty, he carries it over to the center of the room, places it on the coffee table.

"No, that belongs to my ex-girlfriend. I've been—"

"Oh, so it is Demi's? Your ex-girlfriend, Demi," he explains patiently to Ryder who seems momentarily confused.

"No, no. Another ex. Look at the monogram—see that stitching on the top? There is no D for Demi. That bag belongs to my ex, Sophia Magnusson. See—SM."

"So, Sophia is your ex-girlfriend?" asks Klaas, making a note on his little pad. Ryder nods.

"And—Demi is your ex-girlfriend also?" asks Koos. Again Ryder nods, and another note is made.

It is at this moment that Candy emerges from the bathroom, a small towel wrapped expertly around her, revealing everything and nothing at the same time.

"Ryder, who was at the door... oh, excuse me. What is going on?" she asks.

"*Jisses*, man," exclaims Koos. "Now who is this? Another ex-girlfriend?"

"Ryder, are you in some sort of trouble?" asks Candy. "Why are there two policemen in your flat?"

"Relax, Candy, all a misunderstanding I'm sure. Look," Ryder attempts to explain to the cops. "Demi did live here, but no more. We were never married. And now she's gone, moved out. I don't know where. This bag is not hers."

"Then you won't mind if we look inside it?" asks Klaas.

"Go ahead—take the bloody bag with you for all I care," says Ryder, fed up by now. "As I said, it's not mine."

"*Ja, ja*. Belongs to your other ex-girlfriend. We're not *doff (*stupid). Now Mam, what is your name?" asks Koos, as he eagerly turns his attention to Candy. Ryder attempts to stand between him and Candy, shielding her, but Koos is surprisingly quick on his feet and deftly veers around Ryder, then moves in closer for a better look.

Klaas mumbles "*Miskien* (maybe) just call her ex-girlfriend number three, *ja?*"

As Candy is about to reply, Ryder's phone rings. They all turn and stare at it as it buzzes and vibrates across the coffee table. A picture of Izzie appears on the phone along with the caller id.

"*Ag*—another ex-girlfriend I'm sure," says Koos.

"No, no—this is my assistant. I can just let it ring, go to voice mail—"

"No, no *Meneer*, please—answer it. *Asseblief* (please). We want to hear this," says Klaas, a small grin beginning now as he stands with his arms folded across his chest.

Ryder picks up the phone, then listens for a few minutes. The others in the room can only hear sounds of crying and gulping on the far end, providing no clue as to the topic of conversation. They wait in silence for him to finish.

"Look, calm down," Ryder says, as he rubs his head and paces up and down in front of his attentive audience. "I'm sure whatever it is, it's not your fault. C'mon, I can't understand what you're saying. Please, don't get so upset; we can talk later when you have calmed down, okay? I'm sure everything will be all right. Look, I'm kinda busy right now, Izzie—"

At this, Koos nudges Klaas and says "Got his hands full, *neh*?", and they both snicker.

"I'll see you at work. Sorry I can't help. Bye now."

He hangs up, then turns to the cops. "Women—what can I say?" he says as he shrugs. Now Candy excuses herself to go get dressed, and Koos stares wistfully at her naked back as she leaves the room.

"*Meneer—wat doen jy*? (Mister, what do you do?)" He asks. "All these women. *Jissis*. We're going to go now, but maybe we can come back some day, maybe you can learn us how you do it?"

"Wait—do you want this bag?" Ryder asks as they make their way towards the door.

"*Nee* man, you keep it," says Klaas waving a hand dismissively. Ryder hears them mumbling to each other as they walk down the steps:

"Bloody tall guys—they get all the girls. Well, that *oke* is going to need some of that Viagra stuff if he doesn't watch out."

"*Ja*—you should know about that," says Koos as they retreat towards their car.

Ryder shuts the door behind them, then stands shaking his head. *Oh Demi*, he thinks, *I told you no good would come of your fancy financial footwork. You should have listened to me, and to Farrell. But why did you tell everyone you were married to me? Another headache I don't need! Just after recovering from emotional havoc. Now you almost got me embroiled in financial havoc. And criminal havoc too!*

He sighs deeply, acknowledging that his time with Demi was poorly planned, badly executed.

From now on, he decides, *I will think before I act. I will not get involved when my head tells me otherwise.*

With this thought in mind he heads into the bedroom, where he finds Candy buttoning up her shirt.

"Do you have to leave so soon?" he asks as he wraps his arms around her. "Maybe you have to go meet your husband?"

"No Ryder—for you I have all day," she answers as she places her hands on either side of his face. "Listen, let's just pretend the last fifteen minutes never happened, okay? Can we do that?"

"Fine by me," he replies, as he begins unbuttoning where she has just buttoned. "Fine by me."

38: Ryder, Knynsa, Boxing Day p.m. December

The sun is just beginning its descent in the west, and Ryder estimates they have another few hours of daylight, what with this being the middle of summer. He props himself up on one elbow, reaches over and strokes Candy's hair with his free hand. She lies back on the pillow and shuts her eyes.

"Let's take a picnic to the beach," he suggests. "We can sit on a blanket, get nice and cozy. I'll bring a nice bottle of wine, and we can watch the sunset together."

He's eager to prolong his time with her, nervous she's about to leave. Is she ready to go back to her other life, perhaps not exactly to the point she left off, but without Ryder?

"I'm not sure," she answers. "Perhaps we should talk about—"

"Hold that thought," Ryder says as he turns to pick up his ringing phone. "Hmm—unknown caller—wonder who this is now. Hello?"

"*Meneer, dis ons* (it's us). The police, from this *oggend*, ah, this morning."

"I see, you again. Okay, now what is it?" he replies,

while rolling his eyes.

He covers the speaker with his hand, and mouths "Those cops from earlier, Tweedledumb and Tweedledumber—" to Candy.

"*Meneer*, we're at your place of business, your television academy. A bit of a situation here. Do you know a woman named Izzie, and her boyfriend Webster?"

"Yes, yes I know them. She works for me. What situation—is there a problem?" Ryder is becoming concerned now. He throws off the sheets, stands up and starts getting dressed, holding the phone between his cheek and his ear. "What—please, this makes no sense. Hold on, I'm not following. Look, I'm on my way over. I'll be there in less than five minutes."

He pulls on his shoes hurriedly, while Candy looks on quizzically.

"Twice in one day with the cops, Ryder. What is this all about? It can't be good—"

"I'm not sure. Those guys—I couldn't understand what they were on about. Look, Candy, it's probably nothing serious, something to do with the staff at my business. There's always some drama. I have no idea why they want me over there, but I better—"

"Ryder, I thought I was the one who needed to sort her life out; now it looks like perhaps you need to do the same. Probably best if I just go—the two of us together is just going to multiply our troubles. Bad timing between us, I'm sure that's it. Maybe we will see each other again, sometime in the future. Or call me when all of this business is settled. Go, go see what's up—you better hurry. I'll let myself out."

Ryder leans over for one last kiss, then races out the door.

"You'll be hearing from me, soon," he yells over his shoulder, but already his mind is racing. What now, what could the problem possibly be? The academy is essentially closed for the holidays, with the possibility of never reopening again. Why the drama—what could be going on?

He speeds out of the parking lot, veers left towards the main road. Another quick left and there is the school, half a mile away down the hill and off to the right. But then he sees the fire trucks, and the black smoke pouring from the windows. He screeches to a halt next to the front door and between the two police vehicles, then jumps out of his car. The police trot behind him as he rushes indoors, filling him in as he looks over the ransacked interior. He sees the open cabinets with the contents strewn and smashed all over the floor, as well as the obvious signs of forced entry at the back door. Then he notices the empty petrol cans strewn in the fields just a few meters away, visible through the smoke-streaked and broken windows. Obviously this fire was intentional, no accident. On his desk, in his now-destroyed office, are the charred remains of a note, addressed to Webster and Izzie. Still visible is the shaky handwriting, the barely literate demands. "Give my monee back Webster!", as well as the unambiguous threat "I can still make more and worser things happen."

"This makes no sense," he says, as much to himself as to the police, who once again stand before him with pad and pencil in hand. And once again he runs his hands over his bald head, trying to puzzle things out. "Izzie has no money, I know that for sure. Webster—well, he doesn't strike me as one who is loaded either. But why my academy, why my business?"

"*Meneer*, where were you this afternoon? *Ag ja*—I think we know—" Koos, or is this Klaas, seems to recall the scene earlier in the day. Is he actually suppressing a smirk or is that Ryder's imagination?

"I'm sure you have an ex-girlfriend who can vouch for your whereabouts, right? Never mind, we know who did this; you're not a suspect. Caught him fleeing the scene. He's ranting about some missing money—hundreds of thousands of pounds, he says. And he seems to think this is Webster's business, or was before he destroyed it."

"What, who is this guy? And what thousands of pounds—I don't see any money here, do you? What about Izzie, is she okay?" Ryder pulls out his phone, tries calling her number, but gets her voicemail immediately.

"We think the two of them, Izzie and Webster, are long gone by now, *Meneer*. Most probably with the money. We tried picking them up, but their place is empty. Only their phones left lying on the counter."

After much further discussion, Ryder leaves and drives back home slowly. He puzzles over the missing money, wondering where it came from, where it went. But without more information, he's at a loss. He concludes that Izzie and Webster have indeed absconded, and that they will enjoy spending the money in some foreign country. And hopefully he will never hear from either one of them again. Then he thinks about his situation—so much time and energy spent agonizing over the future of this floundering business, when suddenly in one flash all is decided for him. Closed, permanently, no more vacillating and hand wringing. Yes, with things burned to the ground, the shared dream does seem to have come to a definitive end, the final bond with Sophia erased forever. And he can't help it; a feeling of relief starts to overtake him.

"Good bye and good riddance, forever," he thinks. "Time to plan for a bright future, free of any ties to the past."

And although it is now dark outside, he sees his path with a sudden clarity. He knows he's finally free to leave Knysna, free of his self-imposed exile and free of any business-related responsibilities. He sits up a little straighter, feeling a great weight gone from his shoulders. He walks into his small apartment, sees Jack waiting eagerly by the door.

"Good boy, Jack. Ready for another adventure, are you? Yes, it's time—we will be leaving here. Very soon. You and me and the open road—once again."

39: Ryder, Knysna, late December

Once again he closes the simple wooden door, locks it with a quick twist and then examines the key in his hand. No need for any messages, subtle or otherwise, this time. He walks to the Lexus, looking with both appreciation and wistfulness at the blue-green estuary visible from the path. He climbs in as Jack takes his place in the back along with Ryder's clothes, bedding and family pictures. On the front seat there is a camera, a laptop, and a thin personal file, with the rest of his possessions handed on to charities over the past few days. No more need for the excess baggage accumulated this past year.

"Jackie, my boy, the thing about life is that if we're forced to travel, travel light," he says as he buckles up. "In fact, an even better idea—live light. Yes, I know, the future is once again uncertain, but this time, no tears, no bad vibes, no heaviness. The past is past, the future is unknown, all we have is right here right now. Kinda refreshing you know, starting over with a blank check. Anyway, no point in railing against what is, rather accept it all—the moment, the choices, the location, the emotions."

"That's what I'm saying, Ryder. Just rolling with the punches,

that's us."

The Lexus glides down the winding road, and he gazes for the last time at the Knysna heads in the distance. Already he feels nostalgic, thinking of the past good times shared with Farrell, Irene, Demi and Candy here in Knysna.

"Jack," he continues, looking in the rearview mirror at his trusty companion. "Two quick stops on our way out, and then it's just you and me, back on the road again."

He pulls in front of the small police station, runs in to pick up some paperwork waiting for him at the front entrance.

"Meneer, meneer," he hears across the deserted station. *"Hoe gaan dit* (how are you)—is everything ok with you, and with all of your women?"

He looks over and sees Koos walking towards him with his hand outstretched, a big smile on his face.

"Ah Koos—just stopped by quickly, finally moving on," he replies, pausing to shake hands. "So you're on duty today then? Pretty slow around here."

"Ja, lucky I have this to read, fascinating stuff," replies Koos as he shows him the cover of the book he holds in his left hand.

"'Killing for Profit'? What's this all about—looks like a heavy-going book—"

"All about the rhino poaching industry, *Meneer*, interesting and scary. *Ja, ja*, I know there are no rhino here in Knysna," he says, waving his hand. "Klaas keeps reminding me of that, but we do have a few elephants at the local park and hiding in the forests, real shy, *jy weet* (you know). I'm sure you've heard about that—you can take a walk next to the elephants here, even touch them. But *Meneer*, you should read this book, learn all about the poachers. Here, take this copy, a farewell gift."

"No, please, I couldn't," protests Ryder, but to no avail.

"*Meneer*, everyone should know about this—now I insist. You're going where the action is, right? I'll tell you right now, my dream is to save the rhino, to help put an end to this poaching. So if you hear of anyone who needs a good cop, to help with that sort of work, tell them about me. The book is to make sure you remember me. *Tot siens, Meneer*, and remember—"

"*Ja, ja*, drive safe and obey the speed limit, got it. And thanks!" replies Ryder as he walks back to his car, climbs in and places the book on the front passenger seat.

"Well that was weird," he says, as much to himself as to Jack. "Now on to meet Farrell for a quick farewell lunch. And honestly, don't know why I am even bothering. I spend all this time discussing my ideas with him, my thoughts about love, happiness and bond, but I'm convinced it goes in one ear and out the other. And asking him his opinion about these things—I would be better off asking Koos and Klaas to weigh in!"

40: Ryder, Knysna,
Late December

Ryder continues on his way, driving now away from the police station and towards the middle of the town. He reaches behind the seat, pats Jack reassuringly on the head.

"Perhaps you're wondering what I think of Farrell, or indeed of all of your friends in this crazy town, Ryder? No? Well, perhaps I should tell you anyway. I believe there is not a lick of common sense amongst that whole motley crew. Demi, Farrell, Irene, Wendell, Jill, Duane, they all only add to the general mayhem, especially when you misguidedly ask them for their imprudent advice. Good friends, perhaps, but unlikely to help you navigate around any dangerous rocks, or even assist you once shipwrecked against said rocks. Of course, that is just my opinion. I suppose I could be wrong, but that does seem unlikely."

With summer at its peak, the single main road is slow and filled with traffic. As Ryder approaches the square at the center, he drives more slowly, watching for pedestrians walking with car keys in hand. Then outside the post-and-print shop he sees the familiar weathered car guard who waves him in to an available spot. He thinks of the old clothes, towels and food items he usually keeps on hand to donate to this old man, realizing he has none of that with him today.

"*Dag se meneer, gaan dit goed (*good day sir, everything going well)?" asks the old guy.

"*More* (good morning), *ja goed* (yes good), thank you. *Dankie*," Ryder replies.

He thinks quickly about what he can part with this time, his worldly goods packed securely in the trunk and back seat of his car, with the few bags he intends to leave with Farrell for storage in the front under the dash. Then he remembers Sophia's duffel bag, included in that front collection. He decides he will give this to the guard when he returns after lunch.

"*Ek het iets for you—vir die parking diens* (I have something for you—for the parking service). I'll be back— *terug kom*—in one hour. Okay?"

"*Ja meneer, ek sal hier wag (*I'll wait here)," the guard answers patiently. "*Ek sal jou roep* (I'll call you) if I see the cops, okay?"

"*Dankie, dankie,*" Ryder says, while silently congratulating himself for solving two problems at once. With the duffel off of his hands, he need never contact Sophia again. One thing less to worry about as he begins his return trip to Cape Town.

He wanders across the street to the chosen restaurant, Jack on his leash and following at his heels. The location is perfect, overlooking Memorial Square, a small stone column in the town center surrounded by a small semi-circle fenced-in garden. Ryder is led to a table set far back in a secluded corner; it is covered with a long white cloth, and a small water bowl for Jack is tucked under one of the chairs.

The patio has umbrellas scattered about, assisting where the shade from the nearby trees is insufficient. Crystal glasses, heavy silverware and serviettes in pewter rings resting on delicate china plates complete the classic setting. He leans back, facing the street, and indulges in one of his favorite pastimes, watching the passing foot and vehicle parade. He's alone again, on the move again, and determined to absorb the last bit of the atmosphere of this place he has called home. Startled, he realizes that he has spent exactly nine months in Knysna, and he begins to wonder at the significance. Long enough for a rebirth, he concludes. His thoughts are interrupted by the chirping of his newly-upgraded smartphone. Somehow he's hardly surprised when he recognizes the number on the display.

"Farrell—where are you? Not getting any younger, waiting here for you—"

"Sorry *Boet* (Brother) can't make it," comes the reply. Now he tunes Farrell out, hearing the faint blah blah bah as he reflects that this broken engagement is symbolic of all the pleasant but unreliable relationships he has formed with the local town-folk.

"Ah, don't sweat it Farrell," he says. "But you remember I'm leaving some stuff with you, right? I was supposed to give you a few bags to hold on for me at lunch. I'll just leave them for you here, okay? No, I must leave today, the open road is calling me. Anyway, now you know for sure we'll meet up again, if only for me to get my stuff back."

They hang up, Farrell promising to call later while Ryder is on his lengthy drive, although Ryder already knows he won't. A disappointing way to leave town, he thinks, but then he determines to make the most of this farewell lunch. He treats himself to a three-egg smoked salmon omelet on rye, signals for a refill for Jack. A fine meal, sitting in the dappled sunlight watching beautiful women, is not such a bad way to say farewell to Knysna, he concludes. By turns bemused and wistful, he watches the tourists wander by with map in hand, looking confused despite the small town layout with essentially only one main road.

He picks up the book that Koos gave him and reads the back cover. Greed, corruption, depravity and ruthless criminal enterprise. Written by an award-winning investigative journalist, the book lays bare the illegal rhino horn trade. Ryder is reminded of the last time he saw a rhino on an early-morning walk at the Kruger National Park. From just twenty meters away, he and the rest of their small ranger-led walking group watched a rhino mother and baby thunder past. The rhino had gotten wind of their group and was panicking, trying to get away and keep her baby safe. She had stopped and peered at the group, unseeing despite her closeness. Ryder recalls his rapid heartbeat and the slight tremble of his hands as he hurriedly took a picture, excited and afraid from the proximity to the magnificent, prehistoric-looking creature. As he reads the disturbing statistics in the book, he sadly realizes that if the current trends continue, his descendants will never have that same exhilarating experience.

Then he lifts his eyes from the book cover to see a pretty dark-haired woman walking past wearing a short skirt, a large hat and sunglasses shielding her face from the sun. Her low-cut tank outlines her perfectly shaped breasts while revealing her generous cleavage.

Boob job, he evaluates effortlessly, turning his head to watch as she walks gracefully on her extra-high heels, her hips swinging provocatively. He stares at the well-defined calf and thigh muscles, then allows his eyes to travel upwards to her toned rear and slim shoulders.

Just my type, well-groomed, well-heeled, muscular gym-bunny. And apparently interested in nice cars, he thinks, as he notices her looking at his Lexus parked across the street. He's tempted to walk over, introduce himself. Perhaps make a joke or two—that always seems to work.

Cut it out, he admonishes himself. *Just enjoy your lunch, relax and take in the sunshine. You're on your way out of town after this; just let this one go.*

Distracted now, he thinks about how sexy he finds women in heels, wonders if they realize this. If Farrell were here, they would discuss this further, perhaps even wax philosophical about how those heels have walked all over the pair of them, all their adult lives. Out of the corner of his eye he notices the woman in question turn, looking around, and he guesses she's meeting someone. Her husband or her boyfriend, he supposes, now relieved he did not go over there and try make small talk. He turns his attention to the table as the waitress brings out his omelet, and he cuts off a piece, pausing to inhale before bringing the fork to his mouth. Then he's startled by a tap on his shoulder, and he looks up. There she is, the brunette from the street, and she has removed her hat, moved her sunglasses to the top of her head.

"Candy, wow, it's you," is all he can think to say. "Amazing! You look incredible as always, a feast for these tired eyes. I had no idea you were still in town. Where are you going—please say you'll join me for lunch?"

He rises from his chair and pulls out the one beside it but she stands there, unmoving, grinning at him, unspoken words swirling between them. Then she reaches around his neck with her arms, hugs him hard while pressing herself tightly into him. This again, he thinks helplessly, yes please, this again. They cannot resist each other, yet today he knows they must. They exchange a secret glance, acknowledging their mutual arousal.

"I saw your car across the street, knew you had to be here somewhere. What are you doing, Ryder—watching the girls go by? See, I hardly know you, yet I know you so well!"

"And I you, Candy, my delicious Candy. But bad news for us, I'm afraid. I'm leaving town now, today. Packed up and on my way."

"Well then I best join you for your last Knysna meal," she says as she sits down in the offered seat.

Ah Farrell, he offers up silently, *thank you, thank you, for standing me up!*

The waiter brings over an extra plate, and he divides his omelet into two, orders Candy a drink. With their legs hidden from view beneath the cloth, Candy kicks off her heels, then begins rubbing the back of Ryder's calf with her soft foot. He takes her left hand, looks at her ringless fingers. Her nails are perfectly manicured, as he knows her to be all over. He lifts the hand to his mouth, gently bites her thumb and leaves a kiss. Now she holds his hand, guides it down onto her leg, after which she adjusts the table cloth so both their hands are hidden. She moves their hands together to the edge of her skirt, squirms to allow it to ride up higher on her thighs. And she guides his hand so it follows her skirt, then pushes it along to rest on the inside of her smooth upper thigh. Now she crosses her legs, squeezes hard, immobilizing his hand where it lies. He longs to inch his fingers up just a little farther, just a little closer. He feels her warmth and dampness so close to his hand; she leans forward, gently stroking his cheek. Again she stares into his eyes, and he groans.

"Ryder, you have not touched your lunch. Don't tell me I'm making you lose your appetite. Tell me—what do you think about the weather this afternoon?" she asks coyly, then lifts her water glass which is dripping with condensation. She runs it slowly down her cheek, then across her upper chest. "Is it just me or is it awfully hot out here?"

"Ah Candy, Candy. I'm going to miss you so. Dammit—our timing has been off, hasn't it?" he responds feebly.

As the lunch proceeds, Candy squirms closer to him, but pulls away each time he leans forward. Eventually he puts down his fork and gives up on the omelet, opting instead to stare into Candy's eyes.

"What is it about you, Candy? We're not going to end up together, we both know that, and yet I feel like I could sit here with you all day. Even on a day like today, when I'm on my way out of town. You're so ... well, complicated.

Why do we do this, anyway, make things so much more difficult for ourselves?"

"Do you think perhaps instead what you would like is a nice, simple woman? I'm sure that would satisfy your craving for—what is it you told me—love, happiness, bond. A plain uncomplicated yet perfect BLH sandwich."

"You know why that wouldn't work for me, Candy. Because a simple woman would not look like you, dress like you, act like you. Wear heels like you do—"

"So be honest about what you're really looking for, Ryder, just admit it. You're not looking for BLH, you're looking for a quick roll in the hay with an attractive woman. Should I see if the hotel across the street has a room available?"

"C'mon Candy, that's not fair. It's more than that between us. But yes, you're driving me wild here—tell me about what you have on under that skirt—"

"Here, let me get just a little closer," Candy says, a naughty grin overtaking her face. Then she uncrosses her legs, freeing his hand to explore a little farther, a little higher up her leg.

"Why Candy," he says, feigning shock as he realizes. "Is this how you left the hotel this morning? Good thing it isn't windy—"

"Yes, isn't it though," she responds, her eyes glazing over and her breath sharpening as he moves his fingers, exploring slowly. "Um, what were we—"

"Ah, so you can't concentrate now either," he murmurs as he leans forward, this time kissing her willing lips with his.

"*Meneer, mevrou*—if you're done—there is a queue of people waiting for this table." The waitress is standing blocking their view of the square, tapping her pencil impatiently against her order pad. "Please—I need you to pay up. Before I go on break."

"So this is it," Candy says, as she scoots her chair back, then stands up. She adjusts her skirt, smooths it over her rear. "Safe travels Ryder. Hope you have something pleasant to think about on the long drive."

She turns on her high heels, blows him a kiss. Then she walks away, exaggeratedly swaying her hips. Ryder watches helplessly, then extracts a few notes from his wallet and places them on the table.

"C'mon Jack," he murmurs. "I guess we better get going now."

Yet another strange encounter, to add to a rather lengthy list accumulated in his time in Knysna. This time he starts to feel anxious and frustrated, a dangerous mix, almost tempting him to stop in and say a final goodbye to Innocent. A proper farewell, complete with a round or two.

Instead, he walks back to his car, breathes deeply in and out a few times, focusing on his surroundings. The street, the sun, the fresh air. Then he opens the door, and climbs in with Jack, trying to push the dispirited feelings away and recapture the lightness of the moment from just a short while ago.

He starts up the engine, turns on the air conditioning and cranks up the stereo. *Loud music will distract me*, he thinks, as he makes his way out of the lot and back around the corner, not noticing the old wizened guard staring disappointedly after him. He pulls up in front of the restaurant, drops off the few bags for Farrell with the maître d', then drives off with screeching tires.

41: Ryder, Knysna to Buffels Bay, late December

On a day like today, unsettled as I am by the morning's events, it's a good thing this car can virtually steer itself along this familiar road. I glance in the rearview mirror at Jack, once again ensconced on the back seat, comfortable atop my favorite comforter.

"What? Don't look at me like that. This is all your doing Ryder, nothing I could have controlled. We stopped, we had lunch. So far, so good. We were all packed, ready to go. You were resolved, resolute. Is it my fault Farrell called and cancelled? Really, are you even surprised—he probably had one too many, a liquid breakfast."

I put on my sunglasses, readjust my mirror, and then curse angrily at the driver who veers around me, attacking the winding road with reckless speed. Jack raises his head, seems to grunt his disapproval as well.

"Now look, please don't remind me—I know I made a pledge of sorts just a short month ago, to be non-judgmental, your supportive Best Friend. Yes, yes, whatever. I'm sure I will regain this lost ground at some point, but it's hard to avoid some critical thoughts about you and your situation here, Ryder."

I glance out of the left window, remember suddenly about the car guard.

"Dammit, forgot to give him that stupid bag," I think, or possibly say out loud. "So now Farrell will be hanging on to it for no good reason."

"Yes, well, look at you, all hot and bothered, definitely disturbed. You virtually staggered to your car after lunch, all thoughts of that poor car guard banished from your head. Is this how you thank him for a year's worth of service? Perhaps you didn't see him watch in amazement as you simply drove past? Well, that's because you were too busy staring at cool, calm, collected Candy waving from across the street."

The car easily holds the curves as we continue on the beautiful drive, the N2 that runs all the way from Knysna to Cape Town. Over here, the road runs alongside the lagoon on the left, with the hills on the right. Farther on, the lagoon will be replaced by the ocean, and a series of lakes will replace the hills on the right. I'm forcing myself to cruise in the moment, take in the natural beauty, yet I feel the emotional whirlwind begin. To hell with those drinking and driving laws—I place the figurative cognac glass in the foot well where I can glance down at it, use it to keep me calm.

"Watch it, separate it out and away from the pit of your stomach," I coach myself. "Yes, push it out to the glass, just observe it, and let it swirl out there. Now breathe deeply, no need to keep any of it inside right now. Nothing will change on this drive, just let it go. "

I imagine the whirling contents of this emotional dervish, now transferred to the glass and outside of me, and I feel instantly calmer. I can now concentrate on the road snaking over the Knysna River Bridge, then up the hill past the upmarket, secluded suburb of Belvedere. I can even see the famous old church there on the lagoon side, a popular wedding spot for international visitors.

On an impulse, I decide to head towards Buffels Bay, named for the Water Buffalo that used to rest in the Goukamma or "fat water" river on hot summer days.

"What do you say, Jack? How about a stop-over? We have no time constraint, no people waiting for us. Freedom, right?"

"Or possibly nothing left to lose. Oh what the heck—sure, I'm game. Anything you say Ryder."

I turn left and head down the narrow side road, under the railway bridge. Jack gazes out the window in the direction of The Deck, a riverside wooden restaurant with canoes and paddle boats for hire.

"Wait—can't we stop here for bobotie? You know you want to—served in a traditional tin dish, with all the trimmings. C'mon Ryder—it's your favorite! I can smell it from here, my mouth is watering already. Ah too bad, now you've missed the turn-off."

The SanPark Goukamma reserve, our spur-of-the moment destination, lies along the eastern boundary where the river and the sea meet. We cross the entry boom of this unspoiled spot, and Jack bounds into the front seat, then sits comfortably in my lap.

"Well yes, I think a stop here might be best after all. Don't think I haven't noticed you shifting about uncomfortably in your seat, trying to stay in the moment, trying not to dwell on your usual issues. Love, happiness, bond, Ryder, or is that lust, horniness, breasts? Ah poor thing, you never stood a chance, you know that. You were simply a pawn, flung about by the random actions of that wanton woman."

I pull up to the three well-appointed bungalows perched on the hill overlooking the river and reserve, and find the caretaker outside, repairing a canoe.

"Hello—remember me? I've stayed here many times before, with my girlfriend, uh, now ex-girlfriend, and also—" I begin, then stop, not willing to revisit the different times and different partners I've brought out here in the past. "Any chance you have a cottage open for the night?" I inquire instead.

After making the necessary arrangements, I enter one of the little thatched bungalows and put a few selected belongings on the bed. Then I hurriedly change into my trunks, grab the book given to me by Koos and wrap it in the beach towel provided. I put them both inside a plastic bag along with my camera, and with Jack at my heels I make my way rapidly to the river. I select a canoe from the small collection, pull it out into the water. I climb aboard, place my small bag on the seat in front of me and the paddle across my lap.

"Well," I yell at Jack. "What are you waiting for?"

"Yes, what indeed. Best I go along, if only for your protection."

Jack bounds into the shallow water, leaps up on the canoe, then stands with his paws on my lap. He stares into my eyes, licks my cheek.

"So, are we headed upstream, to the hills and trees? That way, we can have a peaceful afternoon, usually not a soul in sight out there. You can read that book you brought along. Maybe I owe you an apology, Ryder, for having failed to protect you from so many sticky situations. All these beguiling bitches, sidetracking you from your self-absorbed misery and depression. But really, all it seems to take is some

attention from one of them, and then it's off to the races. And the next sweet distraction could well be lying just around that corner, so it's best I come along with you now. Frailty thy name is woman, and so forth. Let's push off then, shall we?"

I shift the canoe, pointing it towards the mouth of the river a few miles away. Jack turns, panting, then moves to the front of the American-Indian–style vessel.

"Ah to the shallow pans of water at the vlei (inlet) then. Let's have some fun, swimming and wallowing at the intersection of the river and the ocean. The water should be nice and warm from the sun at this time of day. But please, no splashing with that paddle, there's a good fellow. I don't care for the water in my eyes. And I dare say, after the activities, you'll be willing to relax and watch the sunset under the thatch-roofed patio, back at the bungalow. Perhaps we can have a small braai, Ryder? I'll take mine medium rare, thank you kindly."

I can sense the huge forests out away from the river and closer to the road, the lush pine trees benefitting from the mild climate here.

As I get into the rhythm of paddling, I feel my body working from the core. Left, right, left, right. I sway slightly, balancing the movement of object and person with the slow-flowing river. The water laps gently against the sides of the canoe, and the sun warms my face and back. As the heat builds, I stop paddling and remove my shirt, letting the canoe glide gently along the course, propelled by the pull of the retreating tide. I glance backwards at the ripples left in my wake, realizing anew that by concentrating on the motion, smells, sounds, and sights, I've shifted my focus, allowing me to embrace the blessings of this wondrous place. Even Jack's expression seems altered, his normally cheeky face relaxed and somehow approving. I feel connected, whole, at peace again.

After drifting for some time, we reach the end of the river, where the large tidal pools stop short of the sea. I climb out of the canoe, hearing the waves crashing on the beach, seeing them from the shallow water. I pull the canoe to the bank, then retrieve the *SanPark Times*, a small newspaper wedged beneath the seat by the previous occupant. I walk out onto the sand, sit and begin reading with Jack lying close beside me.

More information about rhino poaching, this time as it affects the Kruger National Park, with its porous border with Mozambique. I read with astonishment of the complexity of the problem, the multiple battlefronts that have opened up. At any given time, there are at least twelve poaching groups active in the park, with up to eighty armed incursions per month. The number of rhino slain in the park alone, for the calendar year, is over five hundred. With more than two million hectares to patrol, the park would need two thousand rangers for adequate enforcement, yet currently only five hundred are employed. Apart from the obvious lack of funding and training, the logistic issues of housing and feeding mean that these resources would be next to impossible to obtain. I read further of the psychological strain on these poor rangers, caught in a losing battle with a violent enemy armed with rifles capable of downing large elephants. It is all too clear—the Kruger Park sits at the exact intersection of supply and demand. The last large remnant of all the rhino in the world; severe poverty; international traffic; huge amounts of money from foreigners convinced that a gram of rhino horn will cure all their ills; corrupt regional and national governments and officials; skillful trained sharp-shooters left over from the days of military strife along the border. Without a systemic approach calling all parties to the table, there can be no hope for any resolution. Time is of the essence as the rhino population dwindles every year.

With the awareness from the river still reverberating through my senses, I start to wonder: could embracing this issue, one that captures my time, my mind, and most of all my heart, keep me grounded, centered, living in the now? Is it possible that this newspaper appeared here as some sort of cosmic sign, and that now my murky path is emerging in clearer focus, around this desperate cause? I rummage in the plastic bag, pull out the book from Koos, and continue reading while Jack slumbers at my side.

42: Ryder, Garden Route, late December

So what is it about this drive along the Garden Route that moves me so intensely? No matter the weather or my mood, the vistas around each bend in the road are guaranteed to leave me breathless. Wherever I pull over, to pause and stare out over the cliffs, ocean and horizon, the majesty overwhelms me. The sun can be rising or setting, or seemingly sitting perfectly still up there in the sky, and I'm filled with wonder, knowing I'm traversing the most beautiful place on the earth. The aptly named Garden of Eden. And today, on this particular voyage, I realize that there is no longer any serpent, any apple, or any wrath to contend with.

It's true, over the past few years, the drive had become a chore: back and forth, forth and back; Cape Town to Knysna; Knysna to Cape Town. Really, I spent so much time in my car, it seems fitting that it's now essentially the only home I have. Looks like we will grow old together, my car and I, both of us raking in the miles, but still chugging along, still in good shape, attractive, desirable. Yeah, I remember buying this car, a time when I had money in my pocket, a clear vision of the future, a desire for a necessary luxury, and the knowledge that I could possess it just because I wanted to, with no current- or ex-wives' opinions, no one else to answer to. Just a beautiful thing that I could own, wholly and completely, because I decided I deserved it. Ah, in those days, I thought I was in charge. Planning for the future, making choices with no basis in reality. The fallacy of it all seems so clear now, on this beautiful balmy day.

Is this a good time to look back to a year ago, to make the inevitable comparison? Do I even recognize that guy, barreling out of Cape Town with no real destination, but with an urgency to get there? Looking for refuge to hide and lick his wounds, a place to rest and recoup before launching a renewed onslaught. Knysna—named from the KhoiKhoi word for ferns—my place of beauty and peace, the sanctuary I needed to find, now that I was no longer welcome at home. Was this my only reasoning, or did I know that to restore my spirit I needed to find my resiliency first?

Jack and I have resumed our journey once more, travelling through the Tsitizikamma forests, then on past Karata, home to local loggers for hundreds of years. Then it's back on National Road Two. Groenvlei Lake appears, the first of the five visible from the car. Groenvlei forms the western boundary of the Goukamma reserve, and is usually populated with only a sprinkling of small boats with silent electric motors. One of many havens for hikers, birdwatchers and fishermen, only accessible by foot.

I pass again through Sedgefield, or Slow Town, but I avoid stopping at the Wild Oats market, instead choose to keep on driving, pressing on past three of the remaining four lakes. Rondevlei (Round marsh), Swartvlei (Black marsh) and Bo Langvlei (Upper Long marsh), each of these embodying a little Eden in their own right. Finally, just before we reach Wilderness, we see Island Lake, named for the small island that is clearly visible and around which small fishing boats, sailboats, wind and kite surfers, canoes and paddle skis are visible, even from this high-up vantage point.

Let's see, got the cruise control set to a perfect eight kilometers per hour over the limit, avoiding any unpleasant encounters with the traffic patrol. Acceptance—I can do this. Eden radio station playing oldies, helping me avoid thinking about Cape Town. Yes I am reluctant to return there, but with my lease in Knysna now over, and my business closed, I must go somewhere where I can rebuild, and where I can afford to live. For all my planning, investing and scheming, I managed exactly one month in the exclusive Thesen Island Portion of Knysna, the place where our retirement dream was to be lived out. Gone, gone. I remind myself that this is all a part of the past and release a deep sigh, clearing my lungs, my heart and my mind. With my focus on the road and the beauty before me, today can only be a good day.

43: Ryder, Garden Route, late December

The drive is well underway. Jack's ears perk up and I look into the rearview mirror. Coming up behind and now flashing past—a gold Mazda MX5—the ragtop folded down, burning up the road. I manage a quick glimpse of the driver, long red hair blowing straight back in the wind, but I see no further details beyond the fast woman, fast car, perking my interest fleetingly, but nothing more.

Minutes later, I see the car off in the yellow painted side lane, cruising now at 120km. What is it with women drivers and talking on the phone? Of course, it's illegal to drive in that yellow lane, never mind talking on the phone without a hands-free device, even if she did slow down to have her conversation. Now it is my turn to pass and I take another look. Okay details are becoming clearer. A pretty face surrounded by wild, whipping hair, a slender arm, with the elbow propped on the window, holding the phone to her ear.

Wouldn't you know it—a few minutes later—the bright gold convertible streaks past me again. I decide to see how fast she's traveling, so I pull in behind her and floor the pedal. My Lexus kicks in and pulls away easily. Did I mention that I love this car? Is it the huge 2.5 litre engine that now fills me with adrenalin, or is it perhaps the redhead, who is leading me on at a speed of 180km? We're both risking handcuffs and jail, no questions asked, if stopped at this rate, with a huge R20 000 fine to boot. Quite frankly, they can take the car too if they want to—the joys of the new South African traffic laws.

What am I, nuts? Risking all this, for what? Good sense takes over and I brake, let her go. Anyone doing that speed must be crazy, and I've certainly had my fill of crazy women, people, and situations. No sense chasing trouble, I resolve, not for the first time.

A few minutes later the same scene is re-enacted. I see the car in the yellow lane slowed to a crawl. Again, with the phone stuck to the ear, obviously an intense conversation. And so once again I creep up alongside, take another peek, getting a good look this time. Her head is turned and she is blissfully unaware of any others on the road. Now I'm seriously intrigued, so I match my speed to hers, drive next to her until she glances my way. I point to her phone in her hand, then wag my finger in a slight chastising gesture. She smiles absently, no pause in her conversation, as she shrugs her shoulders. Ah well, I think, ships passing in the night, that's all this is, as I pick up speed, giving up and continuing my journey. Strangely, though, I'm no longer dwelling on my past, nor dreading my future in a place I don't want to inhabit. Instead, I'm wondering about the redhead. Distracted and intrigued.

Some time later I pull into a garage, a quick pit stop to let Jack out and get us something to eat and drink. I pull in

277

to the parking spot right outside the door, thinking vaguely about the remainder of my trip. I'm halfway back now. Without much enthusiasm, I think about my options. The door is finally closed on my lost dream, and I find myself welling up with sadness. It's one thing to resolve to be happy in the moment, yet another to live that way. And despite knowing I can't have change without suffering through painful transitions, still it stings to reflect on the loss, grief and mourning that go along with that.

I try to distract myself by thinking about the next few days, visiting with Vinnie and Maia at their small holiday home in Betty's Bay. Christmas vacation and New Year's Eve are usually filled with parties, people, big celebrations, but not this year. Jack and I are on the road, and spending the time at their hide-away is my choice, a departure from my usual style. Well, why not? I'm changing, evolving, trying to learn to like my own company. New Year, New Start, New Resolutions. Jack seems to approve—I can tell. I'm striving to become more like him—sanguine and non-judgmental. At peace with my surroundings, happy for precious moments in the present.

I'm alone and single again, and I resolve to look on the bright side, going where I want, stopping where I please. In the store, I get my drinks and decide to treat myself to a Magnum ice cream bar, classic flavor if you please. They make many flavors, all great I'm sure, but I'm a classic guy. If I still choose to buy Coco Pops—the cereal of my youth—despite being given a choice of millions of new brands and flavors, then who can question me in this?

"Um, these ice cream bars are on special. If you buy

two, the second one is half price. What do you think?" The chubby cashier, her exposed navel sporting a flower tattoo, leans forward provocatively. I can see down her shirt, see her ample bosom straining at the buttons. She looks up at me while lowering her eyelids slightly, then licks her lips, trying hard to be seductive.

"I'm single and I watch my weight. Who would eat the other ice cream bar?" A rhetorical question—I've already made my decision.

"I'll eat it, gladly. All of it," she says with an exaggerated wink. Licks her lips slowly and deliberately, then attempts what she seems to believe is a sexy pout.

No thank you! I take my single ice cream, and walk out to the car. Sad, really. She's probably only lonely, just as I am. Is this what it will come down to for me now, meeting girls at random stops along the road of life, not-so-subtle banter over discounted frozen treats? Will it eventually lead to the hasty sneaking into the back room, the sharing of something quick and meaningless? Jack looks at me quizzically as I emerge, sighing.

"No, I will not allow this depressing encounter to throw me off course," I say aloud. "I'm headed back and I'm feeling fine, totally fine."

And as I'm about to climb into my car, I see the metallic gold parked right there at the pump, less than ten meters away, with no one inside. Now curiosity takes over and I just can't resist going back into the shop to find her. The girl behind the counter looks up hopefully, squirmingly readjusting her top as she sees me reenter. But I barely glance at her—I'm looking for and then I see—long red hair, long muscular legs in a short denim skirt at the coffee station. Toned upper arms with a colorful sleeveless vest, a great body. Casual sandals. A mature natural looker, no muss and no fuss, and holding the remembered sunglasses. She looks up and over at me, then points at the remnants of the ice cream bar in my hand, now dripping down my fingers. She waggles her finger replaying my earlier reprimand. Then she giggles slightly, turns and heads to the cash register to pay for her coffee. I walk outside slowly, hoping she will follow me. She does.

"I'm guessing that's your gold Mazda," I say, and she nods slightly. "I was wondering—who pays your speeding fines?"

Am I being transparent? Or perhaps a bit too clever, with my subtle way of asking if it's her car, or if it belongs to some boyfriend or husband?

"I do, who else?" she says, friendly but slightly confused.

What a relief. I think it, but don't say it.

"So, where are you headed?" I ask, a natural question between two travelers. And when she answers that she's going to Hermanus, my heart lifts a little more. That is just over 100 kilometers before Cape Town, and a short distance from Betty's Bay, today's destination for me. We chat a little, and Jack does his usual cute act and earns a big hug and a pat on the head. Dog lover, I note, another check in the plus column. I glance at my watch, realize it is getting late.

"So now—well, I better go. And we may never see each other again," I say, looking for a sign, any hesitation.

And, ah, there it is: she opens her mouth slightly, glances around, and then lifts her eyebrows.

"Unless, of course, we swap numbers—"

I suggest this as though it has just occurred to me, a random brilliant idea, and she smiles, and then nods her head. I hand over my card, complete with a listing of all the good things I have to offer. The front has a great picture of me in a suit, taken from a good angle; my degrees and qualifications listed on the back, along with my contact information. An impressive card, I think, once again congratulating myself.

"Okay will you call me? Please do?" I say, and then I put the car in reverse, take off. I don't take her number because I'm playing it cool, placing the decision in her hands.

I drive away, thinking about her all the way. Now I've forgotten about my misery, my sorrow, Cape Town and all the rest. Wonderful distraction, action-oriented therapy. Of course I no longer believe in love at first sight, but lust and intrigue—well, that is something completely different. Can it really be this simple? That all the lessons around transition, change, and personal growth, can be summarized in such a simple encounter? A good looking girl, some positive attention, the possibility of a future tryst or more, and voila—all problems solved? Perhaps it all goes back to resiliency—a survival skill needed to make a life here on this Dark Continent. Over the past year, there have been so many times when I've doubted that I could ever bounce back; now here comes positivity, taking me by surprise!

44: Jack, Garden Route, late December

Hello, are you still out there? Still with us, following along as we spill our story and tell all the delicious details? We have taken our time, speaking of questions asked and answered, of lessons learned and then learned again. And we have revealed considerable information about the vast array of colorful characters and complex relationships encountered along the way. It's true, together we have experienced much loss, much grief, but in addition, much love.

Our story began in the beautiful Western Cape, an area where one tranquil town after another unfolds from the winding road. We have the beautiful beaches along the Indian Ocean on one side, with the soaring cliffs and mountains on the other. Flowers, water and wildlife—the Garden Route does indeed have it all. But I know you have already caught wind of the seamy underbelly, the crime and corruption lurking beneath the tranquil surface, even in this idyllic place. Drugs, alcohol, money, weapons, poaching—life out here includes all of that too, no denying it.

Ah, but I can already hear you objecting, arguing that this story is not about man's inhumanity to man and beast, but rather a story about the heart. Telling me you will read no further unless we are to continue exploring the eternal quest of our beloved protagonist. That is what intrigues you, am I correct? Reading more about our own Don

Quixote, our mad man riding out on Rocinante to find his Dulcinea? Well in that case, I guess I shall continue in my role as Sancho. There may be some who might think this analogy overwrought, some who might protest that this is no epic tale of a man tilting at windmills. Yet I disagree, for right now Ryder is living a life fraught with both internal and external struggles, looming large enough to eclipse all else.

At the start of our story, we had Ryder and Sophia, involved in a relationship of give and take. Ah yes, you are way too quick, pointing out something that Ryder took forever to comprehend: who was doing all the giving? Who the taking? I see you are following the story very well, most impressive. As for Ryder, my buddy, my pal—as you know, he did catch on to this eventually, then forced himself to face the inevitable.

I'm not sure we have enough time to review the rest of Ryder's relationships on this physical, mental and spiritual journey. Demi, the mistress of deception; Candy, the forbidden confection. I'm sure there were others—how quickly we forget. But let's acknowledge that the part of his anatomy guiding him here was neither the grey matter firmly ensconced in that bald noggin of his, nor the strong organ beating regularly in that hairless chest. Ah no. Think of something located a little farther south, shall we tactfully say.

Ryder's life this past year, aided and abetted by a veritable binder of women—as well as the various merchants, misfits and miscreants he befriended along the way—has at times careened far out of control. Honestly, it is surely for the best that we are now headed away from Knysna, and on towards another, more conventional, place. And I hope you realize we're counting on you to soldier on with us as he continues his quest. You have seen that this wondering and questioning almost led to his total undoing, yet somehow he keeps managing to rally round. Believe me, I wish I knew why he persists in diving headlong into misguided relationships, despite lessons learned and questions answered. Or why he ignores his own misgivings, repeatedly refusing to live by his own light. Small wonder he often finds himself crying in the rain, as it were, the thunderstorm of his own creation.

Can we go on? Do you need a small comfort break perhaps? Stretch those legs, smoke 'em if you've got 'em? That sort of thing? No? Righty-o then, let's proceed—a compelling narrative demands continuous attention—all the way through to the end. In summary, Ryder has learned to navigate the Sophia sinkhole, and to steer clear of the Demi detour. He even seems to have found a way to escape his Candy compulsion. But I'm sure the astute reader can guess what is bound to happen next, and I hear you imploring me to continue. Teach us the lessons, you beg, answer for us the questions. Okay, okay. Down Boy, sit, stay. All will be revealed. We're discussing love lost and found, and in that mode we shall proceed.

Ryder is on the road again, done with life in Knysna, but uncertain of where to go next. Rocinante at the ready, driving wherever steered. Yes, Ryder received no argument from me as we packed up, and then bid a fond farewell to all who had befriended him over the past year. My opinion of that ill-assorted crowd? A bunch of Philistines. I am happy to be off again with my best friend, pursuing the change we both so desperately need—so long and good riddance to the whole lot of them.

You know, it wasn't so long ago that Ryder rescued me from the mean streets of Cape Town, then named me Jack. As he and I travel down this path together, I feel sure the reflexive irony of who rescued whom does not escape his awareness. For now, though, let's not dwell on that particular lesson. I believe it's best to let that particular sleeping dog—well, you know the expression.

45: Jacqueline, Jo'burg, New Year's Eve

Sitting in front of her easel, with a clear view of the path winding its way past her small studio, Jacqueline surveys her latest work with a critical eye. She can scarcely believe how much has changed since her decisive trip to the Aquila game park: a move back to Johannesburg, a new business collaborating with small art dealers and gallery owners, and a whole new focus for her artwork. The rhino on the canvas seems to grin back at her—not quite the effect she was going for—yet lately, she intuits smiles and welcoming glances wherever she looks.

How fortuitous that she had met Mike on the plane ride from George. He had introduced her to this new up-and-coming neighborhood: Forty-four Stanley, a formerly blighted part of Johannesburg, now transformed into an eclectic area. Through the window, she can see the collection of new shops and restaurants, and she notices again the steady stream of customers, credit cards at the ready. She pauses to wipe the paint off her hands with an old towel before answering the ringing phone. When she recognizes the voice on the other end, she moves towards the sofa in the far corner and sits down, ready for a lengthy chat.

"Ah, it's you. I was hoping you'd call," she says, smiling. "Yes, yes, almost finished now. Sure, of course I want you to come see it. I mean him. I think this painting is going to be my best yet."

As she talks of her paintings, she's struck by the parallel progression of her life and her work, from still, inanimate subject-matter to a powerful vibrancy. She attempts to describe this to Mike, but he has other things on his mind.

"Here's what I'm thinking," he tells her. "An auction of your paintings, a huge fund-raiser for your save-the-rhino foundation, some time in the first quarter of next year. Jacqui, some of your pieces could fetch hundreds of thousands of rands. I think you should do it. I already know the auctioneer, a personal friend. I'm going to set up a meeting for you with him. How does next week sound?"

"But Mike, I'm not ready, I think my work is not—"

"Yes, you are. I keep telling you, your work is world class. You can still sell your stuff at those little art shows, and still keep running to all the galleries in town. That's fine, but you know that is not enough for a talent like yours. And now you have collected enough work for your own exhibition. All you need do is stop second-guessing yourself. I'm telling you, Jacqui, the world deserves to see your work."

"Well, tying all of this in with my fund-raising for the rhinos sounds like a win-win, but—"

"Yes, exactly. Now tell me, what is there not to like about this?"

"But," she begins, but then realizes that she doesn't really have any further reason to protest. "Well, then, I guess I better get back to work."

"Yes, but don't stay too late. We have big plans tonight. As long as it's not too much for you. How have you been feeling, anyway?"

"I'm fine Mike. Really. I should never have said anything. No migraine is going to stop me from spending New Year's Eve with my new best friend. I can't wait for tonight," she responds, before hanging the phone up gently. She reflects on her relationship with Mike, how their deepening friendship had provided both support and comfort for her transition back into big city life. And how, although the romance that she had initially hoped for would never materialize with him, his connections and creativity had helped spring-board her into a successful new start. And now, he has introduced the almost-tangible notion that she might use her talent to help ensure the future of the rhino. She feels overwhelmed as she thinks of this good, solid man whose presence has helped keep her loneliness at bay.

"Frank," she says, realizing it has been some time since she last spoke out loud to her dead husband, "isn't it odd how sometimes you get what you need, rather than what you think you want? And I think I'm finally getting what I need to let you go. Bring on the New Year—I'm ready!"

46: Ryder, Betty's Bay, New Year's Eve

The next day, I wake early, and then go watch the sun rise over the ocean. I'm at Vinnie and Maia's beach house in Betty's Bay, glad for their company, but still distracted by thoughts of the girl in the gold convertible. As the day wears on, I wait for her to call, despite telling myself not to. I'm alone without a partner this New Year's Eve, and I can't help wondering what my previous lovers are doing and who they are with. I remind myself repeatedly that I planned for this, and that I enjoy the company of my old friends. But under it all, I pine for a pretty distraction. I resign myself to no call, and New Year's Eve passes with barely a whimper.

Through sheer force of will, I forget about the redhead, and disappointment dissipates. It is now the first day of the New Year and I sit outside with my friend, overlooking the sea and *fynbos*. Once again, I'm reminded of my connection to space and time; I see my acceptance, with the resultant hope and rebirth, as the personification of the phoenix protea flower. I'm surrounded by love, embodying the circle of life that renews with the passage of time.

And just like that, my phone goes ting, indicating a

missed call and a message. Acknowledging that all things will be attended to in time, I decide to wait a while and I close my eyes, absorb some heat from the sun. Then slowly I dial my voicemail, listen to the message:

"Hi Ryder, happy New Year. This is Mazda Girl."

That's it—the entire message.

"I have no idea who this Mazda Girl can be," I say to Vinnie. "I don't know the voice, don't recognize the number."

"But Ryder," he replies. "You told me about the redhead with the gold convertible on the road, could this be that woman?"

"Oh yes!" I say in joyful realization. "She actually called me! Wow—I'm calling her back, right now! "

And so we chat on the phone and arrange to have dinner that night with Vinnie and Maia at a tiny popular restaurant about twenty km away from Betty's Bay. She meets us there, dressed in a short-but-modest black dress, and introduces herself as Chrystal. I can barely hear her speak; my heart is thumping so loudly. Perhaps finally this is it, I think, this woman is the one. Who knows this time? It's possible that my chance for love, happiness and bond is right here, sitting before me and ordering spagbol, no spag. It could happen—tonight my optimism knows no bounds.

47: Ryder, Betty's Bay, January–February

The recent rhino horn trade in sub-Saharan Africa is suspected to have been in motion way back in 1976, when members of the South African armed forces in Angola conspired to trade horns with Asian buyers via American citizens. During this time of war and chaos, all parties were guilty of suspect goals and motives. The ugly history runs all the way through the last quarter of the twentieth century, right into the final days of apartheid.

Ryder is shocked when he realizes how long this problem has existed, and how short the collective memories of the involved parties are. Blame is flung at the Asians, with no acknowledgement of the local "bad boys" who control and maintain the supply of poached horns. He reads with great interest how the pipelines operate, clucking his tongue in disgust at the light penalties doled out to the few who are caught. He discovers there are some 200 or more organizations raising funds for saving rhino, with very unclear unaccountability and even less effect. In recent years, the number of rhinos killed has risen alarmingly, and—as he reads—he feels closer to Koos, sympathizing with his idea of helping put an end to this devastating enterprise.

Ryder immerses himself in this new world of dismal facts and figures in his spare time. He's now living in a small, sparsely furnished, rental apartment in Cape Town, having infrequent dinners with a few friends, and meeting up with his family occasionally. He's withdrawing into a small, circumscribed world, knowing he cannot go back to the Cape Town of old, and realizing that with the exception of some small management consulting engagements, he has little work or income.

Is this the main reason he draws closer to Chrystal? A selfless supporter of his bottomless need for companionship and his overpowering thirst for love, bond and happiness? A gentle peace exists in her home, something he cannot recall experiencing before, either on his own or in a relationship. A long-time orphan with no children, she focuses her full energy on him. Sometimes he contrasts this with his time spent living with Sophia and her parents, and he can scarcely believe how far down on her long list of priorities he had fallen.

Today he sits on the deck overlooking the colorful natural *fynbos* between the garden lawn and the kelp-filled sea and rocky sand, visiting Vinnie and Maia's beach house once again. He picks up the well-worn copy of *Killing for Profit*, then sets it aside, deciding instead to go for a long walk along the beach. He strides away from the house for an hour, setting a vigorous pace, then turns around and looks back. He stands still, the sun warm on his back, recalling his conversation with Chrystal from last night.

"I've never known a woman before who is so totally

supportive of me," he had said, acknowledging how she had once again driven to Cape Town to pick him up, then chauffeured him back to the beach, stopping first to satisfy his request for a double feature at Somerset Mall.

"Oh it's nothing Ryder," she replied, her quiet and reserved manner both soothing and annoying him. "I believe a woman's place is to look after her man, to accept him as he is. You know this—as long as you love me and treat me well—there is nothing I wouldn't do for you."

"So you make my very existence your priority? My diet, my exercise program, even the great massages you provide, are actually more important to you than to me, because they affect my health?" he had asked facetiously, yet she answered him with deep sincerity.

"I told you—all of that is nothing. You do so much for me, making me laugh, taking me out, and enjoying my company without stress or pressure. I love being with you; that is enough for me."

He recalls, too, how both Vinnie and Maia had commented on his appearance when they arrived at the cottage.

"Ryder, you look great. Fit and trim, have you been dieting, working out?" they asked, to which he responded that all the credit belonged to Chrystal, with her cooking and coaching advice. When Vinnie had asked if she was forcing him to go to the gym, perhaps inviting a confidence, Ryder had set him straight.

"No, it's not like that at all Vinnie—truly she wants me to do whatever makes me happy. But she's so encouraging, and such a good and healthy cook, I can't help but improve.

Low carbs, high protein, you know the drill."

Now he gazes out at the curve of clean, soft, white sand to his left, scattered with clumps of kelp and stretching out towards the ocean. To his right, across the small sand roads and out in the distance, he can see the steep incline of the Hottentots Mountain and Kogelberg Nature Reserve. He breathes deeply, then begins walking determinedly back to the cottage. Jack charges off after some birds, then returns to his side.

"*Sorry Ryder—just those silly Egyptian Geese. They are actually just ducks that have never flown north of the equator, if you must know, so-called river birds, yet now found by the sea. I'm just having a little fun.*"

Ryder glares at both Jack and the geese impatiently.

"What? Do you all have an opinion too? My journey from place to place, from woman to woman, there and then, here and now? Perhaps you can tell me what the hell I'm doing here," he demands, then kicks the sand dispiritedly in Jack's direction.

"*Well, I must admit I'm quite enamored of this Miss Ice Chrystal, with her simple lifestyle, her transparent honesty, her willing spirit, and her innate ability to put you first in all things. I quite like that, you know. Seems she allows you the freedom to do as you please, all the while knowing that she will do as you please, too. Seems perfect to me, if I might venture an opinion.*"

Ryder turns to the dunes, scanning for birdlife or nested eggs. Yet he can't help speaking out loud again, this time turning from Jack towards the orange-beaked oystercatchers that strut nearby.

"Maybe you can tell me what this search is all about?

Are there others like me, or am I alone in this? What is this, this bond, love, happiness? Is it real?"

He keeps walking, mumbling to himself, no longer making sense.

"How much have I learned? What is happiness? How do I find love? Do I really need a bond? Why? When do I need to compromise? And should I? Is this bond necessary to stay in any relationship? Is a shared dream important to a bond? What is the best way to handle a fall? How do I manage the pain? What matters when climbing up again? What do men want? What do women want? How do I live in the here and now? How do I blend what is important and what matters with what is within my control? How do I handle intense emotions and not let them rule my actions?"

Suddenly he stops, forcing himself to confront what he has avoided thinking since the start of the year.

"What exactly am I doing with Chrystal? Yes, she's a hot sexy woman, one who cares for me deeply, but what exactly binds me to her? Is this another horrendous mistake? If this is true love, then why do I feel like this, as if there is a problem? Surely if there were a great bond, I would feel totally happy, filled with joy."

"Are you asking me Ryder, or simply rambling on? Because I could seriously help you out here—"

"What if I can never resolve these dilemmas, with her or with anyone? Is this unease because I know that aside from our joint desire for clean living and our enjoyment of the movies, we don't really have anything in common? Are our limited conversations going to sustain me? Or maybe, just maybe, this bad feeling is more about my need for drama and excitement—like craving a drug despite the bad side effects? I had all that noise with Demi and Candy, even way back when with Sophia, but surely I don't want that anymore—to hurt or be hurt! One thing I know, Chrystal will never hurt me."

He thinks about her, so different from the other women he's usually attracted to, with her quiet selflessness and undemanding nature. And as he resumes his walk, with Jack following obediently behind, he ponders the lessons he has learned from the past, determined to figure out how to apply them to the present. He counts them off on his fingers as he walks back to the house.

"I have learned—love and bond alone do not lead to happiness. They don't even lead to each other. Sophia was love and bond but no shared dream. Huh—that dream was stillborn—no long-lasting happiness there. And it doesn't matter how it started, eventually there was no love either, and then no bond. Demi was about love, but let's face it: no trust, so no bond, and with her, I had more unhappiness than joy in the end."

"I have learned—pay attention to early signs of a distressed relationship. I know now this means to pay careful attention when getting involved too, to heed any early-warning behavior signs. It stands to reason: if a woman behaves weirdly in the beginning, things will only get worse."

"I have learned—living in a community and not in isolation is something I need. I get my batteries charged by being part of a group. So what if this means I have to suffer fools gladly sometimes, and maybe I'm not like others in this way. Many would rather live in a limited world of exposure, but not me. People are definitely not all alike."

"I have learned—live in the moment. Breathe, listen, hear, feel. Experience it all as it happens, the seasons, the weather, the mountains, the ocean, the beach. Everything that happens matters deeply during the time and space of its occurrence. To fully experience life, be fully present."

"I have learned—sometimes I have control, sometimes I have to let go. I must distinguish between what matters and what I must simply accept."

"I have learned—sometimes the draw of work, dreams and lifestyle, added or multiplied together, can be stronger than the pull towards a bond and love. A relationship where the situation is not right is doomed. The early bloom of love is not enduring enough to surmount diametrically opposed forces."

"I have learned—a dream not fully committed to by both parties will not survive when the going gets tough. Conflicting factors around finances, physical proximity, travel and work schedules can have horrendous consequences on a relationship. And negative dynamics in blended families can turn any wonderful shared dreams into living nightmares."

"I have learned—the pain of parting cannot be avoided, but must be experienced so as to successfully emerge on the other side. Denial and anger are feelings that help us move onward and forward. Ignoring or running from these or any other emotions can easily lead down the road to addiction. Drinking, doing drugs, excessive sex, gambling, shopping—all are possible."

"I have learned—compromise is often not healthy. Sometimes this involves giving up one's needs a little at time until nothing is left. Far better to remain intact, get what you need, and then find ways to help your partner do likewise, rather than give away bits and pieces of your soul."

"I have learned—clean and healthy living, through diet and exercise, really do create a platform for happiness. I have learned that I'm not always able to stop my excessive behaviors, but that I can always recommit and move towards that goal."

"I have learned—men and women want different things in a relationship. It's obvious really, that we all have our own blend of hobbies, interests, motivators, needs, wants, emotions, lusts, love, bond and happiness desires. When there is enough of an overlap of these, between me and my partner to ensure mutual benefit, then it works. Otherwise it doesn't. A very simple concept."

"And I have learned—men and women are different in what they actually need from a relationship. I'm simple in my needs, wanting only a roof, a shower, a comfy bed, and company to keep me entertained and loved. And yes, plenty of hot sex. Possibly this is true for most men. Women are never so simple in their needs. They crave someone to listen very carefully, to be in tune with their wants and feelings."

Ryder continues this reflective process until the house is just a few steps away. His situation, about to be his here and now, will need to be dealt with, he resolves. Managed in a way very different from the past if he's to prevent any of the same pitfalls. Then, just as he's about to walk up the stairs and onto the deck, he sees her in her cycling gear, returning from her two hour ride down to Pringle Bay and back. She takes off her helmet and shakes out her hair, and his determination is gone, replaced by a flutter in his heart and a stiffening in his shorts. He stares lustfully at her, her toned butt and muscular thighs outlined in the tight black cycling gear. His eyes move past her slim hips and settle on her round, firm breasts, with her nipples hard and clearly visible through the tight fabric of her spandex sports bra.

"Hey there!" he calls out to her as he approaches. "Wow, don't you look hot!"

"What did you say? I look hot? I've been out on the road for hours. Of course, I'm hot, and also very stinky and sweaty. No, get away from me," she says, pushing him back as he approaches. "Don't come near—I'm heading straight for the outdoor shower—meet me on the deck afterwards, okay?"

"Okay," he says, stepping back and retrieving a water bowl, then filling it up from the nearby hose as Jack watches thirstily.

"Thanks, muchly. That was a rather long walk, wouldn't you say?"

Ryder's distracted, picturing Chrystal's legs pumping on her ride, almost able to feel the steep incline of the road as it winds left from Betty's Bay towards Pringle Bay and Rooi Els, then around and past "Dappa se Gat" towards Gordon's Bay. He visualizes the secluded path along Kogel Baai, ten kilometers of nothing but beach to the left and huge mountain peaks to the right. He pictures the "surfing soldiers" on the beach, drawn by the opportunity to ride the blue-green breaking waves alongside the dolphin swimming and fishing there. These daredevils enter the ocean at this spot despite the danger of shark attacks, and despite the warning system erected in memory of the many who lost their lives this way.

The road she has just travelled is carved neatly from the mountainside rock and winds its way back and forth along the smooth curves of the land for thirty kilometers, all the way to Gordon's Bay. The *fynbos* varieties growing on the mountainside are endless, with newly-emerged protea blooms visible from the blackened stems of long-ago fires. The sea is a hundred meters below, the various shades of blue and green topped with white waves and swirling eddies. On a clear day, one can see all the way across False Bay to Cape Point, the ocean expanse dotted with the occasional sailboat. And one can see the silhouetted mountains on the other side, circling around from the point of the Cape to where the road lies ahead. He realizes that when he thinks of Chrystal, she's always located in this magnificent setting, one of the most beautiful and peaceful throughways in the world. Yes, the two images are inseparably intertwined in his mind.

He turns his thoughts back to the present, walking stealthily along the path outside towards the shower. He can see the two-meter-high, three-meter-long curved stone wall, a beautiful natural construction of large grey, brown and sand-colored rocks, smoothed by years of sea wave action. From inside the shower, gazing through the shatterproof glass panel and across the garden, one can clearly see the ocean and the mountains, with the glass-brick doorway cleverly concealed from the neighboring properties. The shower is a large one, big enough for at least two people, and open to the sky. The green colorful plants, selected and placed within by Maia, give it a greenhouse effect. A huge rock forms a comfortable seat beneath the large, square spray-head, completing the practical beauty of this lovingly-made hideaway.

Now Ryder stops in the tallest part of the bush about ten meters away, partially hidden, then peers around and over the wall. Chrystal's head is thrown back, eyes closed, and streams of water run over her face and neck, and then all down her naked body, washing white shampoo bubbles away in rivulets. He watches without moving, entranced, his breath quickening. She turns and grabs the tube of pink shower gel, then squeezes some onto her chest, pausing to let it run down between her magnificent breasts. He stares as her hands spread the soap out smoothly then begin to lather each breast, stopping briefly at the nipples, tweaking them gently a few times. She squirts more into the palm of her hands, rubs them together and then moves the foam down and onto her flanks and stomach. She lathers it with quicker hand movements, adding more gel, her eyes now open and inspecting her body more closely. She turns, props her foot on the rock, seemingly focused on reaching every secret place.

Ryder moves a little closer, trying to get a better view. It's hot in the sun and he's starting to burn up, surely the only reason he's so desperate to join her in that shower. He removes his shirt and shorts and stands naked, harder than the rock where she now rests her delicate foot. He touches himself as he watches her, every unrelated thought in his brain vanished. He can't move, stands there totally mesmerized.

Chrystal has her back to him as she bends over, slowly and sensually washing her thighs and legs, the water and soap running across her muscles and then her breasts in the sunlight, reminding him of an enticing wet t-shirt contest. Sans the t-shirt.

He sees her hand appear between her legs, washing and rubbing, and he opens his mouth, licks his lips at the sight of the gap between those thighs, wet and inviting. Is she washing there a little longer than necessary, he wonders, his neck uncomfortably twisted as he peers through the glass panel. Fuck this, he thinks and moves quietly around to the concealed doorway, certain he will remain hidden by the tall plants.

As he gets there, she turns and sits on the rock with her legs apart, her back against the wall. Her stomach is as flat as a plank! She adds more gel then begins soaping her inner thighs, her fingers kneading the flesh. Her eyes are closed again, the midday sun illuminating her entire body, her leg muscles tense. Her torso is rigid, her mouth open, as her fingers move a little faster, a little higher and onto her smooth mound. He grasps himself firmly, his penis throbbing and wet tipped, his whole body preparing itself.

"You think I don't know you're there," she says suddenly, catching him off guard, her hoarse and throaty voice clearly audible over the running water.

"Chrystal, I—"

"Ryder, I'm so horny right now. Can you see that, too?

301

Are you going to keep standing out there, watching? Or will you come in here, and fuck me? I want to feel you deep inside me, now, right here on this rock."

Ryder enters the shower immediately, pausing only to wet himself under the spray and soap up his body. He applies the gel liberally to his bald head, his chest, arms and legs, then ends up with his soapy penis, wet and hard in his hands. His body is lean and firm, toned from months of outdoor activity. His legs are muscular, well developed, his chest lightly covered in slightly greying hair. He has shaved around his penis, leaving only a thin covering. Now she stands up, grabs him around his neck, pushing her whole body onto him, feeling his strength and hardness.

"Fuck me now. Please, baby. I can't wait anymore."

"Hang on, I think you missed a spot. Let me check," he says pushing her gently back down onto the rock, turning off the water and then getting on his knees, smiling up at her. "I'm going to need a closer look."

He takes her thighs with both hands and holds them slightly open, squeezing her muscles as he goes, his hands almost reaching her womanhood, but not quite touching. He leans up and kisses her lips. Immediately her tongue feels its way inside his mouth and her hands grab for his penis.

"Wait," he instructs. "I'm not finished checking."

He runs his lips across her neck, sucks her wet clean skin and bites her gently below her ear. She moans with pleasure.

"Oh Baby, I'm mad about you. It's not your mind, it's your hot sexy body I'm after," she says, breathing harder.

She pulls his head down onto her chest and he sucks each nipple in turn. Then abruptly she forces his head down into her lap.

"Ryder, kiss me there. Ah, yes, that's it. Incredible, so hot, so wet" she murmurs as she grabs his hand, then uses her fingers on top of his, guiding them inside, touching, pushing and pulling where she wants to feel his touch. "Oh don't stop."

With her feet planted firmly on the ground, her hips start to lift and gyrate and her pelvis swings slowly and firmly back and forth. She pushes her Venus mound on Ryder's mouth and he moves easily with her rhythm. Ryder puts his free hand up under her, holding and squeezing her glutes as she moves. The thumb of the other hand has found her clitoris and is stroking it, moving up and down along the length of the muscle beneath. Between strokes, he tongues her firmly and sucks hard, pulling at her mound, biting softly. She squirms and groans with pleasure, now moving faster and faster, breathing harder.

"Ryder, please. I want you now. Please, I want to feel you inside me. I can't wait...it's too much." she yells as she comes, her body shaking, her breath rasping and trembling.

Now Ryder stands and pulls her up towards him, kissing her and holding her close while she struggles to regain her breath.

"Stand up," he says in a demanding tone as he moves toward the faucet. He turns on the water, pours copious amounts of gel on her back and chest, lathering her all over. He turns her to face the wall, with her hands against it, then stands behind her, his hands moving all over her body. His hardness touches her legs as his hands traverse her defined curves, moving from her breasts to between her legs, one hand in front and one behind. She feels the pressure on the backs and fronts of her legs, travelling between her thighs and then on to her clit and her butt. She starts to move her body to his beat, rocking on her feet to open her legs, spreading herself to let him into her deepest places.

She forces his hands away, turns and bends down, her mouth suddenly on his hard penis, licking and then sucking him. He leans back against the rock, allowing her to take the lead. It's exquisite, he can't ever recall this feeling, the connection, the love, the bond, the sex. He's wild with desire for her, can't even remember how he arrived here, to this place, to this time.

"Come here, I need to kiss you on your mouth. You're driving me wild," he says, hooking his hands beneath her arms and drawing her up.

He lifts her face to his for a long kiss, both of them hot and wet, both pausing just seconds away from orgasm. Staring into each other's eyes, engaging fully in the moment, together.

"Come now, Baby, please," she says, interrupting his stare.

He spins her around and pushes her against the wall again, his chest on her back and his hands holding hers by the wrists against the wall.

"Ryder I want you to take me now, let me feel you inside me. Please, please, now."

"Don't you dare move," he says, remembering her washing and touching herself, knowing he was watching but pretending otherwise. He pushes up behind and against her, his cock hard and upright, curved and long. He enters her from behind and immediately feels the heat of her, the friction on the tip of his penis, all along the sides, holding him tightly, constricting him, pulsing with him. He moves his right hand in front of her and touches her clit, stroking it again. She stands firm with her arms against the wall, bending forward slightly to let him in deeper. Her body starts shaking, her eyes closed and her mouth open, as she feels another climax starting to take hold.

"Ahhhhhh ... Oh God ... oh Ryder, that feels intolerable it's so good."

"Chrystal, I've never felt like this before, you're as hot as a volcano!" he pants into her ear. "I'm gonna fuck you so hard, have my way with you, until you can't even stand up anymore. Over and over again."

"Whatever you want to do with me, Ryder, I'm all yours," she answers, panting and trembling.

Ryder's body moves up and down, in and out, his leg muscles pumping, his biceps and shoulders taut from holding her. His eyes close and with a few last strokes they climax together, Ryder shouting her name, and Chrystal grunts, breathing hard and then screaming at the intensity and heat of him.

After a few minutes, he moves to sit on the rock, taking her in his arms. She curls up in his lap feeling his wetness, his penis now gone soft.

"Wow that was incredible. You make me feel so sexy, so special," she whispers.

"Chrystal, my darling precious," he pants in her ear. "Our relationship is the purest I've ever had. Maybe that's why the sex between us is so intense. Total honesty—I could never lie to you!"

48: Ryder and Chrystal, Hermanus, January—February

Both now spent, they dress then go sit on the upper deck with tall flutes of fresh orange juice and champagne, looking out at the mountains and sea. He spots some dolphin out in the distance, their synchronized curving out and up, in and down, reminding him of his readings about these magnificent mammals and their communal life within the pod. Groups of fifteen or more swim together, caring for and often feeding each other, with these groups joining together in the open ocean, forming larger pods, the members often changing associations. Even among these creatures, he thinks with some pessimism, the social bonds are strong but rarely permanent, morphing as they progress through life. Mother-calf bonds, juvenile group bonds, adult male pair bonds, female multigenerational bonds, with the male-female bonds the most short-lived of all, lasting only through the breeding season. Why is this what comes to mind as Chrystal remarks upon the beauty of their turquoise-gray colors shining in the sun, appearing and then disappearing, emerging and submerging, blending in with the surf? He looks over at her, feeling happy for the closeness they share, yet sadly aware of his increasing isolation from friends, family, and the buzz of a metropolitan setting. He approaches this subject tentatively.

"Those animals out there, Chrystal, those dolphins, and also so many others, they live a community-based life. Do you know when an elephant dies other members of the herd will wait alongside the dead body, mourning and reluctant to leave? All of them, and all of us, are a part of it, you know, this African Ubuntu."

"Wow Ryder—you know so much about so many things," she responds, apparently missing the reference to the spirit of community that binds the animals to each other, and all the people together. Is it possible that she feels none of it, he wonders now, with her total selflessness extending no further than him, his dog and the very few people she allows into her private circle? Just as he's struggling to find words to discuss it more deeply, his smart phone vibrates.

"I must take the call," he explains, looking at the screen. "Could be a consulting job."

After he hangs up, there is no longer the opportunity for insightful observations.

"Chrystal, that was an assignment for me, I have to leave tomorrow. It's good pay, but I'll be gone for two weeks, travelling up north."

The mood is lost, yet he knows that when he returns, he will have to sort out his conflicted feelings, resolve his dilemmas, and somehow manage their relationship, with each other and with the world at large, differently.

49: Ryder, Volksrust, March

It was a rare moment in time for him, his black suit jacket slung over his shoulder, his cleanly-shaven head slightly moist from standing in the hot sun. And a slow, contented smile working its way across his handsome face. He feasted his eyes on the azure sky filled with cotton-like cumulus clouds, on the endless vista of crisscrossing squares of green farmlands, and on the South African town of Volksrust directly below. All fifty-two years of his life had brought him to this point, this stolen instant when his whole world and its timepiece shut down and stopped in its tracks. He was clock-less, timeless, and aware of existing only for that brief second, at one with all that surrounded him. Something had shifted within, a place had opened up. And he realized in that moment that he could feel the love that surrounded and included him. It flowed towards him from all directions, and he felt it—he embraced it! Idly his thoughts strayed to the town's name. Was it significant that after the last long period of transformation, transition, travel, and tremendous un-love, that now this place where people rest was the place where the rare moment out of time was experienced?

He moved into the shade, removed the HTC Sensation from his pocket with thoughts of writing to tell Chrystal about this latest experience. Finding the words to describe all that had gone into his reaching this point of timelessness, this point of sudden insight. And telling of how he now realized that each day was bringing him to a deeper understanding of his inner journey. Yet he put the smartphone back in his pocket, knowing the words would be meaningless to her. First, simply be. Here and now. Absorb it all.

He found a level patch of earth and lowered his lanky six-foot-plus frame to the ground, back against a huge acacia tree. Thoughts swirled through his head—thoughts about beginnings and endings, thoughts about love, life, happiness and the universe. And he wondered—was this the beginning, the ending, or simply a point along the way?

He looked again at the view as the sun began its slow descent; saw the shaded grey hills of the Majuba Mountains. The same mountains where the Boers fought against the British back in 1902. He recalled the details he had discovered earlier in the day in coffee table books in the guest house lounge, the information now coming in handy. He had asked Jan the owner about the local history, eager to learn all he could about this unique place. Now his reverie was interrupted by a grumbling deep in his stomach and he realized that he was hungry after the long day's work consulting at the power station. Dinner time—and the guest house owner waving from the stoep, as well as the anticipation of a hearty dinner, brought him back to his feet, got him walking briskly back down the hill.

A meal worth waiting for! The very best steak; the vegetables and chips all homegrown; everything cooked to perfection by the houseman. Typical fare offered to the diverse, well-paying guests working in the corporate world and stationed in this remote place. Germans, Englishmen, Frenchmen, a virtual United Nations! He glanced over at the Korean technicians, imported to weld the boiler tubes causing the power station problems, and reluctantly staying for months on end. No doubt they missed their home-style food. Ryder recalled his visit to Korea, how he enjoyed the cuisine, but knew tonight's meal was infinitely preferable. No garlicky kimchee on the menu here. And throughout dinner, he continued to experience the conflicting feelings of pain, loss and despair fading away, and now overlaid with incredible excitement, hope and energy.

And perhaps it was the silence he had encountered in this remote place that allowed him to feel this peace, finally; the silence both within and without. Was this why he was now able to keep all thoughts at bay, achieving a yogi-like higher state of consciousness? And was this how he was able to come to a focused awareness of his integral place in the vast universe before him? No past, no future, just here and now.

The guests were talking and the dessert was served. Unobtrusively, Ryder excused himself to return outdoors to the tree, to try to recapture his state of bliss. Yes, it waited patiently out there for him, as ever, ready whenever he was. The light was fading and a consciousness of each blade of grass beneath his body, each pebble scattered beneath his feet permeated his mind. He concentrated hard on his senses, on the mountain shadows, the dark spots among the trees, the shape of the house and the sounds of the night insects and scratching dogs. Momentarily he was distracted, forced away from the present as thoughts and images of Jack floated by. Gently sweeping those thoughts away for later, he found himself once again able to feel and grasp the infinity of the present moment. And, with great clarity and pleasant surprise, Ryder realized that there was no other place where he would rather be. He had everything he needed to feel at peace, right there at hand in that moment.

A newfound clarity of vision and thought, a new understanding of how his life had unfolded to that point. How the physical landscape had mirrored the emotional. The mountains stretched out before him—struggle, strife, obstacles, with the rivers winding below—tears, change, and rebirth. And as he looked closely, even in the fading light, wildlife emerged around each nook and cranny—risk and resilience of spirit. And so he reflected back on his year of tussle and turmoil, realized as well that it had been a year full of insight and reward. And again he was struck by how apt it was that he found himself in Volksrust, a year almost to the day after setting out on his quest. Three hundred and sixty-four days of restiveness, then ending in a restful place. Peace within and peace without.

As the sun ended its slow descent into the mountains in the distance, the river ignited in a last blinding blaze of orange. He thought further about his quest, and is it any wonder that he saw in it the embodiment of that oldest of all stories.

In the beginning, he was created. Without form and

void of consciousness. Yet the spirit of love had always moved all around him. And in ignorance of this love he wandered the earth, until he learned, slowly and painfully, to absorb and ultimately reflect it. To set aside pain and anger. And then finally to be filled with this love, this light, and embrace a newfound purpose—to spread this message of hope, recovery and love to all, and in this way to bask anew in its reflected glow.

50: Ryder, Volksrust, March

Peace. Restoration. Words that until a few months ago were meaningless to me. No rest then, no time for reflection. Instead, constant commotion, movement, bouncing off of walls. How could I have spun out so fast yet remained in the same stuck place? Dead-end plans and foolishness; meaningless answers and irrelevant questions; agonizing decisions and actions never taken. All for naught, and yet all responsible for bringing me here, finally. Physically, mentally, Volksrust.

Serenity. Another word whose meaning escaped me for so many months. Is the sun really brighter than it was last month? The blinding reflection on the river, the many rainbows in the mist as the water crashes over the rocks. And can I really be the same person who wanted to crawl into his closet with the lights off and the door shut? And stay there. Permanently. Now I can see the main permanence will be my link to this land. No more useless contemplation of emigration. My place is here. South Africa. My ancestors came here to escape their fate and now I, too, surrender my destiny to the Mother Country— my past, my present, and my future. So much of me wrapped up in this country. The end of one journey and the start of another with something very clear—I will not leave this land. It is in my blood, a part of who I am. The beauty of this country has helped heal me; I know this now.

The end of this long and torturous year, another clarifying realization. There is no true destination, only a journey towards one. And my life is all about this journey—the trials and tribulations, as well as the rewards and recompenses. What a gift to have spent the past year travelling, exploring and learning. My year of inward focus, travelling inside the country of my birth as well as inside the uncharted territory of my psyche. Now I feel prepared for the next phase, the next journey. Another leap off of the cliff—another emotional and physical bound. Trusting in the universe not only to catch me but also to deliver me to the place where I'm supposed to be.

Yes it is clear that time and place really are interconnected—this time and this place, for me, now. Hope, that elusive feeling that escaped me for so long, now springs eternal. I think about my story—one man's quest. And again, clarity from the universe! This is a love story, a story of love lost, and then found again in far greater abundance. Of how I set out in pain, and how I discovered love along the way. Love for my true best friend, love for the land of my birth, and ultimately an abiding love for myself, so long buried that I had forgotten its existence.

But what of the love of a partner, my need for love, happiness and bond? Have I arrived at some sort of crossroads here too? I think of what I have with Chrystal, of the community of two that only she and I share. I know this is all she needs, yet my connections to society are deeper, my feelings about humanity and my place in South African life so central to me, core components I daren't compromise. Have I created yet another untenable situation with her, or is there a solution I'm failing to see? Somehow, the universe will answer this for me in time, I feel sure of it.

I look down, notice my ringing phone, and debate whether or not to answer. Why allow the outside world to enter this little space of tranquility? But of course when I recognize the number I can't resist.

"Farrell—how the heck are you?" I say, my surprise at hearing from my old friend registering plainly in my voice. "Tell me what's new, how are things in Knysna?"

"Ryder, listen—I'm really busy right now," Farrell says, wasting no time getting down to the business at hand. "We can catch up another day. But I just had to call. Ryder, didn't that Izzie girl—the one with that sinister-looking boyfriend Webster—didn't she work for you at one time?"

"Yes, she managed the education of the—"

"Right, thought so. Listen you won't believe this—she and her boyfriend were killed in a big shootout in the Kruger National Park, near the Mozambique border."

"What—Farrell, slow down. What happened?"

"Ja, Ryder, I'm reading the newspaper today—I'll send you the article. A big picture of the two of them. Plus one of this Vietnamese guy who I think shot them both, right before he was shot by the park ranger. All hidden in the Mopani bushes. Bad, bad business."

"But I don't understand—"

"They were involved in a rhino poaching ring, Ryder.

All of this is so unbelievable. Do you know how many rhino have been killed for their horns?"

Slowly the details unfold, and I realize that this scourge has used its terrible whip, punishing even those seemingly at a remove from the carnage. As I listen to Farrell, and try hard to avoid picturing Izzie's lifeless and bloodied body, I realize that she paid the ultimate price for her devotion to her man. And I begin to understand that she must have been aware, at least in part, of what was going on.

"Farrell, thanks for calling—yeah send that article on to me when you get a chance," I say, after we discuss the rhino poaching problem in detail, then move on to exchange a few pleasantries. "No, not sure when I'll be back in Knysna, but of course I'll see you then. Talk soon. Yeah, yeah, bye now."

51: Ryder, Cape Town, April

On the way home from the airport, he collects Jack from a nearby friend, then drives the short distance to the rented apartment. He turns the key and lets himself in, pausing in the doorway to look around at the small space that has been his temporary home. Two weeks in Volksrust have provided a new perspective, left Ryder feeling different. He has accepted that he must reenter society and find more work, yet he has decided he can do this while maintaining the life he has with Chrystal.

On the flight back to Cape Town, he gazed through the window at the landscape passing below, reflecting on the rapid passage of his life, understanding that he was once again headed for a change. Izzie's death reminded him anew of the transient nature of his past relationships, and he resolved to cling to all precious connection. An internal calmness took over, his eagerness to see Chrystal overcoming his feelings about everything else. Today he acknowledges he no longer feels sadness about the past, nor trepidation for the future, only a willingness to move on.

Jack rushes past him now, then turns back with a quizzical look.

"What is it Ryder? You seem changed somehow."

"Jack, how do you fancy another move, old boy?" Ryder says as he grabs a water bowl, fills it at the nearby sink, and then sets it down on the floor. "What do you say—do you think Chrystal would like having the two of us living with her, fulltime?"

"Oh, I see. So now we're going to move in with Chrystal, is that it? Was everything too perfect the way it was?"

"Perhaps this will work out, only time can tell," Ryder says now as he moves on into the kitchen, pours himself a drink. "Do you hear me Jack? What will be, will be."

"Another mistake here, Ryder. Don't you know—there are still lessons to be learned, still questions to be answered. Shall I simply help you along, is that what you want? I can already tell your need for a community is stronger than your need for a love-happiness bond with Chrystal. She is truly capable of living in the moment, finding happiness in simple circumstances with the two of us, we both know that. But you and I, Ryder, we're cut from the same cloth. We crave a connection to others; we have a deep-seated need for involvement with society at large. Can't you see, we will both become lost without others to be amused by our anecdotes, or taken in by our charming ways? Face it, this is one of the reasons you and I get along so well, my friend. This time of healing and contemplation in the arms of a generous woman is not going to last. We need to rejoin society, Ryder. Even love cannot overcome incompatible lifestyles, and adaptation can only go so far. No compromising on important things—your words not mine! Isn't living as an integral part of a community one of those important things, to me, and especially to you? Ryder, you're going to run into this issue head-on, mark my words."

Within a week Ryder resolutely sets out for Chrystal's

home, Jack once more sprawled on the back seat. He has vacated his apartment, determined now to build a life with Chrystal. He has a vague notion that he will travel intermittently for work, then return home to her, his peaceful and willing partner. And that they will spend their days and evenings together quietly at home or the movie theater, with no agenda and no angst, the whole tenor of their life subdued but happy. He banishes all thought of compromise from his mind, deciding instead that this is a chance to rebuild, to regain his confidence. The temptation to move in and share her peaceful home is too great for him to resist.

As he pulls up into the driveway of her small house in Hermanus, she runs out to meet him, and he's stirred anew by her stunning appearance, her sexy muscular shape clearly visible beneath her faded denim low-riding shorts and multicolored halter top.

"How've you been?" he asks, putting his arms around her waist, kissing her tentatively. He's prepared for a guarded conversation, yet she leans the full weight of her body into him, telling him how she missed him, how glad she is to have him back.

Oh things have changed, he tells himself. *Now she's going to share her thoughts without making me feel like I'm invading her private, inaccessible place. Now she's going to willingly articulate her wants and needs, I know it.*

Feeling encouraged, later in the day he introduces his newest idea.

"Chrystal, I've been thinking. You're so good at devising healthy recipes and developing healthy routines—

just look how you've helped me. I think you could easily start up a fitness consulting business. We could put up flyers, advertise in the local paper. Put your picture on there. Maybe mine too—before and after, perhaps? What do you think?"

She acquiesces, with Ryder staunchly refusing to see this as simply another avenue of compliance. Over the next few weeks, they place a few ads, distribute some fliers and make a few phone calls, but apart from agreeing with all of his suggestions, she has no further input. And as their time together begins to drag, with no work or social activity flowing in or out, he becomes increasingly frustrated with her passivity, her reluctance to engage with others, and her lack of desire to reach for anything beyond her grasp.

So of course, this cannot last—Ryder is too much of an extrovert, too needful of an audience. Chrystal is content to live a life of isolation, and to allow Ryder the latitude to do as he pleases. Ryder realizes more each day that he needs to be a part of a supportive community in addition to part of a supportive relationship. And he begins to notice that Chrystal's unconditional selflessness extends to all of her relationships, that she's not capable of firm boundaries. Little by little, the huge sacrifices made for anyone within her small circle who asks, himself and Jack included, begin to erode his happiness. And he realizes too, that meaningful work will remain in short supply while he stays in this isolation. With reluctance he accepts that there is only one place where he has a chance of rebuilding his business. And that Chrystal would never survive living there, in Johannesburg, away from the coast and immersed in big city life. After only a month, Ryder decides he must address the issue. He cooks dinner, then sits Chrystal down at the table, telling her he has something important to discuss.

"Before you even begin, I know what this is about," she responds. "I've seen that look on your face when we talk, expecting me to reply in ways that I'm unable."

Ryder is stunned into silence, his face becoming flushed as the realization sinks in; in her quiet way, this big-hearted woman understands him more deeply than the others before her.

"You think I don't know what you mean, what you want?" she continues, tears now rolling silently down her cheeks. "Perhaps it's you who can't see beyond your own little window. I do love you Ryder, you know that, but I am who I am, and I can't pretend to be someone else. Not even for you."

"Chrystal, it breaks my heart to talk like this—you give me so much, know me so well. But you also know this about me, how I need the energy of other people around me. I'm an extrovert, I need to charge my battery. I need other relationships, the vibe of a wider community. I can't get that here."

"Yes, and don't forget, you also need more work," she reminds him, "which you cannot get here either. You need to move on, Ryder, go to Johannesburg. I get it." She smiles sadly, dabbing at her eyes. "You know, I would go with you, but only if you really want me to. And Ryder, we both know in our hearts, that's not the case."

Now Ryder takes her hand, gazes with love at her bowed head. "Chrystal, I care so deeply for you. But the restful life you have here, with the sun, cycling and beach, that can't be recreated in Jozi." He feels compelled to continue, despite knowing the matter is already settled. "Look, I really don't know where I'll live, or even how long I'll need to be up there. I can't promise you any kind of security, either financially or romantically. And I don't want to be responsible if things don't work out. Where would that leave us? Both of our lives would be in turmoil.."

"It's really okay Ryder," she replies in her usual generous way. "What we had was good while it lasted, but all along I've had few expectations, knowing everything about you and your life."

Ryder is mesmerized by her words, wondering now if he hasn't made a huge mistake. He gets up from his chair, leaving the unfinished food on the table, takes her hands and leads her out onto the porch overlooking the park and trees. Then he lifts her chin and stares into her eyes.

"Chrystal, you're a truly amazing woman. I don't know if I'm making the right decision, but—"

"We'll stay in touch, Ryder, see what the future brings. I still think you're a great guy, and I'll always have strong feelings for you, you know that. But you're right, this is how it has to be."

"Unfortunately, a long-distance relationship is not part of the here and now we're both committed to," he says, a feeling of resignation and regret already taking over.

Jack stands and moves towards the bedroom, then turns back to glance at Ryder.

"Need any help packing there, old chap? Shouldn't take you too long, you've barely had the chance to unpack. What—is that tactless? Too soon? Sorry, I'll try to be more sensitive next time. In fact I won't even bother to say I told you so, although if you recollect—"

52: Koos, Knysna, April

"Klaas, we have as much chance catching someone speeding out here as we have of catching a six foot rabbit, even if it is the Easter weekend," Koos says bitterly from the passenger seat. "Why sit on the N2 heading out of town? The locals all know we'll be here, they're never going to speed between the hospital and the garage. *Aish*, I'm *gatvol* (sick) with this job, working every holiday, never catching a break. And now, sitting here, barely hidden from view—"

"All of this is your fault, you know. Complaining that you have no life outside work, so no wonder the boss picked you for patrol. I'm the one who should be *gatvol*," comes the rejoinder from Klaas. "And anyway, Koos, catching bad guys. Crooks and thieves. Speeders, drunk drivers. Isn't that what you want?"

Once again they sit in isolation, this time behind an embankment, again hoping to trap speeding or inebriated drivers.

"Yes, but we could be doing something else, something more useful. Like—"

"I'll tell you another thing, I've seen a lot more rabbits

than rhinos out here. So *moenie* (don't) start with your nonsense about poachers today. No more noise for a while, okay?"

They sit quietly now, Koos silently fuming. Then Klaas relents.

"Have you looked at the captain lately? I wonder if he's sick. Losing weight, always out of breath. I heard his wife left him, took the kids—"

"That was a long time ago, Klaas, and can't say I blame her, he's an ugly bugger. But *ja*, 'strue, he looks like something bad is just about to happen. And he's always arguing with the chief—wish I knew what that was all about."

Koos climbs out of the small van to stretch his legs. He walks around it, taking in the mesh screens on the back windows, designed to prevent any locked-in occupant from escaping. He snorts derisively, knowing there is little likelihood he or Klaas will be making any arrests in the foreseeable future. He feels embarrassed to be seen driving this battered police car, with its barely functional siren, and he climbs back in, hunkers down on the cracked seat.

"Klaas, there has got to be a better way. Look at this— the stuffing is coming out of the seat, the spring is digging in to my arse. In the big city they have new cars, with computers and cameras. Micro-technology, Klaas, that's what they have."

"*Wat se jy* (what's that you say), micro-what?"

"Take a look at this article," Koos says, digging in his pocket and retrieving yet another page from a magazine. "See, they can tell from the DNA of a rhino, where he comes from and how long he's been dead. Microchips and whatnot. But still they are losing the fight. Cars with secret compartments, horns buried in back yards. Everyone thinks it's just the Vietnamese, Klaas, but it's not. This here is about a South African landlord with a game farm that offers legit hunting. But then he does this illegal stuff when no one is looking."

"Interesting. But what can we—"

"That's what I'm telling you, Klaas. They need people with brains to stop these *ous* (men), trained guys like us who can think one step ahead of them," Koos replies, a desperate tone creeping into his voice. "I don't know how, but I'm going to do it someday—I can't keep working like this, wasting my time while I'm needed somewhere else."

"All right Koos. Just give me fair warning, okay? Then maybe I can find a better-looking partner—"

"*Ja*, like that new recruit. What's that chick's name?"

"Don't call them chicks, it's not politically correct," Klaas corrects him, but then continues. "But *ja*, a hot chick partner would be a big improvement over you—"

53: Ryder, Jo'burg, July

"Two artists walk into a bar. The first one…"

"Ryder, please! Spare me these jokes. Just come with me already. You've been gone from the Cape for three months now. Don't you think it'll do you good to see these photos and paintings of the land and seascapes? Fine, bring Jack along too, it's an outdoor thing anyway."

Ryder stands up reluctantly, then scowls at Vinnie.

"Can't we just head to the local, around the corner? I thought you were here in Jozi to go drinking with me. And anyway why are you so interested, I thought Maia was the art connoisseur in the family?"

He continues mumbling disgruntledly as he grabs his jacket and throws it casually around his shoulders. "Fine, but after one hour we're headed elsewhere."

Jack waits patiently at the door as Ryder fetches his leash, then they all walk across the garden and climb into his car. Jack emits a low growl.

"No worries, I'll go in the back. No please, I insist."

Ryder navigates his way expertly through the crowded streets, then pulls in to the lot reserved for the art show patrons. Parking is at a premium and he maneuvers into the last available spot.

"Remember…" he says to Vinnie as they clamber out of the car.

"Yeah, yeah. One hour. I got it. Let's start on this side, where the prize-winners are located," says Vinnie.

They wander from one display to the next, set up in this impromptu arts arena. As they walk around, they are alternately bathed in midday sunshine and jacaranda-tree shade. Ryder picks up a wooden carving, inspects it absent-mindedly, and then returns it to the shelf. Jack tugs on his leash, apparently impatient too, and Ryder follows him across the dusty lot. He trots over to one of the larger booths, then stands under the sign, panting in the sun.

"Trying to help you out here, man. Ryder can you please, please, pay attention?"

"Pastels and water colors," says Ryder, finally looking up. "Okay, could be interesting—let's go in Jack."

Then he stares incredulously at the drawing hanging in the entrance, the title and artist displayed alongside the prize-winning rosette. "Jack at the Beach, by Jacqueline."

"What the… Vinnie, come here," he calls out. "Come look at this! It's Jack. Look, there is his yellow smiley ball. Where's this—damn, I recognize it. That's Wilderness Beach. How…"

He looks around, catching the eye of the young man who appears to be in charge of the booth.

"Can I help you?"

"You're obviously not Jacqueline the artist—where is she?" he asks, mystified and intrigued.

"Oh that's her—returning right now."

He points through the crowd, and Ryder spots a slim

woman headed towards them. He takes in her long blond hair held back loosely in a low ponytail, her short African-print skirt, kitten heels, and sleeveless white blouse accenting her slim arms and full breasts. And even from this distance, he spots the ringless third finger on her left hand.

"Wow," he thinks, now turning his attention to her face. Beautiful, with a strong jaw, high cheekbones, approximately mid-forties. And smiling broadly as she negotiates her way back. As she approaches, she sees Ryder, Vinnie, and Jack, all standing in front of her drawing.

"Ryder? Jack?" she greets them. "Is this possible?" She kneels down and Jack bounds over to her, rubbing his snout against her legs. "Jack—where is your ball? Looks like you remember that day, at Wilderness."

"Yes, indeed I remember—do you think it a mere coincidence that I dragged Ryder over here? And I see it's clear you remember me too. Now let's both give Ryder a few minutes to catch up, shall we."

Suddenly Ryder recalls a long-ago walk along the beach, a distant day when his focus had been on Sophia. As ever at that time, wondering how to make her happy, how to restore the fragile peace. And he remembers, too, standing in the sun with this woman, with her clutching her hat in the slight breeze. How had he not noticed her beauty then? he wonders fleetingly.

"That was you—the artist on the beach! But that was almost two years ago—so much has changed since then. And this is your work? Amazing."

For once he's stuck, cannot think of a single witty thing to say. Vinnie comes to the rescue.

"But you must join us for a drink! When are you free?

We'll come back and get you."

They exchange information, make plans. And Ryder feels himself getting lighter and lighter. Another chance, another potential opportunity for love, happiness, bond. But this time is somehow different, more than his usual lust-fueled need to impress. Is it imagination or instinct— he feels drawn to Jacqueline in a way he has not felt in decades. Then Jack pulls away again, wandering to the back of Jacqueline's booth. He finds a warm carpet and curls up to sleep.

"Ah finally –I can lie down here in peace. I think I can safely leave those two to get the details sorted here."

54: Ryder and Jacqui, Jo'burg, July

I look out of the window and I'm startled to see the first rays of winter sunshine appearing on the horizon. Morning already? Jack lies sleeping on a large pillow, an oblivious guard dog situated halfway between the two of us on the sofa and the front door. The small living room begins to be bathed in a soft light, and I can see details I failed to notice last night. A table off to the left, with small stacks of papers, a pen and a stapler scattered on its surface. To my right is the doorway that I assume leads to the bedroom, and here, right here, next to me and within my embrace, is Jacqueline. How did this happen—we have been here all night, neither one of us noticing or caring about the lateness of the hour.

"Jacqueline—hey—I can't believe it is already morning. How long have we been talking now? Forever, or no time at all?" I ask as I shift slightly and readjust my weight.

When did I take her hand in mine? When did she lay her head on my shoulder? Last night's dinner led to a nightcap at her house, and then this. What happened to Vinnie—he melted away tactfully sometime after dessert was served, as I recall. And now, here we are, sitting together as if it had always been this way. How can I explain—it's as if we both opened our heads, poured all of our thoughts out, blended them together, until we could no longer distinguish which belonged to whom. All in the space of one evening.

"I don't believe in compromise," she had said. "Giving away pieces of yourself can never lead to a successful relationship. Only those things that don't matter can be let go of; going further can only drag you down a sad and lonely path."

What? My words, issuing forth from her beautiful mouth; how strange and how wonderful. Next we discussed her journal, still sitting on the chair next to us even now, opened to her musings about Ubuntu and compassion. A deep dive into her insights gathered over the past eighteen months—mirroring my understandings exactly, gathered in the same time period.

"I cannot live in isolation anymore," she had read out loud from the pages. "I'm a part of the collective, Ubuntu. I'm me because of how I exist in relationship to the world. My heart has healed, but I will not be totally happy while still living in isolation."

We talked about grief, love, loss; about anger and denial, our parallel lessons and experiences in our separate pasts, strikingly similar, yet markedly different. Her grief over her husband's death, my mourning over the loss of recent relationships, and our concurrent but separate searches for love, happiness, bond. Was it she or I who said the following:

"Mostly what I feel now is gratitude, for being set on

this path, where I get to live a life of deeper meaning and appreciation. Where I get to experience joy and happiness more fully, without ever taking these for granted."

Perhaps it was I who emphasized a newfound ability to take pleasure in the moment, to focus on the here-and-now. "Jacqui, it took me a long time to learn that I have everything I need right here, right now, to be happy in this moment—especially in this moment."

And still, she matched this sentiment with her own: "Yes, I no longer dwell on a past that is long gone, nor worry about a future that may never arrive. And I've finally realized, there is no should, there is only—"

"There is only what is," I said, completing her thought, my thought, and our thought together. And all of this brought to mind something Vinnie told me, a long time ago:

"Ah Ryder, if it feels wrong, then it is. When it's right, you will know. Your head will know as well as your heart."

And so many times, it had felt wrong, yet I had still persisted. But no, not this time. My head, my heart, my whole being tells me that this is it, this is right. Here and now, in this moment. So simple, so uncomplicated. She looks at me now, stares deeply into my eyes.

"Ryder," she says. "I'm not going to tell you any bullshit about how long it's been, how lonely I've been. That is a poor excuse for starting something up."

"Agreed," I say, thinking briefly of the beginnings of my relationships with Demi, Candy, and Chrystal.

"And I'm not going to think of where this is headed or—" she continues.

"Jacqui, I can't imagine not seeing you again. And again. I want—"

"Please, I need to finish. I feel so close to you now, like we are blended, bonded. I don't want to lose that; I had forgotten what that felt like. This would have me scared, but I think you feel it too. Am I right?"

"Can I tell you what I feel right now? I never want to leave here. But mostly, I just want to do this—"

I lean over and kiss her, and she pulls me closer. She's hesitant, tentative at first, and our kiss is soft and gentle; but after a while it grows harder, more insistent. Then she stands and takes my hand.

"Come with me," she says, and leads me to the right. And I'm correct—this is the way to the bedroom!

55: Ryder and Jacqui, Jo'burg, September

Ryder offers Jacqueline a drink as he takes a Corona out of the outdoor fridge, then cuts a slice of lemon on the wood counter-top and pushes it into the bottle neck. She's lying on one of two white aluminum chaise lounges, next to the *lapa* (cabana) and alongside the sparkling plunge-pool, the emerald cushions framing her tanned skin. Her face is shaded by the huge leaves of the banana trees, with her tall, slim body bathed in sunlight. The bright pink on her polished fingers and toes sparkles in the sunlight as it reflects off the water.

"Itsy, bitsy, teeny, weenie—silver high cut bikini," Ryder hums to himself, thinking of the contrast from their first meeting, when her baggy artist clothes hid her magnificent shape, and when her beautiful face was smudged with pastels and paint.

This woman can do it all. Day-to-day casual, steaming hot at home. Wow, am I a lucky guy or what? he thinks, not for the first time.

He looks at the muscle lines on her flat stomach, then stares hungrily at the flare of her hips and the narrow curve of her waist. His eyes settle briefly on the hollow between her rib cage and solar plexus, then move up and down again, following the droplets of sweat running from her neck to the flat spot between her breasts. And he knows she's wearing this revealing bikini for him alone, that she will change into something more modest before their company arrives later in the afternoon.

"I'll have a lime and soda please, ice and lemon if there is any in the fridge. Drinking a Corona are you—less of the Jack, more of that, huh? Perhaps it's this unseasonal heat wave?"

He carries the drinks out to her as Jack looks on wryly.

"I'm so relieved to share him with you, Jacqui, after having had to take care of him for all this time. You must know, it hasn't always been an easy task. And I'm happy to report, it's not the hot weather keeping him from the hard stuff. No dearie, it's you, and this whole change of lifestyle."

"This rhino poaching problem is even more complex than people think," says Ryder now, as he moves aside the recent copy of the *SanParks Times*, collected from his last trip to the Kruger National Park and spread out on the second chaise, then sits down. "Says here the Vietnamese government sent over some smart, insightful people. They are asking our SanParks guys interesting questions."

"But Ryder, we all know that the Vietnamese are the biggest users and are the whole problem. What questions can they ask? If they stop buying, the market would just die out, end of story."

"Jacqueline, my love, if it only were that simple," he replies with a small shake of his head.

'Well it sounds pretty simple to me. What am I missing?"

"Here's the problem—they need to convince their whole population that rhino horn is of no medicinal value. It's like trying to tell all the rich Sandton *Kugels* (spoiled brats) and Pretoria *Poppies* (spoiled brats) that homeopathic treatments or vitamins don't really help with serious diseases."

"Well, they don't, Ryder. If they see any benefits, it's only because they believe they work."

"Exactly—the placebo effect, but then they keep buying and using the products. It's the same thing here."

"Well, I guess you have a point there, but tell me about those questions they are asking, the ones you find so interesting."

He scans the article, paraphrasing it for her.

"They've sent a member of the National Assembly, the Vice Chief of their Environmental Police, as well as members of the Education for Nature in Vietnam, to see the Kruger Park and learn firsthand what poaching and saving rhinos is all about. This is a first. And the Vietnamese are asking us how we know that their citizens are the principle consumers of rhino horn in the world, probably another first. But here's what I think is the most important—they're asking if there are any studies on the efficacy of treating illnesses with rhino horn. These are questions we should be able to answer easily, but I haven't seen this type of information in the press, ever."

"Yeah well, maybe they have done such studies, but you simply haven't read them, Mr. Expert. Ever think of that?"

"Okay, well maybe. But listen to this: here's this guy

saying that South Africa should apply pressure to the World Health Organization to publicize the fact that rhino horn has no medicinal value. He wants third-party proof so he can go back home and say it's neither a South African nor Vietnamese government point of view, but rather a credible body such as the WHO. Armed with this, he would be able to build an educational campaign back home. Now that's a smart strategy."

"Sounds promising, but what are they going to do to combat the actual poaching here at home? Does it say anything about that?"

"I don't know, that'll be tough. Can you believe this? The value is now five thousand dollars per hundred grams, and a single horn weighs three or four kilograms! Greed, Jacqui, that's what this is all about! How do you combat greed?"

"There is so much to be done and so little time," Jacqui responds, shaking her head sadly.

"Well, at least we have a start. Now the Vietnamese have signed memoranda of understanding to work more closely with our government, and they've started awareness campaigns to educate their people that rhino horn has no medicinal value, or social enhancement potential."

He tucks the pamphlet underneath his seat, then takes a long pull from his beer and reaches his hand out to her.

"Why don't you come over on to my chaise, and show me some love?' she says as she grasps his hand, pulls him towards her. "Please? This sun on my body must be affecting my hormones, it's really intense. I feel so, ummm—"

Ryder finishes his Corona quickly, then moves closer. He can smell the suntan lotion blending with her perfume as he bends his head, slowly licks his favorite flat bare spot between her breasts. With the taste of her sweat salty on his tongue, he lifts his eyes and with a slight nod of his head invites her to join him in the heated pool. Both aroused now, they enter together at the shallow end before wading in deeper. Soon they are completely immersed, mouths suctioned together, kissing deeply, tongues exploring. Ryder stands on the pool bottom, his legs apart, with Jacqui suspended in front of him, her arms around his neck and her legs hooked around his calves. Ryder reaches around her back and pulls on the strings of her small bikini top. It slides into the water, exposing her pink hard nipples in the middle of her pure white breasts, the skin near her armpits faintly reddened from this morning's sun. He grabs the floating top, flings it unceremoniously out of the pool, then reaches down with his mouth and gently tugs at her nipples. Below the warm water surface, he can feel the heat from the sun's rays emanating from her, and he feels her squirming against him as he presses his erection against her, through the two layers of their thin, wet swimsuits. She feels her arousal building, the friction against her mound, smooth from a recent waxing, driving her on. She grabs Ryder's hand, wanting desperately for him to touch her pink, smooth and hairless lips, wanting to feel his fingers thrusting inside her.

"Wait, wait," she says, still clutching his hand but simultaneously removing her bikini bottom. "Ah much better, now I can really feel you."

She presses his hand against her, holding his fingers and then moving them forcefully inside of her.

"Now let's get these fucking trunks off," she says, demanding compliance, and in an instant Ryder's suit is off, bobbing away.

Jacqueline uses Ryder's shoulders to lift herself up, then lowers herself slowly onto his hard penis, groaning as she feels him entering her, then penetrating deeper and deeper.

"Oh Ryder. I feel that right on—Oh my God—"

Now she moves on him in the water, splashing slightly as she sways her hips back and forth. She closes her eyes and Ryder grabs her neck, pushing his fingers into her mouth and sliding them along her white teeth. He feels her lips as she sucks and nibbles his fingers, and he leans his face towards her, and then bites her neck softly behind her ear.

"Jacqui, I can't hold on much longer," he says now, panting and groaning. "Each time you move your body my penis feels like it might explode. Oh God, you're doing it again!"

"Hmmm," she says, leaning her body back but holding on with her arms, staying joined to him beneath the water. "Did you know that 'God' is the word used most often during sexual intercourse?"

She laughs with joy, deep and long, and Ryder feels her whole body reverberate on him, around him, through him. This moment, this woman, this time, this exquisiteness, is too much and he lets go, explodes, just as Jacqueline screams and clutches at him, her orgasm rocking her body.

He feels her alternately constricting and relaxing around his penis in a wave of ecstasy that propels him along farther, drawing him in deeper.

Jack sighs and blinks a few times, the glare of the water and the spectacle before him tough on his eyes. Jacqueline looks over at him, and then rolls her eyes.

"Ryder, it's about that dog of yours. I think perhaps, ah never mind—" she murmurs in his ear. "I get the feeling he thinks it's time we got out of the water."

After drying off at the side of the pool, Ryder wraps a towel around his waist, pads on bare feet to the front door. There beneath the mail slot, he finds and retrieves the day's mail which he inspects casually as he walks back outside.

"Look at this," he says, waving a thin envelope with multiple forwarding addresses on it in the air. "A miracle I received it at all, with the number of places I've lived since it was mailed!"

Shaking his head, he turns it over and opens it roughly with his index finger. Inside there is no note, only the promised newspaper article, mailed by Farrell almost six months ago. He slides it from the envelope, scanning it quickly, and then looks incredulously at the published picture of Izzie and Webster at the beach, taken a few years prior. Slung over Webster's shoulder is a black gym bag with his initials embroidered on the side: WS.

"I'm such an idiot!" he exclaims now. "It's not Sophia Magnusson, not SM, it's WS, Webster Sloan or whatever.

Jeeze—"

Somewhat shaken, he suddenly understands how the bag had ended up in his possession, and he realizes he has unknowingly transported it and its now-suspect contents from one location to another.

"But I don't understand," Jacqui asks, confused even after he tells her the whole story. "Where is the bag now?"

"I left it with some other stuff of mine; all with Farrell, for storage. Jacqui, I have no idea what's in there. It could be anything!"

"Can you call Farrell, ask him to take a look inside?"

"No, I'm not so sure I can trust him that way, and what will he do with the contents anyway? I'm just going to have to go down there myself, sort this out. I'll collect my other stuff from him too—about time for that I think."

"Yeah, probably best to do this in person, but Ryder, the auction is only two weeks away. Do you think you can go there, get this taken care of, and get back to me, before then? I really need you here."

"Jacqui, everything is set up and in place already. I wouldn't miss it for the world. Please don't worry—I'll be back in time, no matter what it takes!"

Now feeling nervous and distracted, Ryder makes a few calls and books a flight to George for the next day. Jack stays at his side as he packs a small overnight bag, then accompanies him to the study, waiting patiently while he prints out his boarding pass.

"There, there Ryder. What is it you told me once—what will be, will be. This too shall pass, and you'll be back before we even have a chance to miss you. Don't fret."

56: Ryder, Knysna, September

Ryder picks up the rented car at the George airport, feeling both apprehensive and excited to discover the contents of the duffel he left with Farrell almost nine months ago. He heads into the center of Knysna, finds a parking spot directly in front of the small café, then spots Farrell already seated indoors, waiting for him. He thinks back to his last time here in town, a broken lunch date, and the ensuing chance encounter with Candy. Ah well, different restaurant, different time in his life. He clambers out of the car, walks in to the sound of the small bell attached to the top of the door. Farrell rises and extends his hand for a shake, but Ryder grasps him in a firm hug.

"Damn, it's been a long time. Farrell—you look the same. Still need a haircut."

"Ryder—you WISH you needed a haircut! Wow, it's good to see you—"

"Right," says Ryder with a grin as he runs his hand over his bald head. He continues to force himself to engage in banter with his old friend, despite being consumed with thoughts about the contents of the bag still in Farrell's possession. "So tell me all the news. There has to be something of interest going on in this crazy town."

"Ryder, Ryder, Ryder. You're so lucky you moved away. Things seem to get just a bit worse with my little circle here, year after year; businesses struggling to make it, and then closing down. Who do you want to know about? Demi is the same as ever—she filed for bankruptcy, then found a new guy who bailed her out—"

"Well, that's good, maybe she'll be happy now?"

"No man, the guy is long gone. She's still hanging on, but it's by the last of her fingernails."

They both sigh, and Ryder sips from the glass of water in front of him.

"What about you, Farrell? What's new with you and Irene?"

"Another sad tale I'm afraid. She went back to Charles. Can you believe it? I guess a thirty-year habit is hard to break. Ah, but you know, I never really thought she was the one—"

"Farrell, you keep waiting for the one. How old are you now? When do you think this perfect woman is going to arrive? Reminds me of the story—"

"Ryder, another story? Nothing's changed with you, I see. Okay tell me," Farrell responds.

"The story about the guy who was stranded on his roof in a flood, facing the rising waters. He asked for help from God. So along came a rescue boat but he turned them away, saying no, he's waiting for a sign from God. Then came the police in a helicopter, but again, he said no, waiting for God."

"I know this one, don't tell me," Farrell says, rolling

his eyes. "He drowned, right? End of story."

"Shush—don't interrupt. He did drown, but then he finally got to meet God. So he asked God why he never sent a sign. God said—but I sent a boat and a helicopter. What more did you want, for pity's sake?"

"Ryder—when God sends me the perfect woman, we can talk again," Farrell replies and they both chuckle, then look over the menu. The waitress walks past and Farrell indicates with his glass that he needs a refill.

"Hey, it's after five pm somewhere in the world, right?" he says to Ryder. "See nothing's changed. Except we're in a restaurant, not the usual bar. Where's Innocent when we need him?"

Now Farrell brings up the newspaper clipping.

"I sent you that article, *Boet*, the one about that woman, Izzie, that used to work for you, from the local paper. Remember how she and her boyfriend Webster were killed in a shootout in Mozambique?"

"Of course I remember," says Ryder. "That was hectic hey! The rhino poaching, guerrilla warfare, the duel-to-the-death of Webster and one of the ringleaders, and with Izzie the victim in all of this, although according to the article her innocence is debatable."

Farrell opens his mouth to speak, but Ryder interrupts him, changing the subject.

"We always talked about women when we got together Farrell. Now you haven't even asked me if I've fallen in love yet."

"You mean again, right? Well, who is she this time Ryder? Tell me all about it."

Ryder begins telling him about Jacqui, surprising himself with how much detail and emotion spills out.

"Farrell, we're actually really serious about each other. We have so much in common, it's quite unreal, and together we've gotten really involved with conservation. She has started a fund to save the rhino population from the poachers. Do you know rhino are now officially extinct in Mozambique? And in South Africa, we're headed the same way really fast, unless something is done."

"Ja, ja," Farrell says, shaking his head and clicking softly, but Ryder feels compelled to continue.

"The key is education, and Jacqui's foundation is trying to do just that, but we have to get our hands on more resources, to spread the word, to tell others. That's why she's doing this huge auction of her art, trying to raise funds."

"Is that right—?"

"All the money from her paintings will go to help save the rhino. Farrell, you know I can't draw to save my life, but we worked together to set this up. Actually the auction is right after I get back to Jozi, really exciting time. Listen, Boet, in all seriousness, this girl, she's the one. This time, I'm totally certain of it."

After all of this soul-baring, Ryder is suddenly anxious to conclude this meeting, impatient to get on with the real reason for his visit.

"Enough of this—I'm not really hungry and it looks like you just drank your lunch," he says, and Farrell shrugs resignedly. "I've got so much to do in Knysna, starting with getting my stuff from you. Let's settle up here and go to your place, okay?"

At Farrell's house, Ryder is directed to the back corner of the garage, where he sees his bags in a small heap. He's relieved when Farrell is drawn into the house by a ringing phone, and he moves immediately to the large black duffel at the bottom of the pile. He yanks it out, opens it and removes the package that has been hidden there for all this time. He tears the corner of the package open frantically, then immediately recognizes that he's holding a very large sum of money in his hands. With his mind reeling, he replaces the package, then transfers all of his slightly dusty belongings to the rental car, wondering what his next move should be. Should he call Jacqui? Should he confide in Farrell? Should he contact that policeman—what was his name again?—or should he keep the money for himself? He makes a decision, shouts a hurried goodbye to Farrell, and then proceeds directly to the local police station, pulls in right in front. As he climbs out of his car, two policemen emerge.

"*Meneer*, you cannot park over there—*dis vir* (it's for) emergencies, *jy weet* (you know)," begins the first cop. He looks Ryder over, then turns to his partner.

"It's him. The Ryder guy, the one with all the women! *Hoe gaan dit, Meneer* (How are you, Mister)? *Dis ons* (it's us)— Klaas *en* Koos!" he says.

"You guys, still here in this station. How fortunate that I ran into you. We need to talk. I have something that might interest you," Ryder begins, as he walks towards them. "I think we should go inside."

57: Ryder, Knysna, September

I'm a little surprised when the officers usher me into the station, then carefully steer me past the main desk, down a hallway and into a deserted room in the back. I notice that they constantly glance over their shoulders, adding to the general strangeness.

"Guys, what is this? I told you, I need to tell you—"

"Shh," says Klaas. "Koos will talk to you here in the back room."

Funny how my path keeps intersecting with these same two guys, Koos and Klaas. And from the start, I have instinctively felt I could trust them. They lead me into what appears to be a small storage room in the back of the station, and then indicate a tiny cleared area within, in front of the door and opposite the unpainted side wall.

"Let's sit—we can chat in here," Koos says, as he walks in behind me and turns on a small radio in the corner, then turns up the volume. "So no one will overhear us…" he explains, excessively slowly and patiently to me. Then he points to Klaas. "Do you remember my partner Klaas? You can talk freely in front of both of us."

He carefully unfolds a chair and hands it to me, then

opens another and places it so it holds the door shut behind him. We both sit, while Klaas stands between us with his arms folded across his chest.

"Koos, Klaas, I need to tell you some things. Firstly, I'm very glad you gave me that book, because—"

I now explain to Koos the whole sequence of events; beginning with my interest and efforts in combatting poaching, moving on to how I found the bag at my now-closed television training school, and moved it from place to place. Then discussing the newspaper article sent to me by Farrell and now held in my hand, and finally ending with today's discovery of the contents in the duffel.

"Yes," says Koos, nodding his head sagely. Apparently, none of this is particularly surprising to him. "But you see," he continues, "we have a problem, and now we think maybe you can help us come up with a solution. That article you're holding there—the one with the picture of that Izzie chick and that Webster *ou* (guy)? Look on the other side. You see the picture there of the other guy who was killed, the Vietnamese guy? He was—wait, let's start at the beginning. Have you ever been to Sirocco?"

"You mean the restaurant?" I ask. "Well, I—"

"Don't be *doff* (stupid). Of course he's been there," says Klaas, giving Koos a dismissive glare. "Look at all the girls he goes out with. Girls like that—you have to take them to the nice places. Hey, *Meneer*, do you think one of your ex-girlfriends would go out with me if I said we would go to Sirocco?"

"*Ja*, like that Candy woman! Or one of your other ex-girlfriends."

Now I'm getting confused, wondering at the turn of conversation.

"Guys, what is all this talk of Sirocco? Yes, I know the place; beautiful restaurant on Thesen Island, an upstairs balcony with a beautiful view of the lagoon. You're quite right. It's a perfect romantic place to take a date, watch the sunset, and have a drink. The decor and the lighting—everything is perfect. Yes, during the time I lived here I took some beautiful women there, to be sure. And the food is amazing—"

"Well what about this one, then," Koos interrupts, a look of inspiration suddenly moving across his face. He removes his wallet from his back pocket, and extracts a piece of paper; unfolding it carefully, he smooths it across his chest.

"*Hierdie vrou*—this woman," he says, pointing at the picture. "*Jissus* man—*praaagtig (*pretty)!! And here's her phone number as well. Tell me, *Meneer*, is Sirocco your secret? If I say I will take this girl to a *lanie* (fancy) place, maybe spend money on her, what do you think? Would she go out with me?"

"Wait a minute. Where did you get this?" I ask, snatching the piece of paper from his hands for a closer look. "This is Chrystal's ad."

"*Ja, ja* Chrystal. My friend from Hermanus sent it to me, told me to lose some weight with her program. *Ag Meneer*—so you know this woman too?" asks Koos, a look of disbelief on his face. "*Asseblief, nee* (please, no), is she really another—"

"Ex-girlfriend. Yes, I'm afraid so," I answer, grinning

guiltily now. "Koos, of course you should call her, ask her out. And maybe she can also help you with this," I say, pointing to his belly bulging over his regulation-issue belt. He slaps my hand away playfully, and Klaas laughs.

"*Ja*, a fitness *vrou* (woman), Koos. She'll learn you a thing or two—"

But now, suddenly, I'm becoming impatient.

"Look, we need to get back on track. I'm here to report something, to turn in this bag, not talk about dating or dining out at fancy restaurants with beautiful women."

"*Ag, Meneer, wag 'n bietjie* (wait a minute). We are about to explain you. You see, about a year ago we saw our boss, the captain, coming out of Sirocco, and he was with that Webster, the *ou* in that newspaper picture you have over there. And they were with the other *ou* too, the other guy killed in the shootout."

"I don't understand—all three of them, together? Well, perhaps your captain was questioning them—" I say lamely, unwilling to accept this story, trying to see it in the most favorable light possible.

"*Meneer, luister* (listen). He was having dinner with the two of them, and we saw him there with the other guy again, just a few months later. Fishy business."

"*Ja, meneer*, this was not—how do you say it?—not kosher."

The cops look at each other, share a glance—I recognize that look. They think I'm not following, that they will have to explain more slowly. Time to cut through all of this nonsense.

"So you think perhaps your boss was in cahoots with

these guys, is that it?"

"*Ag Meneer*, that's it exactly. Now we have a problem. Because the boss already knows about this money—he has talked about a package of hundreds of thousands that has gone missing. If you bring the bag in here, the money will—"

"Go missing again somehow—I get it, but what do you want me to do? I can't keep this blood money, we all know that. But of course I don't want the captain to simply walk away with it—"

"*Luister*, the chief of police is already investigating this, wants to organize a sting. Very hush hush," says Klaas.

"Yes, hush hush," says Koos. "But we are his, what is the word, his—"

"Confidants?" I ask.

"*Ja, Meneer.* The chief told us all about it," Koos says, barely containing his pride. I can almost see his mind spinning, trying to come up with a plan. "Klaas, now we can tell him we have the bag! And he can use it to trap the captain."

An hour later, Klaas opens the door and they quickly usher me out, back to the entrance. Ah Frick and Frack—Klaas and Koos—and their bumbling efforts to do the right thing. Briefly, I worry that our new plan to catch their captain will go awry, but then I feel excited at the thought of helping Koos achieve his dream, of punishing the poachers, and of helping rid the department of corruption. And I suppose the thought of how Jacqui and I could have spent all that money, should I have been inclined to keep it, crosses my mind, but only very briefly.

58: Ryder, Sedgefield, September

Otherwise known as "hot stuff," the Pili Pili extreme sports beach bar sits on and in beach sand, in front of the dunes at Sedgefield beach. On the seaside behind the dunes, beachgoers often walk for miles without seeing another soul. The cliffs soaring above are dotted with large, luxurious homes, the spectacular views from their glass-faced fronts enjoyed year-round by the wealthy owners. These so-called swallows commute between the beach and Johannesburg, catching the five a.m. red-eye out of the small airport at George every Monday morning, then returning Thursday or Friday for the weekend seaside with their family—a way of life involving great sacrifice, perhaps, but ensuring an enjoyable beach life for the spouse and children who remain behind in the slow town.

Today, Koos arrives at the bar complete with his undercover beach bum attire, his considerable belly bulging through the buttons of a loud palm-tree-and-seascape shirt. Although his blindingly white thighs are blessedly covered by his cargo shorts hanging past his knobby knees, his hairy toes are still visible atop his shiny new Woolies beach thongs. Dark old-fashioned teardrop Raybans cover his eyes, barely concealing his excitement about this secret meeting with Ryder. He smiles as he orders a pitcher of mojitos "with two glasses, please," and a pizza, embracing the role of a swinging single waiting for his date. He takes off his sandals, digs his toes into the sand beneath the table.

"No suspicious undercover policeman would do this," he thinks slyly. "Bare feet and alcohol—I'm blending in perfectly over here."

The pitcher is more than half gone by the time Ryder pulls up in his rented car, parking at the far end of the lot and then walking out onto the beach. Some minutes later, he emerges from behind the dunes and enters the sand-filled table area through the wooden gate. His Panama hat and usual dark glasses hide his face, while his nondescript white shirt and Hurley quick-dry beach shorts make him indistinguishable from the usual tourist crowd. Perhaps he, too, is embracing a different role: one of anonymous assistance to law enforcement.

He approaches the table and grabs a slice of Koos' pizza as he sits, burning his fingers and lips slightly as he guides it towards his mouth. Together, these two form quite the odd couple, only emphasized further by their individual attempts at disguise. Seemingly in unison, they turn their heads and watch lustfully as the waitron, barefoot and beach-blonde with muscular thighs, tight shorts and low-cut shirt, bounces past on her way to seeing to her many customers.

"Koos, good to see you," says Ryder after chewing and swallowing his first bite. "Now take your eyes off her tits! You're old enough to be her father."

"*Ja*, you're just as old as I am *Boet*, and you have some nerve tuning me like that, the way you checked her arse out. You think those sunglasses hide that from me?"

"And another thing," Ryder continues, ignoring the comment and good-naturedly ribbing his new friend. "Are you seriously dressed like this as undercover? Are you practicing for a new job maybe?"

Ryder laughs aloud, but Koos frowns in response, unamused.

"Make your jokes Ryder, *ek gee nie om nie* (I don't care). I'm telling you, I've had enough of this small-town police *jol* (game). I've got plans, man, moving on and up. Maybe I won't be a poacher-chaser, but I'm gonna do something different. Did I tell you—?"

"Right, well, I can't be here for too long, so let's get on with it, shall we? Tell me what today's plan is."

Koos goes into great detail, explaining how he has been working with the HAWKS, South Africa's new Directorate for Priority Crime Investigation (DPCI) that targets corruption, as well as organized and other serious types of crime. Through coordination with the National Commissioner of the South African Police Service (SAPS), Koos has arranged that the HAWKS will oversee the sting operation and make any arrests.

Ryder agrees, after some persuasion, to call the corrupt captain and inform him he has the money, and that he has figured out all about the captain's involvement after reading the news article and drawing his own conclusions. Koos instructs Ryder to arrange a meeting at Sirocco the following night, and to claim that he is ready to turn over the money as long as he can retain a generous share.

"Tell him he must wear a carnation in his lapel," Koos says. "So you'll recognize him, *Meneer*," he explains slowly, shaking his head slightly at the perceived lack of comprehension.

"A carnation—don't be ridiculous! You read too many spy novels, Koos. I know what he looks like—everyone knows him in this town. His picture has been in the paper like a million times."

"Fine then," says Koos. He takes a large sip of his mojito and swallows before continuing with the details. "Once the captain agrees to this plan, all our suspicions will be confirmed. And when the HAWKS catch him in the act, they'll have the proof they need to arrest him."

"Well Koos, I guess this little matter could transform your work life hey," Ryder says, trying to conclude the meeting. "You might become a famous cop. All you'll need to do then is lose some of that beer investment you carry around your waist, and the girls will be after you, for sure."

"*Ag nee*, Ryder," Koos says, a slightly wistful air coming over him. "I don't have the luck and charm like you do. Maybe if you have some time now, I can pick your brain about the ladies. Find out how you do it and so forth."

"Great idea, really. Only sorry I don't have all day," Ryder replies, adjusting his shades and standing up to leave.

Sighing, Koos beckons to the waitron for the bill by making a signing gesture. He focuses on her, his eyes beneath the Raybans travelling stealthily down to her deep cleavage. She smiles at him as she bounces over, improving her odds for a large tip immeasurably.

59: Ryder, Knysna, September

It is springtime in Knysna, and after the cold, wet winter, the half-dozen restaurants situated in the upmarket Thesen Island precinct had filled up quickly, the townsfolk eager to take advantage of a balmy evening. Now, closing in on eleven p.m., the parking lot is once again half-empty, and the black BMW four-by-four has no trouble finding a bay directly in front of Sirocco. A burly man, dressed in dark trousers and checked shirt, with a blazer slung casually over his shoulder, emerges from the car.

"Those two bloody fools, going and getting themselves killed," he mutters as he strides up to the entrance, then muscles his way through the door. "That really ticks me off, leaving me to clean up their mess. Didn't I make sure they never spent any time in jail? And now what? Now I have to give this Ryder-character a share of the money. What the heck did he do to deserve any of it? Nothing, that's what."

He wonders briefly at Ryder's ready compliance when he had insisted on taking possession of the entire amount, then providing a payoff to him only after checking and exchanging all of the currency.

Another stupid bloody amateur, he decides. *Well, perhaps he won't be collecting much from me after all is said and done. Stranger things have happened. And every last pound better be there, or else he'll be sorry. No one messes with me.*

Distracted, he doesn't bother looking around, doesn't notice the many eyes on him: two hawkish-like pairs partially obscured by menus, sitting across the way at a table outside the adjacent 34 Degrees Tapas; two uncovered pairs inside Sirocco focused on the entrance, and one more pair squinting in the semi-darkness through the windows of an old car in the nearby loading zone.

Thirty minutes later, Ryder pulls into a distant spot, then checks inside the bag of cash on the seat beside him one last time. He climbs out of the rental, only vaguely aware of his labored breathing and nervous sweat. He looks across to the outside restaurant tables, but notices nothing suspicious, the loud and energetic vibe now slowly fading. He struggles to remain calm as he walks into Sirocco and up the stairs, pausing only momentarily when he spots the beefy captain seated at a table, now paying his bill with great flourish. Ryder tilts his head almost imperceptibly at him, the prearranged signal, then heads immediately for the men's room located in the upstairs back corner. He notices a familiar-looking face a few meters from the toilet entrance, but determinedly shows no sign of recognition.

Klaas is present in deep disguise, dressed to kill in a jacket and tie, with his grey hair dyed black, and an extravagant outcropping of artificial black hair gracing his upper lip and framing the sides of his mouth. He stands casually at ease, holding a sign at the ready. It reads "Out of

Order" on one side, and "Please use downstairs toilet" on the other. He places the sign in the doorway just after Ryder goes through, already convinced that this duty is the most important part of the operation. Indeed, he is pretty sure it is the most significant moment of his entire life. He retreats towards the shadows now, determined to stand guard but keep himself invisible.

Wouldn't want my soon to-be-imprisoned ex-boss to spot me and flee before retrieving the bag, he reminds himself. *No exchange of money means no evidence and that would mean no arrest.*

Ryder finds the men's room empty. So far, so good. He sees the marked booth door and enters it as previously arranged, first through consultation with Koos and then through suggestion to the captain. He tucks the bag beneath the tank near the back wall, then exits and closes the stall door behind him. Mission almost accomplished. He saunters out into the restaurant, past Klaas, then moves rapidly down the stairs and out the front door. Outside he inhales deeply, allowing himself a quick sigh of relief. Then he trots over to his waiting car, climbs in and drives away.

Klaas monitors the out-of-order bathroom in earnest now, standing in a dimly lit nearby corner. A black-and-purple haired woman in a minuscule skirt approaches him, smiling prettily.

Is she looking at me? he wonders, glancing behind him to be sure there is no one else there. He looks at her shapely form moving rapidly in his direction, the smooth, tan skin virtually glowing. Her tight belly is exposed below her super-short blouse, and her gorgeous firm breasts are straining to emerge above the low-cut neckline.

*What? Now she's making sex eyes at me! It must be this lanie (*fancy) *place. Good thing I've got this new jacket and tie. Yeah, the black hair is definitely working, and the moustache too. She is definitely into me. So this must be how it is for that Ryder ou.*

"Hi handsome," she whispers, moving in as close as possible as he stares nervously.

Oh God, she's talking to me, he thinks, panic-stricken. *What should I say? Maybe—*

"My name's Demi. Haven't we met somewhere before?" she asks in a husky voice.

His jaw drops, a thunk so loud it is undoubtedly heard at the police station two miles away. He turns to face her, as she angles her body towards the staircase. He sucks in his stomach, extends his hand.

"*Aangename kennis (*pleased to meet you). I'm Klaas. I'm sure I would remember if I'd ever had the pleasure—" he begins. "You say your name's Demi?"

With Klaas now safely distracted, another figure emerges from the dark corner table where he has been crouched undetected for the last two hours. Finally, Farrell's efforts tracking Ryder and that bag for days are about to pay off.

That hurried call to Demi was brilliant, he thinks now. *Look at her, distracting Klaas with her unique body and her wily smiles. Absolutely perfect.*

He watched carefully when Ryder arrived with the bag and then left unencumbered. Now he walks unnoticed behind Klaas, giving Demi a thumbs-up over his shoulder, confident his plan will work.

That's right, Honey, keep him talking. All I need is two

minutes, and I'm out of here.

He finds the bag in the back stall as expected, opens it hurriedly.

Wow! Even more than I thought. Thank you Ryder! he whistles through his teeth, then chuckles soundlessly as he grabs bundle after bundle, stuffing his large pockets full, and then quickly exits the washroom. Demi is still deep in conversation with Klaas, her hand touching his arm, then squeezing it firmly with her face upturned to his. Her red-lipped pouty smile is just inches from his, and her body brushes subtly against his belt, then presses against his spanking new trousers. She feigns surprise as she leans against his erection straining at the seam.

"Why, Klaas, I do believe you're quite happy to see me," she says with a giggle.

Suddenly, Klaas remembers why he is in Sirocco on this particular night, and he takes a step back.

"Shit, Demi, it was nice to meet you," he says sorrowfully, "but I really, really have to go. Damn, you're so hot—can I find you in town? We can meet again, and next time we can take our time. I think we will enjoy really getting to know each other."

"Whatever you say, Darling," Demi replies, eager to leave now that she has observed Farrell sneaking away and out of the building. "See you soon. You know I can't wait."

She spins around, then blows him a casual kiss as she sashays off, swinging her hips and ass tantalizingly. Klaas looks one last time at her retreating shape, her high heels causing her calf and glutes to contract so spectacularly. And even as he forces himself to turn back, checking his watch and staring at the bathroom door, his head is filled with tantalizing images of the meeting point of those sexy legs; and how he would love to get a closer look.

"That conversation wasn't more than two minutes," he reassures himself now, suddenly noticing the captain headed his way and then entering the men's room. "Well, I obviously didn't miss anything. In just minutes, this will all be over, with my part done best of all. *Jissus*, that was the hottest conversation of my life! I think I'll wear a jacket and tie and hang out here more often!"

The captain exits the bathroom with the bag, then recognizes Klaas standing right in front of him.

"Klaas what are you doing here?" he says. "I suppose your pal Koos was too busy to hang out with you tonight. Don't you think this place and these women are a little too *lanie* for you?"

"Just upping my game," says Klaas, full of confidence after the unexpected Demi encounter and suddenly unconcerned that the Captain has recognized him. "Maybe taking a leaf out of your book, Captain."

He winks knowingly, yet avoids looking directly at the bag in the captain's hands. The captain walks away casually, determined not to draw attention as he crosses the restaurant and returns to his car. The satisfied smirk on his face disappears quickly after he climbs in, opens the bag and begins counting the bundles inside.

"What the hell. That Ryder—he's a dead man. Half of this money is missing. I thought this was too easy. I knew this bag felt too light."

He is startled by a loud tap on his window, and looks

up just as four HAWKS descend on his car, dragging him out and wrestling him to the ground. As they cuff him and read him his rights, they ignore his protests.

"I'm the Captain. You can't arrest me," he yells. "I am on duty here, tracking down missing rhino poaching funds and now there's a lot more money missing—half this bag is empty. If you want to arrest someone, you should go after Ryder. He set me up. He's the criminal—"

The Hawks stuff him in the soundproof back of their car, instructing him to tell it to the judge someday. Then they slap each other on the back, pausing to thank Klaas for his key role, while quietly snickering at his obvious disguise.

Klaas is strangely silent, briefly wondering if the captain is correct about missing funds, and if any of it might have disappeared under his watch. Koos, who has since pulled up in their trusty cruiser, remains silent too, reluctant to think any aspect of his carefully orchestrated plan might have gone awry. The captain is booked and charged, the remaining cash counted and inventoried, and the entire matter put to bed, even as Farrell returns to his small home and empties his pockets, gleefully rubbing his hands together.

60: Ryder and Jacqui, Jo'burg, October

She opens her computer, then clicks on the link for the Voice of the Wilderness, the small community's online newsletter.

"Ryder, look here!" she calls out. "In the Wild News, there's a huge article about the bust, the sting operation you were involved in."

Ryder walks over to her, then reads the computer screen over her shoulder.

"Today, Captain du Toit was charged with theft, extortion, conspiracy—"

He reads further, about how the captain was captured on tape, sneaking out of Sirocco with the gym bag—that same bag that had sat in the corner of Ryder's apartment for all those months, the small fortune hidden in plain sight.

"Wait just a minute," he says as he continues reading. "Jacqui—this says that the captain was raving about the bag being half empty, about how there was a huge amount of money was missing. That bag was stuffed full of cash when I delivered it, I know that."

"What about the other cops, Ryder? Were they there? Maybe one of them decided to help themselves, pocket some—"

"Nah, not those guys. I know they're totally trustworthy. They were trying to get rid of the corruption themselves. That bag was filled with money, and I left it right there for the captain. I'm totally sure of that."

"Well, look, keep reading," advises Jacqueline. "They are dismissing his statement as 'random rantings'. So maybe nothing was really missing after all."

Now Ryder leans in, pulls up a chair, then turns to finish reading.

"What a mess," he says when he's done. "Izzie was in way over her head, I'll tell you that. I could never have imagined she was involved with something like this. Poaching, foreign currency, intrigue, corruption. Well, at least we know the poacher is permanently out of the picture, and the police corruption rooted out—"

"I find it incredible what some people would do for money," says Jacqueline, shaking her head slightly. "But let me just say this, I have all the good fortune I need, right here in this room."

With that, she wraps her arms around Ryder and squeezes him affectionately. Jack grunts softly, then rolls over on his pillow in the corner.

"Amen to that, Sister. You took the words right out of my mouth."

"But now, time to get ready. We have to leave in less than two hours."

###

Jacqui had finally hurried Ryder out the front door, determined not to be late.

"Try to relax, just enjoy yourself tonight," Ryder advised on the drive over, as she told him one more time how anxious she was. "Too much stress is not good for anyone, especially not you."

They arrive at the auction house a few minutes after eight. The parking lot is emptier than expected, not a good sign. He places his arm protectively around Jacqui's shoulders as they walk from the car to the ornate marble-and-glass gabled entrance door, and then both pause on the threshold to look around. The gallery appears busy enough, with people milling about holding cocktail glasses filled with red, white and pink champagne. The large airy space, with its gleaming wooden floors and ornate ceilings, reflects both Cape Dutch and European architectural influences. Works of art hang in the air, all along and close to the walls with barely-visible wires holding them up.

"Am I imagining that these people seem more intent on the drinks in their hands than on the art on the walls? More interested in conversing and glad-handing than in perusing and purchasing?" Jacqui wonders in a hushed tone.

"But you must look beyond that, Honey. The new South Africa is right here in this room tonight. The new Black Diamonds, the Old Mining money, the stock exchange guys, even the sleazy underworld mobsters. Believe me, there is a lot of eyeballing and networking going on. Don't sweat it, it's all good, I promise," he replies, his reassurances just what Jacqui needs to steady her nerves.

As they head towards the bar, she catches a glimpse of

the penguin-suited auctioneer and tries to catch his attention, but he is headed in the opposite direction and walks on, not noticing her.

"And what about him? Seems like he's ignoring me."

"Just in a hurry," Ryder replies. "My guess is, he's rushing into the hall to set up for the actual event."

Jacqui has gone all out for this special night, wearing a couture full-length black gown, the sleeves and side panels constructed of a sheer, intricate lace. The slit up the side, ending high above the midpoint of her thigh, ensures that her long legs and impossibly high heels are on view with each step. At her back, the scooped neckline displays elegant shoulder blades, smooth skin, and an overall bronze tan. With her hair piled in an up-do and a simple strand of pearls around her throat, she combines delicate beauty with cutting-edge designer flair. Ryder, too, has donned his finest, pulling out all the stops. His black tuxedo jacket is complemented by the subtle blue-edged cummerbund and bowtie, and is paired with his carefully pressed black slacks, the waist having been taken in a few inches to account for his newly trim physique.

A few minutes before they left home, he pulled on his fanciest black square-toed boots, smiling as he recalled his chat with Farrell all those months ago. Jack had watched carefully him from across the room.

"Ah I see you remember that too, Ryder. All that claptrap about nice boots, hot women, so on and so forth. So many other mindless conversations." Then Jack scratched his ear with his paw, stood up and walked over to Jacqui's side and looked up at her. *"At any rate, he must have done something right, to have*

landed here with you. My dear, you look positively fetching. Ryder is still playing way above the rim, no doubt about it."

"Ryder, what do you think?" she asks him now, interrupting his flashback. "I thought all that advertising would draw a bigger crowd. How many people do you think are here?"

"Looks like the room is filling up," Ryder says, beginning to feel a twinge of nervousness despite his earlier reassurances.

This auction represents the last chance for Jacqui's foundation, the only hope to secure the funds to keep going. Jacqui and Ryder both know that once the government completes the establishment of its own anti-poaching department, any future donations will be funneled into the gaping maw of corruption, confusion and mismanagement. And that any small organization without a firm financial base will simply fade away with no hope of survival. All of this, coupled with a very public judging of the financial worth of her artistic works, has Jacqui virtually trembling with anxiety.

"Look, here comes Mike. Let's see what he thinks."

They both grin at the handsome man headed in their direction, also outfitted smartly in a tuxedo. His rainbow-colored bowtie matches that of the man walking next to him, providing a definite clue about their relationship.

Jacqui absent-mindedly kisses him on both cheeks in greeting. He takes her arm, discreetly pointing out all of the important moneyed people in the room. Yet his soothing words sound hollow to Jacqui as they make their way into the hall and assume their seats in the reserved area in the front, along with the other artists and agents. The auctioneer takes the stage, explains the procedure to the assembled crowd.

"Is there a rule somewhere that an auctioneer must be so distinguished looking?" Ryder murmurs to Mike. "I mean, if I ran into this guy, in that tuxedo and with that head of grey hair, my first guess would be art-auctioneer."

"Or funeral director," Jacqui chimes in, suddenly awash with foreboding. "Now hush. Pay attention."

Jacqui's ten paintings are reserved for the end, and a few stragglers trickle in as the auction of the other items proceeds. But she keeps glancing back at the many empty seats, noticing with mounting tension the mediocre prices the art pieces are fetching.

Finally, the auctioneer brings out her first work and the crowd murmurs, just as they have all evening. Then the assistant walks up to the stage and climbs the two stairs, walks to the lectern with all eyes turned towards her. She is provocatively outfitted in a flimsy red dress, with a floral tattoo snaking its way up and around her calf, then winding up behind her knee, and then round again to the front and up along her thigh.

"No telling where that tattoo ends—" Mike whispers naughtily to Jacqui, as they all take note of the ultra-short dress, the ultra-high heels. "A highly qualified assistant—no doubt a studious art scholar."

Again, Jacqui tells them to be quiet and pay attention, just as the auctioneer begins to speak.

"This is most unusual," he says to the crowd. "We have a pre-qualified, anonymous bidder on the telephone.

Obviously located elsewhere. He'll be communicating his bids through my assistant here."

Now the assistant makes a small curtsey, leaning forward and giving the crowd a better view. A lone member of the crowd begins to applaud enthusiastically, but his hands are quickly stayed by the woman at his side, her glowering countenance immediately killing his enthusiasm. The audience looks on patiently, their little paddles poised in their hands.

The red-clad assistant holds up the first piece, a stunning scene set on a beach among the dunes and white-topped waves, the blue and green ocean hues shimmering in the reflection of the sun on the water. Ryder looks closely, fondly remembering his days on the Garden Route coast.

"May I have an offer please? Do I have thirty thousand? Opening bids, a great piece, original and not from photographs. Each picture today painted *en situ*. I have thirty, forty over there fifty, now fifty-five, sixty to the left—" The auctioneer begins his musical, mesmerizing chant, the paddles around the room held up hesitantly at first, then more aggressively. The piece sells for sixty-seven thousand rand.

"Mike, I'm shocked, really," Jacqui gasps as the first sale completes. "But you knew this would happen, didn't you? How can I thank you for pushing me into this?"

She clasps her hands, going silent as the auctioneer resumes his sing-song chant. The next hour passes in a blur. With the final bid on each painting higher than the previous one, Jacqui's pieces fetch record prices, over and over.

"And finally, this unique never-to-be-offered-again

painting, the prize piece of this collection," announces the auctioneer, moving towards a huge picture seated on a large easel and covered with a white cloth.

The room is silent, all glasses still, with the waiters assembled in a row at the back of the room, none daring to move. The sexy assistant, her thigh and butt muscles clearly visible through the fabric of her tight dress, stretches up and removes the cover.

The sharp intake of breath from the audience is clearly audible. Ryder steals a glance at Jacqui, trying to gauge her emotions. He can barely contain himself as he stares at her full-lipped mouth, desperate to kiss her, hold her, have her and be with her now and forever. He slips his arm around her waist, squeezes tightly.

This is it, he thinks. *Right here, right now.*

She looks up at him, searching his eyes as she takes in his bald-topped face, and he knows she feels this connection in this moment too. Love, bond, happiness, totally together.

"Do I have one million rand? One million for the opening bid. C'mon ladies and gents, it's for a very good cause, we all know why we're here. That's just the price of half of the average car—well, average for the parking lot outside here tonight!"

Jacqui whole body feels liquid, the room tilting slightly as she holds onto Ryder's arm. She can scarcely believe her path has led her here, to this night with her work, her cause and her man.

Her prize painting is of a dense bush scene, remarkable hues of green, brown and black portraying the tall grasses, the thorn-topped trees, and the fire-burnt sandy patches. In bold and sweeping strokes, a huge white rhino emerges life-like from the canvas, his magnificent battle-scarred skin grey with deep red gashes visible around his neck. He stares peacefully into the distance, regal in his stance, completely at ease in the *bushveldt* (grassland) setting. And there on the canvas, almost but not quite, dwarfed by the giant rhino, is a mature brown-and-white Jack Russell terrier, staring bravely at the enormous creature, his awe apparent in his big brown eyes.

"A million I have, thank you to the gentleman on the phone, one point two the lady in the hat, one point four to the gent at the back, one point seven to the gentleman on the phone."

The bidders fall away, until only the assistant representing the phone-bidder and gentleman in the back remain. The bidding has slowed, the man at the back offering two-point-five million.

"He's a well-known black entrepreneur with interests in the concrete manufacturing business in Africa. He also has game farms and high end lodges in the Kruger park area. Obviously a keen art collector and environmentalist—" Mike whispers, before Jacqui silences him by squeezing his hand.

"Any more offers?" the auctioneer inquires, as he looks to the assistant whispering into the phone. The gent in the back smiles, confident now as he turns to toward the woman on his arm, murmurs something in her ear.

"Going once, going—"

The red-clad assistant nods her head slowly as she

listens to her instructions, then raises her eyebrows at the auctioneer and signals a new bid, holding up three seriously well-manicured fingernails on three very elegant fingers.

"I have three million, three million rand," chants the auctioneer, now looking back at the well-dressed gent.

The gent turns from his conversation and glances around the room, then stares at the painting one more time. Apparently outspent, he turns and walks out of the room, smiling while courteously lifting his hand in a departing gesture of defeat.

"Any more bids? At three million, three million— going once, going twice—" the auctioneer continues. "Sold! To the lady in the red dress, for the gentleman on the phone! Three million rand. I believe that's a new South African record for wildlife art, and let me be the first to congratulate the artist, Jacqui, sitting right here in the audience."

The crowd bursts into an extended round of applause, while Jacqui looks on in a daze. The painting has sold for a price that she needs repeated to her three times before she can finally absorb it.

"I'm sorry—all I keep hearing you say is three million rand. Surely that is not—"

Now, the waiters bring in the pots of steaming hot Kenyan coffee on shiny silver trays as friends, colleagues and strangers swarm forward, eager to congratulate both Jacqui and Mike. Jacqui looks at Ryder and smiles as she chats to the departing guests. She keeps a firm grasp of his arm, not losing contact nor forgetting his presence for an instant as the evening comes to an end. In the car on the drive home, stopped at a traffic light, he turns to her and is surprised to catch her wiping her eyes.

"What is it, Baby?" he asks. "Tonight was a blowout. Incredible, we raised more money than we ever thought possible, and what an endorsement of your painting skills. So what's up? What's got you so upset? Or is it one of your headaches coming on—hang on, we'll be home soon."

"Oh Ryder, it's not that. It's just—" she says, struggling to hold the tears back. "I know it's going to sound really stupid, but—"

"What? Tell me, I promise not to laugh," he says encouragingly.

"I was just so fond of that last painting. I'm really happy, honestly I am, and I know tonight was an amazing success. But I feel like I just sent a piece of my heart out into the world, and now I will never have it back again. All to an anonymous buyer! Am I crazy? I know there'll be more paintings, but this one—I don't know, it was somehow special. Ah, I'm sure I'll feel better tomorrow, don't worry about me."

With Jacqui crying quietly, Ryder continues the drive home, his hand patting her comfortingly on her leg while he struggles to think of something cheery to say.

61: Ryder and Jacqui, Jo'burg, later that year

The thatch-roofed cottage is visible from the pool area. Above it appears the steel lightning rod, a necessary protection from the frequent loud thunderclaps and bright spikes of the fierce Highveld storms that spring up suddenly at this altitude. Jack lies outside beside the warm *braai* salivating in anticipation of the fillets waiting to be seared, hoping he will get more than just a whiff drifting past his damp nose.

In the distance, no beach, no mountain, only the faint glimmer of the yellow "mine dumps," the distinctive landscape feature of Johannesburg. And occupying the chaises around the pool, some new friends sit deep in conversation. The hospitable and welcoming Highveld folks, taking a break from making money to enjoy the holiday weekend. Gauteng, the economic heart of South Africa, is now the old and new home for both Ryder and Jacqueline. Today they are enjoying what is, without a doubt, the best weather in the world.

Jack stares impatiently at Ryder and Jacqui as they laugh and play catch in the pool.

"What on earth is taking so long? The meat is not going to braai itself, you know. You two are so into each other, all this dilly

dallying is becoming most irritating. Time to start the cooking already! And um, by the way, exactly whose ball is that, anyway?"

Finally they climb out holding hands, kissing and laughing, with their hips swaying exaggeratedly in time to the Natalie Cole tune belting from the nearby music station. And as he listens to the words, Ryder hums his own version, recalling his journey through his beloved Garden Route, with his best friend at his side.

> If you ever plan to motor East,
> Travel my way, it's the wild way, it's a beast,
> Get your view on route sixty-two.
>
> Won't you get hip to this timely tip:
> When you make that garden route trip
> Get your view on route sixty-two.

They settle down on the chairs among their friends, all drinking Corona or Darling white wine driven up directly from the vineyard by Vinnie on his last visit.

Ah what a country, thinks Ryder as he takes it all in. He stares over at Jack.

"Well, seems you have given up that Jack and Red Bull thing, despite it being your drink of choice for over ten years Ryder. And what's next—I wonder if you'll change my name to 'Corona with a slice of lemon'? No? Well, what will you change next, Ryder? I just hope it's not this painter woman with the pseudo-French name. I sure hope you appreciate how special she is, how rare a find."

The doorbell rings and Ryder gets up, grabs a towel and walks through the cottage, across the living room to the front door. He peers through the peephole, then opens the door wide.

"Farrell! What a surprise. Come, in come in!" he says as he greets his old friend. "But what brings you to town?"

"Just had some business here," Farrell mutters evasively as Ryder keeps quizzing him.

"Business? Since when do you have clients in Johannesburg?"

"Just had to pick up a package, Ryder. No big thing. But hey, do you mind if I store it in the house? I don't want to leave it in the car."

"Why, what is it?" Ryder asks. "You think it would get stolen from a locked car? Something valuable then?"

"Never you mind, Ryder. Now can I bring it in or not?"

"Sure, be my guest," Ryder says easily as he heads back outside. "Then come join us on the patio, ok? I hope you brought your *cozzie* (bathing suit) for a quick dip in the pool, and your appetite too! I'll pour you a drink in the meantime, a beer, right?"

"Nope, none for me," Farrell says, blushing slightly. "Given up drinking, been almost three months now. Clean living, Ryder. Giving it a try for a change."

Ryder is confused, suddenly aware that Farrell looks quite different without the usual drunken dishevelment.

"Well, that's certainly a change," he says, then steps aside and shrugs. "See you outside."

Ryder returns to the *braai*, busies himself with the food, placing the raw meat on the fire under Jack's watchful supervision.

'That's it, careful now. I'm just keeping an eye out, Ryder, in case you drop anything. Tough job, you know."

Farrell props the front door open, goes out to his car and returns with a large, flat package that he places in the passage between the entrance and the kitchen, leaning it carefully against the wall. He looks through the window to the patio, noticing Ryder and Jacqui engrossed with the lunch preparations of cooking, carrying plates, and setting up the table. They are conversing easily with the other guests, not glancing his way. Without drawing any further attention, he slips out the same way he came in, shutting the front door softly behind him.

Five minutes later the doorbell rings again. Ryder looks at Jacqui and raises his eyebrows, then glances around and notices Farrell is missing.

"I'll get it," he says, moving inside, then calling out. "What did you do, Farrell, lock yourself out?"

But this time, as he opens the door, the surprise is even greater.

"I don't believe it! Koos—look at you!" he exclaims as he stares at the slim, stylishly dressed man in front of him. "You look so different. The last time I saw you was at the Pili Pili Bar in Sedgefield. I almost didn't recognize you."

Ryder thinks back to his trip to Knysna, barely three months and yet a lifetime ago, remembering when he had huddled with Koos and Klaas in the small room in the police station. After that meeting, he had driven his rental car to the central square, seeking out the old parking guard. He had found him easily, hard at work as usual in the hot sun, directing traffic into and out of the cramped and coveted spots. He had pulled up next to another car, then jogged over to the old guy.

"*Meneer*," the guard had greeted him, smiling a toothless grin, the wrinkles in his face almost hiding his small eyes set deep in his face. "Long time no see, *nee? Waar het jy gegaan (*where did you go)?"

Ryder had smiled at him in return, then handed him a huge bag filled with all of Izzie's clothes from within Webster's duffel.

"This is for you," he said to the guard. And before he spun around and returned to his car, he dug into his pocket, producing a small, tightly wrapped bundle of cash. "And this too. I found it in an old coat, forgot I even had it. Here, take it." When he heard the guard call him back, he had turned around one more time and waved him off. "No, it's for you. Keep it. You've earned it," he reassured the old man, trying not to notice the tears of gratitude streaming down his face. "When I come back next summer, you can give me the best spot in town, okay?"

Smiling at the memory, Ryder now turns his attention back to Koos.

"I'm very surprised to see you here," he says.

"*Ja* man—and I have another surprise for you," Koos says as he steps aside. And there behind him stands Chrystal, flowing red hair, short skirt and halter top, looking just as Ryder remembers. "I know you've already met my Fitness *Vrou (*woman)," Koos says, somewhat bashfully. "It's because of her that I look like this."

"Oh Koosie, you did all the work yourself," interrupts Chrystal as she gazes at him lovingly, then slips her arm around his waist. "Ryder, it's really nice to see you again. I hope we haven't come at a bad time?"

"No, no—please come in. We were just about to have lunch—a *braai* (barbeque). Plenty of food. I hope you'll join us?" He turns around just as Jack comes scampering towards the door. "I know you remember Jack—"

"Yes, yes. Lovely to see you again, Chrystal. And you as well, Koos is it? Now do please get a move on, there's a good couple. Dinner is almost ready and we're not accustomed to waiting."

"But Koos, tell me about Klaas. Where is—"

"Ryder, I'm not a policeman anymore, not sure if you know that. I've moved to Hermanus. Chrystal and I—we have our own work over there," he begins to explain. "I have my own detective agency, and Chrystal keeps me in shape. As for Klaas—Captain Klaas—"

"Yes, I saw he got promoted after that sting—"

"Yeah, now he thinks he's a big shot. I'm sure he's doing very well—probably dating one of your exes if I know him—"

Now they both laugh as Ryder shakes his head.

"All your ex'es Ryder. What can I say? You've got good taste," Koos says, and both Ryder and Chrystal blush slightly.

At that moment, Jacqueline enters the room, and Ryder walks over to her, takes her hand. "This is Jacqueline," he says, beaming with pride. Jack walks over to stand at their feet, panting eagerly.

"Yes, and she's best of the bunch, no question."

Then Ryder holds up Jacqui's left hand, and they show off the diamond ring he has placed on her third finger, with her very willing permission, just the day before.

"Soon to be my wife. No more exes, ever again!"

They all murmur their congratulations, and Koos claps Ryder heartily on the back.

"Ryder," Jacqui asks him now, suddenly suspicious as she points towards the door. "What is that?"

She indicates the large object blocking the passageway, wrapped in brown paper and with a red "Sold" sticker sealing the front corner. "This looks like a painting from the auction house. See, that's their logo."

They stand around as Jacqui unwraps the package, then gasp in disbelief when they see the contents.

"It's your multi-million-rand painting Jacqui. Where did this come from?" Ryder asks, frowning in puzzlement. "Wait a sec. What happened to Farrell? He was just here. You don't suppose he was—"

"Best not to ask too many question, Meneer," Koos advises him, wagging a finger knowingly. "Look how happy your woman is, to have her painting back. Maybe that's all you need to know."

Ryder looks over at Jacqui, notices her glowing smile as she crouches down and studies the artwork more closely. She reaches over and puts her arm around Jack, drawing him in and patting him on the head.

"That's you in the picture Jack. Do you recognize yourself?"

"Well, I daresay that's what makes the picture so valuable."

Jack extricates himself from Jacqui's arms, moves over to stand next to Ryder.

"As for you Ryder, do you finally realize what a gem you have here in Jacqui? I am warning you—don't fuck it up. She's a keeper!"

Look how far we've come together, Ryder thinks as he stares at his dog, his silent best friend who has traversed the country of his soul with him. *Jack, my boy, I may have a new woman, a new life, a new home, but you will always be my oldest and truest friend, my best travelling companion. And I honestly believe you understand me best of all.*

Then he winks at Jack as he and Jacqui both straighten up and turn their attention back to their guests.

"Right, everyone, let's head this way—mustn't let those steaks burn," Ryder says as he leads them all out towards the pool.

ଛ End ଓ

ABOUT THE AUTHORS

Nicki Blumenau Bloch grew up in Johannesburg, South Africa and now resides in Columbus, Ohio, where she works as a Software Engineer, Author and Consultant. Her previous book is entitled "Women of the Metro Ballet."

Jeff Lomey grew up in Johannesburg and has spent most of his adult life in the Western Cape. He is both a sailor and a photographer, with a passion for travelling the breathtaking Garden Route. He currently lives in Johannesburg and works as a Strategy Execution and Leadership Consultant.

Visit our website for pictures, South African travel information, and other resources, at
http://nbloch6.wix.com/rydersroute

We welcome your email telling us what you think of Ryder & Jack.
jefflomey@yebo.co.sa
nbloch@columbus.rr.com

And remember to like us on FaceBook at Ryders-Route